BETTY KERSS GROEZINGER

The Davenport Dilemma

Blessings,
Betty Kerss Groezinger

Ps 91

abbott press®

A DIVISION OF WRITER'S DIGEST

THE DAVENPORT DILEMMA

Abbott Press books may be ordered through booksellers or by contacting:

Abbott Press
1663 Liberty Drive
Bloomington, IN 47403
www.abbottpress.com
Phone: 1-866-697-5310

ISBN: 978-1-4582-0733-3 (e)
ISBN: 978-1-4582-0734-0 (hc)
ISBN: 978-1-4582-0735-7 (sc)

Library of Congress Control Number: 2012923421

Printed in the United States of America

Abbott Press rev. date: 01/29/2013

For my Daughters,
Kim and Teresa
Who read my very first effort and didn't laugh at their mom ...
Then strived to keep my computer working, which was no small feat!
And always encouraged me to keep writing!
You make my life joyful.

And

In Memory of the two men of my life,
Bill, whose life inspired the story ...
and
Ray, who encouraged me to write it ...
Who read all the trial runs ...
Forever telling me to make my characters stronger
And the villains meaner ...
For you both, with love.

Acknowledgments

I AM SO GRATEFUL TO everyone who was kind enough to read and critique my story, who kept me going, and who listened to me talk and talk about it, ad nauseam ...

There are not enough ways to say thank you to my daughters, Kim and Teresa, for all the help and encouragement you have given me.

Thank you, Bill Ward, former advertising executive, you were the first reader outside my family and your inspiring words are engraved on my heart. I will never forget your note saying the story was a "Cousin to the *Manchurian Candidate*."

Thank you, Pat, for your encouragement, many critiques, and for your stories and insights about secret agents.

Special thanks to Marsha, Meredythe, Gary, Jane, Ashley, and Marcy for taking the time to read and critique my story, some more than once!

Thank you, Kathleen, for helping me work my way through the maze of publishing, and for Gary who said "He didn't want to put the story down." And for Martha, English teacher extraordinaire.

Many, many thanks to my very special editors, you know who you are, you made my story so much better.

Last, but, oh so important to me, thank you to the rest of my family who uphold me with their love, Patrick and Meghanne, Lauren, Aaron, Ashley, Bob, Thomas and Pam, Connie and Tom, Donnie and Nicole, David and Paula, and Rich and Kristi.

I hope you enjoy the story ...
The Davenport Daughters is already underway!

"*He was given power to give breath to the image of the first beast, so that it could speak and cause all who refused to worship the image to be killed. He also forced everyone small and great, rich and poor, free and slave to receive mark on his right hand or on his forehead, so that no one could buy or sell unless he had the mark, which is the name of the beast or the number of his name.*"
REVELATION 13:15-17 NIV

"*All it takes for evil to flourish is for good men to do nothing.*"
EDWARD BURKE 1729-1797

Prologue

THE MASSIVE MAN SCRUTINIZED the terrain with rapt concentration. From his vantage point in the helicopter, he could see the trail up the mountain would be steep and difficult in the summer months; but, in the winter when the snow was deeper than a grave, it would take a strong, experienced hiker to navigate it. Only one narrow break in the trees was evident. *This will do well,* he thought. *Unwelcome intruders will be at a minimum.*

The chopper zoomed over the treetops then dropped into a clearing fast enough to keep ahead of the re-circulating white-out. Before the snow settled, two uniformed guards shoved a ramp up to the opening door of the chopper. The huge man rolled down in a battery-powered wheelchair.

Impatiently waving the guards away, he maneuvered along a pathway toward the dark-timbered structure perched on the edge of a rocky precipice. Stopping just out of range of the swirling snow, he spun his chair about and gazed at the surrounding area. Mt. Pilatus loomed over the isolated chalet, which was hidden in the mountains high above the small village of Engelberg.

"Have the others arrived?" he wheezed at his assistant, Hans, who was standing nearby.

"Four of the men are here, sir," Hans' voice grew louder, as he struggled to speak over the rumble of the rotors revving up for takeoff. "The helicopter carrying the other eight is on its way."

The wheelchair-bound man nodded. Shielding his face from the icy wind when the chopper lifted off and gasping in the thin air, he signaled the young man to lead the way.

"Your room is midway down on the left," Hans said, as they entered the central hall. "The conference room is at the far end."

"And the other bedrooms?"

"They are on the second floor, sir. The staff is housed on the third.

"Well done, Hans. Make sure everyone knows that the meeting will start as scheduled," the man ordered, peeling off his leather gloves.

Hans made one last assessment of the conference room. Obstacles had been removed leaving ample space for the chairman's wheelchair between the table and the credenza. Within reach was a silver tray holding brandy, Evian water, and crystal goblets. A gold gavel lay beside a leather notebook. Twelve other places were set, all with matching notebooks and pens.

He added another log to the enormous rock fireplace and stirred the fire to a higher blaze. Harsh winter light streamed through the floor-to-ceiling windows that looked up to Mt. Pilatus' 6,982 foot elevation. One guard stood at attention at the entrance to the room and another on the balcony outside the windows. Other guards were placed strategically around the perimeter of the property. All was ready.

PROMPTLY AT 1100 HOURS, THIRTEEN of the world's most powerful men assembled in the richly paneled conference room for the annual meeting of *The Brotherhood*. Five men from the United States, four from the British Isles, and four from Europe circled the long marble table and found their designated places. In the early 1950s, three separate and powerful groups, the Illuminati from the United States, the Inner Circle from the British Isles, and the Alliance from Europe, combined forces and organized a controlling nucleus to be known as *The Brotherhood*. With this convergence, their power became unlimited.

The chairman called the meeting to order and distributed agendas. One by one each man presented an update on his particular field of global concentration: the political infrastructure, foreign and domestic policy, universal values and religion, education, public opinion and media, communications and transportation, food supply, oil and energy regulation, health and welfare, a unified international economic order, a world treasury agency with taxation powers, and military jurisdiction. All were designed and leading to a new world order under the sole control of *The Brotherhood*.

The tall gray-haired man from Lloyds of London was reading his report when a loud knock interrupted him. Conversation ceased and twelve pairs of eyes turned toward the stone-faced chairman in his sixties sitting at the head of the table. All waited for him to respond.

"Enter," he barked, turning the sheaf of papers in his hand face down on the table. His fingers drummed a cadence as Hans hurried toward him.

"This just arrived for you, Mr. Chairman. It's marked urgent." Handing the folder to him, Hans rapidly left the room.

The chairman pushed away from the table and inspected the seal on the folder before opening it. He withdrew several sheets and read through them. Spinning his chair about, he rolled to the window and stared outside for several minutes.

A collective breath was held. All was silent except for the whirring of the wheelchair and the crackling of the fire.

Turning back to the table, the chairman exploded with fury. "Gentlemen, we have confirmation. *The Brotherhood* has been infiltrated. This identifies the man as Joshua Davenport." Throwing the folder toward the center of the table, he roared, "Check it yourself."

Waves of rage flowed around the room, like living organisms. A thin, weasel-faced man on the chairman's left sprang up knocking over his chair. He dashed to the credenza and grabbed a packet marked *Ballots.* "I call for a vote," he shrieked, waving the packet in the air and pacing around the table.

"I second it," came a guttural voice from the man known as the Enforcer.

"A vote has been called and seconded," said the chairman.

The ballots were distributed, completed in a matter of seconds, and flung to the center of the table. The agitated man slowed his pacing long enough to collect and open them, one by one.

"It is unanimous, Mr. Chairman. The decision is termination."

"So be it," the chairman concurred, a vein pulsating in his forehead. Swiveling his chair to the console behind him, he picked up a dark red drawstring bag, dropped one black ball and eleven white ones into it, and drew it closed.

"You know the procedure, gentlemen." He handed the bag to the man on his right. Each man reached in, drew out one ball in his closed fist, and immediately placed it in his pocket.

"You will examine your selection in private. The man who drew the black ball has twenty-four hours to exterminate Joshua Davenport. We'll meet here at 1800 hours three days from now."

The chairman's face prohibited any conversation. He crashed the gavel against the marble table and bellowed, "Adjourned."

The sound reverberated in the ears of the angry men as they stormed out in silence.

3

Thursday
February 17, 1977
ENGELBERG, SWITZERLAND

"MR. CHAIRMAN, THE MATTER has resolved itself without our intervention," drawled the soft voice of the man from Texas. "The infiltrator died of natural causes."

"Proof," demanded the chairman.

"Joshua Davenport died at 0300 hours, February 16, at Baylor Hospital in Dallas, Texas," he stated, handing the chairman a death certificate and autopsy report.

"The cause of death was a subarachnoid hemorrhage due to a ruptured intracranial berry aneurysm. Less than a third of people suffering this condition survive it. It was confirmed by an autopsy later that afternoon. Nothing unusual occurred at the inquest. Burial is scheduled at Sparkman Hillcrest Memorial Park tomorrow morning."

"What about the woman, the traitor's wife? Does she know anything?"

Pausing for a moment, the man thought about the blond woman at the hospital. All he saw on her pale face was panic and then shock. "No, I don't believe she does, Mr. Chairman. She became quite hysterical and had to be sedated by the doctor. Jennie Davenport and her daughters appeared to be completely traumatized by Davenport's death. I saw no signs of collusion."

The chairman lowered his head and was silent for a few minutes. Much too convenient, he thought. If this is a set up, if she knows, future plans of *The Brotherhood* are jeopardized. There was something unyielding in his voice when he looked up and ordered continual surveillance on the wife.

"For how long?"

"Indefinitely, I don't want her to make a move that I don't know about. If she stubs her toe, I want to know and I want a daily report."

Late Friday Night
February 18, 1977
FORT MEADE, MARYLAND

CONSTERNATION CROSSED THE FACE of the man standing at the window. For the better part of two decades, Mason Silverman had been Director of the NSA. This office and his clandestine connection with the Illuminati, the US sector of *The Brotherhood*, gave him almost unlimited power.

He watched his most experienced operative park his car and enter the building. Silverman knew by the man's body language that the mission had not been successful. The man had been trained by Army Intelligence and was highly qualified, but Silverman had an innate distrust of everybody. His very survival depended on his judgment. He turned sharply and glared at the young man coming in the room.

"Good evening, sir."

"Is it a good evening?"

"Not really, sir. No records were in Davenport's office."

"It is vital that the records be retrieved. We know he was operating naked, but word was getting out, a steady stream of names and information. There are records and there is a contact. I want both."

"I understand, sir. I made a cursory search of his home during the funeral but didn't have enough time for a thorough one. The house has been filled with people ever since. I'll go back when I have a longer time frame. I do have access to his safety deposit box and will search it tomorrow."

"What about close friends?"

"I'm checking them, but I have to be cautious. I'm working through the Dallas Ad League, ostensibly doing a biographical story on Davenport for an advertising journal."

"Stay with this. There'll be real trouble if the leak continues. I want you back in Dallas tonight. Report in between six and seven every evening," the director ordered.

A guttural, disembodied voice spoke for the first time from the direction of a wing back chair that was faced away from the room. "Why should there be any more trouble?"

The director started to answer, but the voice growled that he wanted to hear from the operative.

Silverman nervously backed off and looked toward the dark corner from which the voice had come. The tension in the room was almost visible.

"There won't be any trouble, sir. I'll find the records and the contact."

"That's what I wanted to hear," the voice intoned.

Chapter 1

JENNIE DAVENPORT LOOKED WILDLY about her. Just enough light permeated the dark for her to see she was in a bedroom. A scream rose up in her throat when she looked down at the bed and saw a strange man. *Oh dear Lord, who is that ... oh, Lord ...* Terrified, she stifled a scream and backed out of the room hoping he wouldn't wake up. *Where am I,* she wondered desperately. *Calm,* Jennie told herself. *Have to stay calm ... have to get out of here.*

Shutting the door put her in total darkness. She inched along the wall until her hand hit an opening. She slipped in, easing the door shut. Expelling the breath she had been holding, she flipped on the light and caught a movement out of the corner of her eye. Twisting violently, she looked all around the room. Relief flooded over her—it was only her reflection in a mirror. Stomach reeling, her legs gave way and she fell on the bed with a thud.

I was running across a lawn, she recalled. *Josh was right behind me.* Every fiber of her being still wanted to scream, but she didn't dare. She clenched her hands tightly and choked the scream down. *Breathe, just keep breathing.*

What am I doing here? I was outside, and now, this house—that man. I have to find Josh. She had to find out where she was. So scared she could barely move, she forced herself to get up and look out the window. A car was parked in the driveway; it looked like her car. Turning back to the room, she saw a photograph on the dresser and picked it up. It was a picture of her daughters, Kris and Laurie.

My daughters—suddenly she knew; everything kicked in. She was at the lake house. The man in the other room was Nathan. "I didn't recognize my own husband," she cried out in anguish. "I was talking to Josh, but that can't be. Josh died years ago." Jennie started to shake, she collapsed on the bed. *I just talked to a dead man. Breathe … in and out … keep breathing.*

Head pounding and heart racing, she turned out the light, opened the door, and looked in all the upstairs rooms. "Crazy, I've gone completely crazy," she mumbled. No one was there except Nathan, and he was still asleep. Something not only weird but really frightening had just happened.

Josh is alive! I was with him. She had always felt he was alive. *He must be downstairs.* Frantically she rushed to the staircase and stumbled down it. She searched every room, every closet. He wasn't there. She couldn't see anybody out the windows either.

Maybe he's outside. Fumbling with the keys, she opened the door after several tries and dashed out into the misty night. She ran up to the road, but nothing was moving—no cars, not even a headlight; no glimmer of any lights shone through the trees. She ran back past the house and down the hill to the dock and looked across the water for boats; no ripples, no boats. Everything was still and quiet except for the distant thunder. The yard lights from across the lake were making unbroken streaks in the water, so no boats had passed recently. All the houses around the cove were dark. There was no movement anywhere.

"Josh, answer me." Jennie called softly. "Where are you?"

She shivered as thunder cracked and the sky lit up. Rain began to pelt her before she got back to the house. She'd had some strange dreams since Josh died, but this was no dream. She hadn't been to bed; she had been standing at her bedroom window looking at the lake. No one will believe this. Nobody believed her six years ago when she thought she saw him.

She paced barefoot around the room, peering out every window. Cold, wet, and shivering, Jennie put water on to boil for tea and wrapped a blanket around her. Every detail of whatever had happened was vivid in her mind. It had been real. She could still feel his face under her fingers. His voice was ringing in her ears. He'd even sung a song to her, the old pony song; she hadn't thought about it in years.

Irrationally she could remember everything, riding in the car, running across the grassy lawn, but most of all, touching Josh …

Jennie didn't question how she got in the car. The car was going down a boulevard lined with huge trees that overhung the street like a canopy. Moonlight broke through the leaves making patterns on the pavement. The houses they passed were old with double-curved staircases leading up to the front door. Ground level looked like basements. Some houses had balconies. Others had round turrets, lots of ironwork, all quite old and picturesque. It looked like New Orleans.

All of a sudden she realized she wasn't alone. There was a man beside her. And they were in the back of a limousine. There was another man driving.

"There's the old Jung Hotel. Do you remember when we stayed there?"

Startled, she tried to see his face in the darkness. "We stayed there?"

"It's no longer the Jung. It closed years ago," he said.

"Who are you?"

He began to hum a tune that she hadn't heard for years. Recognizing it, she turned toward him and strained to see him in the faint light.

"Who are you?"

She caught her breath when he began to sing the words …

> *Go to sleepy, little baby,*
> *Go to sleepy, little baby,*
> *When you wake, we'll play patty, patty cake*
> *with all the pretty little ponies.*

It was a voice she knew so well, a voice from the past. One she never expected to hear again. And the old lullaby, the nonsense lullaby. Oh yes, she remembered it.

"Look at me," she stammered.

Light flickered across his face when he turned toward her. Her heart stopped. It couldn't be, but it was. He was there beside her. He looked different; his face was fuller with a beard that was almost gray instead of red like it used to be. His hair was streaked with white. He was heavier and looked older. Of course he was older. It had been six years since he died. He died—yet, it was Josh.

The breath she had been holding exploded out of her. "You're dead. You died years ago."

"Hold on, honey," he said as she leaned away from him. "Listen to me. Take a deep breath and listen. "It's okay. It's really me. I'm alive. I'm so sorry about all this."

"Sorry, you're sorry for dying. This doesn't make any sense."

"Think, honey, you remember our lullaby, the one we used to sing to our daughters."

"You died, and we buried you. I saw you buried; you were in the casket."

The memories and the pain of that day flared up in her mind. She had known something was wrong at the funeral home. She combed his hair and that helped, but he still didn't look like her husband. His shirt didn't even fit right. Everything was strange then, out of focus, but he was in that casket.

"We buried you," she kept repeating. "You can't be here."

"I know it seems impossible. Remember Kansas City, we used to say that if we were ever separated we'd always recognize each other by that song. We even joked and said the pony song was our private code."

She looked at him again, right in the face. She touched his forehead and felt the small scar on the bridge of his nose. It was Josh. He was back. With a flood of joy, she threw her arms around him. They rode in silence for a little while with their arms wrapped around each other.

"Tell me about my girls," he whispered hoarsely. "Do Kris and Laurie remember Scarlet Ribbons? Do they remember me singing it to them?"

She opened her purse and showed him pictures of them and of his two grandchildren. As he looked at them, tears rolled down his face. "They're young women now. I've missed so much, so very much."

"What happened?" Jennie asked crying softly. "Tell me what happened."

"There's not enough time to tell you everything right now. The important part is I had to disappear, similar to a witness protection plan."

"Why didn't we go with you?"

"It's a long story, honey," he continued cautiously. "Do you remember when I was in the Army, and was sent to New York to a special information school in New Rochelle? That was the beginning and all that was true, but there was more to it. In 1954, a group of us were flown to an island; we weren't told where it was. It was top secret, paramilitary training. I was classified G-2. You didn't know it then, but G-2 is the Army counterpart of the FBI. I was also trained to evaluate information concerning the war potential of foreign nations and the capability of the United States to defend itself. That's why they did the intensive investigation on you when we were married."

"I remember. The Army came to Dallas and talked to our neighbors where I grew up, the people where I worked, my high school and college teachers. I had never heard of anyone who was investigated like that, but you told me it was customary to check out the wives of anyone privy to top secret intelligence."

"All this was in preparation for my assignment. Specifically, I was qualified to handle sensitive data for the Special Operations Division of the Army. It wasn't just the news releases to the American public; however, that was part of it." Josh paused and touched Jennie's face. Then with a deep sigh, he continued.

"As time went by, I began to be aware of some strange occurrences. A number of them concerned the NSA and other government agencies. Then I stumbled on what appeared to be a conspiracy. I found information about a covert group planning a controlled takeover of our country. Actually, their plans extend way beyond the United States. The group's long-term plans are to control all the world governments. I couldn't ignore it. I started tracing it, unofficially, just on my own. Every time I thought I was closing in, I ran into a brick wall. Someone must have found out what I was doing. Evidently I got too close for comfort because that was when I was called to a meeting at Fort Leavenworth. You remember the week I spent up there? I was questioned; maybe a better word would be interrogated. They tried to convince me I was misinterpreting what I had found. A man I respected and admired echoed this. I received papers shortly after that week stating that I was to be mustered out four months early. I had to agree to stop all investigation and never reveal what I had discovered. In other words, they were getting rid of me. I also had to agree to be reactivated anytime they wanted me back."

"We moved back to Texas, and I didn't hear from them for years. And, for the most part, forgot about it until the spring of 1974 when they contacted me. I was reactivated then. That was part of the agreement I had signed." Josh hesitated, and then continued quietly. "You're never *out* when you are G-2. They had considered me a sleeper up to that point. I was now in a position with the advertising agency to make trips and keep irregular hours without arousing suspicion. The conspiracy I had chanced upon when we were in Kansas City was indeed real. There's not enough time to tell you any more, besides I don't want to compromise you with the details. All you need to know is that when my cover was blown, they had to bring me in."

"Why didn't we go with you?"

"It just wasn't possible. There was no way everybody could be protected from this group: you, the girls, my mom, your parents, my sister, her husband, or my niece and nephew. There were too many ways they could get to me through all of you. The only means they could find to protect the whole family was for me to die. It had to be believable and public. You had to believe it. If

I were dead, there would be no reprisals against any of you. It wasn't what I wanted, but I had to keep you safe."

"I don't understand how all this was done. How you could die right in front of me? How could you be in the casket that still for so long?"

"They gave me medication that knocked me out. I tried to warn you right at the end. If I could have stopped it then, I would have. But it was too late. The medicine had already taken effect. As for the casket, another body was altered to look like me. No one expects a dead person to look right, and you sure don't expect another body to be there."

"I don't know how I could have been fooled. I knew you too well."

"They are really good at what they do, and they counted on shock and grief to do the rest. It would have been easier if you had taken the medication they tried to give you in the hospital. That would have kept you confused through it all."

"What a horrible thing to do to someone. They manipulated me, just like a pawn in a chess game. But this was my life, not a game. Have you any idea of what Kris, Laurie, and I have been through?"

"Oh, Jennie, I didn't do this because I wanted to. It had to be done to protect you, so you and the girls could have a normal life—no hiding, no looking over your shoulder every minute. No watching for strange faces that might be stalking you. It was the end of my life in all the ways that counted. You did have Kris and Laurie."

"Where have you been all these years?"

"They first moved me to a secure zone, then out of the country for a couple of years. I've been back in the States since then, much of the time in New Orleans."

"Who are *they*? Why have *they* allowed you to contact me now?"

"It's Army G-2. They haven't allowed me do this, but I think it's safe. My death hasn't been questioned, and I've been much closer to the situation than operations has. I would never endanger you or our daughters."

Josh hesitated, then with a terrible heaviness said, "I had to see you. They told me when it all came down six years ago it would be temporary, two or three years at the most. I never figured on you marrying again. They didn't tell me until a month ago." His eyes turned cold and steely. "They should have told me. I knew then I had to break free."

"But I'm not free," Jennie cried. "I'm married and have been for a year. I'm married to two men. What do we do now?"

"It was never supposed to go this far." Josh looked sharply at the driver, and then said very softly, "Tell me who you married."

"Nathan Scott. I married Nathan Scott."

Josh's body went rigid. "Nathan Scott," he said ominously. "I know him. How did you meet him?"

"At the country club; he said he'd played in a tennis tournament with you. He's been wonderful to us, and I do care about him. He's a good man, but he's not you. Do you have any idea how much our daughters needed you," she cried in anger. "How could you do this to us?"

"There was no other option at that time, honey, but now is our chance. You have to get away from Scott."

Unnerved, frightened, Jennie panicked and yelled, "Stop the car. I have to get out—right now."

She flung open the door and ran away from the car. Light was shining through the windows of the large building in front of her. Huge trees were surrounding her; their limbs almost touching the grassy lawn. The moonlight created long shadows that stretched like fingers ready to grab her. The wind moved the fingers back and forth.

Josh ran after her. "Wait for me, Jennie."

When she turned to face him, she couldn't see through the dense fog. She was hemmed in by the dark murky night. And she couldn't find him.

Frantic, she called out, "I'm right here, but I can't see you. Please, please, don't leave me again. Where are you, Josh ...?"

All she could hear was the eerie sound of foghorns in the distance.

Chapter 2

THE SHRILL WHISTLE OF the teakettle sent Jennie running. She had to turn it off before it woke Nathan. She didn't want to talk to him right now. It was a couple of hours till dawn and she had to think, try to sort out what happened. She curled up in the corner of the sofa with her tea. She couldn't stop shaking. She pulled the blanket around her and held the hot cup with both hands trying to get warm.

The terror still swirled around in her stomach. Jennie felt cold and queasy. She burrowed deeper into the blanket. "I didn't recognize Nathan ... or where I was," she sobbed, still wanting to scream.

She had seen Josh. "I even touched his face. We were in a car in New Orleans, but I couldn't have been," she cried softly. "Oh, dear Lord, help me. What happened to me?"

There has to be a rational explanation, but what? Yesterday was just a normal day, nothing out of the ordinary. She had looked forward all week to going to the lake house. Nathan came home early and was anxious to get started ...

"WHAT A WEEK THIS HAS been. I'm ready for a break. Are Kris and Laurie coming with us?" Nathan had asked while they were loading the car.

"No, just you and me, I didn't ask the girls. I thought we'd enjoy some time alone. We haven't been down since Christmas and there's a lot of spring cleanup. It's too cold to swim, so there wouldn't be much for them to do except rake leaves and that wouldn't excite them."

The two-hour drive to the lake house always seemed longer on Friday nights. She supposed it was because they were anxious to get there. They had known they wanted the house by the lake the first day the real estate lady showed it to them. It had been a good decision. Everyone loved it and it had helped draw them together as a family.

When they arrived at the lake house, the view was beckoning. They had unloaded quickly and hurried down to the water's edge. The fiery glow of the sunset was spreading over the lake. The night was filled with sounds as water splashed against the retaining wall. Every now and then she could hear the distant droning of a motorboat across the lake accompanied by the mesmerizing chirps of birds and crickets. Yard lights twinkled around the shoreline. The peace of the place washed over her, and she knew Nathan felt it too. He hadn't been very talkative, but that was nothing new. She wished he would tell her more about himself and his job. All he'd ever say was that he had been in the military and now he was a civilian employee of the Army. She knew his office was in the Federal building downtown Dallas, but that was all. He wouldn't talk about what he did. He was very secretive about his past and his job. He had told her many times, "It's a very dull government job, there's nothing to tell." Each time they came to the lake, Jennie hoped that the magic of it would help them grow closer. She yearned for that, but she couldn't break through the armor Nathan held so tightly around him. It puzzled her that he seemed almost afraid to let her in.

Jennie relaxed a little as she remembered racing Nathan back to the house and calling out "Loser has to make the drinks." She liked making him smile. She had cooked dinner and Nathan had opened his favorite wine.

LAST NIGHT HAD BEEN NO different than any other evening they had spent at the lake house, absolutely nothing to cause such confusion. Jennie got up and put the empty cup on the coffee table. The adrenaline rush was leaving and exhaustion was setting in. She really wanted to go to bed, but she knew it was useless. She'd just toss and turn and stare into the darkness. It was a long time until daylight. Better to stay down here with the lights on. Besides, if she stayed here, she could watch the door.

She had touched Josh. She felt the scar on his face. Jennie looked at her fingers and could still feel the moisture of his tears. She had not been dreaming, but what had happened? Maybe she was losing her mind. Her head was pounding. She took a couple of aspirins and stared out all the windows again. She picked up a magazine, sat back down, and tried to concentrate on it. After a few minutes, it fell to her lap as her mind drifted again to the past.

She had never really accepted Josh's death. There were too many loose ends, such as those strange phone calls with the whirring noise that started right after Josh died. They still come at least once a week. She had kept records, but the phone company had never been able to trace or stop them.

Just like the police never found out who vandalized Josh's office. As far as anyone could determine, nothing had been taken. And her house, she knew someone searched it one weekend when she and the girls visited her parents in the country. Nothing had been messed up. It was the little things that alerted her. Papers were slightly out of place on her desk and the stapler was in a different spot. But there was no way to prove to the police the house had been searched. She just knew it had; she could feel it. They said she probably imagined it. Jennie knew different and added extra locks on all the doors and windows. Same thing happened with her safe deposit box. The woman at the bank said that no one could have gotten into it, but the documents were shuffled around.

The door to the past had opened and memories flooded in. There was that time in church when she thought she saw Josh. Maybe she really did. If only she had moved faster she might have caught up with him. And the telephone calls. She heard his voice once on the phone. She knew it was him. She knew it, and once again, no one believed her.

Then there was that TV program when she saw him in a crowd of people. Her friends told her lots of people have these things happen to them after someone dies. She understood they were trying to help and that was how she learned to live with it, but sometimes she still thought *what if…?* The *what-ifs* could drive a person mad. And now this, well, this is a really big *what-if.* Jennie moaned as she wiped her tears away.

It hurt to think on those years. She struggled so hard to leave them in the past. Since she and Nathan married a year ago, she had been content, happy most of the time, and that was good. But acceptance of Josh's death—that was another matter. Sometimes, even after all these years, she would wake in the middle of the night and remember. She would feel uneasy and way down inside her the unanswered questions about his death still demanded answers. Tugging the blanket tighter around her, she wondered what Nathan would think? She knew she'd have to tell him because this wasn't normal. Something peculiar had happened to her and she had to find out what.

Her friends would just laugh and say it was another dream. She had listened to them before and where did it get her? Exactly nowhere, so who would really listen to her now? Someone who knew Josh way back, someone he trusted. Herman Wilkins knew Josh in high school. He had stayed by her side at the funeral home that last terrible day; he might be willing to help. He was a detective with the Dallas police and had told her to call if she ever needed anything. Well, she definitely needed something now. He would at least listen to her. She'd call him and see what he could find out. Maybe she could go to New Orleans and look around. If she could find the place where they were driving, it might tell her something.

This is senseless. She was thinking like it was real, but something had certainly happened. Could there really be such things as thought transference or telepathic communication? She had heard about it on TV, but never paid much attention to it.

Restless, Jennie went outside again. She couldn't quit looking for Josh. She could still feel him. The rain had stopped, and the air smelled so fresh. A night bird was chirping, and water was thumping against the retaining wall. *All very normal except her—but then, her life had not been normal for years and now she was seeing and talking to a dead man.* She laughed nervously.

Back in the house she sat beside the bay window and watched the dawn break through the darkness. Nathan would be awake before long. Sooner or later she would have to tell him because she couldn't ignore this. She certainly couldn't ignore Josh's reaction when she told him she had married Nathan. If this is real and Josh is alive—she wasn't sure she could face it. Her heart pounded so hard she couldn't breathe.

"Good morning, honey. You're up early," Nathan said cheerfully as he came down the stairs.

Startled, heart racing, Jennie stammered, "I, uh, couldn't sleep, bad headache, so I came down here. Took some aspirin, but it hasn't helped."

"You look tired. I'll get the coffee going. That will help."

Later, Jennie went upstairs, showered and dressed. She wanted to look outside for footprints, but logic told her the rain would have washed them away.

Everything was changing again; nothing ever stayed the same. When she thought about Nathan's reaction, she realized she didn't know him well enough to predict how he would respond. They had been married such a short time. Would he laugh and make a joke of it or would he understand that this was something out of the ordinary? Maybe Herman will have an explanation, and she'd never have to tell Nathan.

But amidst all the uncertainty, she knew without a doubt that she had never given Josh up and that she was still waiting for him, even after all these years.

Chapter 3

THE ARMY COMMAND CENTER of G-2 was a hotbed of activity.

The Intelligence and Security Command (INSCOM) was charged with prevention and detection of acts of treason, espionage, and sabotage, as well as the policing of other critical situations.

Suddenly, a loud warning signal blared. A young man bolted back to his station in the monitoring room, sloshing coffee with every step. "What the hell? That's never happened before." Grabbing the phone he punched in an extension. "Transmission's been interrupted on *JDavenport*. The screen's blank."

The senior officer arrived in a matter of seconds. "Is it still off? Did you get a fix on her location?"

"No, not yet. I'm checking to see how long it was off. I'll have to run the backup tape to get the location."

"Get it fast. General Thurman's not going to be happy when he hears about this."

The general charged into the room, red-faced, angry, and out of breath. "How long was transmission off?"

"Looks like about an hour, sir."

"An hour—what the devil was the operator doing all that time? All he's supposed to do is sit there, watch the screen, and alert us if anything changes."

The officer grimaced, glanced at the young man, and said hesitantly, "He fell asleep, sir, then left to get coffee. Nothing has ever happened in the six years we've been monitoring her."

General Thurman stormed out of the room snapping orders as he went.

"This is why she's under surveillance. I want that operator in my office ASAP. Check the satellite and the backup tape. Find the problem."

"Reaves," he yelled, "Get a tail on the Davenport woman this instant. I want to know where she is and what she's doing."

Chapter 4

Monday
March 7, 1983
DALLAS, TEXAS

NATHAN AND JENNIE STAYED at the lake house until early Monday morning. She wasn't able to think about anything except Josh. When they were driving home Nathan asked her what was wrong; he said she seemed so distant. She made up some story about Kris and Laurie and the grandchildren.

A day had passed and the more she thought about it the more certain she was that whatever happened was not normal. Jennie could not get past the fact that she had not been asleep. Dreams could be vivid, but after you woke up they faded. The details were as clear to her today as they had been Friday night. As soon as Nathan left for the office, she grabbed a pencil and wrote it all down.

Next thing was to find Herman's phone number. He had given her his card with his direct line at Josh's funeral, but that was six years ago. "No telling where it is now," she muttered. Starting with the top drawer of the kitchen desk, she worked her way to the bottom. No luck. She would have to call the police department and ask for him. The minute she picked up the phone, she remembered where it was. She sighed in relief when she found it. Anxiously, she dialed. "Herman Wilkins, please."

"Detective Wilkins isn't in," the operator answered. "Do you want to leave your number?"

"Yes, I do. Have him call Jennie Scott. 972-555-2710. Wait a minute— you better put Jennie Davenport Scott. Do you know when he'll be in?"

"Late afternoon, I'll give him your message."

"So now I wait," she grumbled.

The attic was next on her mental to-do list. She wanted to find Josh's

19

Army papers. The attic was dim and filled with cobwebs. Not much light worked its way through the dusty window and the one light bulb did little to brighten it up. Memories of when Kris and Laurie played here drifted through her mind. They were always half scared; perhaps that's what made it so much fun.

She shifted several boxes containing things from Josh's desk away from the older Army trunks. Yes, the attic was definitely filled with ghosts, ghosts of another life.

When she got to the older trunks labeled *Army,* she really hoped the top one had Josh's papers in it. If it didn't, she wasn't sure she could move it to get to the one underneath. She was relieved to find it was filled with papers. She pulled an old chair over to the window, but it was hard to see in the dim light. She found a rag and wiped years of grime off the windowpanes. Gathering up an armload of papers, Jennie began her search.

The papers brought back a flood of memories and a few tears even after all these years. *You'd think it would be easier by now,* she thought, as she wiped her eyes with a dirt-smeared hand.

New Rochelle. Josh had talked a lot about New Rochelle. The Army sent him there. Josh had told her that when he enlisted the recruiting officer was interested in his writing ability and had questioned him at length about it. "There's a possibility you might qualify for a special school that trains men to handle classified information," the officer had said. "This school would teach you to write and process news releases. Upon completion, you'd have a chance to be linked to the National Military Command Center at the Pentagon if you could pass the background check. Would you be interested?"

Josh had realized at the end of his second year in college that he couldn't swing another year even with a partial football scholarship. It sounded like his best chance would be to join the Army, spend his four years there, get some training, and then have the GI Bill to help him finish college, so he signed on. By the time he finished basic training, the background check had been completed. His next orders took him to the Special Information School in New Rochelle, New York.

Jennie knew he was in a special division of the Army. G-2 was familiar, but she had never heard anything about Josh having gone to an island. "I should have asked more questions back then," she mumbled. "Problem was—I didn't know I needed to. I'm always so good at asking the important ones after the fact."

After New Rochelle, he was officially based out of Fort Leavenworth, Kansas. He actually lived in Kansas City, Missouri, and was assigned to the Army Hometown News Center, the clearinghouse for all military information. Top priority clearance was required and the background checks became more demanding. Why didn't she question the extensive investigation that was run on her before approval was granted for them to be married? Would things have been different if she had?

Permission finally came through, and they were married in January, 1956. Jennie smiled as she remembered how they piled all their things in their new Chevy and drove to Kansas City. Good memories. Military life had not been much different for them than civilian life since they were on *per diem* and had an apartment in the city. Their goal during those days had been to save enough money for Josh to finish college.

"I hate these weekends, Josh, when you have to stay at the News Center. It's so lonely here."

"I don't like leaving you alone either, but it's only once a month, honey. It's not like the Army gives me a choice. Believe me, it's dull enough there."

Josh wasn't allowed to tell her anything about what his duties were or what he read and edited. The only thing he told her was that all information about the military had to be cleared through the Center before it could be released to the newspapers, and that some information never made it to the papers.

By 1957, he had become editor-in-chief of the News Center and everything filtered through him. Jennie watched him become utterly consumed with his work. He would forget to come home until she called to remind him of the time. *It wasn't much better when he got home,* she recalled. *He still wasn't with her. He couldn't let go of it.*

In spring of that year, he had received orders to report to the base at Fort Leavenworth. He never told her what it was about, but she knew it was serious and that he was very preoccupied when he came home. Shortly after that, he received early separation papers from the Army. Josh told her he expected them and that he would get full GI benefits even though he was mustering out before the end of his four-year commitment.

WHEN THE PHONE RANG, JENNIE jumped and ran down the attic stairs. She was out of breath as she caught it on the fourth ring.

"Jennie, Herman Wilkins. Are you all right?"

"Yes, just out of breath. I was in the attic and had to rush down the stairs. Thanks for calling me back so soon."

"It's great to hear from you. How are you and your daughters?"

"We're all good. Kris and Laurie are both married, and I actually have two grandchildren. How are you and Molly?"

"Doing great," Herman answered. "I can beat your two grandchildren by two. I heard you married again. Would I know him?"

"I don't think so. His name's Nathan Scott. His wife died several years ago so we have a lot in common. It's been good for both of us. It's really hard to be alone after you've been married."

"I'm sure it would be. I couldn't make it without Molly. What's on your mind, Jennie? After all these years, I bet this isn't a social call."

"I was wondering if we could meet for coffee. There's something I'd like to tell you, and I'd rather not do it at my house. Could you give me an hour sometime soon?"

"Would tomorrow morning be quick enough? We've got a grandson's birthday party tonight. If it's urgent, I could get away later this evening."

"Tomorrow's great," Jennie answered. "Will ten o'clock work for you?"

"Ten's good. I have to check in at the precinct first thing in the morning. What about Kip's Coffee Shop on Walnut Hill near Greenville?"

"I'll be there. Thanks, Herman."

The rest of the day went by slowly. Back in the ghost-filled attic, Jennie searched until she found Josh's military papers. There it was in black and white—he was G-2.

She went through all the papers to see if there was any mention of what Josh told her but didn't find anything. She found his discharge papers. Nothing appeared unusual except for the fact that he had been discharged four months shy of his four-year commitment.

She wondered why he had been released early. Josh had never told her—another unanswered question to add to the list.

Chapter 5

DAYLIGHT FINALLY CAME. ANOTHER sleepless night, her mind had played and replayed what she was going to tell Herman. It was hard to believe she actually called him. "He'll probably think I'm a lunatic."

Jennie dressed early and made breakfast for Nathan. Anxious for him to leave, she tried not to show it. She knew he was sensing something; she caught him staring at her with a puzzled look on his face.

Herman was waiting when she got to Kip's Coffee Shop. They ordered coffee and muffins, chatted about their families, and then he looked at Jennie expectantly.

"What's happened?" he asked, "You look like you haven't slept for days."

"You're right. I haven't gotten much sleep the last few nights. I feel a little silly. I don't know what you're going to think about this, probably that I'm crazy. A really strange thing happened to me last weekend, and I need help sorting it out. Are you up for a weird story?"

"I bet I've heard stranger stories than yours," Herman laughed. "Are you forgetting I'm an undercover cop? Lay it on me."

"Okay, here goes." Jennie paused, took a deep breath, clenched her hands together in her lap, and began. "It's about Josh. Last Friday night something happened to me. It was really bizarre. It wasn't a dream unless you can have one when you are awake and standing up. You know it's been six years and I haven't dreamt about him in a long time. This has really upset me."

"I can tell. Dreams can be pretty graphic sometimes. What else?" Herman said.

"Do you remember when you came to the funeral home after Josh died?

23

We sat and talked a long time about him, and you told me what you had seen happen to aneurysm victims?"

"Sure I do. It was a rough time."

"Did you think that he looked like Josh?"

"Jennie, no one looks the same after they die."

"That's not what I mean. Do you think it was Josh?" she asked.

"Wait a minute, that's an odd question. You better tell me what's behind it. Maybe you should tell me the whole story, if that's what caused you to question if the man was Josh."

Jennie fidgeted around in the booth, folded and unfolded her napkin, sipped coffee, then looked at Herman. "Okay, here goes."

When she finished, Herman just sat there stirring his coffee and avoiding her eyes. She got more and more nervous. Then he looked directly at her and asked, "Was there anything in that episode you didn't know about years ago when Josh was in the Army?"

"The part about G-2's mission, I didn't know much of that. I thought it was just sending out releases to the various newspapers around the country."

Herman thought a minute and pulled out a small notepad. "We can check that and see if it's true."

"Are you saying that you believe that this was real?"

"No. I don't know what happened. What I'm saying is that we can check out those facts. I want you to think about G-2 and see if you could have known all that. All the rest of it was probably bits and pieces of things in your mind. The subconscious can play tricks on us sometimes. About Josh's looks, it had been a number of years since I'd seen him so I can't give you a definite answer. Of course, he looked older and somewhat heavier, but I never thought about it not being Josh."

Herman motioned the waitress to refill their coffees and then continued slowly. "I've been involved in some special projects these last few years that involve subliminal messages and tracking devices. There are ways of communicating that I doubt you've ever heard of. Let me think about this and do a little research. In the meantime, you do some real hard thinking about whether you could have known what the G-2 mission was."

They got up from the table, paid the bill, and Herman walked Jennie to her car.

"My advice right now is that you get a grip on yourself. You know as well as I do that it was probably wishful thinking. I hate to hurry off, but I have to get back to work. I'll give you a call in a day or two. Relax, Jennie, and get some sleep."

"I'll try, Herman. Your help means a lot to me. I know it shouldn't have upset me so much. I guess we never really give up someone we love."

"If you're going to keep dwelling on this, Jennie, tell your husband about it. He needs to know; otherwise, he'll think something else is wrong," Herman advised.

"Okay. But he'll just think I'm nuts."

"That's better than imagining you don't care about him."

"All right, I hear you," Jennie said, as she gave him a quick hug. "I'll be waiting for your call."

Driving away from the restaurant she was relieved and a little surprised that Herman hadn't laughed at her. She should have told him about Josh's reaction to Nathan, but she hated to prejudice him against her husband.

Life was always changing. Pulling into the parking lot at the grocery store, Jennie was grateful for a little bit of normalcy, even if it was grocery shopping and cooking meals.

Later that night she tried to tell Nathan, but the words just wouldn't come. Maybe she really didn't want to.

Chapter 6

TWO LONG DAYS PASSED before Herman called. First thing, he asked if she had told Nathan.

"Not yet," Jennie hedged. "It's hard—I'm not sure how he'll react."

"Well, you better do it. I don't want to meet at the coffee shop. I can be at your house about five this afternoon. Tell him before I get there."

Unable to postpone it any longer she called Nathan and asked if he could come home early, about four. "I need to tell you about something."

As soon as he got home Jennie handed Nathan a drink and launched into the story. He was very quiet when she finished, no laughing or joking about it. "I wish you had talked to me about it before calling Herman," he said after a long uncomfortable silence.

Finishing his drink, Nathan poured another and paced around the room. "I guess it's possible he might have some answers for you when he gets here. Then you won't have to worry about it. I haven't had a dream that vivid, but I've heard it happens. I'm sure it'd shake a person up. Have you been able to remember if you ever knew about G-2's responsibilities?"

"It wasn't a dream, Nathan. That's the one thing I am sure of. As for G-2, I don't remember ever knowing any of that. I'm sorry I didn't tell you sooner, but I was very nervous about telling you. I don't want you to think I'm unhappy."

"I know you're not unhappy, but I also know you still think about Josh. You know I'll always help you if I can, even if it's a dream, and a pretty silly one at that."

Relief was evident on Jennie's face. "Maybe it was a silly dream," she laughed. "On my sensible level, I wonder about that. But on some other level I think, what if it's true. What if it's true and Josh is trying to reach me."

"It may be a good idea for Herman to come," Nathan said after a moment. "Maybe he'll be able to settle it."

When Herman arrived, Jennie introduced him to Nathan saying that she, Herman and Josh were in high school together and the guys had played football on the same team. They talked comfortably while she got Herman a drink.

"Herman," Jennie interrupted. "Did you find out anything?"

"A little bit, enough to make me want to investigate further. First, did you think about G-2 and do you remember ever hearing about its mission before?"

"No—I mean, yes, I have thought about it, but, no, I can't remember knowing any of that."

"That's what I was afraid of," Herman replied. "If it's something that wasn't already in your head, then we have two explanations. Something actually occurred last Friday or you read it and don't remember doing so. What I did find was that everything you said about G-2 is correct. So I went one step further, I called the funeral home and spoke to the director. I had him pull all the paperwork on the funeral. There was no physical description in the records. The director didn't know why. He said there's a mandatory section that describes the person, the cause of death, any abnormalities, or other details. That page was missing in Josh's file. He checked several other files and they were complete. He had no explanation as to why it was missing."

"So why do you think that particular page is gone," Jennie asked.

"That's what I asked. The director said he had no idea. It certainly wasn't the normal procedure."

Turning toward Nathan, Herman asked, "What do you think about this?"

"It's surprising that Jennie doesn't know more about G-2. My guess is she's just forgotten. Death plays havoc with a person's mind. The missing paperwork at the funeral home is much more of a concern. How else can we check on this? Jennie's not going to rest easy until she knows what this is all about."

"I've thought about it all day," Herman said. "I'd like your permission, Jennie, to request Josh's Army records. I can probably get the information quicker than you could. I'd like to see what we can find out from them."

"That's fine. Go ahead. What do you think they'll tell you?"

"I don't know, Jennie, maybe nothing. But I'd like to see them."

"I want to see them when you get them. I know my daughters would like to have a copy of his records." Jennie paused and looked at Nathan. "I haven't been able to get New Orleans off my mind. I've been thinking that I'd like to go there and see if I can find that grassy lawn I ran across. What do you think about that?"

"I think it's a good idea," Herman said. "If nothing else, it'd be a nice little trip. I guess I better confess, I've already requested Josh's records. We should hear something early next week. When I do, I'll give you a call." Herman got up, saying that was all they could do right now.

"Thanks, Herman. So how was your grandson's birthday party? How old is he?" Jennie asked.

"It was wild. He's five and quite a handful. There were way too many presents."

"These grandchildren are really something," Nathan said. "Herman, I appreciate your helping Jennie. You're a good friend. We'll be anxious to hear what you find."

Nathan's face was solemn after Herman left. "It's interesting that Herman is taking this seriously. He must have seen lots of unusual happenings in his line of work. I can't believe he'd investigate something as insignificant as a dream."

Putting his hands on Jennie's shoulders and turning her towards him, he stared intently at her. "Is there anything else you haven't told me?"

"No, nothing, I told you everything. There's nothing else." *Except,* Jennie thought, *that look on Josh's face when she told him about Nathan.*

"New Orleans is a good idea. We're due a little vacation time, and I haven't been there in years," Nathan said.

They checked the calendar. If Herman was going to have some information sometime next week, they might as well go this weekend.

Chapter 7

"HAVE YOU DETERMINED WHERE Jennie Davenport was when the screen blacked out?" General Thurman, Chief of Staff of INSCOM, asked as he stared at the monitor.

"Yes, sir, at a place called Cedar Creek Lake in Texas. It appears to be the Scotts' weekend retreat. They go there often and the signal has never been lost before. We're currently hearing a lot of talk about someone named Josh and whether he's alive or not. Most of the things coming through have been fairly garbled, but that's not unusual."

"Get me a printout of her words. What interrupted the transmission? You've had six days to figure it out."

"We don't know, sir. The backup tape was completely erased."

"How the devil can that happen?"

"Not easily, sir. We've eliminated a power glitch and a satellite problem. The only viable possibility is that the system was intentionally penetrated. It would take knowledge of how it operates and some very sophisticated equipment to break in. Whoever did this also had to know about the backup copy and how to erase it. There's no way for us to trace who broke in."

The general sputtered angrily and yelled for Reaves to get him the latest report from the team tailing the Davenport woman. Perching on the side of a desk, the general read through it. Nothing had gone on for six years and now all hell was breaking loose.

"Reaves, call the Dallas Police Department chief and get a rundown on that cop, Herman Wilkins. That woman is just stirring up things, but the cop could cause some real problems."

Chapter 8

"PULL OFF AT THE Welcome Center, Nathan. It's the next exit. I want a city map of New Orleans," Jennie said when they crossed into Louisiana.

The woman at the center gave them a map and made several suggestions of places to stay. She cautioned them to watch their billfolds and purses and stay on the main streets. New Orleans was having lots of problems with muggings and pickpockets.

Opting not to stay in the French Quarter, they pulled into a Holiday Inn on Interstate 10. After unloading the car, Nathan asked Jennie what she wanted to do first, eat dinner or look around.

"I'd like to drive around before it gets dark," she answered. "It's been so long since I've been here. I know the city has changed a lot but maybe something will be familiar."

"The trolleys are still running," Jennie said excitedly when they exited I-10 onto Canal Street. "I used to love to ride them." Continuing on down Canal, she was shocked when she saw the Jung Hotel. It was dilapidated and a *For Sale* sign was nailed to the door.

"Stop, Nathan. Look, that building with the *For Sale* sign. That's the Jung hotel I told you about. When Josh and I stayed there, it was very nice. It looks just like it did last Friday night. How could I have known that?"

"I don't know, Jennie. You probably saw something about it on television. There's a program every year about Mardi Gras."

Jennie grabbed her camera and snapped a picture before they drove on. "Turn left on Decatur, Nathan. Let's drive through the French Quarter."

They saw the Cafe du Monde that served the wonderful crullers and the strong, chicory coffee, passed by St. Louis Cathedral, and drove up and down the narrow streets.

"We were on a street with lots of trees. Let's go to City Park area next."

"I'd forgotten how beautiful the trees are and how very different from home," she said when they drove into the park. "Look, those trees have limbs bending down to the ground. I wonder how big around the trunks are." They circled through the park and around the lagoon, but nothing looked like where she had been.

"It's getting too dark to see very much, Jennie, and I'm starving. Got any ideas where to eat?"

"I'm hungry, too. Do you remember me telling you about the little cafe where so many of the locals eat? The one that makes the huge shrimp and oyster subs? I know you'd like it. It's somewhere on Canal. I believe the name is *Nina's*."

"That sounds good. Hope it's still there."

"It probably is. It's an institution here. It's the place where dad said he wanted to 'belly up to a bar one more time,' and he did." It was a bittersweet memory. Her mom and dad had been killed in a car wreck a few months before she met Nathan. "I wonder what he would think about all this. I really miss him," she continued.

"Sounds like you had some good times together," Nathan responded. "I think I'd have liked your dad."

The café was definitely open; the line was coming out the door. Finding a parking spot a block away, they walked back and joined the waiting people. It didn't take very long till they were seated in a side room that Jennie didn't even know was there. The food was wonderful, even better than she'd remembered.

"Where do you want to start tomorrow?" Nathan asked.

"I don't want to wait till tomorrow. Let's drive around Tulane University tonight. In whatever happened to me, it was dark and maybe that will help me find the place."

"Good idea, we can do that. I'm ready if you are," Nathan said signaling the waiter.

Jennie juggled the map under the car light to find the university. "Everything looks so different at night. Here it is, follow Canal to LaSalle Street and turn right." Driving through the darkened city felt like it had last Friday night, but maybe she was imaging that too.

"Turn left at Cleveland. It's should be the next block. That will take us down the side of the campus. I don't know where to go after that. Just drive around," Jennie said.

The streetlights were on all over the campus. Students were still walking around; others were clustered on benches and sitting on the ground talking. Jennie was reminded of her college years. The side streets were dark and narrow. She caught her breath when they came to a wide street with large trees. "There, that street. Turn now, Nathan."

Nathan drove slowly. This felt familiar, she had been here before. She could hear a foghorn in the distance, so they must be close to the Mississippi River. She'd heard that sound before.

"Stop, Nathan. Stop right here; this is the spot. This is where I got out of the car."

It was a large open grassy field and beyond it were several buildings. The light from the buildings filtered eerily through the trees. Jennie walked slowly across the lawn and the trees seemed to reach down to touch her. Looking up toward the moon, she watched the fog rolling in and her heart pounded. She turned and looked for Josh, but no one was there.

"Jennie, where are you? Jennie?"

He was there and she ran toward the voice crying, "I'm here, Josh, right here. Wait for me."

"I'm waiting. I won't go anywhere," the voice said.

The wrong voice, it wasn't Josh. She'd lost him. "No, no, not again," she cried, crumpling to the ground. "What's happening to me?"

Nathan's face was angry as he hurried to her, stooped down and lifted her up. He put his arm around her and guided her back to the car. "Hang on, honey, we'll figure this out. You've had enough for today. We're going back to the motel."

JENNIE WOKE BEFORE DAWN AND watched Nathan sleeping. He was a very handsome man. He had been quite patient about all this. It wasn't fair to him. It didn't make any sense that she knew the Jung Hotel was in such a run-down condition and for sale. It didn't make any sense at all that she found the spot where she had jumped out of the car. Could she have seen that grassy area years ago and her mind resurrected it? She had to go back there in daylight. Maybe it wouldn't feel the same. Maybe it was just a trick of the moonlight and fog and her imagination.

During breakfast Nathan said, "We should go back there, you know. We need to see where it is and take a look at it in daylight. Since we're here, we should look at it all very carefully. If there's the remotest chance Josh is alive, we have to find out. Then we'll deal with whatever has happened."

So back they went and the *what-ifs* started plaguing her again. When they turned down the street, she clenched her hands tightly together to keep them from shaking. Nathan stopped the car at the spot where they'd been last night. It was just a beautiful lawn in the daytime, no foghorns, no strange shadows, no trees reaching for her, but she knew it was the spot where she had run from Josh's car.

"This is it, Nathan. I know it is." The distant sounds of the ships on the river and her uneasy stomach confirmed what she had felt. "Maybe we could go to the university and see if they have staff listings or yearbooks or something," she said, anxious to get away from the feelings this place stirred up.

Nathan drove down what looked to be the main drag at Tulane University. "Which building should we check out?"

"See the one on the left. It looks like the student center. A lot of kids are hanging around it. Let's start there if you can find a parking place."

Climbing up the steps made her think of her days at the University of North Texas. Young people were everywhere with their books spread all over the steps and on the ground. They went into the building and there it changed. The walls were covered with graffiti. Jennie couldn't imagine doing anything like that when she was in college. They'd have been kicked out of school. "Everything changes," she sighed.

She found the information desk and asked the young girl there if she had a listing of instructors, maybe college bulletins, catalogs, or yearbooks. No luck, but she was able to direct them to the college library.

The library was within walking distance just down a block and on the right. They studied the directory by the elevators and found a likely place to start their search. The third floor housed the yearbooks and the clerk at the checkout desk was very helpful. She directed them to the correct section and they gathered up yearbooks for the last five years. Jennie looked through all the instructor listings and found that some didn't have pictures. She assumed they would have changed Josh's name. Would they keep the same initials? She looked for names that might have some relationship to Josh's relatives, anything that might be a clue. Paying specific attention to the art, writing, and journalism departments, Jennie found no pictures or names that triggered any recognition.

"Well, that was a waste of time," Jennie said. "I have no idea if he changed his name. I really don't know where else to look. Do you have any ideas?"

"Maybe we could look around the art and journalism departments and talk to people. What do you think?"

The journalism building came first; it was the closest to the library. As they wandered through the halls, Jennie asked a few students if they knew any instructors about forty or fifty years old with streaked gray hair. They giggled saying, "Most of them would fit that description."

They looked in rooms randomly then tried the same thing in the art building with no more success than they had at the journalism building. Jennie felt dejected when they went back to the car. They both knew they would find nothing here.

"I had to try, Nathan."

"I know. It was a long shot at best, Jennie. Let's go back to the place you recognized and take some pictures. We can show them to Herman. You can hang on to that till we can find out more." Nathan circled the campus again, they took a few pictures, but Jennie didn't find anything else from her dream.

"There's nothing for us here, Nathan. Why don't we go to the French Quarter and walk around? It's always interesting, and besides, there are lots of antique shops."

By early evening, Jennie's feet were hurting and Nathan was hungry, so they decided to eat at Diamond Jim Moran's in the Quarter and go back home early the next morning.

THERE WAS NOTHING TO DO but think on the long drive home. Jennie went over the entire trip in her mind. She could see the place where she jumped out of the car. How real it felt when she actually stood there and thought she heard Josh call her again, so real she answered. She knew a person's mind could play tricks, but like this? Nathan's being very understanding. How many husbands would take his wife to find another man, especially when that man has been dead for six years? "Oh, I wish this had never happened," she murmured.

"What'd you say, Jennie? I couldn't quite hear you."

"Nothing, honey, just thinking out loud I guess."

"Let's drop the film off at the drugstore before we go home. That way you might have the pictures when Herman comes over," Nathan suggested, as they drove into Dallas.

"Good idea. We need to pick up bread and milk, too," she answered. "Would you mind if I call Herman tonight and see what he's found?"

"No. I think you should."

As usual, she had to leave her name for Herman to call back. She hoped it wouldn't be too long. She was having a lot of trouble putting it all in perspective, mostly because there wasn't any way to do that.

Herman called quickly. "Hi, Jennie, how was your trip? See anything interesting?"

"Well, sort of. I saw the Jung Hotel where we stayed years ago and it was all run down, just like I saw it last week. We also found a place that looked like where I got out of the car. We took pictures of both."

"How'd it feel when you saw it?"

"I lost it. We were there at night and I got out and walked around. I recognized everything, sounds and all. Then I thought I heard Josh call me and I answered him. Now how crazy is that?"

"I want to see the pictures when you get them back. Did you find anything else?"

"No. We checked out the library at Tulane, walked around and talked to people, but found nothing. I described him to some students and they said most professors were forty or fifty with gray hair, so no luck there. It was just a waste of time. The Jung Hotel, well, that was freaky. Did you find out anything?"

"Not much, we'll talk about it when I see you," Herman said. "I can't come by tonight. I'm on call. What about tomorrow evening?"

"That'll be fine. We should have the pictures back then. Can you eat supper with us?"

"Sounds good, what time?"

"Six would work for us. We'll look forward to seeing you."

Chapter 9

THE DAY CREPT SLOWLY by. Jennie was finding it difficult to act normally. She kept busy with everyday things that had to be done, vacuuming, dusting, shopping, and cooking, but it didn't occupy her mind. When she picked up the pictures, she was excited to find that the Jung Hotel and the grassy area ones turned out well. Six o'clock finally got there and Herman arrived.

They tried not to talk about Josh during dinner, but the weather just didn't fill the gaps. The stilted meal finally over, they sat down with coffee and Herman looked at the pictures. "Jennie, have you been back to New Orleans since the time you and Josh stayed there?"

"One time, I went with my parents a few years ago, and I'm sure I pointed the hotel out to them. It was one of the historic hotels there."

"So you had no way of knowing that it had closed, at least that we know of. Were you ever in that grassy area?"

"No, I don't remember being around there. It's not a tourist spot. It's sort of hidden in the back of the university and off the major streets."

Herman thought for a moment. "Okay, hang on to the pictures. We may want them again."

"What did you find out about Josh's military records?" Jennie asked anxiously.

"Not much. I contacted the National Personnel Records Center in St. Louis and was informed that on July 12, 1973, a fire at NPRC destroyed approximately sixteen to eighteen million official military files. It affected the Army records for personnel discharged November 1912 to January 1960. You said Josh mustered out in '57. They stated that his record was one of the destroyed ones. Also, no duplicate copies of the records were kept anywhere else. This means that they have no record of him."

"That doesn't sound right. So what do we do now?" Jennie asked.

"It leaves very little along this line. However, an odd thing happened. John, my partner, told me that the chief had questioned him about why I requested Davenport's military records. He told John that I had no authority to be accessing them. Then he ordered John to make sure I stop all investigations regarding Davenport. I asked John what else the chief said. The only thing he told him was the orders were from higher up and it was final. Now, there is no way that the chief could have known about this unless someone notified him. I figure it must have been the NPRC. So my question is why do they care? Anyway, as far as the department is concerned, I can do nothing else."

"Now this makes me more curious than I already was," continued Herman. "Why would anybody care about a military record of someone who has been dead for six years? It makes me wonder if Josh's records were burned up as the letter said or if that was an evasion. I've been trying to think of some other way to get into the records without going through the department."

"Maybe I should try to get them as his widow," Jennie said.

"I don't think it would make a difference. You'd probably get the same form letter I did. What I'm thinking about is contacting an old friend of mine in the Army to see if he can find out anything from the inside. He'll know Army procedures. I'll give him a call tonight at his home. I don't want to call him at the base."

"It bothers me," Nathan said, "that the records at the funeral home had information omitted and now this. The obvious question is why are the records missing?"

"That's what I'm wondering, too" Herman answered. "Couple this with Jennie recognizing the place in New Orleans. It's not adding up. I'm anxious to talk to Carl, my friend in the Army. You should remember him, Jennie. Carl Kendall, he played football with us in high school. He's made the Army a career, and I think he'll help us, if he can."

"I do remember him, Herman. I even have an old picture of Carl and Josh in football uniforms somewhere around here. Tell him hello for me, and that I'll be grateful for his help."

"Will do, I'll be back in touch after I talk to him." Herman stood up and walked toward the door. "I need to get on home. Molly will be looking for me and I want to call Carl tonight. Get some rest, Jennie. You don't look like you're sleeping very much."

"I'll try, Herman. Talk to you tomorrow," Jennie answered, as they walked outside with Herman. Nathan bent down and picked up the newspaper. Lost in thought, they went back into the house, automatically turning off lights and locking the doors.

"Nathan, did you see that car drive off without any lights?"

"Yeah, I did. He'll remember to turn them on when he gets away from the streetlights. Some people don't pay any attention to what they are doing. It's a miracle that we don't see more accidents than we do." Neither of them thought any more about the car that had pulled away from the curb a few seconds after Herman did.

"What did you think about what Herman found out? You know, I wonder if the records were really burned up? It's hard to believe that the military has no backup records on microfilm or something. The Army's bound to have copies somewhere," Nathan continued thoughtfully.

"It doesn't make any sense," Jennie replied. "The individual branches must keep their own records. What if they needed to find someone or reactivate someone?"

"Wait a minute," Jennie said excitedly. "Reactivate someone; remember Josh said that he didn't hear anything from the military until 1974. Nathan, that's a year after the files are supposed to have burned up. Herman said the letter from the NPRC stated that in 1973 all files were burned up for men discharged between 1912 and 1960, so how could they contact Josh if they had no records? There must be records somewhere. The NPRC is lying to us. And I want to know why."

Jennie headed for the phone. "Where is Herman's card? He wrote his home number on it for me. I need to get hold of him before he calls Carl." Nathan hurried over to the desk and handed Jennie the card.

HERMAN PULLED AWAY FROM JENNIE and Nathan wondering if they had picked up on the discrepancy of the date of the fire and the reactivation date of Josh. He sighed, here he was chasing down information based on a woman's daydream or hallucination or maybe just plain wishful thinking. "Absurd, absolutely absurd," he muttered aloud.

He could hardly tell that to the chief, he would put him on permanent leave of absence. But Herman's gut was telling him something was going on. He didn't trust coincidences. He couldn't figure out if Jennie's episode had anything to do with it, or if an event from her past had broken through her subconscious and now triggered a memory, perhaps something that hadn't made sense to her six years ago. At least, a memory wasn't as irrational as a daydream.

Well, something's going on behind me, Herman reflected, as he checked his rear view mirror again. He had been watching a car following him since he left Jennie and Nathan's. He decided to make a few quick turns and see if he could lose him. "Nope, he's sticking like glue." He pulled in a service station to see what the car would do next. It slowly went on past. When Herman left the station he kept an eye out for the car, but didn't pick it up for a couple of blocks. Then he saw it pull out of an alleyway and continue to follow him. Another thing he could chalk up. Too many coincidences just aren't coincidences any more.

The car was obviously following him but didn't appear to be after trouble, so Herman drove on home. He hoped Molly was still up. He wanted to get her view on this. She had a knack of picking out things he hadn't thought about.

"MOLLY, THIS IS JENNIE DAVENPORT. Is Herman home yet? I need to talk to him before he calls Carl."

"He just came in, Jennie. I'll put him on." Molly handed the phone to Herman whispering, "It's Jennie."

"I was going to call you and see if you noticed the car with no lights on that pulled off after I did. It followed me all the way home."

"Someone followed you home? We saw a car without lights leave right after you left. Was it really following you? Could it have anything to do with us?"

"I don't know what it means yet, maybe nothing."

"Herman, we thought about something after you left. You said the records burned in 1973. Have you thought about the fact that Josh told me that he was reactivated in '74?"

"Yes, Jennie, I wondered how long it would take you to pick up on the dates. But you need to realize that date may not be real. I don't know how much we can trust that. I want to call Carl before it gets too late. You get some rest. Talk to you tomorrow."

Jennie hung up the phone and watched Nathan staring out the front window. What was he thinking? Was he wondering if all this was only her imagination?

"Have I got a story for you tonight," Herman said to Molly. "You're not going to believe it. I want to tell you about it because I believe it, and I don't believe it, and the chief thinks I'm due for a rest."

"Bad enough that the chief thinks you need a rest. Well, well, what else is new? I'm looking forward to this story!" Molly laughed.

Herman dialed the phone and said, "It is quite a tale. Maybe that's all it is, but it's puzzling, and to complicate things someone followed me home tonight."

"Carl, Herman Wilkins here, have you got a minute? I know it's late, but I've a favor to ask of you. It's about a mutual pal of ours from high school, Josh Davenport. Yeah, that's right. He died about six years ago. Jennie, his wife, called me last week and she needs to get Josh's military records. I've tried through my office, but they tell me that their records were destroyed in a fire in '73. Common sense tells me that the Army has to have copies somewhere. Could you check that out for me?"

"I know. I know it's not customary, but there's a good reason. I'll tell you about it privately, but not on the phone. Thanks, Carl. I'll be waiting for your call. By the way, Jennie said to tell you hello."

Molly came back into the den with two hot chocolates instead of coffee. She curled up on the sofa saying, "Okay, I'm ready for my bedtime story."

Herman looked at her thinking that she was prettier than a grandmother had a right to be and wondered what in the world could ever make him leave her. Remembering how close Josh and Jennie were in high school, he couldn't believe that Josh would leave Jennie either.

He started slowly. "Do you remember when Josh Davenport died six years ago? The chief called me in and said that he wanted me to go to the funeral home and keep my eyes open for anything unusual regarding the Davenport death. He said I was not to do anything, just watch and report to him. Imagine my surprise when I got there and it was Josh. When I saw Jennie, she just assumed I had heard about Josh's death and had come to be with her. I don't think she ever questioned why I stayed at the funeral home with her for two days. Of course, she was under lots of stress. I didn't see anything unusual, nothing that triggered a reaction in me. I do remember some very military-looking types around and, of course, lots of people were in and out. However, nothing seemed out of the ordinary about that. I just assumed they were all friends of Josh's. That's what I put in my report to the chief. I don't think I ever told him I knew Josh. It just never came up in our conversations."

40

"At the time, I don't remember thinking anything about it other than what a coincidence it was. Jennie was pretty broken up and moving around in a daze. Josh was only in his early forties, and they had two young daughters. I really felt sorry for her. She was so lost, and I kept thinking what if it was you. I left her my number and told her to call if she ever needed help, but she only called once about some crank calls they were getting."

"The next strange thing was that I was ordered to patrol the neighborhood she lived in with special attention to her house. Now that was really unusual. They had me on patrol duty along with two other guys so that the house was covered twenty-four hours a day for several months. I never knew what that was about."

"That's the background and I haven't told Jennie any of it yet. Now this is where it gets weird. She called me last week and asked if we could meet, said she needed to talk to me. I couldn't imagine what about after this length of time, but I met her, and here's her story."

As MOLLY LISTENED, SHE PICTURED Josh and Jennie in her mind. She had known them but not very well. As best as she could remember, they were just nice, average people. Jennie didn't seem like a person to go off the deep end. However, you never really know.

When Herman finished the story and asked for more hot chocolate, Molly knew they were in for a long night. She had been there before while Herman wrestled with a problem. She was getting a feeling that there was a lot more to this than they knew about.

"I'd not be too impressed with this if the chief hadn't sent you to the funeral home to keep an eye on things," Molly stated. "That's very unusual unless you're dealing with a president or some celebrity. Security is not the norm at most funerals. Is that what made you curious in the beginning?"

Herman answered, "Yeah, I've always wondered about that. Josh wasn't a celebrity and wasn't that important, at least, not that I knew about. But, at the same time, there had to be some reason why I was there and also why the house was under surveillance for a couple of months."

"Didn't you ask why or try to find out what was going on?" Molly questioned.

"Normally I would have been more curious, but that was the time my partner was out with his back injury. I was so busy I didn't have time to think about it. Also, the chief implied that his orders came from higher up, and I'm not sure he knew what was going on. So often, we just do the job we're told to do and never know the whys or the outcome of many of them. Right now, I'm feeling a lot of responsibility," replied Herman. "What do you think about this, Molly?"

"I'm not sure. I know I've never had a dream or anything that seemed that real. However, I haven't lost a husband and that would certainly account for lots of emotional turmoil. And on top of that, having your parents killed in a car crash, that's enough to do damage to anybody's head. She's had a lot to deal with. I guess it could cause some very realistic episodes. But six years later, that's a long time."

HERMAN WONDERED IF HE SHOULD tell Molly about the Implant Surveillance System that was developed years ago. The ISS was used to keep track of agents in enemy territory. He knew of several instances where it had been used and information had been retrieved after the agent died in the field. He hesitated for a few minutes.

"Molly, there is a way that someone could have tracked Jennie and transmitted images. I can't quite understand how it could transport her to New Orleans, or if it could. I don't know much about the technology of it, but some years ago a microchip implant was developed that could be injected into a person. It enables the people involved to monitor the whereabouts of a person who has it. The ultimate bug, you might say. I just don't know what else they could do with it. The life of the chip was indeterminate because it was new technology and no one knew for sure how long it could function. I'm wondering if Jennie has the microchip in her. If so, who put it there and who's monitoring it? And that leads me to a more important question, why would she be monitored? Josh was in advertising in Dallas, but he must have been into something else. I don't know what to think at this point."

Molly stood up, stretched and said, "Well, I do. It's one-thirty, Herman. You're on duty tomorrow, and we need to get some sleep. Besides, this is turning into a scary story and if I hear much more, I'm not going to be able to sleep. But I do have to ask if you told Jennie about the implant. If you haven't, you better talk to her about it and see if there was a time when it could have been injected." Molly yawned. "I think I've lived a very sheltered life. This is all way too *007* for me."

"You're right, honey. I should have asked Jennie about the microchip. It's probably much too far-fetched. You know, a little knowledge is a dangerous thing. Let's go to bed." He put his arm around Molly and held her close as they walked to the bedroom.

He couldn't get it off his mind. He knew that if he told the whole story it would help him see something he was missing. It was always that way with Molly. She had a way of asking a simple question that would trigger a new thought for him. What would he do without her? He sure didn't want to find out.

Morning came too fast and with it a whole pot of coffee. He really should quit drinking so much of it. As Molly opened the pantry to get the cereal for breakfast she asked, "Herman, since I've had a little time to think, I'm concerned about the car that followed you home last night. If it's connected to all of this, that's scary. They know where we live. Do you have any idea who followed you?"

"Not yet. If we knew that, we might have lots of other answers. It could be totally unconnected with Jennie. There's no way to know at this point," Herman replied. "I'm anxious to see what information Carl can get for me. Someone has to have Josh's military records. If he calls here today, find out where I can reach him and let me know."

"My main problem, Molly, is that there are coincidences and that always spells trouble."

Chapter 10

NATHAN WAS WATERING THE sprouting ferns when Jennie joined him in the backyard. The daffodils were already blooming. Everything looked so pretty this year. He smiled at Jennie, saying that it was going to be a good year for the yard. He had put a large swing back under a tree in the corner flower bed and this had become her favorite place.

"It's looking wonderful already," she said. As Jennie ran her hand over a fragrant rosemary bush, she heard the phone ringing. "I'll get it," she called, running for the house.

She was breathless when she answered. "Hello ... hello ..." All she heard was a whirring noise. "Either say something or hang up," Jennie said angrily. The whirring changed to clicking, then the dial tone returned. Nathan came in just as Jennie slammed the phone down.

"I'm getting really tired of all these calls where no one says anything. I know someone is on the other end because I hear noises. I wish they would talk."

"You've gotten these crank calls for years, but it seems like you've had more than usual lately," Nathan said.

"I haven't kept count, maybe five or six this past week. It's maddening. It's been going on since Josh died. I even changed my number last year when we married."

The phone rang again. Jennie grabbed it, ready to do battle.

"Hi, Mom, What's wrong? You sound like you're about to hit someone."

"Oh, Kris, I'm sorry. Remember those phone calls we used to get, the ones where no one would answer us. Well, I just hung up from one and thought this was another. Sorry, honey."

"That's okay. I'm calling to see if you had a good time in New Orleans," said Kris, her oldest daughter. "I hope these calls aren't ruining it."

"Yes, we did have a nice trip. The food's always a treat there," Jennie answered.

"Did you do anything special or go through any of the plantations?"

"No, we just rode around sightseeing. We did eat at the little place where I took your grandparents several years ago. It's still excellent. The shrimp and oysters were wonderful. Of course, I eat my oysters fried, not on the half-shell like you."

"Remember the trip, Mom, when I was with you and we stayed in that small hotel in the French Quarter? It had a certificate hanging on the wall dated many years ago licensing it to be a house of ill repute. That was so funny. And I loved going to Preservation Hall and hearing the band play jazz. I wonder if they still do."

"I'm sure they do, honey, but we didn't go there."

"Well, what did you do, Mom?"

"Not much. Drove around the park with the big trees and looked around Tulane University. That's about all, nothing special."

"Mom, what's wrong? Lately you have sounded depressed. What's going on?" asked Kris.

"Just going through a mood, I guess," she answered, wondering if she should tell Kris and Laurie what was going on. Kris had a good life now. It seemed wrong to disrupt it, and this would sure stir up old memories again. And Laurie, she'd already had enough problems to deal with.

"Mother, I know your voice. Something's wrong, I can tell. Are you and Nathan having problems?"

"No, Kris, we're fine. There is something I should tell you about, but not on the phone. Come out for supper about six and we'll talk. I'll call your sister and see if she can join us. I guess you two will have to know about this eventually and I don't want to tell this story but one time. Can you come?"

"Of course I can. I have to know why you're being so mysterious."

"Okay. Let's hang up so I can call Laurie and get supper started."

"Nathan," Jennie called, "I've asked the girls to come eat with us tonight. I think I'd better tell them about my so-called daydream. Kris is picking up on my mood."

Jennie couldn't decide how to tell them. It all seemed so silly. Maybe she should just let them read what she had written down. After they read it, she could fill in the rest. That is, if they could quit laughing and thinking their mother had gone senile.

Jennie washed her hands and looked in the freezer to see what she could cook. It did help to do the normal things. Deciding to make her daughters' favorite meal, she was cooking the meat for stroganoff when Kris arrived.

"You sure got here fast, Kris."

"Well, wouldn't you be curious if you were me? Okay, start talking and tell me what this is all about."

"I'm not going to tell the story but once. We'll wait for Laurie. However, the problem is, I don't know what it's all about," Jennie responded. "There's Laurie, go let her in."

"Wow, something sure smells good," Laurie said when she walked in. "What's this command performance about? Are we in trouble?"

"Not yet, unless you have something you want to confess," Jennie teased.

"Laurie, mom's been depressed lately, I'm sure you've noticed. When I asked her about it she said she's still getting those phone calls like we used to. She's had several calls this week. You remember, when someone would call and we'd hear them breathing or hear whirring and clicking noises, but they wouldn't answer us."

"Oh, I remember. They drove us nuts for a while. Did you ever find out anything that you didn't tell us, Mom?" Laurie asked.

"No, I never did."

Kris, never long on patience, pushed, "Okay, Mom, Laurie's here. Tell us what's going on. No more excuses. You've got our attention."

"I don't mean to be mysterious, but this is just so strange. Two weeks ago, Nathan and I were at the lake house and something very odd happened to me. I don't know what to call it. It wasn't a dream because I wasn't asleep. I've never experienced anything like this before. I can't forget it," Jennie said slowly, "nor can I let it go."

"Would one of you get the place mats and set the table for me, someone put ice in the glasses for tea, and I'll get our supper finished."

"Mom, don't stop now. Keep going," urged Laurie.

"Well, Nathan went to bed early, and I stayed up reading. About midnight I went upstairs. I still wasn't sleepy and I was standing at the window thinking about all the leaves we needed to rake up. Suddenly, I was running through a grassy field, and I heard someone calling me. When I turned around I was

46

so disoriented I didn't recognize Nathan. I didn't even know where I was. It really scared me—it was a while before I realized I was at the lake house. When I did, I ran downstairs and outside and looked all around. That's how real it seemed. I even went up to the road and looked for car lights. I wrote it down so I wouldn't forget the details, but I didn't have to. I haven't forgotten any of it. The pages are on the desk. Go ahead and read it. But first, I need to warn you. It's about your dad."

Jennie stirred the sour cream into the stroganoff, poured it and the rice into serving dishes, and tossed the salad while Kris and Laurie read her notes. By the time Jennie put the bread on the table and called Nathan, they had finished reading it.

Kris quickly whispered, "Have you told Nathan?"

"Oh, yes. You can talk freely with him. We have more to tell you."

Nathan gave them a quick hug and sat down at the table. "Glad you could come. I guess your mom has been telling you what's been going on?"

"Sort of, we just read what she wrote down. That's quite a story, Mom. What do you think it means?" asked Laurie.

"I'm relieved that you're not laughing at me," Jennie said. "I thought you'd think I was senile or crazy."

"No, Mom, we're not laughing," Laurie said, glancing over at Kris.

"The strange thing about it, Laurie, is that it wasn't at all like a dream. I was wide awake. I felt the scar on your dad's forehead. I rode in the car with him, then got out and ran across a field. It was so real. I don't know what else to say about it. I didn't tell Nathan at first because I felt pretty foolish. But I couldn't forget it. When we got home from the lake house I called Herman Wilkins. Do you remember him? He was a high school friend of your dad's and was at the funeral. Anyway, he's an undercover policeman with the Dallas Police Department. He told me at Josh's funeral if I ever needed anything to call him. So I did. To make a long story short, I talked to him and he didn't laugh at me. He said he'd do some checking."

As Jennie told the story, Kris and Laurie put their forks down and just listened. Kris poured them all more iced tea. Jennie finished telling them about the missing information at the funeral home, the missing military papers, and about the last visit with Herman when they saw a car follow him as he left the house. Kris and Laurie both sat very still for a few minutes looking at each other.

Kris spoke up and said, "Mom, Laurie and I have had several things happen through the years that we've wondered about, but we were hesitant to say anything to you. We didn't want to upset you. I think we'd better tell you about them."

"Let's go sit in the den," Jennie said.

"I wanted so much to talk to you years ago, Mom," Kris slowly began, "but you seemed to be in such a fog all the time."

"Oh, Kris, I'm so sorry. I know I wasn't any help to either of you. It seemed all I could do was to live through the next hour, and I didn't do that very well."

"I know, Mom, I know. We both understood; we were like that, too." Kris quickly responded. "What I want to tell you about is when the patrol took us to the hospital that night. You were already there and, as I was walking down the hall to meet you, I thought I heard daddy talking. I stopped and walked over to the door and started to knock, but the patrolman said, 'This way, please.' So I just followed him thinking daddy must be all right."

"Then Laurie and I found you and everything started happening. When I remembered it later, I assumed it must have been someone who sounded like him. Then when I saw him in the funeral home it all came back and I knew it wasn't daddy. I can't say what it was except inside me I just knew."

"I really didn't listen to you, did I," Jennie said, as she began to softly cry.

Laurie moved over to Jennie and put her arm around her saying, "Mom, none of us were in any shape to help anyone then. We were all trying to survive the best way we could."

"I tried to tell everyone it wasn't daddy, but no one paid attention to me," Kris continued. "Granddaddy thought I was imagining it and after a little while I guess I did, too. However, I kept remembering daddy's voice at the hospital. I couldn't make any sense out of it. Well, time passed and the sharpness of those horrible days faded a little."

"Then several years later, there was that time I went to dinner with Mark at the Chateaubriand Restaurant. You remember that restaurant, Mom? It was daddy's favorite. Well, while Mark was checking our reservation, I saw a painting on the wall across the room and it reminded me of daddy so I looked closer. It wasn't signed, but it definitely looked like his work. I asked the hostess where it came from, but she didn't know anything about it. The next week I told Laurie and we went to see it, but it was gone. The hostess said that someone comes once a month and changes all the pictures in the restaurant, but she didn't know who it was."

Jennie interrupted, "What was the picture of?"

"It was a castle on a hillside."

"Do you remember that your dad and I were planning to build a home like a castle on our acreage out in the country? You probably heard us talking about it through the years. We had lots of ideas. Your dad was even designing a maze for you two to play in and a rose garden for me. He also wanted a moat and drawbridge. Was it anything like that?"

"Yes, Mom, it was. It looked just like a medieval castle with turrets. Now that you've reminded me, I think there was a maze at the side of it."

Laurie chimed in, "I used to hear you talk about it. You had a file on castles that I loved to look through when I was little."

"Did you ever go back and check on the painting again or try to talk to someone in the restaurant's office about it?" Nathan asked.

"We did. They told us that it had been there on loan from a private collector, but they could not or would not tell us his name. So we hit a dead-end."

"And that's not the only thing, Mom," Laurie said. "I know without a doubt that I saw daddy on a news program on TV one night a few years after he died, and I certainly wasn't dreaming. I called Kris instantly and she turned that station on, but it didn't show him again. Kris called the station and asked for a copy of that news program and they said they'd send it to us."

"That must have been the same program when I thought I saw Josh," Jennie exclaimed. "Did you get a copy?"

"No. When it didn't come after a few days, we called back. They said they were unable to locate the master copy. They didn't know what happened to it."

"The painting probably went back to the owner, but TV stations don't usually misplace the master copy of the news programs," Laurie mused. "There are a lot of odd happenings that we can't explain. It makes me wonder if they're connected in some way."

"I know, honey, it does seem like this has gone beyond mere coincidence," acknowledged Jennie. "There's just too many unusual things coupled with what has happened to me. That's why we're checking this out."

Nathan went to the kitchen and came back with a bottle of wine and glasses. "What I can't figure out is why Josh would pretend to be dead. If we knew that, we might find some answers."

Chapter 11

HERMAN HAD BEEN STUCK in the office all afternoon. He didn't like paperwork; he would rather be in the field. Besides that, he was anxious to hear from Carl. Herman was stewing about the coincidences, too many things weren't adding up. He was relieved when Molly called and gave him Carl's phone number.

He dialed the minute Molly hung up. "Wilkins here, Carl. Did you locate any of Josh's military papers?"

"Found a few, but the main papers are in the top secret files. I don't have clearance to get into them. How about telling me what is going on?"

"I don't want to do that on the phone, Carl. Can you get away this evening? Say seven at my house. I'm anxious to get your take on this."

TWO DAYS A WEEK, MOLLY picked up the grandchildren at school while her daughter Cindy worked at a bookstore. Backing out of the driveway a little before three, she had to maneuver around a dark blue car parked directly across the street. She collected the children and stopped at the grocery store which always took longer with the little ones. When they got back home, Molly was surprised the blue car was still there. She'd been gone almost two hours.

As soon as Molly stopped, the children jumped from the car and ran to the back yard calling, "Can we swing, Grandma? Can we swing?"

"Just don't leave the yard," Molly cautioned, as she carried the groceries into the house. They were later than usual and Cindy would be by to pick up the children in about forty-five minutes, so they might as well play outside. It was too late to start homework now.

On Thursdays and Fridays Herman pushed to get home in time to play with the grandchildren. They were the best stress reliever he'd ever found. Giving Molly a quick kiss, he barreled to the back yard growling he was going to get them. Shrieks of laughter drifted through the kitchen window. Smiling, Molly put the potatoes in the oven, seasoned the steaks, and joined the fun. She asked Herman if he'd talked with Carl.

"Yeah, I did. He's coming by tonight," he answered, as he crawled around the yard with both children on his back.

"I thought I heard voices out here," Cindy called out, coming around the corner of the house. The children went wild when they saw their mother. They ran to get hugs, both trying to talk at the same time.

Herman was still laughing after they left. "Wow, that's a whirlwind if I ever saw one. What's for dinner?"

"Steaks, baked potatoes and salad," Molly answered with a smile. "Pour us a glass of wine. It'll be ready shortly."

"What's the occasion?"

"You're home and you're laughing. That's occasion enough for me. What time is Carl coming?"

"About seven, he said he couldn't get much information, but I rather expected that."

Carl arrived just as they were finishing dinner and joined them for coffee. "What's going on, Herman?"

"Let's take our coffee to the den, and I'll tell you."

After Herman told Carl about Jennie's experience and what they had found out, Molly asked if either of them had noticed the dark blue car parked across the street. "It's been there all afternoon. I assumed the man in the car was waiting for someone, but it's been a long time. You'd better take a look, Herman."

"What time did you see it, Molly," Herman asked. He got up and looked out the side of the curtains. "It's still there."

"I first noticed it about three when I left to pick up the children."

"Is it the same man as you saw earlier?"

"I can't tell. There's not enough light to see clearly."

"Do you think it's the same car that followed you home last night? Have you run the tags?" Carl asked.

"It looks like it. No, I haven't run the tags yet but I will tomorrow. If it's following me, why would he park outside the house all day? This is what I mean, Carl. Too many odd things are going on. Regardless of whether this was a daydream or Jennie's imagination, something's happening. Tell me what you found today."

"Not much. I did find that Josh had been discharged four months early with the proviso that he could be reinstated any time, which is standard procedure with G-2s. However, there's nothing there to indicate he was ever reactivated. The only things in the file were his original papers when he joined the Army and the discharge papers. Nothing else, not even his basic training location. Nothing shows what rank he was or where he'd been stationed. Just the dates, that's all. Next I checked the lists of the top secret files. I found his name there and requested his records from the day officer. A couple of hours later, he came back to me and said that Josh's file was sealed and labeled *Special Clearance Required*, so he couldn't give it to me."

"How can we get them?" Herman asked.

"We can't. I don't have clearance. I've been thinking about this all day. What do you need these for?"

"I know this is strange, Carl, but think about it. Forget Jennie's experience for now. That just got us looking. What we have here is a lot of missing information. First, the funeral home is missing a physical description of Josh. Then the NPRC told me that all his records were burned up in 1973 and there were no records anywhere. Now, you find that he is listed in the top secret files and special clearance is required to get them. Just why do you think that is? I'm getting the feeling that there is something to hide, and I want to know what. Next, my chief told me yesterday he'd received orders that I was to stop investigating Josh Davenport, so I can't do anything else through the precinct."

Herman paused. "There's a thread forming. Seems it started six years ago at the funeral. I was sent there to keep an eye out for anything unusual. Now, how often does that happen? After that, I was put on a surveillance team to watch Jennie's house for a couple of months. I never did figure out why they had me do that."

He filled Carl's cup again and emptied the rest of the pot in his.

"During this time period, Jennie started getting crank calls where someone would call and she could hear breathing, but no one spoke. She says she'd hear a whirring noise and then some clicking sounds. This continued for about a year. She contacted me because the calls were scaring her and the girls. The phone company told her they couldn't trace the calls unless she documented them with dates and time. She did this, but they never came up with who was calling. I turned in my report and when I followed up on it, the chief said it had been taken care of. Jennie tells me that most of the calls stopped shortly after that, but not completely. Was this coincidence? And now they've started again, several times a week."

"What are you thinking about, Herman, the ISS? Are you thinking she was being monitored?"

"Maybe," Herman answered. "Could be they were listening to see who would contact her. She said she continued to get about one call a month, but chalked those up to wrong numbers. Do you know how that thing works?"

"Yeah, it works off a satellite and can give you the location within three feet of the person who's carrying it, plus a lot of other stuff."

"What other stuff, Carl?"

Carl thought a minute. "This is a pretty sensitive area, Herman. I could get in serious trouble for passing this type of information along. Do you know if it's possible that Jennie has an ISS in her?"

"No, I don't. Molly asked me that last night. Is it correct that the microchip can be injected with a needle?"

"It can. It's a bit painful. You'd know you'd been shot, but lots of shots hurt. This is awkward, Herman. You're asking me to divulge classified information. That could get me in big-time trouble. Keep talking to me."

"Well, in Jennie's episode, she said Josh told her he was reactivated in 1974, which is one year after his records were supposedly burned up in the fire at the NPRC. Remember they informed me that there were no other records, yet you found some. Jennie says Josh was G-2, so we know he was in the security arena. She didn't know exactly what that meant. I want to know what those records say; I want to know if it confirms he was reactivated. If he was, it could explain why I was sent to the funeral. And that brings up another question. Whose body is in that grave?

Carl stalled, got up and looked out the window again, and asked Molly for more coffee. "Let's take a walk, Herman, and see what that car does."

Carl and Herman were gone when Molly brought the fresh pot of coffee in. She looked out the window just in time to see the car pull off without lights. Turning the lights off in the den, she saw the car go slowly down the street and turn east at the corner. In a few minutes Carl and Herman came back on the opposite side of the street. They crossed over and walked up to the front porch, stopped, talked a little while, then came in.

"Sorry, Molly, we didn't mean to run out on the coffee, but we thought we'd see what that car would do if we went walking," Herman said. They stood at the darkened window and watched the car slowly pull up the block and park a few houses away. It was still without lights, evidently trying not to attract attention.

"Well, now we know for sure that someone is watching you, Herman, and they're not trying to keep it secret. At some point, you may want to approach that car, but for now just keep an eye on it. Run the tags tomorrow, let's find out who we are dealing with." Herman drew the drapes and turned on the lights.

Carl poured more coffee and picked up a couple of cookies before continuing. "There is a way I could get into the top secret files. It's a little risky, but it might work. On the weekends, we only have a skeleton crew in place at the base. They're usually shooting pool in the game room, nothing ever goes on late at night and they can answer the phones from there. I've been in several times before to pick up something and just waved at the guys. They never questioned me. Of course, those times were legit."

"Can you open the locked files?"

"Yes, I have the code for emergencies. Under normal circumstances, I'd never touch those files without official sanction. Let me think a little more about this. I stand to lose a lot if I'm caught. I'd not consider it if that car weren't tailing you, but I do agree with you, something is going on. This whole thing has a bad smell. Also, check with Jennie and see if anyone gave her a shot during that time period when Josh died. We won't know for sure if it was the ISS, but we'd know if it was a possibility or not."

"You never answered my question about what else the ISS can do, Carl."

"Leave it alone for now. If we find out that she could have the implant, well, we'll talk about it then. As they say, 'it's on a need to know' basis, and you don't need to know yet. My neck's stuck out far enough already," Carl continued, as he got up and started toward the front door.

"Fair enough," Herman responded, "I'll check the precinct files tomorrow. Maybe something will still be there about the surveillance of the funeral or the house. It's probably been put in storage, but you never know. Call me if you find anything."

Herman watched Carl drive away. Caught up in his thoughts, he turned away too soon and missed seeing the blue car drive by without any lights.

SEEING HERMAN AGAIN SURE BROUGHT back lots of memories, Carl couldn't think of anyone he was closer to in high school than Josh and Herman. He and Josh had remained friends while they were at Del Mar Junior College in

Corpus Christi. They lost track of each other after Josh enlisted in the Army. When Carl graduated, he joined the Army and hoped they would run into each other someday, but it never happened.

He remembered the last high school reunion he had gone to. It was a few months after Josh died and Jennie was there looking so lost. They had gone to dinner afterwards and reminisced about old times. After he returned to the base at San Antonio, they corresponded a few times. He'd always had a fondness for Jennie, but she could never see anyone except Josh.

Looking in his rear-view mirror as he turned into the base, Carl spotted the blue car under the streetlights slowing to a stop. He waved at the sentry and drove around to his quarters relieved that he couldn't be tailed on base. As he was walking into the building, his mind was working out the details for getting into the files, hopefully Friday night. He'd have to see who was on the duty roster Friday and Saturday nights. Really don't want to breach those files with any of those hotshot young kids around; they would love to catch him doing that.

Carl wondered what Jennie looked like now; she had been so pretty. If he could help her, he would. But what the hell had Josh gotten involved in?

The blue car pulled into the base after he did. It drove slowly around the parking lot and finally parked in the lot next to Carl's building.

Chapter 12

HERMAN PULLED OFFICE DUTY and luck was with him. The chief had taken a couple of days off, leaving him in charge. The office usually cleared out at lunch except for a sergeant at the front desk. This was the best opportunity he would have to get in the files.

It was quiet as a tomb as he walked down the hall to the main file room. Where should he start? Shuffling through the files he found a section labeled *Incomplete–Do Not Store. Looks promising,* he thought. It was filed by years and filled with short synopses of cases labeled *Incomplete.*

Herman found 1977 at the back of the bottom file. Flipping through the files, he found Davenport. Excited, he pulled the folder out, only to find it was sealed and marked confidential. Now, why would this be sealed shut?

Quickly, he left the room and went to the lunchroom intending to steam it open over the coffeepot. A couple of guys were there so Herman poured a cup of coffee and went back to his office, locking the door as he went in. He set the coffee down on his desk and held the file over the steaming cup wondering how much time he'd get for this if anyone found out he was opening sealed files. The glue was softening a little; yes, it was going to open.

He removed the contents paying special attention to their order. He'd have to replace them exactly as they were. Starting at the beginning of the file, he found a paper dated February 16, 1977, with orders for an undercover agent to be stationed at Sparkman Hillcrest Funeral Home to provide security for the Davenport funeral. Full reports were to be forwarded on to INSCOM. It was signed by the Chief of Staff, Intelligence and Security Command (INSCOM), U.S. Army.

"Whoa, INSCOM, this is getting weird," Herman mumbled. The next paper was dated February 20, addressed to the Chief of Staff at INSCOM, stating that nothing unusual occurred at the Davenport funeral. Attached to it were the daily reports that Herman had turned in. After that was a communication from INSCOM ordering surveillance by the local authorities on the Davenport home for the three-month period, February 20 through May 1977. All his daily reports had been forwarded on to INSCOM. The last paper in the file was the report he had turned in about the nuisance calls Jennie was receiving along with a cover page forwarding it to INSCOM.

He carefully replaced the contents of the file and resealed it. Jennie had told him that most of the calls stopped after that. He hurried to the file room, put the file back, shut the drawer, and got the heck out of there.

Back in his office Herman dropped in his chair, leaned back, and closed his eyes. Why would INSCOM be interested in the funeral of a guy who had been out of the Army for more than ten years? Josh's file must have been tagged for the NPRC to notify INSCOM that an inquiry had been made about his military records. That also means they know who made the inquiry.

"Yeah, I'm in deep muck now," he muttered to himself, wondering what ramifications would come out of this. Jennie may have imagined all this, but something was definitely going on and it looked like he was right in the middle of it.

FRIDAY WAS SO BUSY CARL didn't think about Josh. It was like that sometimes. He was reminded when the duty roster crossed his desk in the afternoon and was pleased to see several friendly names on the list. Those guys would be shooting pool all evening long. *Tonight's looking good*, thought Carl.

About six, he closed up and left for dinner. He liked being stationed in the DFW area. There were lots of good places to eat, and he really liked to eat. Actually, if he had a hobby, eating would be it.

About eleven, he headed back to the base. There would only be a skeleton crew now so this would be the best time. He signed in at the night desk, talked a minute with the young man on duty, and walked purposefully down the hall to his office. Turning the lights on, he sat at his desk and rifled through a few papers. Everything was quiet, so leaving his light on and closing his door he went down the hall past the game room. The guys were laughing and shooting pool as usual. No one looked up. He was home free.

He slipped in the file room, eased the door shut, then went to the top secret files and punched in the code. Davenport should be in the top drawer. It was there, but when he opened the file a surprise awaited him—it was empty with the exception of one page. That page stated that all contents of the file had been transferred to the Little Washington facility outside of Denton. Now that made no sense at all. Why would the files of a deceased Army veteran be sent to that facility?

Carl replaced the file, locked the cabinet, turned off the lights, and opened the door a crack. No one was in the hall. He stopped by the game room and talked with the guys for a few minutes. After turning his office light off, he signed out and left the building.

Where there's smoke, there's fire. And there's lots of smoke around, Carl mused. This wasn't like any procedure he'd encountered in twenty years in the Army. It made no sense that Josh's file was sent to one of the control centers for the government.

"Wonder if Herman is home tonight and if he found out about the car tags?" he mused. Checking the time, he decided midnight was too late to call.

It would keep until tomorrow.

Chapter 13

JENNIE HURRIED TO ANSWER the phone. She hoped it was Herman. There was only silence at the other end of the line. "Who's there? Josh, is that you?" The connection was severed with a sharp click.

"Nathan," Jennie called. "That was another one of those calls. I asked if it was Josh and they hung up instantly. Do you think it could be possible? I'm scared, Nathan," sobbed Jennie. "I don't know if I can stand the answer."

Nathan wrapped his arms around her and said softly, "It will be okay. There's no reason to be scared. It's the not knowing that's so hard. Let's see what else Herman has found."

When the phone pealed again, Nathan snatched it up. "Hello, talk to me."

"Nathan, this is Herman. You sound angry. What's wrong?"

"It's those damn crank calls, Herman. Jennie's had a couple more today and she's really spooked about it. Do you know anything?"

"Yes and no. Carl just called and he's on his way over to my house. Can you and Jennie come? Molly says to come for supper if you don't mind burgers."

"We're on our way," Nathan answered. "We're anxious to hear what you've found out. Where do you live?"

Jennie listened intently. Nathan hung up the phone saying, "Carl is on his way to Herman's house. He asked us to eat with them tonight. I told them we'd leave shortly. Maybe we'll learn something tonight.

Jennie dressed quickly and they left without saying very much. She watched Nathan get in the car, and she wondered what he really thought about all this? She knew he was humoring her at first, but it had gone further than she ever imagined.

"Nathan, what do you think about all this?" Jennie asked. "Don't answer quickly or just politely, what do you really think?"

GLANCING OVER AT JENNIE, NATHAN saw the vulnerability in her face and his anger grew. He answered slowly, "I don't think Josh is alive. However, something is going on, possibly some type of cover-up. I can't even begin to guess what or why. Maybe Carl and Herman will have some answers tonight."

He really hoped that they would have some explanation. Jennie's nerves were stretched thin. It reminded him of when he first met her. His thoughts were racing. What would he do if he found out Davenport was still alive? He and Jennie had made a good life together, but if Josh is alive, he wasn't sure what she would do. Well, he would have some say in that matter. And he'd want to know why. Actually there were lots of things he wanted answers to.

Nathan exited the freeway and turned right at the first red light. "Herman said to turn right at the third street. It's the fifth house on the left. Help me watch for it," Nathan said.

Driving down the street, it flashed through Nathan's mind that the car in front of him was dark blue. "Lots of blue cars on the streets lately," he said. "I guess I'm noticing blue ones since that one tailed Herman. The blue car was still in front of him when he turned onto Herman's street.

"That's it; the red brick." Jennie said. "I'm looking forward to seeing Molly. I haven't seen her since high school."

Nathan pulled in the driveway and watched to see where the blue car was going. It turned in a driveway several houses down the block. Maybe they live there. He was beginning to put sinister meanings on things that were probably just everyday happenings.

Herman saw them drive up and was waiting at the front door. "You made good time in getting here. Come on in. Carl's in the kitchen talking to Molly and I'm pouring wine. Red or white?"

"White for me, please," answered Jennie. "Thanks, Herman. This is so nice of you to invite us. I wish it were just for fun."

Molly and Carl came in holding out empty glasses. "Hi, Jennie, it's good to see you. And this must be Nathan," Molly said as she and Jennie hugged.

After refilling their glasses, Herman led Carl and Nathan to the backyard where hamburgers were already on the grill. Molly and Jennie went into the kitchen to finish things up there. No one mentioned anything about Josh until after dinner was over and they had settled down in the den.

JENNIE WAITED ABOUT AS LONG as she could stand it. "What have you two found out? Somebody start talking."

"Relax, Jennie, the wheels turn slowly, but they do turn," laughed Herman. "How about it, Carl, what have you found?"

"I found nothing, but that tells me a lot. When I got into Josh's file, it was empty with the exception of one page stating that the contents had been transferred to the Little Washington facility."

"Little Washington, what's that?" Jennie asked.

"There are several alternative White Houses. It's one of them," explained Carl. "They each have the capability of running the government. One is an underground facility outside of Denton commonly known as Little Washington. There's another underground facility in Colorado, several other secret locations, and then the 747 White House called the E4B. This plane can stay in the air almost indefinitely. Everything necessary to run the government is duplicated in each facility. I can't imagine why Josh's file would have been transferred there. There's no reason to have records of deceased veterans at these facilities. And I don't have a clue why his file at the base was empty. When files are transferred, a copy is always retained. I've never seen this happen before."

"One more mystery," commented Herman. "And I'm about to add another. I found something else extremely unusual, some communications from INSCOM." Herman looked over at Jennie saying, "INSCOM means the Intelligence and Security Command of the Army. It was on orders from INSCOM that I was at Josh's funeral; however, I wasn't told this or why I was sent there. That's part of the reason I felt there could be something to your episode, Jennie."

Nathan twisted around sharply. He got up and paced about the room. Jennie started to respond, but stopped abruptly when she saw Nathan's reaction. She just nodded at Herman to continue.

Watching Nathan, Herman explained what he had found in the sealed file. "It appears that I have been in the middle of this all along."

Carl opened his notebook and said, "Ok, slow down. Herman. I know you started looking at this because of Jennie's episode, but I don't know the background the way you do. Jennie, I need you to go back to when this started. I want you to tell me all you remember about the night Josh died."

"You mean everything?"

"Yes, as best you can."

"Well, Josh woke me up in the middle of the night. He could hardly talk. He was mumbling for me to get a doctor, said his head was roaring. I fumbled for the light and when I looked at him his face was ashen. He was holding his head and rocking back and forth. I ran to the phone and called for help, then ran back to the bed. His head had fallen forward. I told him help was on the way, and I held him. He tried to say something, but I couldn't really understand him."

"What did it sound like? Think, Jennie."

"He mumbled *remember* a couple of times. But that was all. He never opened his eyes again."

"Have you tried to figure out what he wanted you to remember?"

"Oh, yes, for years. It has troubled me ever since that night, but I have no idea. There are just too many things it could mean."

"What happened when the paramedics got there?"

"They said he wasn't breathing, that there was no heartbeat. They got him out of the house and to the ambulance in a matter of minutes. They wouldn't let me go with them, and I chased the ambulance a long way down the street. The security patrol for our area pulled up and said he would take me to the hospital. I was still in my gown so I had to go in and dress and see about our daughters. It all happened so fast."

Molly slipped over to Jennie and filled her wine glass, then sat down beside her.

Carl nodded at Molly and said, "Keep going, Jennie. Tell me what happened when you got to the hospital."

"They wouldn't let me in to see Josh. I had to wait all by myself in that dismal hall outside of his room. Lots of other people kept running in and out of his room."

"Who was going in and out, Jennie?"

"I guess it was hospital personnel. Doctors, nurses, people in uniforms. A time or two I could see in the door when someone opened it. I tried to get in but they wouldn't let me. They told me I was in the way. A man in a dark suit came by and went right in the room. No one stopped him. I thought he might be the hospital chaplain because when he came out of Josh's room he came over to me and asked if I had any family there. I told him my daughters were on their way, and he said he would look for them. He came back shortly saying they had just arrived. No one told me anything, but I knew Josh was dead. Inside me, I knew."

"Did the chaplain stay with you?"

No, my aunt and uncle and the girls got there. I tried again to get in the room to see Josh, but several men blocked the doorway and wouldn't let me. I asked the doctor who those men were in Josh's room, but he never answered me. Then a police officer came and made me sign papers for an autopsy. He said it was mandatory when someone dies at home. That's how they told me Josh had died."

Jennie's eyes filled with tears as the feelings flooded over her. "After that everything started going out of focus and I couldn't stand up. My legs gave way, and I just sat down on the floor. Then a doctor tried to give me a sedative, but I knocked the pills out of his hand. I guess I was a little hysterical by then."

"What happened next?"

"The doctor took me into his office and made me sit down. He told me I was in shock and he shoved a needle in my arm before I could stop him. He said it wasn't a sedative, but I think it was because it made me woozy."

"Who else was there?"

"I don't know. I wasn't thinking about anything but Josh."

"It's in your head, Jennie. Think a minute. Close your eyes. Visualize the scene. Listen to the voices. You're at the hospital. You are sitting down and there are people around you. Who do you see?"

Jennie closed her eyes and tried to picture it. "My daughters and my aunt and uncle were in the hall. The doctor handed something to Kris and told her to give two pills to me every day."

"Who else do you see, Jennie? It's in your head."

Jennie dropped her head into her hands, eyes still shut. She didn't want to remember what she had worked so hard to forget. She breathed deeply and tried to go back in her mind. "People were moving around, almost in slow motion. I heard the doctor telling me to quit fighting it; just relax. My head was spinning, the lights were getting dim, and I was struggling to keep my eyes open. I saw the chaplain backing away—he never came over to me. No one helped me. There were several strange men in the room wearing dark suits, not hospital uniforms. One of them asked if I was out yet and if the doctor had given me the shot."

Then those men had asked another question, she couldn't figure out how they knew about it. Jennie opened her eyes and looked up at Carl, "I heard one of them ask 'Do you think she knows what he was trying to tell her?' How did they know Josh was trying to tell me something?"

"Keep your eyes closed, Jennie. Keep looking at what is happening."

"The voices were fading; I felt like I was floating. Those men were all around. The very last thing I remember was someone saying 'Tell everyone, it's over. Let's pack up and get out of here.' Everything went black after that. That's it, Carl. That's all I remember. I don't even remember the drive home."

Jennie looked at him expectantly with tears streaming down her face. "Did any of that help?"

"You did really well, Jennie. I know that was hard, but you remembered some important things," Carl answered. "That injection was important. The people were important. Molly, why don't you take Jennie out to the kitchen and get her something else to drink? She needs a break from all this."

NATHAN'S FACE HAD TURNED SEVERAL shades of red. Carl had been watching him and hoping he wasn't going to interrupt Jennie when she was talking. It must have been tough on him to watch her break down like that and not help.

When Jennie and Molly came back with cookies and hot tea, Carl asked Jennie if she was up to answering a few more questions. Jennie glanced over at Nathan, then nodded she was.

"Let's go on to the funeral. Jennie, you told Herman you didn't think Josh looked right. Herman said it had been so long since he had seen Josh that he wouldn't have been able to notice anything different." Carl paused and looked intently at Jennie. "Exactly what was wrong?"

JENNIE CLOSED HER EYES AGAIN and she could see Josh lying there. She still remembered how cold his skin felt and how sick it made her feel. He didn't look like her Josh. Maybe it was the lack of emotion, maybe it was that way with everyone when they died. The only definite thing was his shirt didn't fit right.

"Just little things," she said. "Things I thought looked a bit different. I assumed it was because he was dead."

"What things, Jennie?" probed Carl, staring at her.

"Well, his face didn't seem exactly right. It looked a little longer. His eyes were different, maybe rounder and larger. You remember the scar on his nose, the one he got playing football in high school. It was crooked, but it looked straight after he died. That was strange, but the main thing that sticks in my mind is that his neck was thinner. I couldn't understand that. I had bought a new shirt and I know I got the correct size. It was the size I always bought for him, but the neck was loose. It stood out and looked funny, I tried to fix it, but it never did look right. I can't think of anything else. He just looked different."

Jennie looked up at Carl then continued slowly. "There is another thing. When Kris saw Josh at the funeral home she kept saying, 'That isn't daddy; that isn't my daddy.' My dad took her out of the room because she was so agitated and she never came back in. Josh must have looked different to her too. Another strange thing Kris told me recently is that when she got to the hospital the night Josh died, she thought she heard him talking and she tried to go in that room, but someone stopped her."

"Who stopped her?" asked Herman.

"It was the patrolman who drove her to the hospital. My daughters told me a couple of other things I better tell you about." Jennie told them about the painting Kris saw and about the time Laurie thought she saw her dad on television.

"Okay, that helps put me in the picture," said Carl pulling out a small notebook and pen.

"Let's put the facts in sequence. Kris thought she heard Josh's voice at the hospital the night he died. Jennie was given an injection. Herman was ordered by INSCOM to provide security for the funeral. Jennie thought Josh's shirt collar was too big. Kris didn't think it was her dad. Next, more orders from INSCOM have Herman keeping Jennie's house under surveillance for the next few months. Jennie received phone calls the next year where no one spoke. Kris thought she saw a painting that was Josh's but when she went back to see it, it was gone. Laurie thought she saw him on television and tried to get a copy. The TV station said the master copy had disappeared. Jennie had what we are calling an episode with facts in it that she was previously unaware of. The funeral home has records missing pertaining to the physical description of Josh. Jennie went to New Orleans and found the place where she jumped out of the car in her episode. When she got back home, the calls started again with the clicking noise. The NPRC said all records had burned up in 1973, but in Jennie's episode Josh said he had been reactivated in 1974. His records from the Army have been transferred to Little Washington. Herman's chief has ordered that he cease all investigations about Josh. And, last but not least, a dark blue car has been following Herman. What did you find out about the tags, Herman?"

"Ran them—report said *Classified*. I haven't encountered that before."

Nathan interrupted, "Blue car, that reminds me; there was one in front of me when Jennie and I came. It turned in a drive about three-quarters way down the block. Herman, does one of your neighbors have a car like that?"

"Don't know, but I think I'll go out front and get the newspaper." Herman returned shortly with the paper in hand. "There's a dark car parked at the end of the block facing our way. It appears to be back. Did you get the license, Nathan?"

"Sorry, I should have. If it had been following me, I guess I would have paid more attention to it."

"We now have a few questions to answer," Carl continued. "Most importantly, why is INSCOM involved? Next, why were the Army files on Josh sent to Little Washington if he's deceased? Classified tags are generally government, so is the dark car G-2? Should we approach the car or wait and see what they do next?"

"Valid questions, Carl. I have a few I'd like answered," Herman responded. "Jennie, can you remember anything about what Josh found out when he was at the News Center in Kansas City? That appears to be the key. Did he have any special friends at the News Center?

"I've racked my brain trying to remember if Josh ever said anything else, but nothing has come to mind." Jennie thought for a minute. "There was one couple we used to visit with. I'll have to think about it. It's been so long that I don't know if I can remember their names."

"Try, Jennie. If you can, we may be able to find them. It's a long shot, but they might remember something helpful. So what's your opinion, Carl?"

"I think that there are too many unusual occurrences and too many things missing to call it mere coincidence. The thread is getting longer. I'm not convinced that Josh is alive, but I'm not completely sure anymore that he is dead. It all boils down to why would his death be faked and why all the deception?"

NATHAN SHIFTED UNCOMFORTABLY. HE GOT up and looked out the window, red-faced and furious. His mind was racing. With a supreme effort, he composed his face, turned and studied Jennie.

Chapter 14

THE ANGUISH OF JOSH's death washed over Jennie like a tidal wave leaving her raw and aching. Could he really be alive? Carl said he wasn't completely sure. She had touched him at the funeral home and he was cold, the man in that casket was definitely not alive.

"How dare you do this to me, Josh," Jennie cried. "I can't go through this again."

And then there was Nathan. He'd been really ticked off at her preoccupation, but she couldn't help it. Drawing a deep breath, she had to admit that she had never fully accepted Josh's death. Maybe nobody ever does.

As soon as Nathan left for the office, Jennie ran out of the house. All morning long she had been fighting the compulsion to go to the cemetery. As she was driving there, all the past years she had sat by his grave flashed through her mind. She usually took three roses, one for her and each of the girls. Yellow ones, if possible. Sometimes it had been a peaceful thing, other times it left her in agony.

Stopping at the flower shop she bought her flowers and asked for a paper cup to carry water in. "Here you are," the lady said. "The yellow roses sure are pretty this year."

Jennie parked the car near the grave and saw that the vase had been pulled up and one flower was in it. That's odd. No one ever took flowers except her and she hadn't been here in a long time. When the flowers are dead, the groundskeeper takes them away and lowers the vase so the flower couldn't have been there very long, maybe a day or two.

She stopped at the hydrant, filled the cup with water, and took it to Josh's grave. There was one fading yellow rose in it, only one, and it wasn't from her. She pulled it out and put the fresh roses and water in the vase. Maybe one of the girls had been there. She knew they came sometimes, but they seldom brought flowers.

She sat down on the ground and told Josh what was happening, about her strange experience, about Herman and Carl. Rubbing her fingers over the carved marker she traced his name *Joshua Edward Davenport* and then the date, *February 16, 1977.*

"Oh, Josh, what is going on? Is it possible you could still be alive? If you are, then who did I bury? We had so many dreams and hopes, so many things we wanted to do. Remember that morning after our wedding—we had breakfast in bed, fed each other wedding cake and drank orange juice. It was so much fun." Picturing that, she couldn't hold back a smile. They had laughed and searched through the newspaper to find the announcement of their wedding. *Do you still remember?*

What could have been so bad that you would have left us? Were you protecting us like you said in the dream? "You should have told me," she mumbled aloud. Her anger was close to the surface and all mixed up with feelings she'd forced aside six years before.

"Remember, remember what?" she agonized again. She had never figured that out. Her tears came hot and fast.

Jennie struggled up from the ground, wiped her eyes and looked at her watch. She was shocked to see that she'd been there for over an hour. She had to get back home. Looking down at the grave, anger flared again.

"Damn it, Josh, I have to know if you are here even if we have to dig you up." She wondered if a positive identification could be made after all these years.

Driving home, she mentally went through the episode again. If Josh is alive, could she be putting him in danger? Maybe she should have tried to find out things for herself. From now on she would have to be careful what she told Herman, and Nathan, too. If Josh was trying to contact her, she'd have to make it easier for him to do so. That's assuming that the impossible has happened and he is still alive. She would have to be more vigilant.

When Jennie arrived home, the phone was ringing and she answered it expectantly, but it was only a sales call.

Herman had asked if Josh had any special friends at the News Center. She couldn't remember any names, but her old address book should have their

Army friends in it. She dug it out of the bottom of the file cabinet and started flipping through the pages.

When the phone rang again, Jennie absentmindedly answered it. There was silence for a moment and then she heard a muffled voice singing …

Go to sleepy, little baby,
Go to sleepy, little baby,
When you wake, we'll play patty, patty cake
with all the pretty little ponies.

Shocked, she dropped the phone then grabbed it back up shouting, "Hello, hello, Josh, is that you?" All she heard was a dial tone.

"I'm trying, Josh, but you have to help me," Jennie yelled in frustration.

Who else knew that song and what it meant to her and Josh? Nathan, Herman and Carl don't know it. Kris and Laurie probably don't remember it. More than that, none of them would do this to her. There would be no reason for them to play such a nasty trick. If it was Josh, maybe he's trying to tell her he was alive without letting anyone else know. If he doesn't talk and is sending signals, it might mean her phone line was tapped. Jennie unscrewed the phone, but couldn't find anything unusual.

Restless, she went out in the backyard and sat in the swing thinking about the song and when Josh first started singing it. She thought it was when they lived in Kansas City long before they moved back to Texas. He definitely sang it to Kris and Laurie. He probably made the song up; he was always making up songs and stories for the girls. Is that what he wanted her to remember? Josh said the pony song was their private code; they would always know each other by it.

Could he have put the single rose in the vase at the cemetery for her to find? The rose was yellow; he had sent her yellow roses the morning of their wedding.

"Please, please call again," Jennie prayed fervently. "Give me another chance." *Remember*, he said the night he died. Remember the song, the past, the Army, his jobs, our friends, maybe just remember him? No, it had to be the song. And that would mean he is alive because no one else knows about it.

Excited and scared all at the same time, Jennie went back to the house and picked up the old address book she had dropped. Josh had played chess with a friend by mail. Roger, his name was Roger. He had a funny last name. Zenor, that's it, Roger and Dottie Zenor. He'd been in the service with Josh.

She couldn't remember any of the others. She flipped to the *Zs*, no luck. She would have to search some more, but it would have to wait until tomorrow. Nathan would be home soon. She reminded herself—no more impulsive decisions. She had to stop and think before she acted.

Nathan got home a little early and Jennie was already cooking supper. "Smells great," he said. "That has to be spaghetti."

"You could say hello," Jennie teased in an effort to smooth over the tension of the morning. "Yes, it's spaghetti with meat sauce, garlic toast and salad. I felt like comfort food tonight."

"Anything going on that I should know about?" he asked abruptly.

After seeing the look on his face Jennie hedged on the truth and didn't mention the cemetery. "Not much, just another phone call with no one there."

Giving Nathan a quick hug she asked how his meeting went, but her mind was focused on the muffled voice that had been singing.

She didn't hear his answer.

Chapter 15

CARL KENDALL TOOK I-35 north toward Denton. He had gone over and over it in his mind. He couldn't find any reason why all the information on Josh had been sent to Little Washington. What he needed was to get his hands on Josh's file. He knew several men stationed there but not well enough to ask for this kind of favor unless he could devise a credible story of why he needed it and there just wasn't one.

Several months ago, he'd been officially invited to tour Little Washington but had put it off. Now he had a reason. He decided the only thing to do was to see who was based there and then play it by ear. "You never know," Kendall mumbled, "I may find someone who owes me a favor. It's worth a try. I've been lucky before."

Arriving at Little Washington on the east side of Denton, he stopped at the gate, showed his ID, and was waved in. It was some facility. No one would never know that it was anything more than several nondescript buildings with a few soldiers stationed here. He found a visitor parking space and went in the nearest building. It looked like a miner's shack the way it backed up to a grassy hill.

The guard at the entrance took Kendall's ID, found his name on the list of authorized visitors, and summoned a guide to take him around. Watching the young soldier come briskly down the hall to meet him, Kendall was reminded of himself at that age. You think you know it all, but eventually you realize you really don't know anything, especially when something like this comes up.

"Welcome, sir, I'm Private Daniels, and I've been instructed to show you around. If you'll come with me, we'll begin the tour." Kendall followed the confident young man to the elevators. When they entered, Daniels inserted a key and punched the descend button. It was quite a different sensation to enter at ground level and go down. They exited at level ten, the official Command Center. He paid special attention to everyone he saw, but there were no familiar faces.

As they continued from level to level, he was astounded at the magnitude of the compound. The five levels beneath the Command Center consisted of living accommodations for several hundred people with food supplies and water to last a number of years. There were living areas, gyms, game rooms with pool tables, PX, theater, post office, snack bars, kitchens and cafeteria, and a fully staffed hospital. The lowest level was reserved as living quarters for the president in case of nuclear attack.

Going back to level ten, he was taken to the office of the commanding officer where he had the opportunity to ask a few questions. He asked if all records were automatically forwarded here. If not, what was the determining factor?

Lt. Colonel Graves said that only vital information was sent here, anything expedient to the survival of the nation. Most everything was put on microfiche and stored until needed. Data was constantly analyzed for need, sorted, and then prioritized. They had a very large clerical staff, all military personnel with top secret clearance. No civilians were allowed in the facility. Training was continuous. They were trained to be able to locate and retrieve any file within a matter of minutes.

Lt. Colonel Graves said that white noise was piped throughout the facility, which made it virtually impossible for any sort of bugging. It was an entirely secure zone. He told Kendall that it housed several special rooms that were reserved for visitors. These visitors were generally military who needed a safe haven or were a security risk.

Kendall asked if anyone was living there now. Lt. Graves replied," That's classified, so I can't answer that question. However, I will say that the rooms are rarely empty. Now, if you'll excuse me, Private Daniels will escort you to the exit."

He followed Daniels down the long hallway to the elevators. As they entered the elevator, Kendall asked the young man if he had ever met Josh Davenport. Daniels turned his head sharply to look at him then dropped his eyes and said, "I'm not allowed to answer any questions about personnel." Not even blinking an eye, Kendall thanked him and said that the tour had been most enlightening.

It was almost dark when Kendall drove away. He had much to think about. Through the years he had developed an instinct to people's responses.

And he was rarely wrong. Private Daniels either knew Josh or knew something about him. That much he'd bet on. And it had to be relatively current, not from the past. Daniels would have been in high school six years ago.

That slip of the tongue was a dead give away. He said he wasn't allowed to answer any questions about *personnel.* He definitely said *personnel.* Could Josh be in one of those secure rooms? Or could he have been there some time in the last year or so? Maybe he is stationed out of Little Washington.

Kendall decided Jennie's episode was definitely no ordinary dream. Whatever was going on was highly secret. Oh, yeah, he needed to tell Herman about Daniels' slip of the tongue as soon as he could.

Lt. Colonel Graves sat still for a few seconds after Major Kendall left with Pvt. Daniels; then turned to the large equipment bank behind him. Punching in a few buttons, he listened to the conversation in the elevator between the young private and the major.

Graves whirled around to the phone and dialed. "You asked to be alerted if we had any unexpected visitors, particularly anyone asking about Josh Davenport. Major Carl Kendall came in for a tour of the facility today. He had full clearance. He asked me if anyone was staying in the special rooms right now. I evaded saying that the rooms are rarely empty."

"When he was in the elevator he asked his escort if he had ever met Josh Davenport. Pvt. Daniels answered that he wasn't allowed to talk about personnel. Kendall is sharp; he'll pick up on that. He just left the facility, and I assume is on his way back to base in Dallas. Daniels will be taken care of from this end."

WASHINGTON, DC

GENERAL THURMAN SLAMMED THE phone down. The Davenport situation was intensifying, but he couldn't get a handle on it. Whatever it was, it was spreading. He hit the buzzer for Reaves.

"Reaves, I need several things. I want to see this past week's backup tapes for Jennie Davenport ASAP. Next, Lt. Colonel Graves from the Little Washington facility just called me. Major Carl Kendall has been nosing around. I want him neutralized tonight and while you're at it, take care of that nosey cop in Dallas."

Chapter 16

THAT LONELY YELLOW ROSE at the cemetery was keeping Jennie awake, that and the song. No way was finding the rose and receiving a call with someone singing the pony song a coincidence. She must have been watched while she was at the cemetery. She quit trying to sleep and sat up in bed. If it was really Josh she wished he would just talk to her. Or maybe he did. The voice on the phone was so muffled she wouldn't have recognized it if it were her own.

Josh joked around saying if they were ever separated, she would know him by the pony song, their private code. Maybe he wasn't kidding. Well, we're definitely separated, Jennie reasoned. She wished she could remember why he told her that and if it was before or after the Army.

Trying again to sleep Jennie pulled the covers snugly around her, but it was useless. All the sleepless nights she had spent through the past years kept flooding her mind. Nights when she tried to picture exactly what Josh looked like, to bring him back in her mind, to hear his voice, to recall their life together, and never finding him. Sometimes, she'd been plain angry with him for dying and leaving her to take care of everybody. Other times she felt almost frantic to see him. So how would she feel if he was alive—angry, maybe hurt? Both, she would feel both.

She needed to know what made him leave, if that's what he did. What she did know for sure was that he would never have left unless he had no choice. She knew too well how he felt growing up all those years without a father. He had always hated going home alone while his mother was working. He would not have put her or his daughters through all this willingly.

It had to be connected with the Army, with G-2. Wonder if anyone else from Kansas City knows about this? Or if any of the guys from the News Center have died or disappeared. She definitely had to call their old Army friends, Roger and Dottie Zenor, if she could find them. She couldn't remember the names of any of the others, but they might.

Jennie flipped over again and realized she had done that a dozen times in the past few minutes. It was going to be a long sleepless night and she hated to keep Nathan awake. She gave up and moved to the couch in the den.

She would call the Zenors in the morning, but she wasn't going to tell Herman or Nathan about it until she found out what they knew. There was one absolute, however. She had to find out if Josh was in that grave.

Jennie finally drifted off. She woke to the sound of rain and distant thunder and the smell of coffee brewing. *Umm, rain and fresh coffee,* she thought sleepily when she rolled off the couch and headed for the shower. Her thoughts continued to bombard her as the water pounded her body.

"Nathan, that coffee smells great. You are wonderful. Just listen to the rain; can anything be better than the sound of rain and the smell of coffee in the morning?" Jennie said giving Nathan a hug.

He hugged her back tightly. "I'm glad to see you're feeling okay this morning. You were so fidgety during the night I figured you'd be wiped out today. You tossed and turned nearly all night."

"I did have trouble sleeping. Too many things tumbled around in my mind. I wish we could find out something for sure. Knowing what it is has to be better than this uncertainty."

"Whatever it is, Jennie, we'll deal with it. We both learned a long time ago that nothing remains the same for very long. I can't help but think about how I'd feel in your place. I'd have to find out. Whatever happens, well, we'll work it out."

"Oh, Nathan, thank you," Jennie cried and turned back into his arms. "I've been afraid of hurting you. There's such a war going on inside of me. He was my life for so long, my daughters' father. I know that he wouldn't have done this unless he had no choice."

"Sit down, Jennie, and drink your coffee. I have to be at the office early today so I need to leave soon. You know how slow traffic can be when it rains. Why don't you take your coffee and a book and just relax. There's nothing to do this early anyway."

Jennie did just that after Nathan left. It was much too early to call the Zenors on the west coast; they would still be asleep. It felt good to sit on the couch and watch the rain. Looking out the French doors at the back yard, she thought it looked like a greenhouse. All Nathan's plants were glowing vibrantly in the rain. The blooming flowers and the ferns were beautiful. The little birdhouses he had built and she had painted were so cute. The birds weren't flying in the rain, but they would when the sun came out, flitting in and out of the little houses. The rustic bench nestled in a corner of the deck among the plants and flowers was so inviting. It beckoned to her, even in the rain. She wished she could sit out there.

For a little while, she forgot the past few weeks. She read only a few pages before her eyes closed. When the phone rang she was so deep in sleep that it was difficult to wake up. Laurie wanted to know if she had learned anything new. Jennie didn't mention Roger. After all, she might not be able to find him. She told Laurie there was nothing new, and they talked about her grandchild.

After she hung up, Jennie went upstairs and looked through her desk hoping the old Christmas card list with the Zenors' name would be there. Otherwise she would have to go to the attic and dig through the boxes from Josh's office. She went through the desk twice and it wasn't there. Jennie groaned as she wearily climbed the attic stairs. She looked at all the boxes wishing she had labeled them better.

Starting with the one she could reach the easiest, she opened it. It was like opening Pandora's Box. After Josh died, she had gone to his office and tried to pack up his things. At first, she looked at each item, thinking and crying about them. Finally, she had just dumped each drawer. So, most of the boxes were a jumbled mess and she had no idea what was there.

The first box was organized and full of the items that had been on top of his desk. There was the in-and-out box, a heavy gold ruler that she had given him one Christmas, a small desk set holding paper clips and erasers, and some old magazines. Why on earth did she keep those magazines? The next box must have been from the credenza. It was full of photographs, layout sheets and old seminar brochures, all things that were not used every day.

"You'd have thought the address book would have been in the box with the desktop things," Jennie fussed, not wanting to go through any more boxes. It wasn't much easier now than it had been six years ago, but she had to find the number so she kept searching. Maybe it will be in the next box, she prayed.

"Oh, my, this is a real mess. I must have dumped an entire drawer into it." She shuffled through the papers, brochures, layout sheets, letters, and small pieces of paper with pictures drawn on them. No wonder she dumped it. It still hurt to look at the little cartoon pictures he always drew. Her eyes misted over and she quickly closed that box and pulled out another one. At last, she found the address book and flipped through the pages. "Yes, there's Roger," she cried in relief. His name had a star and Army written beside it.

Brushing the dust off her clothes, she rushed down the narrow attic stairs. After saying a little prayer that she would find out something, she made the call. It was answered quickly, but it turned out to be a wrong number. Jennie's heart plummeted. She had really hoped to talk to them. Information had several Zenors, but no Roger.

What now? She knew the library had lots of phone books from all over the country, so she called to see if they had an Oregon one. They did, however, they couldn't look up the numbers. She would have to come in and do that.

It took her about twenty minutes to drive downtown. Luck was with her, and she found a parking space near the library entrance. She dug in her purse for change to feed the meter and found enough for thirty minutes. She hurried in the building.

It didn't take her long to find the section with the phone books and locate Portland, Oregon. She thumbed through it and found four Zenors, all with different initials, and copied them down hoping that one would be the right one or maybe a relative. With a name like Zenor, it almost had to be, certainly a better chance than a name like Smith or Jones.

When she pulled in the driveway at home, she glanced at her watch and saw that her whole trip only took a little over an hour. She had lots of time before Nathan got home. The first number she called didn't know Roger and the second was no longer in service. Fearful that she might not find them, she dialed the third number and asked to speak to Roger. "Roger doesn't live here," answered the voice. "Who's calling, please?"

"Jennie Davenport, my husband was in service with Roger in Kansas City. Dottie and I were friends. Do you know them?"

"Sure do. I'm Ted, Roger's brother. It sounds like you did know them. May I ask what years your husband was stationed in Kansas City?"

"Josh was there in '54 through '57, and was stationed at the News Center."

"That sounds about right," answered Ted. "Dottie and Roger moved out to North Plains, a small town just north of here, several years ago. I think it'll be okay to give you the number." Jennie breathed a sigh of relief as she wrote the number down and thanked Ted for his help.

Her hand shook as she dialed the number then waited for what seemed an eternity. Finally, she heard a soft, still familiar voice answer and knew she had the right number.

"Dottie, this is Jennie Davenport, Josh Davenport's wife from the Army in Kansas City. Do you remember me?"

"Of course I do. It's good to hear from you."

"I know you're wondering why I'm calling after all these years. You probably don't know, but Josh died six years ago."

"I'm so sorry, Jennie, I didn't know. What happened?"

"It was an aneurysm and it came without warning. He wasn't sick at all, just died suddenly in the middle of the night.

"How are the girls, Kris and Laurie, isn't it?"

"Yes, you've a good memory, Dottie. They're married and I have two grandchildren. I'm calling because I need to find out some information about the News Center in Kansas City. I thought Roger might be able to help me. At least, I'm hoping he can. May I talk with him?"

"Sure you can, Jennie. He's at work now, but I'll tell him you called and give him your number. I'm grabbing a pencil. Okay, I'm ready. What's the number?"

Jennie told her then she and Dottie reminisced a little about Kansas City. It was good to know that their life had been uneventful. Dottie promised to tell Roger immediately and she was sure he'd call back quickly.

Anxious to talk to Roger, Jennie had to find some way to pass the time. All those papers were scattered around the attic and she knew she should go back and put them away. It would be better than just sitting and thinking. Maybe she'd find something that could help her.

It was still cloudy and the attic was so dim she had to get a lamp and long extension cord. The ghostly atmosphere retreated with the bright light and she could see what a mess the attic was.

Jennie organized and replaced the papers in the box. As she had nothing to do but wait for Roger to call, she pushed the boxes to the far corner of the room. Why she had left them in the middle, she hadn't a clue. She decided the heavy Army trunks should also be moved to that area. Bending over she shoved and strained and finally got them against the wall by the boxes from Josh's office. That's better. At least they're not in the middle of the room.

She was carrying the last box when she stumbled and fell with a thud. Rubbing a skinned knee, she looked to see what had tripped her. It was a loose board. She was surprised she hadn't tripped over it before. Then she realized that wasn't possible because the trunks had been sitting on it. Jennie tried to push it level with the other boards. When it wouldn't go down, she got on her knees and pushed harder. It still wouldn't go back into place. Opening the box from Josh's office, she got the heavy ruler, pried the board up, and peered in the hole.

It was so dark she hesitated to stick her hand in it. Pulling the lamp closer, she could see something shoved way back away from the opening. She would never have seen it without the light and having moved the trunks. Reaching in, she pulled out a small package wrapped in plastic. She shook years of dust off it and pulled the plastic away. It was a notebook.

Sitting cross-legged on the floor, Jennie opened it and was shocked to find Josh's handwriting. It was dated February 15, 1977, the day before he died. It contained a list of names and addresses, several cities in Europe with dates after each one, and then some odd entries, like some sort of code. What was this? Why would Josh hide it?

Oh, dear, this must be what his office was searched for. And the house too, it had been searched more than once. It has to be important for Josh to have hidden it. Was this what he was trying to tell her? Josh must have pulled the trunks over that loose board.

Not knowing what else to do with it, Jennie wrapped the plastic around it and put it back where it had been all these years. She went downstairs and got a hammer and pulled the crooked nail out of the board and was able to push it flush with the floor. Hammering the nail back in, she stood up and looked at it. It looked too clean so she took her rag and shook dust over the spot. Until she knew what it was, she wasn't telling anyone about it. Not Herman or Carl, not even Nathan. Jennie's heart was pounding as she went down the attic stairs.

She heated water, made a cup of tea and curled up in the recliner in the den. That book had to be what someone was looking for when they searched his office and their house. Maybe that's what Josh had tried to tell her about …

FEBRUARY SIX YEARS AGO—JOSH'S FUNERAL was finally over, but the house was still full of people, family and friends that had come home with her. She didn't want to talk to them right now, she needed some time alone. She grabbed her purse and keys, slipped out the side door, and got in her car. Everyone was busy eating and Jennie knew it would be some time before they missed her. If anyone did, they would assume she'd gone to her room to rest.

The afternoon skies were overcast and it looked like it could snow. She didn't care. It was February and things couldn't get any worse. She knew exactly where she was going, Josh's office.

Josh Davenport had been in advertising for most of his career. One year before his death, he had started his own company, the Davenport Advertising Agency, and had bought an office building. The agency did very well that first year. Jennie knew because she kept the company books and did the payroll.

She wanted to look around his office, to sit in his chair, to be alone and think. Most of all, Jennie wanted to find his Day-Timer and anything else that might give her a clue as to what he had been trying to tell her. There had to be some hint, some message, something to help her figure out what he wanted her to remember. She had already searched his desk at home and found nothing.

The last two days had been a nightmare of decisions, constant activity, and scores of well wishers. All telling her they understood how she felt; that life had to go on, that she had her daughters to live for. All talk, they really couldn't understand. Jennie knew they meant well, but what she needed was to be left alone.

The parking lot at Josh's building was almost empty. She really hoped no one would be in the office. When she opened the car door the cold wind hit her with a fury. Her unbuttoned coat billowed around her as she ran inside.

Nodding at the security guard, Jennie walked faster so she wouldn't have to talk with him. He had recognized her and signaled the elevator from his console and it was waiting for her. When the elevator door opened on the second floor and the hall was deserted, Jennie sighed in relief. She guessed everybody was at her house.

"I should have brought boxes," she murmured. "I could have taken some of his personal things home."

She went directly to Josh's large corner office, opened the door and came to a dead halt muffling a scream. It was in shambles. Papers were everywhere. The desk drawers pulled out and the contents dumped on the floor. Books had been pulled off the shelves and scattered all around. Chairs were turned upside down and the console pulled away from the wall. The couch had been flipped over and the bottom slit open. Even the lamps were on the floor, the shades torn and crooked. Nothing had been left untouched.

Enraged she stormed in. How dare someone do this? Jennie's mind shifted into high gear as her eyes searched the room. What had they been looking for? Could this have something to do with what Josh was trying to tell her? She had to find his Day-Timer for sure now. She pushed books aside with her foot, dug under papers and shoved the couch toward the wall before she spotted it. Grabbing it, she looked furtively around to see if anyone had come in and then thrust it in her purse.

Now she could call the security officer. He arrived in a couple of minutes and immediately dialed the police. He checked the rest of the agency and found no one else there. None of the other offices had been disturbed.

"I'm Jim Logan, Mrs. Davenport. I don't understand this. The cleaning crew came in early, and I'm sure they'd have called me if it'd been torn up then. The receptionist also came by this morning to program the answering machine. A couple of artists stopped by later to check on something, I don't remember what they said. None of them were up here longer than a few minutes and no one else came past me. I doubt that any of them came in Mr. Davenport's office. From what I was told, everyone was going to the funeral."

He paused then continued, "I'm very sorry about Mr. Davenport. He was always so nice. Not everyone is, you know."

"Thank you, Jim. Will it take the police long to get here?"

"No ma'am. They'll be here soon, don't worry. I better get back downstairs and let them in. You gonna be all right here by yourself?"

Jennie nodded.

The police arrived in about ten minutes and, much to her relief, Jim had already told them about Josh's death.

"I understand your husband was the owner of the company. Do you know who'll be in charge now, Mrs. Davenport?" the policeman asked.

"I think it will be David Stanton. He's Executive VP."

"We need to get him here and see if we can find out if anything is missing."

"I've already called him, officer. David and several others from the agency are on their way," Jennie said.

"Thank you. I know this is a difficult day for you, so tell me why you've come here now?"

"I needed to get away from the house. I guess I thought I'd feel close to my husband here."

"Did you have any particular reason?"

"I wanted to gather up some of his personal things." She didn't mention the Day-Timer.

"Why today, of all days?" the officer pushed.

Jennie paused and took a deep breath. "Right before he died, my husband tried to tell me something, but I couldn't understand him. I wondered if it had to do with the office."

"I'm sorry, but you can't touch anything right now. We'll have to dust for fingerprints. The team should be here shortly. There's no reason you have to stay around for this. It'll take a couple of hours." The man nodded toward the other officer and said, "Give your phone number to the officer there, and we'll call you when we're finished."

Jennie met David at the elevator and they talked briefly. He was shocked and had no idea why anyone would be searching the office.

Snow was falling rapidly when she left the building and the streets were already icing over. It seldom snowed in Dallas, but when it did it was a wet snow and the streets became coated with *black ice*. You couldn't see it, but it was there and driving was a nightmare. The drive home took a long time.

When she finally got there, the crowd had thinned out and the house was quiet. Relief washed over her. Her dad met her at the door and helped her out of her coat. "I was worried about you, honey. You should have told me where you were going, and I'd have gone with you. That was a bad thing to face alone."

Jennie hugged him and tried to avoid seeing the anguish in his eyes. "I'm okay, Dad. Sorry I worried you. I didn't think."

"We're all right, dear," Jennie's mother said. "Do you think you could eat something? There's a lot of food here."

"Not right now, Mom. I'd like to put on my robe and lie down for a while."

Anger was overshadowing Jennie's pain as she stretched out across the bed and flipped through Josh's calendar. It didn't take long, only January to February 16. She found nothing out of the ordinary. Several small sketches were scattered on that last day. Tears trickled down her face as she looked at the drawings. Josh had a habit of doodling while he talked on the phone, some realistic, mostly cartoons. She noticed that several pages had small ponies drawn on them

JENNIE WAS YANKED BACK TO the present. The small ponies, that's what Josh wanted her to remember. She whispered the words ...

> *Go to sleepy, little baby,*
> *Go to sleepy, little baby,*
> *When you wake, we'll play patty, patty cake*
> *with all the pretty little ponies.*

That had to be it. He wanted her to remember the pony song. "Is he trying to tell me he's alive or is that just my wishful thinking?" she whispered.

When Nathan got home that evening he told Jennie that Herman had called him. Herman had checked out the requirements for disinterment. "He was afraid you'd be upset and thought it would be easier for me to tell you. He thinks this is our next step, but I hate putting his job in any more jeopardy."

"I don't want to do that, either. If he tells us how, maybe we can do whatever has to be done so he won't have to be involved."

"I think that would be best. Are you going to tell the girls?" Nathan asked.

"They'll have to know eventually, but let's find out first if it can be done. It's upsetting to even think about it, much less actually digging up Josh's grave.

Chapter 17

CARL KENDALL WOKE BEFORE the alarm went off. If he didn't catch Herman before he left for work, he might not be able to talk to him until tonight. He wanted to set up a time to get together. What he had to tell was best not told on the phone.

Herman sounded groggy when he answered and asked if Carl had found out anything.

"A few things," Carl hedged. They made plans to meet for lunch at Red Bryans BBQ, one of their old hangouts from high school.

While coffee brewed, Carl listened to the morning news. He grew up in Dallas so this felt more like home than anywhere he'd ever been stationed. It was nice being around his family, especially during the holidays.

Taking his coffee with him, Carl walked across the base to his office. He had a busy schedule and the morning passed quickly. Hunger pains reminded him it was almost time to meet Herman. Quickly clearing off his desk, he picked up his keys and headed for the parking lot.

As he was getting in his car, two men in dark civilian suits walked up to him asking, "Are you Major Carl Kendall?"

"Yes, I am."

"Please lock your car and come with us," said the taller man, flashing his military ID.

"What's up? Where are we going?" questioned Carl, as the two men led him to their car.

"We have orders to escort you to G-2 headquarters."

Anxious to talk with Carl, Herman arrived at Red Bryans early. He waited in line and was eventually shown to a booth. *Good thing I came early or we might not have gotten a place to sit.* Red Bryans had been in Dallas since the fifties and had a loyal following.

The waitress kept asking Herman if he was ready to order. Hating to tie up the booth too long, he ordered. He ate his sandwich slowly wondering what had delayed Carl. He was really anxious to hear what he found out. He had been evasive on the phone, but said he had something important to tell him.

By the time Herman finished his lunch, he knew Carl wasn't going to make it. "Damn," Herman muttered. He couldn't call him from the precinct so he had to find a pay phone.

Dialing Carl's direct number, he was put through to the base operator and was told that Major Kendall was no longer stationed there.

"What do you mean? He was there this morning," retorted Herman.

"I don't know about that, sir, but Major Kendall is not listed in the base directory," the man said.

Herman froze. Someone must have found out that Carl breached the top secret files. He said there would be trouble if he was caught. Scowling, Herman slammed the phone on the hook. He had no way to reach him now. He would just have to wait until Carl called him.

Herman was ill-tempered when he got back to his office, and then things got worse. He was instantly aware that some papers on his desk had been moved. Checking the drawers in his desk, he could tell someone had gone through them. Nothing had been taken, but it had definitely been searched. He felt sure they meant for him to know because it was a messy job.

His temper accelerated, he could do better in his sleep. The phone rang as he was rearranging his desk; the chief wanted to see him immediately.

Grabbing a handful of Tums, Herman stalked into the chief's office. "Sit down, Herman. We have a problem. I don't know why you've been checking on Josh Davenport, and I don't want to know, but it has to stop. Whatever you're doing, no matter why or what you're finding, it has to stop today. And you better stay away from Jennie Davenport. If you keep this up, you'll be back pounding pavement in Deep Ellum. Do you understand what I'm saying?"

"No, Chief, I don't," Herman snapped back, still mad about his desk. "Why should anyone care if I check out some things about Josh for his wife?"

"That's not the point, Herman. We've been friends for a long time, and I'm trying to do you a favor. I can only say that this has to stop. Do yourself a favor, do Molly a favor; quit investigating Davenport. It's only going to make trouble for you, more than you've already stirred up. You could even lose your pension over this and you're only a year away from getting it. Listen to me, Herman. Stop what you're doing. I can't say it any plainer or put it any stronger. It's completely out of my hands. I can't protect you. I will tell you that this comes from higher up. This is the last warning."

"Thanks, Chief, I hear what you're saying. But I have to tell you, someone searched my desk and that makes my blood boil." The chief's eyes dropped to the papers on his desk. He picked up one and started reading.

Herman stormed out.

JENNIE WAS COOKING SUPPER WHEN the phone rang and she ran to get it before Nathan. "I've got it," she called.

"I was surprised when Dottie said you'd called," said Roger Zenor. "How are you, Jennie?"

She looked to see where Nathan was before she answering. "I'm fine, Roger. It was really great talking with Dottie today and hearing that everything has gone well for you and your family. I appreciate your calling me back so quickly."

Jennie hesitated a moment then continued very softly. "I've been thinking a lot about the time we were in Kansas City. I wanted to see if you have kept in touch with any of the guys from the News Center."

"No, we lost track of each other a long time ago. I've often thought we should have a reunion and see how everyone has fared through the years. Jennie, I'm sorry about Josh; that must have been rugged."

"Yes, it was. I have a question for you. Do you remember when Josh spent the week at Fort Leavenworth?"

"Yeah, I remember."

"Do you know what it was all about?"

"Why are you asking now? It's been more than twenty-five years since we were there."

"Some things have come up, some really odd things. They have made me wonder about what happened there. I hesitate to tell you what they are, but believe me, it's very important or I wouldn't have tracked you down."

"Jennie, if it's important enough to track me down after all these years and if it's about G-2, I don't want to know any more about it."

Roger paused. Jennie heard him take a deep breath before he continued, "What I'm going to tell you is really odd, particularly now that I know Josh died six years ago. Right now, I'm standing at a pay phone because a few weeks ago I received a letter with instructions that said if you ever called me with questions about Josh that I should call you from a pay phone, not from my house or office. It contained a sealed letter addressed to you. My instructions are to mail it to you if you asked about Josh. I don't know who sent it, but it looks like Josh's writing. However, it's been a long time and I could be wrong. It said that I shouldn't mail it to your house, but to somewhere not personally connected with you. Can you give me such an address?"

Jennie sat down abruptly, took a deep breath, and tried to get her hands to quit shaking. "That's really strange—what do you think it means?"

"I don't know, Jennie. And, as I said, I don't want to know. I do know that when Josh came back from Fort Leavenworth he had changed. He was very serious, like he had something heavy on his mind but he never told me what it was. He did his job and that was it. He was different, no more joking around; he was all business."

Roger stopped. He paused again so long Jennie was afraid he was going to hang up. Finally, he sighed and said, "Give me an address, Jennie, and I'll send the letter on to you."

She thought a minute about her friends, thumbed through her address book, and gave him her friend Lorraine's address. There would be nothing to connect her with Josh. She never knew him.

"The instructions also say to tell you that you should tell no one at all. So, Jennie, don't. My advice to you is to keep quiet until you get the letter and read it. Maybe you'll have a better idea of what you're dealing with once you read it. I don't know anything else and Dottie doesn't know about the letter. I haven't told her. I hate to say it, but you'd better not call us back. There must be a reason I was told to call from a pay phone."

"Jennie, listen to me. We were always finding out secret information regarding the government and the military at the News Center, and, as a rule of thumb, it's generally safer to stay away from all this. You better think twice about getting involved or digging any further. Remember, this is G-2 and national security is involved here. I wouldn't want to dig into it. Please, Jennie, don't do anything foolish. Better yet, my advice is don't open the letter. Throw it away."

"Thanks, Roger. If it's something silly or a joke or something like that, I'll let you know. Otherwise, I won't call you again. Thank you for your advice and for being a friend to us. You and Dottie say a prayer or two for me. Will you mail it today?"

Jennie hung the phone up and sat there staring into space. She stood up slowly hoping her knees would hold her. After taking a few deep breaths, she walked back into the kitchen, stirred the food cooking on the stove, and started setting the table for supper. But her mind was elsewhere. She didn't notice Nathan watching her.

For the first time, she faced the very real possibility that Josh might be alive.

Chapter 18

"DON'T HOLD OUT ON me, Jennie. I've been real patient with all this stuff about Josh. You sulked around last night and I didn't say a word. Now this morning you tell me nothing's wrong. I know better than that, you're holding something back and I want to know what the hell it is," Nathan exploded, yanking her around to face him.

"I want to know who you were whispering to on the phone last night," his fingers digging into her arms.

"You're hurting me, Nathan. Let go of me."

"I asked who you were talking to last night." He waited a moment and when Jennie didn't answer, he shoved her roughly against the wall, grabbed his briefcase and stormed out the back door snarling, "You better think it over today. One thing I won't tolerate is secrets."

Dazed, Jennie watched him drive away. She couldn't move; she was stuck in the doorway. Tears streaked down her face as she rubbed her arm and tried to figure out what had just happened. His face was cold and hard and angry, almost as if he hated her. He'd never been like this before. She knew it bothered him last night when she was preoccupied, but she hadn't been able to think of anything except what Roger had told her. And she couldn't quit thinking about Josh's reaction to Nathan in that weird episode. Josh had that same hard, cold look on his face when she told him she was married to Nathan.

Doubts attacked Jennie. She obviously didn't know Nathan as well as she thought she did. He had no right to talk about keeping secrets. He wouldn't even tell her about his work. "I will not be intimidated," Jennie muttered. "If he's going to act like this, well, he better do some thinking today."

The sky was overcast and the trees were shaking with gusts of wind. *That figures*, Jennie thought, *a tornado just went through my house*. She closed the door on the wind wishing she could close the door on what just happened. She stood with her back to it wondering what had gotten into Nathan. She had tried to please him; she even redecorated when they married. She wanted him to feel it was his home, too.

The house would look very different to Josh if he came back. She and Josh had so much fun going to Mexico and finding the heavily carved dark wood furniture and hauling it back. She changed all that for Nathan. Now it was big, comfortable overstuffed furniture in muted tones of tans and browns and deep reds. With the addition of some antiques and lots of family pictures, it had a softer and more conventional look. She got another cup of coffee and wandered around, but she couldn't calm down, her nerves were raw.

What would Josh think about her now? She had changed as much as the house. She was older for one thing, six years. But that was only external; the important changes were inside her. She was more confident, she knew what she liked and didn't like, and she didn't like Nathan right now. *So much for trusting him, he turned on me.*

"What a mess," she murmured out loud. And there's another messy problem to consider, if Josh is alive, who was she married to? She had married both of them in church. She wanted to stick her head in the sand like an ostrich and wait until it all went away.

Continuing to pace, she looked for things that were left from her old life and found the picture albums on the library shelf. She took one to the couch and held it a few minutes, half scared to open it. When she did, the past took on life and she remembered things she hadn't thought about in a long time.

Oh, Josh, do you remember the day Kris was born and how poor we were. Or when Laurie was born and how she slept all day long, how we wondered if she would ever wake up. And all the fun we had at Christmas time with presents, and Santa, and food, and songs, and laughter. Staying up most of the night on Christmas Eve putting together doll houses and bicycles was always fun.

And the laughter, lots of easygoing fun. The contrast jumped out at her.

Nothing about Nathan was easygoing. That was what she missed most, the fun and the good-natured humor. She wondered if Josh was still like that.

"Do you still sing?" Jennie whispered aloud. The tears stung her eyes as she remembered him strumming his guitar and softly singing *Somewhere My Love* and *More* to her. Kris and Laurie still talked about Josh singing *Sunrise Sunset* to them. She could almost hear his voice from deep within her. His face eluded her, but not the feelings. If he's alive, where has he been all these years? Could he have another family?

Anger and pain rolled over her and she admitted the thought of Josh still had the power to hurt her. It hurt terribly.

HERMAN HAD BEEN IN TOUCH with Nathan during the day. That evening Jennie, Nathan, Kris and Laurie met he and Molly at Denny's on Beltline Road. He told them about Carl, that he had no idea what had happened and he would try to reach him at his quarters later tonight. The only thing he knew for sure was that Carl had gone to Little Washington yesterday for a tour of the facilities.

Getting angry all over again, Herman went on to tell them about his desk being searched and how the chief had told him once more to back off. He ended by saying that he was not about to back off now. Someone had involved him when they assigned him to the funeral and then to patrol Jennie's house and neighborhood.

"Herman, you have to stay out of this." Jennie said. "You're jeopardizing your job and your pension."

"I know, Jennie, but I can't quit now. My desk was searched and that's never happened before. I don't like it. They shouldn't have done that."

Molly watched Herman's red face intently as she said, "I've thought about this all afternoon since Herman told me. My first reaction was that he had to stop, but after thinking about it, I know if I were in your position, Jennie, I'd want someone to help me. I can't abandon you now any more than Herman can, and I know he has to know what's going on. What we have to do is make sure the chief doesn't know he's still helping."

Nathan jumped in quickly, "That's what I'm thinking, too. It's gone too far and become too involved to quit now. However, I think it would be better to contact each other through my office and your home, Herman. I suggest we meet at different places and be on the lookout for that blue car that's been tailing us."

Jennie flinched as she watched Nathan take control. "Oh, Herman, this is causing too many problems. I should never have followed up on that stupid experience."

"If Josh is still alive, it would have surfaced sooner or later. I'm thinking that he's been trying to make contact with you in ways that no one can identify except you. Hopefully, we'll know more when I talk to Carl."

Looking intently at Jennie, Kris and Laurie, Herman spoke softly, "I think its time to talk about disinterment. If we find Josh is there, all this can stop immediately."

Laurie's face paled as she gasped, "You mean dig daddy up?"

"Yes, Laurie, that's the only way we can ever be for certain," Kris snapped impatiently. "We can check the dental records. We could also do DNA testing."

"What do you know about that, Kris?" asked Herman.

"I've read a lot about it. It's a way to identify people. It seems everyone has certain patterns that are inherited. If there is no match at all with Laurie and me, then we'll know that the wrong man is in the grave. I don't know if we can do DNA testing yet; but we can definitely compare dental records. When can we get started?"

"I think it would be wiser if I tackle this instead of Herman," Nathan stepped in again, leaving no room for discussion. "I met with an attorney friend of mine yesterday and he looked up the regulations on disinterment. Since we don't have to remove the body from the cemetery we may not have to have a permit. We will need the authorization and cooperation of the funeral home. If we have a problem, we'll have to get a permit from the Coroner's Office. In order to open the casket we have to have a medical certificate stating what he died from. It seems that there are some viruses and diseases that can remain active for decades after death, so the Department of Vital Statistics reviews all applications carefully. Texas Code says that Jennie can give written consent as she is Josh's surviving spouse. The funeral home wants forty-eight hours notice so their schedules can be arranged."

Nathan looked directly at Jennie and asked, "Do you want me to go ahead with the arrangements?"

Kris said defiantly, "Yes, but only on the condition that I'm there. I have to be there."

"So do I," echoed Laurie and Herman.

Jennie nodded and remained silent staring at her cup of coffee. When

Nathan picked her up earlier, he acted as if nothing was wrong. Now, he was taking over. He was pushing Herman out. This doesn't feel right; she wasn't at ease with Nathan anymore.

"I'll start the arrangements tomorrow," Nathan concluded. "I can coordinate this, Herman. You don't need to be involved."

"Sounds like a plan, Nathan. Let me know time and date. I guess that's all we have to cover tonight unless one of you has something else. If not, Molly and I will leave now. The rest of you might wait about ten minutes so if anyone is watching it won't look like we're together."

"We'll do that. Drive carefully and be observant."

HERMAN DIDN'T SPOT A TAIL on the way home. Hopefully they weren't followed tonight. As soon as he got home, Herman called Carl's home number and found it had been disconnected.

"It's really not like Carl to just take off. If he had been transferred, he'd have called me. I don't like this," Herman grumbled.

He and Molly watched the ten o'clock news before going to bed. When the phone rang at three in the morning, Herman came up fast, the result of long years of police work. "It's probably the precinct, Molly. Go back to sleep."

Grabbing it he heard Carl saying, "Herman, just listen, I don't have long. G-2 picked me up when I was on my way to meet you. All they told me was I had been reassigned, no other explanation. I'm being sent to the weather station in Greenland. Talk about putting me out of commission. They asked a bunch of questions about Josh, how long had I known him, when did I see him last, and did I know he was dead. Herman, listen carefully. I went to Little Washington yesterday and a Private Daniels escorted me around. That's some impressive place and it got real interesting."

Carl quickly told him about Daniels' double take at the mention of Josh Davenport. "I'd bet next month's pay that he knows something about him. Daniels is much too young to have known him six years ago. I think it's possible that Josh is alive. The facility is huge and has living space for several hundred people. They could stay down there indefinitely. Everything is provided."

"Herman, my gut tells me you need to be very careful and my gut's not often wrong. The way this is going, there are some powerful people involved. If they took him out years ago, they don't want him found. Just look where

I'm headed. So watch yourself, Herman. Tell Jennie to be very careful and not to worry about me. Look after her if you can. I've got to hang up now, but I'll call you when I get another chance. Good hunting, pal."

Molly sat up in bed watching Herman. "That must have been Carl."

"Yeah, it was. He's been transferred to Greenland, the weather station. Someone really wants him out of the way. He said G-2 picked him up today when he left for lunch to meet me. He thinks it's possible that Josh is alive and whatever he's into involves some very powerful people."

Molly watched Herman pace around. His blood pressure was way too high and his face had stayed red all evening. She wished he hadn't gotten involved in this. She was worried about him.

Chapter 19

SLEEP WAS ELUSIVE AS usual. It was dawn before Jennie closed her eyes. Even so, she got up early and took her first cup of coffee outside. It was cool and peaceful there. Nathan hadn't slept well either. Maybe his conscience was bothering him. It should. He couldn't miss the bruises on her arm.

Nathan soon joined her. "You were very quiet last night. Are you nervous about the disinterment?"

"Of course I am. Digging up a grave isn't exactly an everyday occurrence. I can't believe someone searched Herman's office. It's everything, Nathan. It's all making me nervous, and now you—you hurt me yesterday."

Ignoring her last comment, Nathan said hesitantly, "It is overwhelming when I think of all the ramifications of this. You know, if Josh is alive, we're probably not legally married."

"I know. That's been on my mind, too. Do you think I could be prosecuted?"

"I don't know the laws on this, but you thought he was dead. When you bury someone you naturally assume the person is dead. I think this would qualify as extenuating circumstances. I wouldn't worry about it now."

"I'm not. It isn't the most important thing on my mind right now." Jennie purposefully looked at her arm. "I'm concerned about how you've been acting. What's going on, Nathan?"

"I'm stressed, Jennie. I'd be less than honest if I said anything else. I don't want to lose you."

Sitting down on the bench beside Jennie, Nathan took her hand and continued. "Being real honest, I have to say that I've thought and thought about this, more than you know. If the situation were reversed, I'd have obligations to find out the truth. Morally, I guess she would still be my wife, regardless of the legal issues. I guess I'd have to go one day at a time and find out what really happened. And I'd sure have to know all the whys."

"I know this is hard for you too, all the uncertainty. Was that what happened yesterday morning?"

Nathan's face hardened again. "I can't stand you not telling me everything. If I know what's going on, I can deal with it. Don't keep secrets from me, Jennie. I want to know who you were whispering to on the phone Tuesday night. What were you saying that you didn't want me to hear?"

"I'm upset too, Nathan," Jennie said, ignoring his questions. "Don't you ever hurt me again, I can't and I won't tolerate that." Nathan winced as she continued. "Speaking of secrets, you keep them, too. You've never told me about your work. You need to think about that."

Jennie stood up and walked around. "Everything is so mixed up that I don't know what is right or wrong anymore. I used to feel when Josh first died that I was falling off a mountain, and now, I'm falling again. I'm not sure where I'll land." She felt she was being ripped apart. "I don't know if what Josh did was right or not or if he even had a choice. Something very extreme had to cause this. I think about Herman and what happened at his office, and then I get worried about Kris and Laurie. Could I be putting them in danger?"

Nathan put his arm around Jennie's shoulder and they walked toward the house. "I don't think so. Let's just pray that we find him in the grave and all this can stop. I'm going to the funeral home this morning. Do you want to go with me?"

"Do you think I should?" she asked, pulling away from Nathan.

"You may have to sign the papers. Yes, I think you should."

THE PEOPLE AT THE FUNERAL home were very professional, acting as if they did this sort of thing every day. It must be more commonplace than we realize, Jennie realized. They knew exactly what needed to be done, got the necessary papers ready, and she signed them. They explained to Jennie and Nathan they would check with the Vital Statistics Office about opening the casket. If there were no problems, disinterment would be Friday at two o'clock.

They had a quick lunch before Nathan dropped Jennie off at home. She went in the house feeling like she was living someone else's life. All she ever wanted was to have a normal life, whatever that was. Going directly to the phone, she called Lorraine to see if the letter had come, but she wasn't home.

Frustrated, she put a load of clothes in the washer and started cleaning the house. The bedrooms needed vacuuming and dusting so she had plenty to do. Jennie had to keep busy; she didn't want to think about the notebook in the attic. Or about what Roger would think about it. He'd probably tell her to get rid of it.

HERMAN WAS STILL STEWING ABOUT his office being searched. When he got back after lunch, he found a message waiting for him from the chief saying he had been assigned a new case. Some new leads had surfaced on a drug dealer that they had been after for a long time and he was to check them out. He liked being in the field and this would keep him out of the office. He got the feeling that was the chief's plan.

He wanted to get back in the main file room and see if anything had been added to the Davenport file. Pulling files on the drug dealer would get him in the room, but he needed a time when no one else was there so he could check the old files.

Late in the afternoon the office was almost empty and Herman had his opportunity. He first pulled the files on the drug dealer and spread them on the worktable. Going back to the bottom drawer where the Davenport file was located, he opened it, found 1977, but the file wasn't there. Assuming it was filed wrong, he looked in 1976 and 1978, and the current files. No luck, the file was gone. "What the hell is going on," Herman exploded.

He gathered up the files on the drug dealer and traipsed back to his office thinking that too many things had gone missing. Josh is gone, the paperwork at the funeral home is missing, Army records are missing, Carl's missing, and now the precinct's files have disappeared.

"What's going to vanish next," he questioned.

Chapter 20

THE MAN SLAMMED HIS fist against the wall. He felt like a pressure cooker ready to explode.

Something was brewing. She was holding out on him. This was exactly why he had been placed where he was. They didn't pay him the big bucks for nothing. Hitting the wall again, he turned and staggered across the room.

His head was pounding when he dialed the phone. The disembodied voice on the other end of the line went through the customary spiel he'd heard for years.

"Identify."

"Code name, Watchman."

"Report at the beep."

He cleared his throat. Instead of the usual "Status Quo," he choked out, "Help needed."

"Elaborate."

He explained that disinterment of Josh Davenport's grave had been scheduled for Friday, March 25, at Sparkman Hillcrest in Dallas, Texas.

"Stay on the line."

The man paced as far as the cord would allow, his face masked with bitterness.

"All will be taken care of, report at the usual time tomorrow."

He hung up and stared out the window for a few minutes. Decision made.

With hollow eyes and without hesitation, he dialed another number.

Chapter 21

JENNIE WAS UP AND dressed before Nathan even woke up. "What a month this has been," she mumbled. She wandered aimlessly around the house. Three days, it had been three long days since she talked with Roger. How much longer could she stand it? The letter has to get here soon or she was going to lose it.

It would have been much simpler if Josh had picked up a phone and called her. Still, there must be some reason for the subterfuge. Carl and Herman said that there were some tracking devices, but they didn't tell her what all they could do. Carl seemed interested in the fact that she was given an injection the night Josh died. The doctor could have injected something like that into her, how could she have known? She wished she could remember that night better, but it had always been foggy.

Assuming he has been alive all these years and hadn't contacted her, why now? The only thing she could think of was what he said, that they just told him she had married again. Had that upset him enough that he wanted her to know he was alive. Was it safe now? Or was he endangering her and the girls? If it was really Josh, it had to be important because he would know how much this would upset her. Jennie turned and stared out the window, not really seeing anything.

WHEN NATHAN WOKE, HE WASN'T surprised Jennie was up. She was so upset yesterday at the funeral home. It wasn't going to be any better this afternoon at the disinterment.

While he showered and shaved, he wondered about how it would be done. He had never seen a body exhumed. He was curious if they would use a backhoe or dig by hand. Maybe it wouldn't actually happen.

When Nathan got to the den he found Jennie just staring into space. He went over to her and put his arms around her, but she pulled away. He wondered how long he'd be able to hold her. Not long, if her reaction right now was any indication. Sighing, he knew she had not forgotten the other morning. How could he have let his emotions get the best of him? He knew better. Well, most of the time he did.

"We need to let Kris and Laurie know the time. And we promised to call Molly so she could tell Herman," Nathan said.

"I know. I'll call them," Jennie responded, obviously hesitant.

KRIS'S VOICE WAS SHAKY AFTER Jennie told her the plans, but she said she would call Laurie and they'd be there by two o'clock. Jennie was even more upset when she hung up. Kris was usually so strong. Then she called Molly.

By the time they sat down to eat breakfast, neither of them had much to say. The silence was awkward, tension separated them. Jennie picked at her food until Nathan left for the office. The headache that had been threatening all morning hit full force.

She got up and dumped her breakfast in the trash. This was going to be a dreadful day.

IT WAS A LITTLE BEFORE two o'clock when she and Nathan got to the cemetery. Jennie drove to the place where she had parked for so many years. "I guess we're early. I thought someone would be here working."

"They are evidently running late," Nathan said. He got out of the car and followed Jennie across the grassy area.

Jennie went directly to Josh's grave with the intention of telling him what was about to happen. She had formed a habit over the years of talking to him. She knew this would anger Nathan, but at the moment she didn't care. Looking for his headstone, she wondered if she had gotten mixed up. No, she hadn't. She knew where his grave was. She was here just a few days ago when she found the yellow rose. Her stomach lurched and she felt nauseous. The headstone was gone. It was gone.

"Where's Josh's grave?" Nathan asked as he walked up.

"It should be right here."

"Where? I don't see a headstone."

"Right where I'm standing—the headstone should be right here by this tree and bench, but it's gone," Jennie answered.

"I think you're just confused. The ground here hasn't been disturbed in years. You're probably at the wrong tree."

"I'm not. I know where his grave is," she cried indignantly. "I've been here too many times."

Nathan walked around to the other side of the tree, but the grave wasn't there, either. Jennie followed him to another tree. She was not confused. She knew where the grave was.

"Are you sure this is the right area? Maybe you parked at the wrong place."

"No, no, I did not park at the wrong place," she retorted, her voice rising. "Someone has moved him, and I've got to find him." Panic set in and Jennie started rushing around reading all the headstones.

When Kris and Laurie drove up, they saw Jennie walking, almost running, all around the cemetery.

"What in the world is mom doing?" Laurie asked.

"I can't imagine," said Kris, pulling to a stop behind Jennie's car. "We better go find out." They caught up with Nathan first and asked him what was going on.

"Your mom has gotten confused about where your dad is buried. She can't find his grave."

"Well, that's not a problem, we know where he is," Kris responded. "Mom, come over here. Dad's right there beside the bench."

Herman walked up and heard Kris calling to Jennie. He watched Jennie running about. "It looks like the stress is really getting to Jennie, Nathan. Do you think she's going to be okay or should you take her home? This isn't going to be pretty."

"I don't know, Herman. She can't find Josh's grave. Her nerves are definitely getting the best of her. I hope Kris or Laurie can find it."

Jennie saw the girls and ran toward them. "Someone's moved Josh's grave. I can't find him."

"Right here, Mom, by the big tree and the bench. Laurie and I have sat here for years," Kris said, as she went toward the bench.

Laurie got there first and screamed, "Daddy's grave isn't here. Where is it?"

"I told you, it's gone. And I'm in the right area. I can prove it because my mom and dad are buried right down there." Jennie stated firmly, as she went over to her parents' graves. Everyone followed her and the graves were exactly where she said they would be.

"I'm not crazy, at least not yet, but I may be if we don't find him soon. His grave is not here." Jennie went back to where Josh should be, reading each headstone along the way.

"What have they done with him?" she cried.

HERMAN WAS STARTING TO THINK that maybe Jennie wasn't confused. His thoughts went back to a few days ago when he found the paperwork missing at the precinct and he had wondered what would vanish next. Now he knew. Josh's grave.

"Let's go to the office and find out what's going on," Nathan said. "They may have already exhumed him and moved him somewhere else. Let's go check."

When they got to the office, everything was quiet and solemn with the hushed stillness of death. A tall somber man approached and asked if he could assist them.

Jennie blurted out "Yes, you can, I want to know what you have done with my husband. I've come for years to visit him. I know where his grave is and now it's not there. I want to know where he is."

Accustomed to dealing with distraught people, the man remained calm. "Please come in my office and have a seat. We'll see what we can do."

After they all went in and sat down, he said, "If you'll tell me your husband's name, I'll look in the records and find out where he is buried."

"I know where he was buried," Jennie said angrily. "What I want to know is what you have done with him."

"What is the name, please?"

"My dad's name was Joshua Davenport. He died and was buried here in February 1977," Laurie answered.

"We came in yesterday and filled out all the papers for disinterment. Yesterday, so find your records and tell me where you've taken him," Jennie demanded, as she stood up and started pacing.

Nathan and Herman sat silent as the man got up from his desk and left the room saying he would get the records and be right back.

It was a very long fifteen minutes before the man returned. He was accompanied by the director of the funeral home who introduced himself as Howard Taylor. "Just what is the problem and how may I assist you?" he asked.

"You can tell me where my husband's grave has been moved." Jennie said abruptly.

"Is Joshua Davenport the correct name?" Taylor asked.

Herman motioned to Jennie to back off and he intervened. "I'm Herman Wilkins, Dallas Police Department. I came in and checked his records a month ago. They were here then. Yes, the correct name is Joshua Davenport. Jennie and Nathan were here yesterday and filled out all the paperwork for disinterment. Your office told them that they would check with Vital Statistics and, if no problem was found, they would set the disinterment for two o'clock this afternoon."

Herman paused. When Taylor made no response he continued. "We just came from the grave site and the headstone is not there. We want to know if Davenport has already been exhumed and where the casket has been taken." He pointed to a folder that Jennie was carrying. "Those are Davenport's dental records. I'm officially here to confirm the identity of the remains. We'll appreciate your help in this matter."

Taylor looked puzzled and replied, "We checked our records and don't have, and never have had, a Joshua Davenport buried in this cemetery. There are no records for anyone named Davenport in our files. We really don't know who you are talking about."

"We were here yesterday and filled out all the paperwork," Jennie repeated. "Mrs. Johnson helped us."

"We don't have anyone by that name on staff here." Taylor answered. "Could you have confused the cemetery?"

"No, we could not have." Herman said, his face turning red. "I want to know what is going on here. It appears Davenport's body has been stolen."

"I'm really very sorry, Officer. If you want, you can look at the records yourself." Taylor said nervously.

Herman turned to the group. "Wait here for me. I'll take a look. I know where the records are, I looked at them before. Please try and relax. Someone's just filed it wrong."

Taylor and Herman left the room quickly.

JENNIE SAT FROZEN, FINGERNAILS DIGGING into her palms, mind racing. She should have known Josh was not here and never had been. This was scary. That letter from Roger has to have some answers. He was so nervous about G-2, even to the extent he told her not to call him back. So what now? Should she tell her daughters and Nathan? No, she definitely wasn't about to tell Nathan.

It was obvious someone was wielding lots of power, enough to make a grave disappear overnight.

"I can't sit here any longer," Kris stated impatiently. "I'm going out in the hall." She got up and left the room with Laurie following her.

NATHAN LOOKED AT JENNIE AND knew that she was already far away from him. His anger, never far from the surface, flared. She was still concealing something; she was entirely too quiet. She had gone from sheer panic in the graveyard to a very unexpected and odd calmness.

He never meant to fall in love with her. He knew better. Now he wondered what the rest of his life would bring. Change, always change, that was the only consistent thing in this world. You either adapt or you die, and he'd already done that several times. Could he do it again? He didn't know.

Looking over at Jennie and how tranquil she had become in the last few minutes, he had no doubt that she'd come to a decision. He raged inside because of what she knew that he didn't. He clenched his fists and stormed out.

FINALLY, HERMAN AND TAYLOR CAME back in. The look on both their faces told Jennie that no records were found.

"We need to talk," Herman said brusquely.

Turning back to Taylor, he extended his hand. "Thank you for your cooperation. I don't understand what has happened, but I appreciate you allowing me to look through the records. One more favor, is there somewhere private we can talk for a few minutes?"

Kris, Laurie and Nathan joined Herman and Jennie as they walked down the hall to the room Taylor had indicated they could use. It was evident by their faces that the news wasn't good. Herman motioned them over to a corner sofa and pulled up a couple of chairs.

"Taylor's right. There are no records in the files for Davenport. I can't explain it nor can Taylor. We know they were here yesterday, but they are not today. We even checked the burial plot records. They don't show that a plot was ever purchased by a Davenport."

"I have the sales papers at home, there's a certificate of ownership, too," Jennie replied. "And probably the cancelled check, but I guess that doesn't matter at this point."

"No, I don't think it does," Herman said scooting his chair closer. "Listen carefully. I don't want to talk too loud. I need to bring you up-to-date."

"Carl called a couple of nights ago about three in the morning. He told me to just listen, that he couldn't talk long. He said G-2 picked him up outside his office and told him he was being reassigned to the weather station in Greenland. He went on to say that he got up to Little Washington. When Carl mentioned Josh Davenport to the young private who was escorting him around, the guy gave him a startled look and said he couldn't talk about personnel. Carl is sure he either knew or had heard of Josh, and he was too young to have known him six years ago. Carl also said if they took Josh out years ago, they don't want him found. He said to be very careful because something very strange was going on. Carl thinks he was reassigned because he was getting too close to Josh." Herman ran his hand through his hair and stood up.

"Yesterday at the precinct, I had to go to the main file room to pull paperwork for a new case I've been assigned. I took that opportunity to check the Davenport file to see if anything had been added to it. Not only had nothing been added to it, but there was no Davenport file anywhere in the cabinet. It appears that all references to him have been removed, along with Carl. We're evidently making someone very nervous. There are too many incidents for this to be coincidence. The question is—where do we go from here?"

A pale-faced Jennie sat very still as everyone turned and waited for her to say something. She looked at each face and thought how much she loved them.

Nathan's expression was grim, his eyes cold as he stared at her. Her daughters, her precious daughters, were watching her expectantly. Herman looked ready to fight someone and she had no doubt that he would do so for her.

Roger said don't do anything foolish, don't tell anyone, so there was nothing she could do until she got the letter from him. Then she'd decide what, if anything, to tell them. Something very frightening was going on. Roger warned her that if it had anything to do with G-2 to stay away from it. Lost records were one thing, but a missing body, well, that was quite another matter.

Her mind was jumping all around, but she knew what she had to do.

"We need to back off for a few days. One thing remains constant in this mess. Josh either died or left six years ago. Regardless of what else has happened, he's not here so nothing has really changed. Herman, don't do anything else. Don't get in any more trouble at your office, just do your job.

Go back to Molly and play with your grandchildren. Kris, Laurie, I want you to go home and take care of your families. Nathan and I are going home, too. I have some thinking to do."

NATHAN AND JENNIE DROVE TOWARD home silently. They were both lost in their thoughts. Nearing home, Nathan asked Jennie if she wanted to get something to eat.

"Is it that time already?" she asked, glancing at her watch. She was surprised to see it was already past seven. "The time really got away from me this afternoon. I had no idea it was this late. Yes, let's eat somewhere. It's too late to cook. What about Angelo's?"

"That's fine," Nathan answered. "It's quiet there and I always like their steak and spaghetti." And he turned the car in that direction.

After they had ordered, Nathan asked Jennie what she thought about this new occurrence.

"It's hard to put into words. So many things are going through my mind. I did buy a plot there, and I buried a man I thought was Josh. I stood by that grave and cried and watched the casket lowered into the ground. Nathan, I saw it go down. And I went to the cemetery just a few days ago and the headstone was there. I sat on the ground beside it and talked to Josh. I even rubbed my fingers over Josh's name."

Nathan eyes softened. He reached across the table to take Jennie's hand. "That's why you were upset the other night. You didn't tell me you were going to the cemetery. I'd have gone with you."

"I know, Nathan, but I needed to go by myself. Now this, I don't know what to think. The ground looked completely undisturbed today. Maybe we should go back and look again. I'm curious if the grass is growing or if it's new grass that's been rolled out. I wish I had felt around where the stone used to be. Maybe just the stone is gone and Josh is still there. Do you think that could be it?"

"It's possible, Jennie. At this point, I guess anything is possible." Nathan avoided her eyes and opened a package of crackers. "What I do know is that someone doesn't want his body exhumed and has gone to a lot of trouble to see that it can't be."

Jennie fiddled with her salad. "I've been thinking that it would take someone with unlimited power to remove a body from a cemetery, not to mention the files at the police department, and to send Carl away, that had to involve the military. That is scary, Nathan. We keep talking about the 'someone' who makes things happen and who doesn't want other things to happen. Who do you think it is?"

"I haven't a clue," Nathan said, looking down at his plate. "I know when we first started talking about your experience I thought it would make you feel better to check things out, so I went along with you. But I never expected it to be anything. In all honesty, I didn't take it seriously. I was surprised that Herman did."

"I shouldn't have told you about it. I should never have involved Herman and Molly or Carl or the girls. But I did, and now I have to live with that. Do you remember when we first started seeing each other I told you I didn't have anything to give and didn't know if I ever would? I told you then that I didn't feel Josh was dead."

"I remember. Everyone feels like that after the death of someone they love."

"True, but I still feel that way. I feel like my life has been a lie. I've been betrayed, manipulated, confused, hurt, and probably drugged by that doctor in the hospital the night Josh supposedly died. Now here it is six years later, and I don't know if he's dead or alive."

Jennie fell silent when the waitress served their steaks. She ate a couple of bites and signaled the waitress for more coffee.

"Nevertheless, with all these bizarre things happening, I have to know why and I have to know what happened. If he had decided to leave me, he couldn't have done anything as elaborate as this on his own. Whatever occurred took lots of planning and deception. It would have involved the paramedics that came to the house, the hospital staff, the doctors that talked to me, the one who gave me that shot Carl asked about, and the doctor who signed the death certificate, to name a few. Then the biggest deception of all had to be the body in the casket. Think about it, Nathan, a dead body was in that casket, I know because I touched him and that body looked like Josh. Someone had the power to get a body and alter it. That's not a simple thing to do. Plastic surgery would have been necessary. So where did they get the body, who was it, and why did this all-powerful somebody do this? Deception on this scale would have to involve many people and people with extreme authority. It's terrifying.

Once more Nathan reached across and took her hand. The waitress chose this moment to refill their water glasses so Nathan didn't answer her. Jennie smiled weakly at him and pulled her hand away. How could Josh have done this to her? She wasn't sure whether she loved or hated him. She only knew that she hurt. It hurt her, it hurt Laurie and Kris, and it hurt Nathan.

"I don't know what to do or think at this point." Her voice quivering, Jennie stared directly into Nathan's eyes and said, "I need time to think about it, to try and understand, and to see what else happens. Most of all, I really need you to be patient and not get angry with me, Nathan. I am sorry. I'm sorry to put you through all this."

"I know that, Jennie. I'm trying. I really am, but I'm afraid of losing you." Nathan looked at her untouched plate. "Please eat something," he said quietly as he watched her pull a tissue out of her purse.

Jennie obediently cut a bite of the steak and put it in her mouth and chewed without tasting it. She should have paid more attention to Roger when he told her to think twice about digging any further, that he didn't want to know anything about it. Especially when he said don't call him back. He must have had a good reason to say that. He seemed anxious to get off the phone, almost unfriendly. She really should have thought more about his reaction. All she had been able to focus on was the possibility that Josh was alive. That was still all she could think about.

"Here's our bill, Jennie. Are you ready to leave?" Nathan asked.

She looked at her plate and realized she'd hardly eaten anything. "Yes, I'm ready." Jennie covered her plate with her napkin and they left the restaurant.

As if by mutual agreement they didn't mention anything else about Josh the rest of the evening. They watched the ten o'clock news and went to bed early.

LAURIE AND KRIS WERE BEWILDERED when they left the cemetery. They rode silently for a little while until Kris asked what Laurie was thinking.

"Well, like mom said, nothing is different. Whatever the reason for all the peculiar happenings, we're in exactly the same place we were a month ago. And if mom hadn't dreamed, or whatever it was, about daddy, none of this would have started. But this thing today, Kris, you and I know daddy's grave was there and now it's not. Someone really doesn't want us to check the dental records. It seems to me this is strong proof that he's alive."

"He must have wanted to leave," Kris answered. "He had to be involved in the plans."

"That makes me feel unwanted, Kris."

"It makes me mad," Kris retorted. "What makes me the maddest is the night he allegedly died. He had to agree to put us through all that. It infuriates me that he would leave us. Do you really think he would have done that on purpose? Just abandon us like that. I have to know if he had a choice."

"Don't be so mad, Kris, remember how he used to sing *Scarlet Ribbons* to us," Laurie said tearfully. "Daddy loved us. He would never have hurt us on purpose." She paused and watched Kris' face. "Herman seems to think G-2 is involved. We know they took Carl away. Maybe they took daddy away."

"Good point, Laurie, maybe they did, but I'm not sure how to find out. Mom said she wants us to back off and do nothing so I guess that's it for now. We're at a stand still, but it's going to eat at me."

"Do you think we could find out anything else about the painting you saw at the restaurant?" Laurie asked.

"I doubt it. Let's give mom a few days to think about it. She has to be awfully upset. She really loved daddy a lot. She's not going to leave this alone forever. There's something she's not telling us about, I feel it."

When Herman arrived home, Molly was anxiously waiting for him. "What did you find out?"

"What we found was nothing. And I do mean nothing. The grave was not there, no headstone, no records, nothing."

"What do you mean no grave?"

"Exactly that, it wasn't there. I even checked the records at the funeral home and the paperwork on Davenport is no longer in the files. It's all disappeared since yesterday, along with the lady who helped Jennie fill out the disinterment papers. It's like Josh never existed. Can you imagine, Molly, how much power it would take to do this? The average citizen can't just go into a cemetery and remove a body or take the records."

"What do you think is happening?" Molly asked.

"Some sort of a cover-up. Somebody doesn't want us to find out if Josh is alive, and they are willing to do whatever it takes to keep us from finding out. They have to know our suspicions because all concrete evidence keeps disappearing. They also know that unless we can prove it, it doesn't mean anything. I wish I knew how to get in touch with Carl. I'd like to tell him about this and see what he thinks."

"What did Jennie say?"

"That was strange, too. When I got there Jennie was frantically running around the cemetery trying to find Josh's grave. Then after we found out all the records were gone, she was the calmest of us all. She made an interesting comment—she said that she wanted everyone to back off, that nothing had changed, Josh was still gone. She told us all to go home and not do anything else, to get on with our lives. She said she needed time to think."

"She sounds a little too calm," Molly replied. "Wonder why?"

Herman turned and looked at Molly. She had done it again. She had picked up on the obvious. Jennie was much too calm.

"I wish I knew, Molly. I'd bet my pension that she knows more than she's telling us."

Chapter 22

As soon as Nathan left for the office, Jennie got out the old picture albums and flipped through them again. She found the one she made when she and Josh were in high school. Oh, how young they looked, so long ago. It was like looking at two other people that she vaguely knew. He was so slim and handsome in his football uniform. How little they knew back then.

Shifting the books around, she found their wedding album, took a deep breath, and opened it. There they were, Josh in his tuxedo, she in her wedding dress. "We looked so happy, we were happy—no matter what has happened, we had a good marriage," she said aloud. "I know we did."

Jennie turned the page and found the picture where they were running from the church to the car. She was shielding her face from the rice and Josh was trying to shield them both. He did love us, he was protective of us, and he wanted to take care of us. He would have tried to shield us from anything harmful. Was that what he did? Jennie dropped her head into her hands and cried.

"No, this doesn't do any good," she said, slamming the album shut." I can't just sit here and cry. I have to do something." Restless, anxious to get the letter from Roger, she wandered through the house looking out the windows. It was a beautiful day, the sun was shining, and suddenly she wanted to be outside. Grabbing her purse and keys, Jennie ran out the door and got in the car.

Instinctively she set out for the home she had grown up in. Turning into the old neighborhood in Oak Cliff brought back memories of how simple life was then. Everything was black and white, right and wrong. She passed the

112

houses where friends had lived and where they had played their childhood games. She and her friends loved to ride the bus to the public library. They did that a lot, especially during the summer vacation. She turned the car in that direction. When she got to the tree-lined street she pulled to a stop by the library, a small red brick two-story building surrounded by a lovely park.

"I can't believe the library is so small," Jennie exclaimed. "When I was a kid it looked so huge."

Continuing slowly down the street, she saw the church she used to attend. It was still beautiful. She looked at the wide steps leading up to the massive front doors and remembered her wedding day; the day she and Josh were married. Maybe she could go in and look around. She would love to see it again.

She parked in front and went up the steps to the main entrance. It was locked so she walked around to the side of the building and found a sign that said *office*. The door was open and a lady was at a desk at the far end of the room.

"Would it be all right if I go in the sanctuary for a little while?" Jennie asked.

The lady smiled, welcomed her, and told her to go on in. Jennie went through the door the lady pointed to and it took her into the side foyer of the sanctuary. She recognized it instantly. It was where she and her dad had waited before her wedding. She wondered why she had never come back to visit. It was such a wonderful old church.

She went through the double doors into the sanctuary and down the same aisle that she had with her dad the night of her wedding. She could almost hear her dad whispering to her that she could always come home. Oh, how she wished she could right now.

"I guess it was as hard for dad to give me away as it was for me to give my girls away," she sighed. "Funny, I never thought about that before. Somehow this makes me feel closer to dad. If only he were here, I bet he'd know what to do."

She stood still and looked toward the altar. The church hadn't changed much in all these years. The light was dim, but it was glowing with color as it filtered through the stained glass windows. Lifting her eyes up, she caught her breath at the magnificent pipes above the organ. She wished she could hear it played.

Jennie moved quietly to the altar and stood right in the center where she had stood so many years ago, the very spot where she and Josh had promised to love and honor each other the rest of their lives. She couldn't hold the tears back any longer. Dropping to her knees at the altar she let them flow and cried for all the lost years, all the lost times and love that she and Josh had missed, for Kris and Laurie and what they had lost, for what it was doing to her and Nathan now. Pain and confusion engulfed her.

A tall, gray-haired man came in the back of the sanctuary, looked around, and saw her kneeling at the altar crying. He quietly walked down there and laid his hand on her shoulder. Startled, Jennie jumped and looked around then tried to get up.

"Don't get up. You're welcome to be here. I'm Joel Johnson, pastor of this church. Is there any way I can help you?"

Jennie turned toward the man and felt his compassion for her. "I don't think you can help me."

"Maybe not, but I'm a good listener."

Jennie rose and they moved to a pew and sat down. When she wiped the tears away, she looked at him and was reminded of her dad. Maybe it would help to talk.

"My name is Jennifer, Jennie, and I do have a problem. One I bet you've never heard before."

"You'd be surprised. I've heard most everything. Why don't you tell me about it?"

"It's so complicated. I don't know where to start."

"Just start anywhere and I'll ask questions if I need to."

"Well, I was married in this church, many years ago. We had two daughters," Jennie started hesitantly. "My husband died in 1977. My girls and I struggled so hard just to survive. It was like swimming underwater and running out of breath, and not knowing how to get your next breath."

Pastor Johnson covered her hand with his as Jennie's voice broke and the tears started again. She had to find a tissue before she could continue. "I married again a year ago and it's been good. But now, through some odd circumstances, I have reason to think my first husband Josh might be alive. My second husband, Nathan, and a friend who is with the police department have been trying to check it out. We found out last Friday that Josh's body has been moved from the cemetery where he was buried and the records of his burial have been removed as well. Nobody knows where he is."

Jennie continued and told Pastor Johnson about Herman's help, about Carl being sent away, the police department records disappearing, about her call to Roger, and that she was now waiting for a letter from him.

"You're right. I haven't heard this before. Have you told Nathan about the letter?"

"No, I don't want to hurt him if I don't have to. Besides, Roger urged me not to mention this to anyone. You're the only one I've told."

"When are you supposed to get the letter?"

"Hopefully, it will get here tomorrow or the next day. I'm really scared. I don't know if I am strong enough to open it when it comes.

"Do you know of any reason Josh would have gone away? And if he did why he should reappear now?"

"No to both questions. I do know that Carl was concerned about an injection that had been given me the night Josh died. He felt it could have been some type of tracking device. It's all mixed up with Army security. If that thing is in me, I guess someone could know I'm here with you now. Maybe I'd better leave."

"No, stay a little longer. I'm not worried about that. Tell me what your main concern is?"

"I guess I'm afraid I'm married to two men at once. What do I do if Josh is really alive? Which one will I really be married to? Where is my allegiance?"

"God says that when we marry it is forever until death do us part. It doesn't say separation or disappearance; it says until death do us part."

"I know that, but what about my husband now—about Nathan? I thought Josh was dead when I married him."

"If your first husband is alive, you are still married to him. I understand that you thought he was dead and remarried in good faith, but morally, you would still be married to Josh. How do you feel about that?"

"I feel angry, betrayed, like my life is totally out of my control."

"I'd say that's a normal reaction. Now, for a moment, put the emotions away. Do you think Josh would have done this deliberately to hurt you? Or, do you think there were circumstances beyond his control?"

Jennie started sobbing again. "It would have been circumstances out of his control."

"What brought you here today?"

"I couldn't sit at home any longer. Waiting is terrible. I had to get out of the house. I've been driving around the area where I grew up. When I passed the church where Josh and I were married, I just had to come in."

"Maybe you felt the need to try and get closer to him. Are your parents still living?"

"No. I really, really wish they were. I could use their support now.

Sometimes I want to start driving and keep on going and never go home again."

"Now that wouldn't help your daughters or Nathan, would it?"

"No, I guess not. They would just worry about me."

"Sometimes we have to make very difficult decisions. I can't tell you what to do, but I can give you God's Word. Regardless of the circumstances, God's Word says that if Josh is alive you are still married to him. I think you've felt this and it's been bothering you. Perhaps that's the real reason you came in the church today."

"You're right. I have been worried about it. I just needed confirmation."

"Your Nathan must be a very good man."

"Yes, he is, at least I thought so before all this. And that confuses me. I've never seen him as angry as he has been the last few days. He even lashed out at me," Jennie said, looking at the bruises on her arms. "I know he's hurt and wondering what will happen if Josh is alive. If he is alive, are you saying I should go to him?"

"No, what I'm saying is that you would still be married to him. What you decide to do is up to you. However, you and Nathan would not be married in the eyes of God. I'm not sure of the legal status. You need to check with an attorney about that. I suspect Nathan has realized this."

"What should I tell Nathan?"

"The truth, always tell the truth. I suggest you wait until you get the letter and see what the real truth is. At this point, you are just assuming Josh is alive. He may not be."

"And my daughters, what should I tell them? They are married and each has a little child."

"They are grown women with families of their own. What you owe them is a mother's love. With that in mind and remembering that Josh was their father, you'll have to determine how much you should tell them. I always believe the truth is best."

Jennie paused and thought for a minute, then asked softly, "Even if it puts them in a dangerous situation?"

"Now that's a different question. That needs serious thought and prayer to decide what's best. I don't think you should knowingly put anyone in danger. However, you don't know any of this for sure yet. In the meantime, I promise you I'll be praying that when you find out what the truth is, you'll know what to do."

Jennie sat very still for a few minutes and then said, "Thank you for talking with me. I've needed to talk with someone outside the family. It does help."

"You're very welcome. If you want to talk again, I'll be here. When you get the letter, if you want to come here and read it, I'll sit with you. In the meantime, I'll pray for God's direction for you and for you to have the strength to do whatever is right."

Jennie walked slowly out of the church wishing she didn't have to leave. It was the most peaceful place she had been in a long time.

As she neared her car, she saw two men in dark blue suits walking toward her. The peace disappeared. She turned fast and ran toward the church. The men caught up with her and took her by the arms

"Don't be frightened, Mrs. Scott, we just want to talk to you," one of them said, showing her his identification. It was an Army ID card with the G-2 insignia. She recognized it; it was like the one Josh had carried. They walked Jennie over to a dark blue car, opened the door, and put her inside. As they were driving off, Jennie saw that another blue-suited man was going toward the church.

The interior of the car looked like the one she had been in with Josh, only Josh wasn't here. Instead, there were two strange men, one on each side of her. Squeezing her hands together to keep them from shaking, she demanded, "What do you want and where are you taking me?"

"We just need to ask you a few questions. You were married to Josh Davenport, were you not?

"Yes, years ago," she answered.

"What happened to him, Mrs. Scott?"

"He died in 1977."

"Are you sure?"

"You don't normally bury someone if they are alive," she said evasively.

"Have you ever had any reason to suspect otherwise?"

All Jennie's senses came alert. She answered with caution, "When you bury someone, you certainly don't think they are alive."

"I'll ask my question again. Do you have any reason to suspect Josh is still alive?"

"None other than I guess I'd like for him to be." Jennie sidestepped the question again saying, "His daughters have always needed their dad." This was G-2 and they were asking her if he's alive. They should know that. They took him away. Perhaps they were testing her to see what she'd learned.

"Of course they do," he said smoothly. "We have had reason to suspect that you might feel he's still alive and that you're looking for him. A Dallas policeman recently requested some documents from the National Personnel Records Center. What do you know about this?"

"There's nothing very strange about that. I wanted copies of Josh's military records for my daughters and an old friend offered to help me. My daughter is interested in genealogy and wants to include these in her records. It was her dad." Jennie paused a moment, her mind in high gear. "My guess is that lots of families ask for the records. However, we didn't get them. I was told that the records were destroyed in a fire years ago."

"What do your daughters know about their dad?"

Jennie swung around to face the man and answered heatedly, "The normal things children know about a parent, that they loved him and miss him. That's a very stupid question. I don't think you have any right to question me."

Looking directly in his eyes, she demanded, "I want you to take me back to my car right now."

"One more question, Mrs. Scott. What were you doing in the church back there?"

"What do you usually do in a church? I was praying. That's another stupid question. Now take me back to my car or I'm going to start screaming."

"Does the minister know Josh?"

"How should I know? I sincerely doubt it. And I can't ask Josh, can I? Take me back to my car right now."

The man made a motion with his hand and the driver pulled over to the curb. "Your car is in front of us, Mrs. Scott." He opened the door, slid out and reached for Jennie's hand to help her. Evading his hand, she jumped out as fast as she could and ran toward her car feeling as if she had just escaped from the devil himself.

She could see the church and her car from where they had stopped. She thought about the man who had been going toward the church when she had been pulled into the car. Wonder what he asked Pastor Johnson and if the pastor told him anything? Did she dare go back in, was that man still there? No, no way was she going to chance that. She got in her car and locked the doors.

Driving quickly away Jennie watched the rear-view mirror and was close to panic. She must have triggered something for G-2 to question her. She didn't know if they believed her answers. She slowed down; she certainly didn't need to add a speeding ticket to her problems. What she did need was to find someplace safe where she could think. If the church wasn't safe, probably nowhere was safe. They must have been following her, or even worse, tracking her like Carl and Herman talked about.

Where could she go that was safe? If that tracking thing was in her, they could find her. So it had to be somewhere public with lots of people? She wished she had asked Carl about what else it could do. Could it read her thoughts? Could it hear her talk? Fear rose up inside her.

The closer she got to home the more she didn't want to go there. Anxious to get someplace where no one else would be implicated she pulled into the library parking lot. Lots of people were there and she could find a quiet corner. Afraid to park in the covered parking garage, she kept driving around until someone pulled out of an open air space near the entrance. Before opening the car door, she looked to see if anyone was near her car, then she darted in.

There were several benches in the foyer where people were sitting and talking quietly. Jennie chose a bench near the door and waited to see who came in after her. All she saw was people with books in their hands. After a few minutes, she began to relax and went into the main part of the library. Passing a display area for mystery books, she grabbed one without even looking at the title and walked over to the magazine section. It was a large area with several couches and she sat where she could keep an eye on the front entrance.

Jennie sat still trying to get her breathing back to normal. She searched the room carefully. An elderly man sat on the sofa reading a magazine. A couple of teenagers were studying at a desk across the way. Every now and then they laughed happily. "How wonderful it is to be that young and have no problems. They don't have a clue what's ahead of them."

"Looks safe enough," she said softly to herself. Her mind was so cluttered with the events of the past weeks that she didn't know how to sort it out. Jennie's pounding heart gradually slowed down. She opened the mystery so it would look like she was reading, glanced at her watch, and was relieved to see it wasn't yet four. She could sit here in neutral territory for another hour at least.

Those three G-2 men really scared her. But what could they do to her? Nothing, she decided, they couldn't do anything to her. She wasn't in the military so she had no reason to be scared. Those questions about whether Josh was alive or not, they were testing her. They wanted to find out what she knew. Well, she didn't know anything except that stuff keeps disappearing, even Josh's grave. *Could it be,* she wondered, *could it be that they don't know where he is?*

THE BLUE CAR PULLED SLOWLY to the front of the church and stopped.

"Why do you think she came to this old church here in Oak Cliff? Surely she goes to a church nearer home. No need to come this far," the G-2 agent with the blond hair said. He wished he didn't have to do this. Davenport had been a good friend. More than that, Davenport had saved his life and that's something a man doesn't take lightly. He owed him and now he felt like he was betraying him. *Where's the loyalty,* he questioned, and not for the first time.

"Must be some connection to Davenport," said the other man.

"Could be."

"She's obviously questioning whether he's dead or not."

The car door opened and the third man slid in asking, "What did you find out from her?"

"Nothing, she sidestepped all questions, but she's hiding something. How about you?" the blond man asked.

"About what you'd expect—the minister is Joel Johnson, somewhere in his early sixties, and has been at this church about five years. Not long enough to have known Davenport or Jennie. He was very close-mouthed. Said she'd come to visit the church because she had gone there as a child. Could be true, I suppose. He wouldn't say anything else, except to invite us to come to church Sunday."

"What else can you expect? If she told him anything it would be a matter of confidentiality. At least I think a minister is something like my priest. They can't tell what anyone tells them."

"Well, the ball is rolling. I'd say she's spooked pretty good. Maybe she'll get careless and we'll find out Davenport's location, or at least get a lead."

Chapter 23

"WHAT DO YOU MEAN you've lost him? A G-2 agent gone rogue and on the loose can cause trouble not yet thought of," roared General Thurman at INSCOM headquarters, his well-known temper barely under control. "I told you to find him and bring him in."

"We're trying, sir. Right now the only lead is his wife. Something has made her question his death. We know she thinks Davenport might be alive, but she doesn't know for sure. We've cut off all avenues available to her," responded Reaves. George Reaves was a small bookish man who had been attached to the general's staff for years. His expertise was getting things done in spite of the general's temper.

"What about the two daughters?"

"They don't appear to know anything about this. They were teenagers when he died. They are married now and pretty much out of the loop. I don't think we can find out anything from them."

"Absolutes, Reaves, I don't want any 'I think' business. Has Blakely reported in yet? He should know all Davenport's habits and hideouts. They were partners."

"He was scheduled to talk with Jennie Davenport today. They're still tracking her with the transponder. However, the signal is weak. We don't know how much longer it'll transmit."

"Have you considered bringing her in for questioning?"

"Yes, but Blakely felt he might get more out of her in a less formal setting. By bringing her in, we'd be confirming that Davenport's alive and we don't want to do that."

"No, we certainly don't. Major Kendall is out of the picture now; he was easy. But that policeman, Herman Wilkins, is still a concern. He is not going to leave it alone. Let me know if he makes any more waves. We may have to take him out. So what about the husband, do you think she's confided in him?"

"Probably a little, but I'd be surprised if she has told Scott everything she suspects. Right now, we're waiting for Blakely to report in."

"Don't wait, get hold of him now."

"Yes, sir," Reaves responded. He returned to his desk and put in another call for Blakely. Tapping his fingers impatiently, he waited while they located him. Davenport had been around long enough and was smart enough that if he didn't want to be found, he wouldn't be. And it wouldn't matter how mad General Thurman got.

"Blakely here."

"George Reaves. General Thurman wants an update on Jennie Davenport immediately. Hold while I get him on the line."

"General Thurman, here's Blakely. We're three-way."

"What did you find out from the Davenport woman today? Blakely, I'm waiting," the general warned after a couple of seconds of silence.

"Sorry, sir, I was thinking about the talk with Mrs. Davenport today. We picked her up at a church in Oak Cliff on the south side of Dallas, the part of town where she grew up. She was cooperative but wary as if she didn't understand what was going on. And I don't believe she did. She may have some suspicions about Davenport, but she doesn't know anything for sure. She's hurting and defensive." Remembering the fire in her eyes when she left the car, Blakely continued hesitantly, "She could be holding something back."

"Anything solid?"

"No, sir, all avenues have been removed and she has no concrete information."

"What about the body in the grave? Did you take care of that?"

"Yes, sir, all records have been removed as well as the grave itself. She hit a dead end there. No DNA confirmation can be made."

"What's your personal opinion about Davenport? What's he doing?"

"I think he'd had enough, sir. I feel he's gone underground and doesn't want either side to find him."

"Do you think he could have turned?"

"No, absolutely not, he's loyal. That's based on years of working with him. His situation when he was reactivated and brought back in as a double agent was intolerable. He's lasted longer in the field than any other G-2 outrider. Six years, that's almost unheard of. When he found out that his wife had remarried, well, that's what did it."

"Do you think we'll find him?"

"No, sir, I don't, not unless he wants us to. He knows all the tricks we do, and then some. If he wants to disappear, he'll do it. He gave up his life and family in '77, and he's worked long and hard with us. You remember that a couple of years ago he requested to be released. He was tired and wanted out then."

"Tired won't matter if the wife leads *The Brotherhood* to him. Don't let her get any closer. She could blow everything we've accomplished. All hell will break loose if they find out he's still alive."

"Yes, sir, I understand."

"Do you really, Blakely?" the general asked. "We may have to pull her in to find Davenport. We'll use her as bait if we have to. If that doesn't work, if she gets too close, you'll have to stop her." General Thurman paused a moment. "Under no circumstances can we let her lead them to Davenport."

The general didn't even want to think about the reprisals that would take place if she did. No way could he let that happen.

He continued very softly, "You have to stop her, Blakely. Any way you can.

DALLAS, TEXAS

O WEN BLAKELY HUNG UP the phone, turned and stared out into the dark night. He stood at the window for some time. He could hear General Thurman's fondest speech, the one he repeated again and again. "Look at the big picture, men, not the nitty-gritty. We have to make our judgments based on the big picture."

He'd had some strange orders in the past, but this was going too far. To order him to stop her any way he could, well, that wasn't right. She's not part of this. To question her or protect her was one thing, but to do anything else would be the ultimate betrayal of Josh. "I won't do that. I'll just have to work it out some other way," the tall blond man said out loud. "I owe my friend my life."

When they partnered in Europe he had learned so much from him. Josh Davenport had the quickest mind of anyone he'd ever known. "He could figure the odds and have a plan by the time it took me to understand the problem," Blakely muttered. "There was the time he came in and got me out when the Tribunal picked me up." He didn't have to; he wasn't supposed to put himself in jeopardy; outriders don't do that. The Tribunal never knew Davenport was there. He's like a damn ghost when he wants to be. For all he knew, Davenport could be watching him now.

General Thurman can spit and spew all he wants, but if Davenport has decided to disappear then he will, and it'll be a snowy day in hell before we find him. The general has no idea of who we're dealing with now, or who Davenport has become. Furthermore, if Davenport wants out, he had his blessing.

Blakely wondered if the general even knew that it was Davenport who figured out who and what *The Brotherhood* was. Blakely remembered when he first met him that it had taken a long time to win his trust. There were many reasons for him not to trust anyone. A wife and two daughters, plus a lot of other family who thought he was dead. They were still at risk if anyone found out he was alive. Blakely knew that, but he also knew he couldn't let Jennie lead *The Brotherhood* to her husband.

Davenport stumbled on that covert faction when he was editor-in-chief of the Army Information Center in Kansas City, Blakely recalled. As editor and a G-2 with a top secret rating, Davenport could access more information than most others could. He also had an uncanny ability to put bits and pieces of information together.

When the pieces of the puzzle fit, Davenport had realized *The Brotherhood* was comprised of three different groups of the most powerful men from around the world. At first he only knew the name of the group in the United States, the Illuminati, and that it was comprised of five men who had the finances and power to control just about everything in America. Then he happened on the date and location of the next yearly meeting and the other two names of the trilateral commission, the European Alliance and the Inner Circle in the British Isles. Their goal was for a unified world under their control. Their power was limited only by their desires. They were the real decision makers, the invisible world government, and they were already controlling much of the economy, including politics, military, presidents, prime ministers, and other key venues, leaving the ordinary people just an illusion of choice.

It started in the early '50s and *The Brotherhood* had gained power every year since then. The thirteen elite meet once a year in a secure location to make decisions about the coming year. They had only one rule: "Whoever owns the gold rules the world."

At that point, his research caught the attention of the NSA, and Davenport was pulled into Fort Leavenworth by INSCOM in cooperation with the NSA. It was determined that he had not penetrated far enough to be a threat. However, he was mustered out of the Army a few months before his term was up. Someone wanted him out of the way, where he could do no damage.

The man Davenport called *John Doe*, who had talked to him at Fort Leavenworth, turned out to be a double agent planted in the NSA by the Illuminati. Davenport didn't know that for a long time even though he knew *The Brotherhood* had informants in the military and all the vital areas of every government in the world.

When G-2 contacted Davenport in '74, he was surprised. A lot of coincidence had played into his recall. His home in Dallas happened to be across the street from one of the five members of the Illuminati. He said his girls had asked about the mysterious goings-on in that house. They joked and called it the *mafia* house, which was not far off base. Since he was in a unique position to do surveillance, he was reactivated. G-2 wanted him to document everyone who came and went. As a former G-2, Davenport had no choice.

Still staring out the window, Blakely watched the flickering lights of the city. He realized that he had already committed himself, that he had never really had a choice either. He knew where his loyalty lay.

I'll have to go through all the motions, he thought, *but I'll do all I can to help Davenport and protect his wife. I owe him that much and more.*

Owen Blakely moved slowly like an old man. He had some serious thinking to do. He knew the dangers and the problems involved in regard to *The Brotherhood* and G-2.

All those times Davenport dropped out of sight, Blakely assumed he had a safe haven. So that's what he had to figure out; he had to find where it was. And he had to find Davenport, for himself and for Jennie. The tricky part would be finding him without leading *The Brotherhood,* or the general, or anyone else to him.

Chapter 24

THE SMALL CABIN WAS situated high in the mountains near Blackhawk, Colorado. For the past few months it had served as home base for the large, bearded man with graying hair. Josh Davenport liked it here, but he would have to leave soon. Nowhere was safe for very long.

It had been years since he had thought, rather allowed himself to think, about Jennie and his past life. He hadn't been able to afford the luxury of thinking about her. Sometimes he wondered if he had any real feelings left. It seemed as if that life with Jennie belonged to another person, at least it did until he found out she had married Nathan Scott. Everything changed that second. Control was lost and emotions flooded in and he knew he could not continue what he was doing.

He could not, would not leave Jennie with that bastard. With that damned transponder in her, he couldn't contact her directly. Against all protocol, he broke into the INSCOM tracking system. He had to alert Jennie and it was the quickest way. He knew it would scare and confuse her and he was sorry for that, but at the same time he knew it would impel her to look more deeply into his death. He wanted to contact her again; but INSCOM would be on high alert. He could only get away with breaking in one time.

For the first time in years he totally let his guard down and allowed himself to remember. When he did his arms ached with emptiness and the loneliness of the last six years almost overpowered him. All he could remember was feeling empty, except for those few years when he had Jennie beside him. He remembered his lonely childhood, growing up without a father, his mother working long hours every day, and how much he hated to enter a dark house. He could still remember his fears as he walked up on the front porch and opened the door. Irrational, he knew, but kids have great imaginations. In some ways he had never gotten over this. He still hated empty houses, except now, the fears were real. Sometimes empty houses hid horrible things.

Davenport automatically checked the window and door locks then peered out into the midnight blackness. No moon tonight. He wondered what Jennie was doing, was she looking out at the same darkness and wondering about him? He tried to picture her in his mind.

Enough, he was through. He had done his part for his country. He had given all he had to give, and more, much more. "I've pushed down, subdued and conquered almost every human feeling, but it's over," he railed at the night. He knew he had operated longer than most others. The physical and emotional toll had been tremendous. He had lived under too much stress for too long and that was dangerous, that was when most errors in judgment occurred. He couldn't, and certainly the president couldn't, afford for that to happen. The president understood this.

The air blew cold when he opened the cabin door and went out. At nine thousand feet elevation, it would be some time before the nights warmed up. He sat on the steps and listened to the night sounds. The day he had been reactivated, he never imagined what it would lead to. They had explained that it would be a simple surveillance of the house across the street from him, not even a whisper of the dangers of the job. But either way, he was given no choice. As a G-2 with top secret clearance, he had always known he could be called back in. However, most were not.

"If I'd just left it all alone when we were in Kansas City, our lives could have been so different," he mumbled wistfully. "It was the challenge to see if I could figure it out." He had never been able to refuse a challenge.

He thought about those first days when it was fun and exciting to watch the *mafia* house. He had to admit it added a zest to life that his job in advertising had not provided. The assignments kept coming and he had been very good at handling them. Then there was the day that he began to question, he began to wonder why the surveillance, why the trips to New York and Chicago and Paris, and he had put his nose where it didn't belong.

He wasn't sorry about that part. It might have been worse if he hadn't. The president had maintained a little control, mostly because knowledge is power. Looking backwards, he wasn't sure where he could have gotten out. There was always that next urgent thing that had to be done.

Once he began to question the orders he had been given, he started profiling everyone he came in contact with. It was another mystery, another puzzle he had to solve. After a while the pieces started to fit. As the picture took shape he realized that the director of the National Security Agency was a double agent and was being paid by the Illuminati for information.

The NSA was working closely with G-2 and INSCOM during this time and was directing most of his activities. The scary part was that the NSA was not accountable to any authority other than itself. The director reported to no one except the president, and the president was told only what the director wanted him to know. Davenport had trapped himself with this knowledge. No one else knew about Silverman and, to compound the problem, Silverman was the president's close friend. At this point it became imperative for Davenport to talk to the president alone. It was some time before he found a way to do this and to present the facts to him.

The president had been aware for a long time that there was an information leak at NSA, and had asked for INSCOM's help in finding it. It was a lucky roll of the dice that INSCOM sent him to Camp David under the guise of analyzing security systems. He was able to get into the president's quarters late one night, explain that he was G-2 and that INSCOM had sent him in answer to his request. It took a lot of talking to convince the president that Mason Silverman, the Director of NSA, was involved with the Illuminati. He presented all his proof, and then he and the president spent the rest of the night hashing it out …

AT DAWN, THE PRESIDENT LEANED back in his chair, closed the folder, placed his hands on the table in front of him, and sat perfectly still for a few minutes. Davenport opened his mouth to continue his arguments, but the president lifted his hand for silence and closed his eyes. After what seemed to be an eternity, the president began to speak very softly and slowly.

"You've told me things I didn't want to hear. I didn't want to hear that my good friend, my comrade, has betrayed me and America." He paused and cleared his throat, his face blotched with emotion. "However, I can't deny the evidence. Everything fits. It answers all the questions I've had these past years. I knew information was leaking and I placed a few false facts with the NSA to test it. I called the general at INSCOM for help when I found out for sure, but I never dreamt Silverman was the problem. I'm sure he has no idea of what you've put together."

The president got up and poured brandy into two snifters. He handed one to Davenport and sipped the other. "Be assured that I will deal with him," the president said angrily. "From here forward I want you to report directly to me.

I'll give you a number so that you can always reach me. I want you to continue in your job just like you've been doing. I need to have reliable information on what is happening. The powers of the Illuminati and *The Brotherhood* are undeniable. I've known this for years, but haven't had a way to penetrate it. This may be my only chance."

Davenport was astounded to hear the plan the president set forth. He wanted Davenport to take all this information to Silverman saying that he felt it was in the both their best interests for him to know what he had discovered. His goal was to become Silverman's friend and to infiltrate the Illuminati.

In other words, Davenport would become a double agent, but with his allegiance to the president. He would receive his orders from G-2 and INSCOM as always. However, he would report everything straight to the president. In this way the president would be alerted to what Silverman and the Illuminati were doing.

"It will be walking a tight rope. You'll have to be very careful." The president turned and looked directly at Davenport before continuing. "No one at G-2, INSCOM, or NSA or anywhere else can know that you're reporting to me. No one, I repeat, no one can know. We can't trust anyone. I'll have a chance to neutralize part of the Illuminati's actions with your input. If I get rid of Silverman, they will just find someone else to take his place, only I would be in the dark again. We're in a very unique situation here. I might be able to exert some measure of control."

The president studied Davenport intently then lowered his voice. "I am asking for your help. You are the only one who has ever been able to slip past the secret service and get to me since I've been president. I can't imagine how you did that. You must have turned invisible. As impressive as that is, even more so is the fact you figured out Silverman's connection to the Illuminati and were astute enough to bring this information straight to me before telling anyone else. You have already demonstrated you have the capability to do what I'm asking. However, the question is—will you do this for me, for your country?"

Davenport sat down abruptly in the leather chair thinking about what this would mean to his life and to his family. The president quietly waited for his decision. Looking out the window of the president's study at Camp David, Davenport sipped his brandy and watched the secret service men patrolling the area. He'd be a part of this, all the secretive, underground activity that went on, and it stirred his imagination. He would continue on with G-2 and INSCOM taking their orders, but with a difference, and it was a big difference—reporting secretly to the president as well. What loomed huge in his mind was that by infiltrating the Illuminati, he would be more alone than he had ever been.

Could anything really be accomplished? Would it be worth the cost? He recognized it would be great. It could cost him his family.

Brandy at dawn, he reflected. He lifted the glass to his lips and locked eyes with the president, he could not refuse.

HE HAD KNOWN HIS POSITION was unique, but every day since then he had regretted that decision. With INSCOM as his control, he had done as the president asked and infiltrated the Illuminati. He had actually been inducted into the top echelon of *The Brotherhood*. It had indeed been a precarious balancing act. He had reported everything to the president as well as INSCOM. The president had been able to sidetrack some of the subversive activities of the covert groups. Nevertheless, he had become more and more aware with each passing day that an outrider, a double agent operating alone, could not last very long. He knew his cover would be blown someday.

And it was, three years later in '77. Both he and the president knew the Illuminati, empowered by *The Brotherhood*, were merciless. Davenport also knew that they would never rest until they exterminated him. He knew too much and they never left a loose end. Just disappearing wouldn't do it. They would use any and all means to get him. No one was safe, not his wife, his children, or the rest of his family.

He watched, but had been powerless to stop what they had done to the president. Realization of *The Brotherhood's* power and of his lack of power had come over him full force during the Watergate trials. He had to sit back and watch them destroy the president's credibility. After the president's resignation, Davenport remained in close contact with him. The next president had been briefed on his activities and Davenport continued to work behind the scenes.

As soon as Davenport knew his cover was blown, he contacted both the president and ex-president. After considering all possibilities, the only way they could absolutely insure the safety of his family was for him to die. The current president took over and along with G-2 made all the arrangements for his death. Only the president and three men inside INSCOM knew he didn't actually die.

If the Illuminati and *The Brotherhood* ever found out he was alive, they would be after him, no holds barred. He had their master plan all in his head, plus a notebook filled with names, places and schedules. They would also be after his family. He knew they would never give up. *The Brotherhood*'s power was unlimited and they never hesitated to use it. Simply put, they didn't play by the rules or subject themselves to the laws of America or any other country. Because of their merciless domination, they were able to stay invisible. He knew all about this first hand.

When the Illuminati and *The Brotherhood* found out he was a double agent, he knew he was dead, one way or the other. What they had not known was that he reported to the president and that he didn't really die. Davenport had known for a long time that dying would be the only way to protect his family.

His misconception was that he would be able to return home someday … but nobody comes back from the dead.

BY DAWN, REASON AND CONTROL kicked in along with a blue norther. Davenport wrapped a wool blanket around him and stirred the ashes in the fireplace. Reviving a few embers, he tossed in some kindling and a couple of sticks, then stoked the wood stove and got coffee brewing. In the time it took to perk, he had his things in a bag and was ready to leave.

Jennie should get his letter today. If he was right, she would be on her way. He wished he could join her, but her only protection was ignorance and anonymity.

Chapter 25

JENNIE CLUTCHED THE LETTER postmarked Oregon to her heart. She pulled away from Lorraine's house with ambivalent feelings of anticipation and dread. Roger's words loomed up in her mind like a stop sign—*you better think twice about getting involved. My advice is don't open the letter, throw it away.*

"No, I can't do that," she cried aloud. "I can't throw away a letter that Josh might have written. I have to read it no matter what."

Going back to the church was out of the question. She couldn't involve Pastor Johnson again, or Herman, or the girls. Definitely not Nathan, he had made her too uneasy the last few days. This was between her and Josh. She had to read it alone.

Once again, Jennie sought refuge at the library. It seemed as neutral and safe as anywhere she could think of. She hurried into the building, took the elevator to the second floor, and looked around. Grabbing a couple of reference books, she found a desk in a secluded corner where she could see out the window. Looking out at the trees helped counteract the turmoil inside her.

Jennie stared at the envelope on the desk and couldn't help debating with herself. If she didn't open it her life could go on as before. She could just tear it up and go home to Nathan. No one would have to know.

Could she live with that? Could she forget? No, she knew she couldn't do that. Her memories were real and alive and strong. If Josh was somewhere thinking about her, she had to know.

Thoughts raced wildly through her mind. When Josh died, she had *Love never changes* carved on his headstone. She had known then her love wouldn't change. She still loved him in a way she could never love anyone else. He was part of her very being and that part of her still cried out in desperation for him.

But what about Nathan, he had literally brought her back to life. He was good and strong and had given her the strength to start again. They made a decision to share their lives and to love each other, but it was a whole different set of emotions. She had never been able to get as close to him as she wanted. Sometimes it seemed like he had something to hide, something he didn't want her to know. He had changed in the last few days. He had scared and hurt her, and that stuck in her mind.

"I think you can only love once the way Josh and I did," whispered Jennie. "Maybe it was because we were so young when we fell in love.

Gazing out the window, the trees faded until all she could see was Josh's face. Jennie realized more fully than ever before how very much they had become one. Even death could not remove him from her. Physically yes, but emotionally no. She knew in her heart that he was still alive, and, more than that, somehow she had always known.

With a gut-wrenching sigh, she opened the envelope knowing her life was about to change forever. She unfolded the paper and recognized Josh's handwriting instantly. Hand over her mouth and afraid to breathe, she read his words ...

My dearest Jennie,

I know this is a shock. I know you are confused, hurt, and probably angry. I am hoping and praying that you will read this letter and understand that I had no choice in what happened. When I heard you married again, I had to reach you. We now have some decisions to make.

Our Oregon friend knows nothing about what's in this letter. All he was asked to do was to mail this envelope to you if you called him; then call a phone number and leave a message stating the date the letter was mailed. Don't call him again, Jennie. That is very important.

When we left the Army, it was under a cloud of political unrest. I had stumbled on some information that was so highly secret that only a few men in the United States knew about it. I'm sure through the years you have heard rumors of a mysterious group that controls the economy of America. This is real, Jennie. It's not a myth. It is part of a larger and more fanatical secret group, whose agenda is a one-world government under their sole jurisdiction.

What I found was a list of men's names along with the dates and locations of their future meetings. More importantly, it included the master plan for taking over America's banking and finance, television and communications, food distribution, and even the health system. In other words, everything necessary to people's lives would be under their supervision. I found all this in bits and pieces in various places. When I put it all together, I knew our country was in crisis.

When this information came across my desk in Kansas City, I started investigating and was just realizing the enormity of the plan when I was ordered to Fort Leavenworth. The man, we'll call him John Doe, who talked with me at Fort Leavenworth turned out to be a double agent. I'll not go into the names because that could still put you in jeopardy.

At the time we left the Army, I signed papers agreeing not to divulge what I'd found out. I was grateful to be out and hoped nothing else would ever come up; however it always worried me. A lot of coincidence played into all this. When we built our home in Dallas, a member of that secret group happened to live across the street from us. You probably remember that we laughingly called it the *mafia* house because of the strange things that went on and the fact the people who lived there did not talk to anyone in the neighborhood.

It took me by surprise when G-2 contacted me in 1974. They wanted me to do surveillance on that house. By accident, I was in a unique position to help, and so I was reactivated. I was not allowed to tell you anything. It was much later when I found out John Doe was a double agent. That was when I realized how I was being used. I had to take action. I tried to find a way out, but there wasn't one. I was forced to continue by becoming a double agent myself—but with a huge difference, my loyalty was to America. The effective life of a double agent is always limited, and I was eventually discovered. That was when I had to die. You know about that. This is a much abbreviated version, but it tells you a little about what happened.

You now have a decision to make, Jennie. You've made a lot of waves and people are getting nervous. If this group ever has any idea I'm still alive, they won't hesitate to use you to get to me. I'm hoping you haven't told our daughters yet. If you haven't, don't tell them and don't show them this letter. Please understand that any knowledge is dangerous. Let's try and give them a chance for a real life. I'm afraid it's beyond that for you. They will come after you.

I still love you, my Jennie, as much as I did the day I *died*. That has never wavered nor has my determination to keep you and the girls safe and secure. That has been my most important motivation. It's always been in my mind that you would join me someday. I guess I'll never know if I did right or wrong, but at the time I had no choice. I had to keep all of you safe and the only way was to die. I don't know if you will hate me, or if you can forgive me and possibly still love me.

I'm sure my enemies know exactly what you've been doing. They will only wait so long before they pick you up. I'm afraid it's not a matter of *will they*, but *when will they*. So we have to get you out of there.

Here are the steps you have to take right now—today, this minute. First, I need you to get something, but don't let anyone see you. Go to the attic of our home, move the old army trunk, and you will see a loose board. Under it is a small notebook containing names, addresses, and the master plan. Put it in the addressed envelope attached to this letter. It will need four stamps. Don't take time to pack, you can buy clothes later. No suitcases. Just walk out with your purse like you're going to the grocery store, get in the car and drive away. Be careful, Jennie, but act normally. Find a drive-up mailbox and drop the envelope in.

Next, and this is absolutely vital—a transponder chip was injected into your upper left arm at the hospital when I died. INSCOM has monitored you throughout the years. You need to find a doctor that you can trust implicitly and have the chip removed because it's still active. An x-ray should show exactly where it is. It can be removed under a local anesthetic, it's a simple procedure. Take the chip with you when you leave the doctor's office and throw it in the back of some truck or pickup. This will keep INSCOM busy following someone else.

Once that is out they will no longer be able to track you. After that, go to the city where we spent our wedding night, find the main post office and ask for general delivery for Suzanne Smith. The letter will contain further instructions, money, an airline ticket, and a driver's license with a new name for you. Make sure you aren't followed. Don't use any credit cards, only cash. Leave no trails. I know this seems unnecessary, but please trust me, honey. We have to get you out of there without leaving a trail they can follow.

You know the recognition code we used to kid about. Don't go with anyone who doesn't mention it to you. Above all, understand that the only way you can protect Kris and Laurie is not to tell them anything. Someday, we will get word to them.

I'll be waiting for you—with a yellow rose.

The letter ended without a signature, but with a drawing of a little pony.

Cymbals clashed in Jennie's ears. He had sent her yellow roses the day they were married. He was waiting with a yellow rose the time she joined him in Paris. Josh must have put or had the yellow rose put in the vase at the cemetery. *Remember the ponies ...*

"He's alive. He's not dead. I've always known it. He's really alive. And he had no choice in what he did," she gasped. Joy spread across her face. She wanted to jump up and dance. "He didn't want to leave. He never wanted to leave me." She couldn't sit still. Jennie got up and walked around.

She had to tell Nathan something. She had to tell her daughters something. But what, what could she tell them? In her anguish about Kim and Laurie, Jennie sat down and closed her eyes. "Oh, dear Lord, thank you. I prayed so many times in the past that Josh would be alive. But my daughters, oh, Lord, what do I do about them?"

Lifting her head, she stared out the window. The trees were gently moving in the wind. Everything outside looked so normal. She thought once again how all she ever wanted was a normal life. "Maybe this is normal," she murmured, her face glowing with a hope she hadn't felt in years.

She had known the minute she saw the little drawing of the pony that she would go to Josh, no matter what. She had to. Her mind was flying in all directions. We've lost years, but now we have a second chance. "I can't, I won't let him go again. My memories will be real because he'll remember them, too. Oh, the precious feeling of becoming me again. I won't be lost anymore." Tears flowed uncontrolled down her face.

Kim and Laurie are grown and have their own families. She loved Nathan and he loved her, but it hadn't been the same for either of them. It was not the wild falling in love feeling that they each had during their first marriages. It was a decision to love and join their lives together, not that overpowering elation of first love.

Josh is alive. Pastor Johnson said that in the eyes of God he would still be her husband. Her heart pounding, she walked up and down the aisles of books. She would have to tell everybody something and prepare them for her disappearance or they would call the police. She sure didn't want them to do that. And Herman, he could make a big commotion and who knows what else. Feeling almost queasy at the thought of what he would do, she had to stop him from searching for her and Josh.

Okay, first things first. She couldn't do anything until she got the notebook and mailed it. Then she had to get that chip out of her arm. *Josh said they are tracking me.* Herman and Carl talked about an injection. They suspected this. Who could she trust to remove it? Not any of her regular doctors, they would ask too many questions and make a big deal about it. They would probably want to put her in the hospital. Jennie rubbed her left arm trying to find the chip, but she could feel nothing. She suddenly remembered her cousin in Ft. Worth. She could trust him. He was a dermatologist and he could do it.

She read the letter again; she had to make sure she wasn't forgetting anything. Plan in mind, she folded the letter, put it in her purse, and looked around to see if she had dropped anything. Forcing herself to walk and not run, Jennie left the library and drove home.

As she neared the house she panicked when she saw Nathan's car in the driveway. What's he doing home in the morning—does he know something? She drove a few blocks away from the house, parked, waited ten minutes, and then went back to the house. His car was gone, he must have forgotten something.

She went straight to the attic, pried up the board she had nailed down, grabbed the notebook, and nailed the board back. Running down the stairs she ignored the ringing phone, she didn't know what to tell anyone. After stamping the envelope, Jennie gathered up a few pictures, her address book, and stuffed them in her purse.

There was one more thing she had to take with her. She had to get the wedding ring Josh had given her and the one she'd given him. She started to leave Nathan's ring on her dresser but decided that would tell him too much. She could mail it back someday. Josh said no suitcases, no clothes. Looking wistfully around her home, she wondered if she would see it again. Her stomach churning, she closed her eyes for a moment before leaving.

"I'll be back, I just don't know when," she cried, blinded by her tears.

Jennie grabbed a handful of tissues on her way out. She backed out of the driveway, drove to the shopping center and dropped the envelope in the mailbox. That's done, now to Ft. Worth. Turning west, she thought about the fastest way to get to her cousin's office.

"First thing though, I have to stop for gas or I am not going anywhere," she muttered.

Navigating the 820 Loop to the University exit in Ft. Worth, she passed the beautiful gardens of the park area and remembered the time she and Josh wandered through them. Would he still remember? It was on their honeymoon and they were so happy, so completely free of worries then. Everywhere she looked memories kept surfacing, things she hadn't thought about in years.

Hurrying into the office, Jennie asked, "Is Dr. Edwards in? I don't have an appointment, but I'm his cousin and thought he might have a moment to visit with me."

The receptionist smiled and said she'd check with him. Jerry came out quickly, smiling and hugged her, "I don't know to what I owe this visit, but I'm glad to see you, Jennie."

"I was just in the area and thought I'd stop and see if you had a minute to visit."

"Come on back to my office. I have a little while before my next patient is due. This is good timing. How are Kris and Laurie?"

They talked about family for a few minutes while Jennie tried to figure out what she could tell him. Finally, she decided to tell as much of the truth as she could.

"Jerry, I have a little problem that I'm hoping you can help me with. You may not remember, but years ago when Josh was in the Army, he was in a top secret division. When we married they checked me out very thoroughly. I thought it was strange, but it turned out that it was the area of service Josh was in. Everyone in the division and all their families had to have top secret clearance. More than that, they implanted some kind of chip in our arms. The division was highly secret and kidnapping was considered a possibility. This chip would have allowed them to find us if that ever occurred."

"I've never heard of such a thing," said Jerry.

"I hadn't either, pretty impressive for way back then. When we left the service they said the chip would naturally dissolve in a few years. But I don't think it has because my arm has been sore for a long time now, and I want to know if that thing is still there. Would you take an x-ray of my arm and tell me what you see?"

"Sure, we can do that, right now if you want to."

When Jerry had developed the x-ray and looked at it, he pointed to a small spot. "That looks like a foreign object. That could be it."

Jennie looked closely at it. "It's awfully small. Do you really think that's it?"

"Possibly, it's definitely not natural."

"So, it's still there. It looks too small to make my arm sore. What do you think?"

"Anything foreign to the body can become infected."

"Do you think you could take it out? I really don't like the thought of it being there."

"I don't see why not, it's barely under the surface of the skin. Let's go into the examining room. I should be able to remove it with only a local. Are you brave enough to let me try?" Jerry teased.

"Sure, let's do it. Would you put it in a little jar so I can keep it? I'd like to show the girls."

Thirty minutes later, Jennie walked out of Jerry's office with a small bottle in her purse and a band aid on her arm. He hadn't questioned what she had said. Now, the next step was to find a place to leave it, maybe a car from another state. If this would keep them trailing some other person for a while, it would give her time to get away from Fort Worth.

She was near the Kimbell Art Museum, so she pulled into the parking lot and drove around. Spying a pickup with plates from Illinois, she parked, got out of her car, opened the bottle and dropped the chip in the bed of the truck as she walked by. No one would ever see it there. Then Jennie went into the museum, discarded the bottle in the trash, and asked the lady at the desk where the main post office was located.

It took her only a short time to drive downtown. The directions were easy to follow. Parking in a ten-minute zone, she went in and calmly asked for General Delivery for Suzanne Smith. The clerk turned and walked to the back counter, then returned with a small package.

"One moment, please," the clerk said, as Jennie started to leave. With her heart thumping in her throat, she turned back to the clerk.

"You'll have to sign for this."

Jennie sighed in relief as she sped away from the post office. They couldn't find her now, the chip was gone. Her eyes riveted on the rearview mirror for dark blue cars. She wanted to put more distance between her and the tan pickup where she had thrown the chip. The elation of the morning was wearing off. She was starting to shake, part nerves and partly because she had missed breakfast. She needed food and to open the package.

About twenty minutes east of Ft. Worth, she spotted a cafe with lots of cars around it. That looks all right, should be lots of people inside and she could get lost in the crowd.

Jennie slipped into a corner booth clutching the envelope to her body. Her stomach had been flip-flopping all day. First the letter, getting the chip out, then the post office. No wonder she had the shakes. After ordering, she sipped her coffee and searched her purse for aspirin. Headaches had become a way of life. She looked around; no one was paying any attention to her.

Unable to wait any longer she tore open the package in her lap. It contained three envelopes. She opened the bulky one first and gasped in disbelief—well, so much for being nonchalant.

It was filled with hundred dollar bills, lots and lots of them. She certainly wouldn't have to worry about money. Slipping it quickly back into the package, she took the next envelope out and found a driver's license issued by the state of Vermont. It had her picture on it, a current one, and her height and weight were correct. *How was this possible? Could Josh have been close enough to me to take my picture? Maybe that day at the cemetery when I found the yellow rose. Well, I don't know how, but I have a new name. I'm now Angela Simmons. Hope I can remember it.*

The next envelope contained an airline ticket leaving at midnight from Austin, and a car rental reservation all in the name of Angela Simmons. Josh had to know she would open the letter today. She couldn't help but wonder if he was nearby watching her. She looked around the café again.

Good thing she started early today. It would take three hours or more to drive to Austin. First, she had to pick up the rental car, but what about her car? *More coffee, I need more coffee.* She signaled the waitress, and gripped her shaking hands under the table.

She had to talk to her daughters and Nathan and Herman and stop them from doing anything else. She needed clothes and a suitcase before she boarded the plane, otherwise she would look out of place. When she paid her bill, she asked for her change in coins. She had some phone calls to make.

"Hi, Laurie, what's going on?"

"Not much, Mom, just the usual stuff."

"Do you think you and Kris could meet me in the food court at the Valley View Mall at three? I need to tell you about something."

"Sure. I can make it."

Next Jennie called Kris. Kris immediately wanted to know why, but Jennie stopped her saying she'd explain when they met. Nathan was out of the office when she called him. She tried at home, but no answer there either. She would try later if she could.

The last call was to Molly and Herman. When Molly didn't answer, Jennie left a message. "Tell Herman to stop the search for now, that I'll get in touch with him later. In the meantime, tell him to call Kris or Laurie. It's important."

Jennie arrived at the mall about one-thirty and knew she'd have to do some very fast shopping. She rushed to Foley's department store and quickly picked up two pairs of slacks, a long skirt, a pair of jeans, several blouses, a sweater, a couple of jackets, one tan, one navy, and went into the dressing room. Everything fit well enough, not perfect, but they would do. She paid cash and went next to the lingerie department. Choosing underwear, gowns, a robe, and house shoes, she continued on her shopping spree.

It didn't take her long to find what she needed including a few cosmetics. The sales clerks were so slow it was making her anxious. As she was leaving the cosmetic department, a forgotten memory struck her. Impulsively, she turned back and bought Josh's favorite perfume, *Hope*. She had quit wearing it after he died.

Not knowing where she was going or how much walking she would have to do, Jennie bought two pair of comfortable shoes, and then went upstairs to the luggage department.

Loaded down with packages, a suitcase and a makeup bag, she struggled to her car and put everything in the suitcase. Then she pulled her billfold out of her purse and removed her driver license and everything else that had Jennie Davenport Scott on it. She replaced it with the new license named Angela Simmons, put part of the money in her billfold, and the rest in a money pouch she had purchased in the luggage department. Almost as an afterthought, she took Josh's letter out of her purse and put it in the money pouch. She put it around her waist and tucked it in her slacks. It was bulky so she slid it to her side where her sweater would cover it, and hoped no one would notice.

When she put her old driver's license and ID in the glove compartment of her car, it really hit home that she was actually leaving and that she was no longer Jennie Davenport. Digging in her purse for a pencil, she scribbled a quick note to Nathan saying she needed to get away for a few days. When Nathan checks the car, and he will, he'll find this and understand."

Finally, Jennie was ready to face Kris and Laurie. She got a coke and chose an isolated table in the food court. It was good to slow down, but when she did her nerves came back. She took several deep breaths and watched for her daughters. At last, she spotted them and waved them over to her table.

"I've already got a drink. Why don't you two get something?"

As soon as they got to the table, Kris looked at her mother and said, "You seem to be making a habit of these command performances, Mom. This was a quick one. I had to find a babysitter."

"I know, sorry I rushed you, but it couldn't be avoided. It's important. You remember that I told everybody I needed time to think. Well, that's what I've been doing. I have also found out a little more, and this has helped me make a decision. I need you to listen and understand." Jennie paused and looked intently at Kris and Laurie before she continued. "You're going to have to take a lot of things on faith from me today. First and most importantly, I'm asking you to quit searching for your dad. I need you to stop Herman from doing anything else. He'll be calling one of you."

"What do you mean, Mom, you found out something more?" asked Laurie.

"I mean that I opened a hornet's nest when I started searching to see if your dad was still alive. It was a foolish thing to do just because of that incident at the lake house. I need you to promise that you will stop looking. Promise me, please."

"Okay, okay, Mom, don't get mad. We'll do whatever you say," Laurie quickly responded.

"I'm not mad, honey, but there are very important reasons for what I'm asking, including your safety and your family's safety. You have to realize, as well as I do, that if papers can disappear from the NPRC and a body from a cemetery, some powerful forces must be involved. And whoever it is doesn't want us to know about your dad. A few new things have come up that I can't tell you about right now because it would be dangerous for you to know. This is where you have to trust me and my decision. For all intents and purposes your dad is dead. He died six years ago. He has been gone since and he is still gone. Even Josh's grave has disappeared. This is all you need to know and all you should say if you are ever asked."

"We were there; we know the grave is gone. We want to know where daddy is," Kris said.

"You have to trust me right now. Please know that your dad did not leave willingly. That he did not want to die, that he loved you beyond anything you can imagine, and that he would have done anything he had to in order to protect you. Can you be satisfied with that for the time being?"

"I don't know," Kris said. "I guess we have to. It doesn't sound as if we have a choice."

"Not any more choice than your dad had, Kris."

"Wait a minute. Are you saying dad is alive for sure?" asked Laurie.

"No, I'm not saying that. I'm saying that whatever happened, he had no choice in the matter of his death. If you are ever asked, you know nothing except that he died six years ago. I need your promise that you will say and do nothing more. Do I have it?"

"Yes, Mom, I promise and Laurie will too. I think I know what you're saying. But I wish you'd just say it out loud."

"I know you do, Kris, but I can't. I made a promise, too. I also made a commitment many, many years ago, and it's a commitment I intend to keep. Kris, Laurie, know that I love you with all my heart. I will explain everything as soon as I can."

"You're scaring me, Mom. I don't like what I'm hearing. It sounds like you're going away," gasped Laurie. "I will do whatever you want me to, but, please, Mom, tell us what's going on."

"I will, as soon as I can. That's a promise I intend to keep to both of you. Now, will you do me an enormous favor? I need some help. First, I'm going away for a while so will you check on Nathan from time to time. He's been there for us and I want you to be there for him. I haven't been able to reach him today. Next, will one of you take my car back home? I won't need it any more today."

Kris and Laurie just stared at their mother until she asked again, "Will you do this for me?" With questioning eyes, they both nodded.

Jennie and her daughters walked out of the mall without talking. There was nothing left to say. When she reached the car, Jennie quickly hugged each of them, got her suitcase and makeup bag out of the car and handed the car keys to Laurie. "Please, please understand and just love me. I have to go now.

If anyone questions you about where I am, just say that I needed a break, a little time alone, and I'll call soon."

Jennie turned from their tearful faces and walked back toward the mall. She hoped she could keep that promise. Looking up through her tears, she was surprised to see Nathan standing at the mall entrance.

"I came as soon as I got your message, Jennie," said Nathan, staring at the suitcase in her hand. "You're crying. What's happened?"

Jennie hurried toward him saying, "Give me just a minute." Nathan reached out his arms and drew her in. He held her until her crying quieted, then pushed her back so he could look her in the face, and asked again, "What's wrong, Jennie?"

They walked over to a bench and sat down. Jennie avoided looking at Nathan's eyes when she told him she was going away for a few days; that she needed some time alone.

"What did you tell Kris and Laurie?"

Jennie felt him tense up. "I just told them I'm going away for a while. They're taking my car home. Oh, Nathan, I didn't think I'd get to see you. I was so upset when I couldn't find you. I put a note in the glove compartment."

"What does the note say, Jennie?"

"That I'm going away and I'll be in touch."

"Can you tell me anything more? Have you heard from Josh?" he asked.

"No, I can't tell you anything right now. I'm so sorry, Nathan, I do care about you."

"I know you do, Jennie. I've always known that." He reached over and hugged her. "You do what you have to do. Just go, think it through, and make your decision. I'll be right here if you need me."

"I know you will. I really have to go." Jennie stood up abruptly, saying, "Please, please, don't be mad."

"I'll be all right, Jennie. Promise me that you'll keep in touch. I have to know that you're okay."

NATHAN WATCHED JENNIE AS SHE walked away. He had always known something would go wrong—he just didn't know what it would be. He deluded himself most of the time, but he had always known.

With a deadly calm, Nathan whispered, "Just don't make me wait too long."

Chapter 26

Early Wednesday Evening
March 30, 1983
WASHINGTON, D. C.

Reaves was desperately trying to find Owen Blakely. He had never seen the general in such a temper. He was a prime candidate for a stroke.

Jennie Davenport had been spotted carrying a suitcase by an INSCOM operative at a car rental place near DFW airport. The man then committed an unpardonable offense; he lost her in traffic. "Sure wouldn't like to be in his shoes," mumbled Reaves.

The phone rang and he grabbed it before the first ring was finished.

"Where are you?" he answered.

"Dallas, as always," said a voice.

"Sorry, was expecting another call. Identify."

"Watchman," the voice answered.

"What do you have today?"

"Jennie Davenport is on her way out of Dallas. I have no idea where she's headed. She left her identification including driver's license behind, so the assumption is she has a new identity."

"Can you tell us anything else?"

"No, that's all I know. Do you have any instructions for me?"

"Not right now. Stay where you are. Check in tomorrow as usual."

Reaves hurried to the general's office and related the conversation to him.

"That ties in with the car rental. She's on her way to Davenport. Get that inept operative that lost her back here. He's useless. Has Blakely reported in yet?" roared the general.

"No, sir, he's en route to Dallas."

"Watchman, is he reliable? You know, we've questioned that in the past."

"Relatively so, the problem we've had with him is that he fell in love and lost objectivity. If she's left him, my bet is he'll work with us now or he wouldn't have called in. He wants her back. Yes, I believe we can depend on him at this point."

The general turned and stared out the window. "I want Watchman on the next plane here. I have to make sure of his loyalty. Find out what's going on with the daughters—get a tap on their phones. She'll be in touch with them eventually. And find Blakely."

Chapter 27

SEVERAL URGENT MESSAGES FROM General Thurman were waiting for Owen Blakely when he checked in his hotel. Tired and irritable, he hurried to his room and called. Reaves said the general was really hot. "It appears that Jennie Davenport is on her way to Davenport and the operative lost her in traffic."

The general came on the line roaring, "We've got her on the transponder, but the signal's getting weak. This may be our best chance to find Davenport, so don't screw up. I want a report every two hours. And watch your backside. We're not the only ones watching her." Reaves gave Blakely the location of the car rental place where the operative lost Jennie.

Blakely splashed water on his face, ran his hands through his hair, and left quickly. "I'm not often thankful for traffic, but this was sheer luck," he mused. If the operative had checked the rental place to find out her destination, he would not have lost her.

Grateful for that bit of stupidity, Blakely drove directly to the rental facility. "Luck is with us, Josh, but you should have brought me in on this. I'm working in the dark."

Flashing his badge, he asked his questions and found that Jennie Davenport had not rented a car. He did find a blond woman named Angela Simmons had picked up a small black Ford a short time ago and had asked for a map. The guy said she mentioned something about the Austin airport. That was a stroke of luck, if she had boarded a plane under that name, he would have lost her.

A fast look at the map showed him the best route and he burned off. With any luck at all he'd catch up with her before she boarded a plane. If she was going to Davenport, he had to make sure no one else followed her. The Illuminati had eyes and ears everywhere.

Blakely settled in for the long drive and began thinking about where Davenport could be. Going back over the past years, he knew that Davenport periodically disappeared. They all needed some down time. However, Davenport never told him where he went. Blakely thought about conversations they had, what books he read, what newspapers, but nothing gave him a clue. He could be anywhere in the world now. Blakely knew better than anyone how invisible his partner could be when he wanted to. For a big man, he had an uncanny ability to blend into the crowd.

Bank accounts; Davenport's salary was deposited in a Swiss account, so that was no help. That could be accessed from anywhere. He should have a sizable amount on deposit. Blakely knew he did; he was almost always on an expense account. Davenport had also talked about an investment paying off unbelievably big, so money was not a problem. Their last assignment together had been in Great Britain. Davenport loved the countryside there. Maybe that's where he has gone to ground. England, Ireland, Scotland—he could be in any of those places.

Pulling in a gas station, he filled the car up and phoned in. He told Reaves he didn't have time to talk, but was on her trail and hoped to find her. He hung up before Reaves could ask his location. Blakely was not about to tell him they were headed for Austin, and he didn't hang on long enough for a trace.

Chapter 28

THE INSCOM OPERATIVE MONITORING the movements of the *JDavenport* transponder had specific orders to alert George Reaves of any unusual activity. The blip on the screen had moved out of Dallas to Fort Worth then back to Dallas. Late afternoon, it had turned north. It had been moving steadily for the last couple of hours and was now well into Oklahoma.

"Get a fix on the location," Reaves said, "and let me know of any directional change or if it stops."

"General, it appears that Jennie Davenport Scott is driving north. The monitor has picked her up in Oklahoma. We are trying to pinpoint an exact location."

"Blakely should be in Oklahoma following her. Watch her closely. See what data you can pick up. When Blakely reports in again, get his location."

Reaves went back to the screening room and ordered the operative to zoom in and identify the location.

Chapter 29

WAVES OF PAIN ENGULFED Jennie as she fought to see the road through her tears. She had to pull over and stop. Part of her was full of sorrow and another part of her was elated beyond words. She was full of sorrow for her daughters, for Nathan, and all that she was leaving behind. She had said *a while*, but she had no idea how long or even where she was going. She couldn't let herself think about Kris and Laurie's hurt faces when she had handed the keys over and walked away. She knew how hard it was to be in the dark.

She could not shake the feeling of guilt, of disloyalty. So much pain all around her, no matter what she did someone would be hurt. She could always go back home, but right now she had to find Josh. "I have to keep going. I can't be in the dark anymore." Jennie said to herself. She thought the girls understood even though she didn't exactly tell them their dad was alive. At least this time, they knew she was alive.

Tears under control, she pressed the gas pedal and took off.

She should be about halfway to Austin. The map showed the airport on the northeast side of town. She felt sure there would be exit signs. If she could get there by ten and check in, maybe she could find something to eat. Suddenly, she realized that she hadn't even looked at the airline ticket to see where she was going. Both fear and excitement tugged at her.

Jennie pulled off I-35 at the airport exit. She was in luck; it was well marked. Following the signs, she stopped and filled the rental with gas, then drove several more miles before she saw the airport. She found the car rental area, turned the car in, and got on the shuttle to the main terminal.

Close behind her a dark sedan pulled in. A man got out and boarded the same shuttle. Jennie noticed him because he didn't have a suitcase. She guessed lots of people traveled back and forth on the same day. He probably came for a meeting.

THIRTY MINUTES LATER BLAKELY PULLED into the car rental return, looked around, and spotted several small black Fords. Hopefully, one of them was the one she had been driving, but he had no clue which terminal she had gone to.

The man in the rental office confirmed a woman named Angela Simmons had just returned a car. Blakely asked about the route the shuttles took then jumped in his car and raced off for the first stop.

Chapter 30

STUDYING THE LARGE DEPARTURE screens, Jennie found her flight and gate number. It was Denver so it wouldn't be a long flight. She looked for her gate while keeping an eye out for a place to eat. She had more than an hour until her midnight flight and it had been a long time since lunch. Spotting a brightly lit area she headed for it.

There was only prepackaged food, but she was hungry enough to try. She picked a not-too-limp-looking salad, a cheese sandwich, a chocolate brownie, and hoped they would be edible. Nothing was very fresh. Choosing a table where she could look down the long corridor, Jennie sat down, bone weary.

She felt a little better after eating. She walked around the gift shop, picked out a magazine, a couple of candy bars, some chewing gum, and Dramamine tablets, then looked for the water fountain. She had never been a good flyer.

BLAKELY PARKED AT THE FIRST shuttle stop, went in and examined the flight screens. Planes were going to Denver, New York, and Seattle. Deciding to go to the New York gate first, he checked the waiting area, the gift shops, and places to eat. He went next to the Denver gate. Fortunately, it wasn't a large airport like DFW so he would have time to check out all the flights leaving after midnight if he had to.

Relief flooded over him when he saw her come out of the gift shop and go toward the Denver gate. Cautious as to what she would do if she saw him, he leaned back against the wall and watched. A man left the gift shop right after Jennie did. A couple in their mid-sixties were talking and laughing. Several other people were reading newspapers; others were just staring out the darkened windows. The man kept looking at Jennie. *Coincidence,* Blakely wondered. *Don't trust coincidences.* He stood still and watched.

Jennie went to the desk and got her boarding pass. The man continued to watch her, but he didn't check in. *Red flag,* Blakely thought. *What's he doing here?* When she sat down, the man picked up a newspaper from a chair and sat near her. *Something wasn't feeling right. The man didn't get a boarding pass.*

The stewardess announced it was time to board and everyone in the area crowded toward the door. In the confusion of boarding, the man grasped Jennie's arm and started pulling her away from the area.

Backing away from him, Jennie said, "Let go of me. What are you doing?"

"Just come with me. There's been a change in plans. I have to talk with you."

"Leave me alone. I'm not going with you." She tried to get away, but he had a tight grip on her arm.

"Yes, you are, and be quiet about it," he answered, tightening his hold on her arm.

"You're hurting me. Let go," she yelled, trying to pull away.

At that moment, Blakely stepped up and blocked their way. "Let go of the lady. I don't think she wants to go with you."

"No, I don't. My plane's boarding," Jennie said, recognizing the blond man. "I don't know this man."

"Get on the plane. I'll take care of this," Blakely ordered. He pulled her away from the man and stepped between Jennie and her assailant. He put his hand on the man's chest, "Back off. I don't think you want me to call airport security, do you?"

GRABBING THE MAKEUP CASE SHE had dropped, Jennie ran to the boarding line. That was the blond man outside the church. She looked around fearfully, but didn't see any of the other men who were with him. His identification said G-2; could he be helping her? Or following her? The line was moving and she would soon be on the plane. Josh's letter said, "Don't go with anyone who doesn't mention the *pony* song." She wasn't about to—if she could help it.

Jennie handed her boarding pass to the stewardess and mingled with the crowd that was going down the long ramp to the plane. She found her place, pushed her makeup bag under the seat in front of her, and sat down with a sigh of relief. She looked around and didn't see either man come on board.

Who was that man who grabbed her and why did he do that? Nervously, she scrunched lower in her seat wondering what was going to happen next.

BLAKELY PROPELLED THE MAN TOWARD the security gates saying, "Don't make a scene here. It won't do you any good." Seeing a guard standing near the gates, Blakely signaled him over, told him that this man had been harassing a lady as she was trying to board, and would he please hold him for questioning. Flashing his ID, Blakely left the man there saying he would be back shortly.

Rushing to the ticket desk, he gave the clerk his ID and credit card, told her it was imperative for him to get on the plane to Denver. While she was getting his ticket, Blakely asked her to call air control and have them hold take off until he could board.

All the passengers had boarded by the time Blakely got back to the gate. He glanced over at the guard holding Jennie's assailant and hoped he would detain him until the plane took off. Slipping into a seat near the door, he decided it would be a good idea to wait until they took off before he tried to talk to Jennie. She couldn't run away from him then.

JENNIE RELAXED WHEN THEY WERE airborne and released her seatbelt. She placed the pillow the stewardess had given her against the window and curled up in the seat, very grateful no one was sitting beside her. She was exhausted. Maybe she could sleep for a little while.

Waking with a start, Jennie sensed someone had sat down beside her. It was the man that had helped her at the airport. What was he doing here? She sat up straight saying, "I guess I should thank you for helping me back there. I don't know who that man was."

"I was glad to help. What did he want?"

"He said he wanted to talk to me," Jennie said, feeling a bit more comfortable with the man since he had helped her. "Are you with G-2?"

Glad for the opening, Blakely answered quietly, "Yes, I'm attached to the Army, but I'm not here officially."

"Oh, vacation? Colorado's a beautiful state."

"Not exactly, I'm here because I'm concerned for you."

"Why? Why is G-2 concerned with me? I wondered about that when you asked me all those questions."

"I know your husband."

"You know Nathan?"

"Not Nathan, your first husband. I worked with him for a long time."

Blakely tried to think of some way to convince her he knew him and that he wanted to help her. He lowered his voice to a whisper, "I know you are traveling under the name of Angela Simmons."

Jennie caught her breath sharply. "How did you know that?"

"It's a long story; maybe I need to tell you a little about myself." He looked at the people around them, and then lowered his voice. "First, my name is Owen. Your husband and I are in the Army together. We have been partners for a long time."

Her face told him she wasn't accepting any of this—he realized he had to reveal more. He leaned toward her and his voice was so low Jennie almost couldn't hear him. "I know Josh is alive."

Why is he whispering—maybe that other man is on the plane? Jennie struggled to make sense of what he was saying. *Could he really know Josh? Or was he still trying to find out what she knew?* She moved closer to the window, not trusting him at all. "Then you know more than I do. I assume you're testing me to find out something about Josh. All I know is that he died six years ago," she repeated softly.

"Jennie, when we talked at the church it was official. This is not. I'm on my own now, as his friend and partner."

"You haven't said the right thing to convince me," she said, thinking about the *pony* song.

"Let me say that I know he is missing. The general doesn't know where he is and they are trying to find him. The man at the airport is not G-2. I'm not sure who he is, but it tells me someone else is trying to find my partner. I also know there's an order to bring you in to headquarters. They want to keep you from getting to him."

Getting more and more scared, Jennie asked, "So why did you help me if you're G-2? Aren't you going against orders?"

"Yes, in direct defiance. I'm supposed to take you in, but I'm not going to. I know you're trying to get to Josh. I haven't reported your new name, that you went to Austin, or that you're going to Denver. What I want to do is help muddy the trail you leave so that you can get away safely. I have an obligation to my partner that overrides the one I have to G-2. Do you understand what I'm saying?"

"I don't know, but I do know you helped me get away from that man. What do you mean by an obligation?

"There's no time to explain to you now. We'll be landing in Denver in about twenty minutes and I'm not sure who'll be waiting for you there. I was able to detain the man at Austin, but he may have called ahead by now. Someone else could be waiting for you. Do you know what you do next?"

Realizing that she'd just assumed she would meet Josh in Denver, she answered that she had no idea either.

The stewardess interrupted them saying, "Excuse me, Mrs. Simmons, I'm supposed to give you this envelope before we land in Denver. Jennie reached for it with a shaking hand wondering if it was more instructions. *Should she open it in front of Owen? No, no way.* Thanking the stewardess, she put the envelope in her purse and asked Owen to let her out so she could go to the restroom.

Hurrying toward the restroom, she wondered if this was what Josh's life had been like. The lack of trust, the looking behind her to see if someone was back there, being afraid of strangers, not knowing if she was doing the right or wrong thing. Maybe Josh had been right to protect her years ago. Could she have handled all this then? She would have been terrified for the girls. But no matter what, it was never right to leave her. He should have explained to her. She deserved that much.

Balancing against the sink, she opened the envelope. There was a short note telling her that as soon as she arrived in Denver to destroy, actually tear up and flush all the documents with the name of Angela Simmons, then use the new ones with the name of Carla Martin.

She had another flight scheduled to leave Denver for Chicago at four o'clock in the morning. There was barely enough time to do as Josh asked. She had to pick up her suitcase at baggage claim then get to the next terminal. She didn't have a clue how far away that was. Slipping the new papers in her purse, she got back to her seat just as the descent into Denver was beginning. Owen was looking up at her expectantly.

Jennie sat down and buckled up. She had no intention of telling him anything. He had not mentioned the ponies so he could not be from Josh, no matter what he said. She would have to find some way to get away from him in Denver.

Sighing, Blakely said, "Please, Jennie, I want to help you. I don't know how else to prove it."

Jennie smiled sweetly and said, "Thanks. You did help me and I appreciate it."

Chapter 31

WHEN DAVENPORT ARRIVED AT the Compound he was exhausted and completely keyed up. The last twenty-four hours had been non-stop. Getting down the snowy mountain from Blackhawk to Denver had been a feat in itself. He had called in all the favors due him, laid on security, and completed the remaining plans to get Jennie to the Compound. She would be safe here.

Josh Davenport, known in Scotland as Alexander Cameron, had the quiet demeanor and look of a college professor, but that was deceptive. He was intense and driven and it wasn't in his nature to wait. This was going to be an excruciating day. There would be no rest for him until Jennie arrived.

Several identity changes as well as plane changes would make it almost impossible for anyone to trace her. *Almost* was the problem. It was driving him crazy that he was not with her, but he knew his presence would make them much more visible and only endanger Jennie. So, he gritted his teeth and prepared to wait. With luck, she could get to the Compound late Friday night or Saturday, more likely Sunday.

The president wasn't happy about Davenport stepping down although he wasn't surprised. He approved the choice for a successor. They agreed that Josh would continue until he got his replacement up on everything, at least a year or so, with the understanding that Josh would be turning more and more over to his successor. The man Davenport had chosen didn't know yet so he still had that hurdle to get past. He anticipated no great resistance. After all, he would be on hand. The new man would never have to operate naked the way he had. As far as INSCOM was concerned, he didn't plan to tell them anything until Jennie was safe in the Compound.

Everything had been ready for him when he arrived; the changes and additions to the security systems were up and operating. All areas could be monitored by camera from his office; the castle itself, the adjacent grounds to the far perimeters of the property. Anyone stepping foot on the Compound property would set off an alert. The installation had taken almost a year to complete.

He stood at the huge window in the library. Time at the Compound was six hours ahead of Texas and he was already seeing the glow of the sunrise. It was a spectacular sight breaking over the mountains and the lake. "Incredible," he said. Tired as he was, it still thrilled him.

He looked down at the gardens he loved and had so carefully tended over the last couple of years, and then to the maze he and Angus, the gardener, were working on. He never imagined he would get such enjoyment out of gardening, but there was a wholesomeness about it that had been missing in his life. It was clean and pure and undefiled. Jennie will love all this. She had always wanted a pretty yard and this was so much more.

Beyond all that was a lake, or as Angus called it, the loch. The mountains soared wildly upwards in jagged peaks. He loved rising early in the morning and walking outside in the cool air. It was so different from the hot steamy air of Texas. Even in the midst of summer it was only about sixty to seventy degrees. The castle represented total peace to him.

Exhaling noisily, he wished for Jennie as he had every day for the past six years and even more so since he had bought the castle. Remembering how they had planned on building one on their property near Denton, he could visualize her excitement. More importantly, she would be safe here. They would finally have their dream. Settling down in the big leather chair by the windows, he forced his body to relax and let his mind wander …

WHENEVER HE HAD LEAVE TIME from G-2, he would take off on a walking trip. It had proven to be the most anonymous thing he could do. After he discovered this remote area in the Highlands of Scotland he never went anywhere else nor had he ever told anyone about it, not even his partner, Blakely. Hiking in the mountains had kept him sane; there was purity about it. It had been the only place he could get completely away from the political arena.

He still remembered every detail of that day when he first saw the castle. As he topped the mountain, it burst upon him like a bolt of lightening. Never had any place so completely called to him; it was what he had been searching for all his life.

The mountains were purple with heather, the loch was azure blue, and the trees around it were brilliant green. It took his breath away and made him want to paint again. It made him feel human. From that first view the castle didn't look very large, but distance could be deceptive. He could see pale colored rock, three round turrets and many other peaks in the roof. Nestled in huge green trees, the castle looked like it was growing out of the mountain. One side sloped sharply down to the lake.

Something deep inside him recognized it as home. He had to get closer.

Picking up his pace, he tramped down the pathway, across the valley, and up the hill to the castle as fast as he could. From where he was, he couldn't even tell if it was the ruins of a castle, which he saw often on his walks, or an intact structure. It didn't matter. He wanted it.

When he drew near, he found a narrow gravel road that twisted and turned up the hill to iron gates which were open and in good repair. Enormous trees hung over the lane like a canopy and the sun made beautiful mosaic patterns on the ground as the light streamed through the leaves. When he reached the last curve of the road he saw the castle and caught his breath. It wasn't a ruin. It looked lived in and well maintained. It reminded him of a painting he had done years ago, when he still had dreams.

Nearing the front entrance he saw a large black wreath hanging on the door. While he was standing there debating with himself as to whether he should intrude in a home where someone must have died, the front door opened.

"May I assist ye, sir?" asked the man at the door.

"Possibly, I was trying to decide whether it would be an intrusion to knock," Josh said as he indicated the wreath on the door.

"The master died several weeks ago."

"You're not the owner, then?"

"Nae, sir. I am Duncan, the butler. Are ye lost? Nae a body ever comes by here unexpectedly."

"No, I'm not lost. I rather think I've just found my way for the first time in a many years," he said, thinking how much Jennie would love this place. It was so like the castle they had dreamed of building. "Would you know, Duncan, if the property is for sale?"

"Aye, sir, it is. The family is packing and in the process of moving to the city. It's much too isolated here for two ladies. The mistress is meeting with the real estate folk this afternoon."

Davenport introduced himself as Alexander Cameron, the name he had used since he had been coming to the Highlands. He had known from the beginning that it would be necessary to get out someday and had established another identity. His passport and international driver's license in this name had been in place for a couple of years as well as a local bank account in Inverness. He always stayed in the same small, family-run hotel in Tain. He was well known as Alex Cameron, the very private and wealthy professor from America, who loved to walk in the Highlands. He had made a number of friends in Inverness and the little village of Tain.

Davenport and Duncan walked around the grounds of the castle with Duncan telling him all about it. Davenport stopped, stared with disbelief, and then laughter rolled out of him when he saw the little ponies in the stable. *Perfect, even the little ponies are here.* He visualized his daughters riding them until he remembered they were young women now. *Maybe the grandchildren,* he thought sadly.

Duncan invited him inside and introduced him to Mrs. Sinclair and her daughter. They talked for quite a while. Originally from Glasgow, she was planning to move back to her family home there. The estate was much too large and remote for the two of them. Davenport talked about the possibility of buying it, but she had no idea of the value of it. She said she would have to discuss that with her solicitor and the real estate people. However, she was anxious to sell the estate. If he wanted to look around, Duncan could show him about. With that, she excused herself.

The entrance of the castle opened into a great hall featuring a massive rock fireplace in the middle and dark paneled walls that were hung with enormous tapestries. Several heavily carved benches and chests filled the area. The floor was ancient, rose-colored flagstone worn to a fine patina with a large oriental rug in the middle. The staircase curved upwards from both sides of the fireplace and the arched windows on the center landing of the staircase were brilliant with light coming through the stained glass. Duncan said the castle dated back to the 1300s in the oldest sections.

On this first level was the drawing room where he had tea with Mrs. Sinclair, a dining room, a billiards room, and several other rooms. The kitchens and servant quarters were on a lower level. Below that were the dungeons, but no one goes there anymore Duncan told him.

As they climbed the stairs to the second floor, Duncan recounted some of the history of the house. People that Davenport had read about in school textbooks had been guests of the castle.

Davenport was excited to see the magnificent library on the second floor. It ran almost the length of the castle and was filled to capacity with leather bound books, very likely first editions. It was all he could do to keep his hands off them. Several leather couches and overstuffed chairs formed three different sitting areas. Along the end of the room was a massive library table with books scattered on it. The arched windows looked toward the loch and the mountains.

"Would you know, Duncan, if Mrs. Sinclair plans to sell the furniture with the castle? And the books, will she sell them?" Josh asked hopefully.

"I don't know, sir. But I assume much of the furniture will bide with the castle. My guess is most of the books as well. She will nae have room for all these at her parent's home in Glasgow. I would venture to say that she will take the more personal items and leave the remainder."

"That's perfect. I'm interested in whatever she doesn't take."

"I assume, sir, that ye are an American on holiday. Were ye looking for a place to buy?"

"In a way, I've taken walking trips through this part of Scotland for a long time. This is the most peaceful place that I've ever seen. And if you're asking, yes, I have the means, Duncan."

"I apologize, sir. I did nae mean to be rude, but I would nae want the mistress to get her hopes up. Estates this large don't usually sell quickly. She is nae well, and it would be a godsend for her."

"Do you know how much land is connected to the estate?"

"More than a thousand acres, sir, it's nae as large as many estates in Scootlund, but all ye can see in any direction belongs to it."

"That's amazing. I must have been walking on Sinclair property for hours. What are your plans, Duncan, when the estate is sold? Will you be going with Mrs. Sinclair?"

"Nae, sir. Her parents' home is fully staffed. We have nae got plans yet. My guidwife is housekeeper and we've been here for almost thirty years. This has been our home since we were first married. Our bairns grew up here. The master was very guid to us and left us enough to buy a wee cottage somewhere for our retirement, but Mrs. Duncan says it will nae be home."

"If I am able to purchase the estate, would you and Mrs. Duncan consider staying on with me? I do a great deal of traveling and will need someone to help me and live here as caretakers."

"Mrs. Duncan does nae want to leave, sir. Nor do I—this is home. I don't think we could stand living in the city."

"Well, Duncan, if you're willing, let's shake on it," said Davenport. "Where I come from a handshake is as good as a contract."

"Are ye sure, sir? Ye have nae met Mrs. Duncan."

"I'm sure. I'm very sure. You know this castle and the grounds in a way I cannot. I'll need you here, Duncan."

Duncan smiled broadly. "In that case, Mr. Cameron, I will gab with Mrs. Duncan about it, but I think I can say, we would be glad to bide."

Davenport gave him his address in Tain and told him to please ask Mrs. Sinclair to have her solicitor call him. Reluctantly, he left the castle and walked down the steep road toward Tain. He knew he wasn't going to rest until he could return.

"I'm sorry to disturb ye, sir, but there is a telephone call on your private line," Duncan said, as he entered the library. Duncan had more than lived up to Davenport's expectations and had become a friend as well as butler. He had proven to be exceedingly loyal and had been trusted with a limited version of Davenport's situation.

Davenport went instantly to an almost invisible door on the side of the fireplace and entered a hidden room that he had made his office. It looked like a small, modern corporate office. He had the latest computers, copy machines, fax equipment and phone lines installed at the same time he had made renovations to other parts of the castle, including modernizing the bathrooms and the kitchens, which had firmly established him in Mrs. Duncan's affections.

Quickly picking up the phone, Davenport heard the words he had been waiting to hear. "The package for Suzanne Smith was picked up at the post office just before noon."

Standing very still, it was hard to believe she was actually on her way. Once again, he thought through all the next steps of Jennie's journey, carefully analyzing her safety. He knew the trickiest part would be getting out of Dallas without being followed, but hopefully his colleague would block anyone following her at the car rental.

"Thank you, my friend. Your help is greatly appreciated," he answered.

He had orchestrated the plans with extreme care using dependable contacts he had made in past years; calling in favors. No one had any idea of what they were transporting, or for what reason, so he was comfortable with all the package deliveries. The problem was the accidental element, the one he couldn't predict.

He returned to the library wondering again if he should have confided in his partner, Owen Blakely. Maybe, he thought for the hundredth time, he should have had Blakely follow her. But there was an additional danger in that. He knew beyond a doubt that Blakely was loyal to him, but if anyone was watching her, they would be quick to spot a tail and wonder why.

Unable to sit still, he made the rounds of the castle checking to see if everything was ready for Jennie. He realized how confusing and difficult this would be for her. He knew she would never have married again if she'd had any idea he was alive. He also knew she wouldn't have married again if she hadn't cared deeply for the man. And that was driving him crazy.

"Oh, Jennie, can you understand why I had to do this? Will you be able to forgive me?" he agonized, as he prepared himself for the long wait until the next call.

Several anxious hours after the first call, he received a second one. The second envelope had been delivered to Mrs. Simmons shortly before landing in Denver.

He was told there had been a slight altercation in the Austin airport. It appeared some man had accosted her at boarding time, but a tall blond man had intervened. Jennie had boarded the plane without further mishap.

Davenport stormed around the library. The chances of it being a random attack were slim to nothing. The unpredictable had already shown up. The blond man must be Blakely. How could he have found out that Jennie was leaving?

"Damn, I should have pulled Blakely in to begin with. Now he's operating in the dark, and Jennie's scared. She won't know to trust him."

Chapter 32

JENNIE HURRIED AWAY FROM the plane, anxious to get where Blakely couldn't follow. She could feel someone watching her. She didn't know if it was him or someone else.

Grabbing her suitcase off the turnstile, she rushed in the nearest women's restroom and into a stall. Jennie used her manicure scissors to cut up the driver's license for Angela Simmons and tore the rest of the papers into small pieces. She watched as they flushed away. She didn't want any bits and pieces to remain.

When she came out, she didn't spot Owen, however, that didn't mean he was gone. She was sure he was someplace nearby. Checking the big screens for departures, she found her gate number. As she trekked down the mile-long terminal, she was thankful she had on comfortable shoes. She made it to the gate just in time to check in. Holding her boarding pass firmly in her hand, she stayed by the desk not wanting to risk what had happened in Austin. *Just stay with the crowd.*

Boarding went smoothly and she didn't see Owen again. If he was really with G-2, she figured she wasn't rid of him yet. Looking down at her paperwork, she wondered if she could keep up with all these names. She was Carla Martin this time, returning home to Chicago after vacationing in Colorado. Take off was good and when the plane leveled off she looked at her watch. It was a three-hour flight. She was still tired and that was long enough for another nap.

Jennie woke up about an hour out of Chicago and looked around. Nothing had changed; she didn't see Owen or the man from Austin as she went to the restroom. It was tiny, hardly enough room to turn around. Splashing water on her face, she opened the makeup bag and tried to cover the dark circles under her eyes. She left feeling better and asked the stewardess for coffee and something to eat. She had been asleep when breakfast was served, the stewardess said, but she could bring coffee and a sweet roll.

The plane landed on schedule in Chicago. She walked through the tunnel and into the lobby on alert to everyone around her. After the Austin incident, she was a little scared of what might happen. Her instructions said to go to passenger assistance and ask for messages for Carla Martin. It felt good to walk after sitting in the plane for three hours. Jennie located the baggage claim area, retrieved her suitcase, and was really glad she had gotten one with wheels. Hooking her makeup bag to the handle, she hunted for passenger assistance. She hesitated to ask for directions.

It took a bit of searching but she found it and asked if there were any messages for her. The clerk checked her book and said, "Yes, we have a package for you. It's at the passenger assistance counter in Terminal B."

"Terminal B. How do I get there?" Jennie inquired.

"The clerk pointed to a moving sidewalk on her left. "The easiest way will be to go on that until you reach Terminal B. Passenger assistance will be just on your right when you get off. I'll let them know you're on the way." Dejected, Jennie thanked her.

The sidewalk moved much faster than she could have walked and it was certainly easier. She wasn't sure she could have made it all the way. Arriving at the counter, she gave the clerk her identification and was handed the package. Thanking her, Jennie turned away, and once again she ran into trouble. One man stepped in front of her, another came from behind. They grabbed her arms.

"Leave me alone," she yelled angrily. "Get out of my way. I'll scream if you don't let go of me."

"Be quiet, Mrs. Scott. You're coming with us."

"No, I'm not. Someone will help me." And with that Jennie yelled as loud as she could, "Help me, these men are hurting me—help me." Then she started screaming and struggling to get away.

Several people stopped and looked, but no one offered help. The two men started pulling her faster and she kept on screaming. She could see people reacting now, and she yelled at them to find a guard. Then as she was being pulled outside, she saw a welcome sight—a tall blond man was bearing down on them with fury in his face. When he got there he grabbed the man on her left. The tension and frustration of the day was in Jennie's arms when she swung her purse at the other man. He let go of her arm to shield his face, and Jennie slammed her knee hard into him.

Down he went, just like they had taught her in self-defense classes. She was elated. Grabbing her suitcase, she started running down the sidewalk toward the taxicabs. As she was getting in, Owen caught up to her, told her to scoot over, and he scrambled in.

"Get out of here as fast as you can," Owen ordered the driver. "Take us to the Drake Hotel. Are you all right, Jennie? Did they hurt you?"

"No, I'm not hurt. Actually, I feel good. I defended myself, and I didn't know I could. I've never had to before."

"You did great. I would have had a hard time with two of them. What have you got in that purse? That man went down in a flash."

"Just the usual stuff—I think it was my knee that did it." Jennie laughed. "When they came up and grabbed me, I suddenly remembered what I'd been taught. They told me never to go quietly, to scream and keep screaming. To swing my purse at his face if I got the opportunity, then bring my knee up as fast and hard as I could and run like crazy. So I did it and it worked."

"You did great, Jennie. I'll have to remember to stay on your good side and away from your knees."

"Thank you, Owen. I owe you again." Jennie said quietly, clutching the package to her chest. "I think I'm ready to listen to you, but first I have to see what is in here."

"Go ahead. I won't look unless you ask me to. I know you are getting instructions from Josh. I've tried to think of some way to reassure you, but I don't know where he is either. I'm not out to get him or you, Jennie. Please believe me."

"I want to, Owen. You have helped me twice now. I'm sorry, but I can't help thinking, what if you set this up to make me trust you?"

"I don't know how to get around that, Jennie. Except maybe to say that I could take that package away from you, but I won't. What I can tell you are some personal things about Josh that others wouldn't know. Josh and I were partners for several years. He saved my life once in an impossible situation. No one else would have come for me. I owe him my life. That's why I'm trying to protect you. I know he loved you and your daughters and deeply regretted having to leave you. Do you know why he had his death faked?"

"I know a little. He told me in a letter that it was the only way he could protect all of us from a group that was after him."

"That's right, Jennie. As long as they thought he was dead, you were safe. And you were monitored constantly."

"What do you mean monitored constantly?" she flinched, thinking about the phone calls and the chip in her arm. Her hand unconsciously rubbed the spot where the band aid was. She was grateful the chip was gone.

"A microchip was injected in your arm. It's called a transponder. G-2 could track your location and also record things you said. The phone calls you got when no one answered downloaded what was on the chip."

"You mean everything I said was there, even private things?" Jennie questioned.

"Yes, unless it malfunctioned. You should know that Josh didn't agree to the chip being placed in your arm. He was told about it after the fact."

"That's invasion of privacy, big time. That has to be illegal."

"Probably, but legality wasn't their major concern. You're probably being tracked right now."

Wondering whether she should tell Owen that she had the chip removed, Jennie asked, "Didn't you say it was G-2 following me?"

"No. Those guys were definitely not G-2. I'm not sure who they were. There's more we need to talk about, Jennie, but right now you better check your instructions and see what you are supposed to do next. I've got the cab headed for a safe house unless your instructions say you need to get back to the airport for another flight."

Jennie had been anxiously fingering the package. She tore the paper off the shoebox-sized package and the usual envelope was there containing a drivers license, passport and airplane ticket in the name of Christine Logan, and a bulky parcel on the bottom. The departure time was nine o'clock tonight. The instructions said to go to a hotel, get some rest, change her clothes, and wear the wig that is in the bottom of the box. The last words of the note warned her to be very cautious.

Deciding it was useless not to tell Owen since he had found her again, she told him that her next flight was tonight at nine o'clock and she would welcome a bed and bath and change of clothes.

But, she didn't tell him about the wig or her new name.

Chapter 33

MASON SILVERMAN SWIVELED HIS chair around to look out the window. Something was wrong, he could feel it. His sense of survival had been his greatest asset. Without that, he wouldn't still be here after all these years. He trusted his gut feelings.

Unable to concentrate on the job he needed to do, he let his mind dwell on what he was feeling. He had felt a reserve from the president for some time, but hadn't been able to identify exactly what the problem was, or if there actually was one. However, his gut wasn't often wrong.

Located in several large complexes in Fort Meade, Maryland, NSA operates in relative obscurity analyzing intelligence data from all over the world. Formed in November 1952 by President Truman and the National Security Council, its main function is to assist the president in formulating foreign policy and intelligence priorities. The president, as commander-in-chief, is the final authority over all the data and NSA was responsible only to the president.

In effect, Silverman answered to no one but the president, and he worked diligently to control what the president did and did not hear. Surviving several administrations and investigations, the closest he'd ever come to having his cover blown was back in '77 when Davenport died. A most convenient death for everyone, he thought once again. Silverman swung around in his chair and stared out the window. It had been too convenient, and the possibility of Davenport being alive had worried him for years.

Davenport played him like a novice, and he couldn't forget or forgive that. He would have killed him with his own hands if he could have gotten to him. If the Illuminati had any inkling Davenport was alive, well, that didn't bear thinking about. His life wouldn't be worth a plug nickel.

Something had always needled him about Davenport's death, but he had never been able to put his finger on it. It was altogether too timely and in this business coincidences were always suspicious. It disturbed him so much that he had placed a permanent surveillance on the wife.

It had taken a bit of doing to get his man in with G-2, but it finally came together, and his agent had kept him informed of all her activities. His connection with Silverman had been kept secret from G-2, and, of course, it had cost him, Nathan Scott was money hungry. But that was a good thing. Scott would never do anything to jeopardize this extra income. Besides the money, Silverman held a power card in his safe and Scott knew it. If he ever got out of line he'd send it on to G-2, and Scott would be in the brig before nightfall.

Silverman got up and went to a bar in the corner of his office. Watching the amber liquid trickle into his glass he smiled. Scott would demand more money if he had any idea that Davenport might still be alive. Even though the fool fell in love with the woman and actually married her, Scott had still alerted him about the investigation the wife started. Until this happened, there had never been anything real about his fears that Davenport was alive. Not completely trusting Scott, Silverman had sent another agent to watch her. This man had provided him with critical information about her movements.

He knew exactly when she arrived at the Austin airport and boarded a plane to Denver. The problem was, the man who was tailing her got a little aggressive and screwed up. He was only supposed to follow her, not question her.

"Fools, I'm surrounded by fools. You'd think they could follow a simple order. I didn't tell him to interfere, just watch her," Silverman muttered. He swallowed his scotch and poured another one.

"Now, she's alerted. And more than that, it sounded like Blakely from G-2 was also tailing her. That's another scenario—why is G-2 having the Davenport woman followed? What do they know that I don't?"

Washington, D. C.

REAVES HAD BEEN STANDING behind the operative that was monitoring *JDavenport* for some time. He watched the signal growing fainter. There was no way they could predict how long it would keep transmitting. What a time for it to die. General Thurman was not going to be happy.

"Lock in the location before it fades completely," Reaves ordered.

"I'll try," was the response.

"You'd better, or both our heads are in a noose," said Reaves.

"I got it. The signal is coming from around Tulsa, Oklahoma."

The operator honed in on the location while Reaves watched anxiously.

"Okay, here's the best we're going to get. It's stopped moving on the south side of Tulsa in a small town called Sapulpa at the intersection of I44 and State Highway 33."

"That's good. Keep watching. Let me know immediately if it changes."

Bracing himself for the explosion, Reaves told General Thurman that Jennie Davenport's signal was fading and it had stopped moving in a small town just south of Tulsa."

"Get a team there immediately," ordered Thurman. "And find her. Check all motels and hotels. She's probably stopping for the night. Give them her description. I want her brought in. She's our best chance to lure Davenport out of hiding. He'll come for her. "

"Yes, sir, that signal's not going to last much longer."

"Damn," muttered the general. "Get our people there before it quits."

DALLAS, TEXAS

HERMAN WILKINS PACED BACK and forth in his office at the precinct. He had listened to Jennie's message to back off and her thanks, but now he was more worried than ever. That message didn't sound right, she sounded nervous, maybe scared, he wasn't sure what. He had tried to call her all day and had left several messages for her or Nathan. He had not been able to reach Kris or Laurie either. He didn't know what the hell was going on.

What he did know was that he had gone back to the grave last night and looked at it carefully. The only spot where the ground had been disturbed was where the headstone should be. He dug around with his hand and found that he could lift out a square of grass. The marker had been removed. He'd bet his pension the casket was still there.

Herman knew he was going to get himself in trouble, but he couldn't stop. He had arranged for a crew to go in there tonight and open it up. He also had a dental technician coming to look at the skull and take pictures of the teeth. Then the crew would close the grave up and put the grass back as best they could. If they were real lucky, they would get in and out before anyone found them.

He picked up the phone again and dialed Kris. He had to reach one of them and find out what was going on with Jennie.

Chapter 34

THE TAXI PULLED UP to the front door of the Drake Hotel and the doorman hurried to greet them. Blakely tipped him, grabbed the luggage and took off across the lobby toward the elevators without checking in. Jennie had to run to keep up with him. Taking the elevator to the second floor, he went to the exit door, and then down the staircase to a service entrance that led outside.

When they emerged from the hotel they were in a sort of alleyway. Blakely stopped, looked around then walked rapidly away from the hotel saying, "Only a little further, Jennie."

They rounded a corner and she saw several old, rundown buildings on both sides of the street, definitely not a very desirable part of Chicago. She followed Blakely to the second building on the left and up the crumbling front steps to the entrance. He punched the doorbell impatiently. It wasn't anywhere she wanted to stay; she would rather go back to the hotel. The door opened a crack then closed and Jennie heard a chain being removed.

An elderly woman opened the door wide and greeted him with a smile. "It's been a long time since you've been here. I got your rooms ready as soon as you called me, the usual ones. You know where they are. Let me know when you want to eat."

Blakely motioned Jennie to follow him. They went toward the back of the hall and up a narrow staircase. The hallway was dimly lit with faded, peeling wallpaper and dull wooden floors so it was a real surprise when she walked into her room. It was cheery and clean and bright.

"What is this place, Owen?"

"It's the safe house I told you about. We should be fine here until your next flight. Let's freshen up and grab a couple of hours sleep, then Dora will bring us some food and we can talk."

Jennie agreed. She looked longingly at the bed, but a hot shower and a change of clothes won out. She was so tired by the time she crawled into the bed, she was asleep before her head hit the pillow.

Chapter 35

IT WAS ALMOST DARK when she woke. Relieved to find it was only a little after five, she turned over and was half dozing when a loud crash brought her straight up; something slammed against the wall. She jumped up, shoved her feet into her loafers, and listened. There was scuffling sounds and men yelling. One voice was familiar and shouting, "Get the hell out of here."

That was Owen. Not pausing to think, she grabbed her things and ran

WHEN THE DOOR CRASHED AGAINST the wall and the two men stormed in, Blakely shot up from the bed yelling. He hoped Jennie could hear him. He had to stall and give her time to get away, "What do you think you're doing bursting in here?"

"Where's Jennie Davenport?" demanded the big man.

"Who's that?" Blakely stalled. *Get out of here, Jennie,* he kept thinking.

"Don't play dumb with us. Where is she?"

"Not a clue. Who are you?" he asked dodging the fist that came toward him.

"One more time, where is she?"

Blakely didn't answer him and the man slugged him. He saw it coming, but couldn't get out of the way. That was the last thing he knew for some time.

When he came to he was alone and flat on the floor with what felt like a broken jaw. He pulled up and staggered to the bathroom and splashed water on his face. He hurt like hell and looked worse. Then he remembered Jennie.

Running to the room next door, he yanked the door open without knocking. It was empty, the bed rumpled, but no sign of a struggle. Her suitcase was gone. Hopefully she understood his yelling to get out and those thugs hadn't taken her. He dropped down in the chair and rubbed his head trying to stop the pain. It was hard to think.

A moment later Dora tiptoed through the open door and gasped when she saw Blakely's face. "What happened here? Do I need to call for help?"

"No time, Dora. But you can help me clean up. Did you see the two men who came in?"

Dora went into the bathroom for a wash cloth as she answered him. "No, I went out for a few minutes and when I got back the door was standing open. Someone must have picked the lock."

"Did you see the lady that was with me?" Blakely asked, still rubbing his jaw.

"No. I haven't seen her. Let's go downstairs. Your jaw is swelling, but I don't think it's broken. You're talking pretty good. We need some disinfectant and bandages for your face."

Dora cleaned off the blood and bandaged the cut. She told him he needed a couple of stitches but she'd put a butterfly bandage on it for now. There wasn't anything she could do about his bruised jaw. It was already discolored. He wasn't going to win any beauty contests for a while.

Blakely thanked her and ran out to find Jennie. He wouldn't want to face Davenport if anything happened to her.

Negotiating the narrow staircase was not easy with the suitcase and it took Jennie a couple of minutes. Finally down the stairs, she cautiously poked her head out of the dark stairwell. She didn't see anyone there. She quickly darted outside and looked frantically around. She turned the way she and Owen had come.

She hurried as fast as she could, her footsteps echoing eerily in the narrow passageway. When she reached the service entrance and pulled on the door handle, it wouldn't open. Scowling in frustration, she looked behind her to see if anyone was following, but it was so dark in the alley she could barely see. She wanted out of this scary place.

She ran toward the lights, but slid to a rapid stop when she saw the doorman of the Drake Hotel. It was the same man. She didn't want him to see her coming in again with her suitcase. She waited a moment until he was busy helping some people out of a taxi and then rushed in. She saw a sign pointing to the public telephones and Jennie hoped that the restrooms would be near them. Her stomach was churning. She had to get out of sight, somewhere.

The ladies room had a small sitting area with a sofa and vanity. Jennie dropped her bag and bent over trying to catch her breath. Had Owen told her to get out or was he telling someone in his room to get out. She wasn't sure. Maybe he was talking to her hoping whoever broke in wouldn't realize what he was doing. It must be those men from the airport. Either way, she realized, she was on her own.

Jennie sat down at the vanity and opened her makeup bag where she had stuffed the dark wig. She brushed her hair back and slipped it on. "Wow, it does make a difference, but I look too pale." She added blush, more eye makeup and a darker lipstick. That's better. The dark hair needed brighter makeup. With that and her change of clothes at the safe house, she didn't think she would be recognized.

She checked her new airline ticket, driver's license, and the passport that had been added this time. "I'm now Christine Logan. Maybe Christy will do if someone asks my name, sounds a little more natural. Christy Logan. That'll do." She cut up the Carla Martin ID and flushed it. Her next plane was supposed to take off at nine. If the men that accosted her were the ones at the safe house, they would more than likely go back to the airport when they didn't find her. So, the airport was out.

But what about Owen, she should have checked on him, even though she probably couldn't have done anything to help him. She hoped he was all right. He sounded like he did know Josh and he had helped her when she needed it, but he never said the right words. He didn't mention the ponies. How did she know the safe house wasn't a trap? Well, she wasn't going back there.

She was going to be off the schedule that Josh had set up for her, but there was lots of money so he must have anticipated she might have to change something. Pulling out her instructions she read through them once more. Leave Chicago on the nine o'clock plane for London, arrive at Gatwick Airport, and take the train to Victoria Station. Then find the lock boxes, use the enclosed key to open it, and retrieve the next set of directions.

Putting all but the key back in the money pouch around her waist, she pinned the key inside her bra. No matter what else happens, she couldn't lose that key. That was her only way to find Josh.

Right now, she had to get out of Chicago without being recognized. The train was a possibility, but where should she go? Whoever was following her would probably check both the Chicago and New York airports so flying was out. Where else could she get a plane to London? Miami is too far away. Dallas is definitely out. Atlanta—Atlanta is international, yes, that could work. Train to Philly and then south. She could rent a car, but that would be a long hard drive. What she needed was a travel agent; too late in the day for that. So it has to be the train to Atlanta. Maybe not what Josh would have planned, but it's the best she could think of. She closed her bags and left the ladies room.

On her way to the front door she passed the hotel gift shop and saw several raincoats in the display window. That might be a good idea. She found a tan one that fit, and then noticed some large duffel bags you could sling over your shoulder. She grabbed a dark tan one and took it and the raincoat to the cashier. She paid and ran back to the ladies room.

Jennie found she could get everything in the duffel bag, including her makeup case. She would be much more mobile and wouldn't have to check any baggage. She shoved her suitcase behind the sofa. Stepping back, she couldn't see it without bending over and she thought that it might not be discovered for several days unless the hotel had some really efficient cleaning people.

With the raincoat on, the bag over her shoulder, and the dark wig, Jennie knew she didn't look like Jennie. She was now Christy and she felt like her. Excitement rose up in her. "I can do this. Nothing is going to stop me from getting to Josh."

With that thought in mind she walked confidently out of the hotel, nodded to the doorman, and walked briskly away. When she approached the corner, she saw a very rumpled and anxious Owen hurrying toward her. Not slowing her pace she kept going. He never gave her a second glance.

"Yes! Yes, I did it!"

BLAKELY STOPPED AS HE ROUNDED the corner and scanned the street. He saw the doorman unloading luggage from a cab, a couple walking into the hotel, and a dark-haired woman rushed past him.

Running his hands through his hair and straightening his jacket, he made himself walk slowly into the lobby. This was the only place in Chicago that Jennie had been and she might have come back. He looked around the lobby. He checked the hallway, the phone booths, the restrooms, and then he noticed the gift shop. Maybe the clerk had seen her.

"Excuse me. I wonder if you could help me. I was supposed to meet a friend here and I'm a bit late. She's a small, blond woman in her forties but she looks younger. She may have gotten tired waiting for me and come in here to browse," Blakely told the clerk.

"No, sir, it's been a slow evening. The only person who came in was a dark-haired lady. She bought a tan raincoat and duffel bag."

Blakely's antennae went up. "Did she have a suitcase on wheels with her?"

"Yes, she did. I assumed she had been shopping and needed another bag. You'd be surprised how many people have to buy another one when they visit here."

"Thanks for your help," he called, running out the door.

The box Jennie opened with Josh's instructions had to contain more than new ID. He'd lay money that the package had a wig in it. She would have to get somewhere she wouldn't be seen to move her clothes to the duffel bag—the ladies room. He bolted down the hall, knocked loudly on the door and hollered *attendant,* then barged in. He could see her putting her suitcase on the couch and transferring her clothes to the duffel bag. Bending over he found the suitcase behind the couch.

"Good job, Jennie. I like your style," he said.

Leaving the hotel, he settled into a fast jog in the direction that he had seen the dark-haired woman going. She'd been wearing a tan raincoat. She'd thought fast and reacted well when the men approached her at the airport. It seemed she had done it again.

Chapter 36

IT TOOK A COUPLE of hours for the G-2 team to fly into Tulsa. Then more time to drive to Sapulpa.

They went directly to the location where the transponder had quit moving. Two motels were at the intersection. The men immediately started trying to pick up the signal with a hand-held sensor. Walking in front of the rooms they aimed the sensor toward each one then around the parked cars. The Days Inn was huge and had at least a hundred cars around it. Nothing showed up at this motel so they moved to the Best Western across the street.

They followed the same pattern. Near the back of the side wing of the motel they picked up a faint beep. Holding the sensor closer to the door, the signal faded. They backed off and walked around the cars. At last, the signal got stronger near the back of a pickup. Flashing a light around the bed, the man spotted a tiny reflection. Calling to the team, they climbed in the truck, moved the sensor around until they found the minute-sized transponder and carefully secured it.

The night manager of the motel took his sweet time studying the identification the G-2 men showed him. Muttering that he better not get in trouble over this or he'd sue the government, he reluctantly checked his records, found the Illinois license, and gave the uniformed men the room number.

Running to the room, they banged on the door. A sleepy-eyed man peered out at them. "What's going on?"

"Open the door, sir," the agent said, flashing their ID.

"Let me see it," he said waving his fingers through the cracked door. "G-2, what's that?"

"We're a division of the Army, sir. We need to know if you're traveling with a woman."

"No, I'm alone," he said. He slipped the chain off and opened the door, then handed the ID back to the men.

"Do you know a Jennie Davenport or a Jennie Scott?"

"No, never heard of either one."

"Where did you drive from today?"

"Fort Worth, I had business down there. I'm on my way back home to Illinois. What's this about?"

"Exactly where did you go in Fort Worth?"

"Well, let's see. I got there about ten this morning, went to the stockyards, met with some men about cattle, and then dropped a package off for my wife. Her sister works at the Kimball Art Museum, and I took her a birthday present. What's this about?"

"We need your name and address in case we need to contact you again. Thank you for your help."

The rumpled man ran his hand through his hair, yawned, got his billfold, and handed over a business card saying that the least they could do was explain what was going on. The G-2 agents thanked him again and left.

"Damn, the general's going to explode," said the sergeant, as he dialed headquarters. "We found the transponder, General. It was tossed in the back of a pickup. She evidently had it removed. No sign of her here. The owner of the truck said he had been to the stockyards in Fort Worth and at the Kimball Art Museum delivering a package. He appears legit. She probably threw it in his pickup."

With several expletives, the General yelled, "Get back here now. We've been had—and by an amateur.

WASHINGTON, D.C.

THE GENERAL SLAMMED DOWN the phone and yelled at Reaves, "Someone's coaching the woman. She didn't know about the transponder. It has to be that rogue Davenport, possibly Blakely, they were partners. Or Nathan Scott, who knows what he's up to. I knew he would cause problems, trouble has always followed him. Get Blakely and Scott in here tonight. I don't care how you do it, just get them here. She has to be contained before she blows everything to hell and back."

Chapter 37

Thursday Evening
March 31, 1983
CHICAGO, ILLINOIS

J ENNIE HURRIED ON TOWARD the bright lights ahead of her. Seeing Macy's
department store in the distance, she knew she could find a cab there.
When she got there an idea hit her. Neiman Marcus in Dallas had a travel
department, maybe Macy's will. They did, and it was still open.

Jennie told the agent she wanted to go to London by the quickest route.
The woman checked several airlines, found one out of Chicago tonight, but
it was fully booked. Then Jennie asked her about tours, thinking that no
one would look for her on a tour. What would be leaving for London in the
next few days? Maybe she could join one. Late bookings were usually very
reasonable. She should have enough money.

"You're right," the woman said. "They even discount the last minute ones
to almost the cost of the airfare and you have a hotel to stay in." She found
several leaving from Chicago and Atlanta. Not wanting to appear anxious,
Jennie asked about the one leaving from Atlanta tomorrow and found it
actually stayed in the Victoria Station Hotel in London.

"I like the sound of that one. It would work well for me. I don't mind
going to Atlanta. However, I don't want to fly. What other choices can you
give me," she asked.

The agent handed her a train schedule as she made the tour reservation.
The late booking cost was only half what was printed in the tour book, and
Jennie easily covered it. "If you're in such a hurry" the woman said, "wouldn't
it be faster to fly to Atlanta?"

Jennie looked her straight in the eye and said without flinching, "I have a
very violent ex-husband that I'm trying to avoid and he's looking for me. My

family's in England and I'll be fine there. I'd really appreciate it if you would promise not to tell anyone about me. It's possible he might ask."

Understanding quickly showed in the woman's eyes, "You can depend on me and for what it's worth, I understand your situation. Good luck, my prayers will be with you."

Gripping the paperwork tightly, Jennie left and found a cab. As they pulled away from the department store she told the driver to take her to the Hilton Hotel, there had to be one somewhere in Chicago. She changed cabs at the hotel and hoped it would muddy up the trail. At least it was worth a try.

At the train station, Jennie looked cautiously around before getting out of the cab, but didn't see those men or anyone watching her. She hurried in and booked a sleeper on the Atlanta train. She went to the snack bar, picked up some coffee, sandwiches, cookies, fruit, and a couple of drinks for the trip. She found a seat where she could sit with her back to the wall and see the entire waiting area. She sipped her coffee and waited for her train to be called. Everything looked safe, at least as far as she could tell

THE SIDEWALK IN FRONT OF Macy's was crowded. Blakely had to slow to a walk to keep from bumping into Thursday night shoppers.

He stopped by the bus stop and was looking around when a dark-haired woman caught his attention. She had on a tan raincoat and was carrying a duffel bag over her shoulder. It was Jennie. She almost fooled him. He might have missed her if the gift shop lady hadn't told him about the coat. That was a stroke of luck. The change was dramatic. Davenport would be proud, she had done really well.

Aware the men who had invaded the safe house were probably somewhere around, Blakely wasn't about to approach her and tip them off to her disguise. He'd follow and try to lose them; better yet, find out who they were. She got in a cab. He hopped in the next one telling the driver to follow the one in front, but not to be obvious about it. Leaning back in the seat, he rubbed his aching jaw and wished for aspirin and a cold pack.

Those men weren't G-2, so who else was after Jennie? Only the general, Reaves, the president, a couple of senior G-2s knew Davenport was alive. The general didn't even know of Davenport's connection with the president. Could the Illuminati have kept a tail on her all this time? Doubtful, but possible, they had long memories.

Blakely's cab slowed and he watched Jennie switch cabs at the Hilton. He continued following the new cab. Keeping close watch behind him, he knew he'd picked up a tail. Someone had found him.

When Jennie's cab stopped at the train station, Blakely told the driver to turn the corner fast, slow down, but not stop. He handed some bills to the driver and plunged out of the moving cab and into a dark doorway before his tail turned the corner. He watched the car continue down the street following the cab. Waiting a few seconds to make sure it didn't stop, he ran back around the corner and into the train station.

Blakely kept his eye on Jennie while she waited in the ticket line then went to the lunch counter. He went to the ticket counter, flashed his ID, and asked about the destination of the woman in the tan raincoat. The clerk was reluctant, but Blakely kept tapping his ID on the counter until he had her destination and compartment number.

Ticket in hand, there was fifteen minutes before the train was due to leave. He had to let G-2 know the safe house had been compromised, even if it meant giving his location away, and he had to find out who else knew Davenport was alive. Blakely went to the bank of telephones and stepped in a booth.

"General Thurman, Blakely's on line one," called Reaves. "What's your location, Blakely?"

"Chicago."

"What the hell are you doing in Chicago?" yelled General Thurman, as he joined the conversation.

"Following your orders, sir, and tailing Jennie Davenport. First, you need to know that the safe house on Baker Street has been busted. I was there with her when two men broke in. Jennie got away, I wasn't so lucky."

"Details, Blakely, I want details."

"I followed her to Chicago. When she was leaving the airport two men accosted her. I didn't recognize them. I intervened and we got away safely. That's when I took her to the safe house and before I could contact you, the same two men broke into my room. I was slugged and when I came to, she was gone. There was no sign of a struggle in her room. I think she heard the fight, got scared and took off. I'm still looking for her, but I need to know who else is on her tail. Have you any idea, sir?"

"They're not ours. Our men followed the transponder to Oklahoma. She had it removed and threw it in a pickup truck where we found it. Someone has to be coaching her. Davenport must have told her about it and how to have it removed. This pretty much confirms she's on her way to him. You have to find her and stop her. We can't let her lead anyone to Davenport."

"I know, sir. I'm looking for her now. Who do you think they are?" Blakely asked expectantly.

"Don't know at this point. We're working on it, possibly the Illuminati. We know it's not Scott; he let her get away. Call in again in a couple of hours. I just issued orders for you to be brought in, don't wait so long to call next time. If I have to bring you in, you'll be in for good, Blakely. This is a team and I won't be kept in the dark. Understood?"

"Yes, sir, I'll call. Find out who these guys are. One has a fist like a baseball bat."

"Two hours, Blakely."

Blakely watched Jennie from a distance. In case the two men spotted him, he didn't want to get too close. The general was going to be mad again because he wouldn't be calling in any time soon. He would be on the train to Atlanta.

At least he'd have some time to think about who was tailing them and, more importantly, think about where Davenport could be. Copying Jennie, he went to the lunch counter and stocked up on food, aspirin, coffee, and a cup of ice. He swallowed some aspirin with his coffee and held the ice against his throbbing jaw.

The Atlanta train was announced and Jennie went straight to the boarding line. She had her supper with her, and Blakely hoped she wouldn't leave her compartment until the train arrived.

He saw her board, but he waited until the train was pulling out of the station. He jumped on at the last second. Leaning out, he watched for late boarders until they were out of the station and well down the tracks. He was satisfied their tail wasn't aboard. He'd have to be on alert if the train made any stops.

JENNIE FOUND HER COMPARTMENT WITHOUT a problem. Locking the door and pulling the window shade down, she collapsed gratefully on the small couch. She put the duffel bag on the floor and slipped out of her raincoat. Then she made sure the key was still pinned in her bra.

"So far, so good," she sighed.

FINDING A SEAT NEAR JENNIE'S compartment, Blakely settled down for a long, uncomfortable night.

Chapter 38

Thursday
March 31, 1983
CAMERON COMPOUND, SCOTLAND

DAVENPORT LOOKED ANXIOUSLY AT his watch again. It was seven in the morning in Chicago and her plane should be setting down. He worried about this connection. People had been known to disappear in Chicago. "It's a big city. I'll feel much better when I know she's out of there."

Catching movement out of the corner of his eye, he turned to see Darcy coming in the room with her hands full. "What have you got there, Darcy?"

"I'm sorry to bother ye, sir. I know ye are very worried about your wife's trip. Cook says ye did nae eat lunch, and I thought ye might like some tea and sandwiches here in the library."

"That's very kind of you. Put it on the table and I'll eat there. I don't want to get very far from the phone."

"She'll be guid, sir. If she's anything like ye, she's able to make a journey on her own. My guess is that she's quite capable. Now ye just quit worrying and have some tea. Ye will feel better for it."

"Thank you, Darcy. I couldn't do without you and Duncan and Cook."

Darcy quietly left the room wishing she could do more to relieve his anxiety. She had prayed that Mrs. Cameron would have a safe trip. She reflected on the past few years and how glad she and Duncan had been to get to stay with the castle. They had come to love and respect Mr. Alex. She would be hard put to find a kinder man anywhere, or a more lonely man. She didn't quite understand why Mrs. Alex wasn't with him. Mr. Alex said it wasn't her idea, that he had a job that would have put her in danger had she been with him.

185

"Strange do'ins," she muttered, "when a guidwife can nae be with her guidman." She had been working these past few weeks getting things just right. Mr. Alex wanted everything perfect. What he wanted, Darcy did too.

Davenport sat down at the library table, ate the sandwiches and drank his tea. He wasn't hungry but didn't want to upset Darcy.

The call finally came saying that the Chicago package had been picked up on schedule. Now it would be hours until her plane would take off for London. He did feel better after he had eaten and knew he had to do something. He wouldn't hear anything else until late tomorrow morning.

Grabbing a jacket he went down the stairs, out the door, and started toward the loch. He would check the perimeter fencing. When the bulk of the renovations were made he had electric fencing installed around the inner grounds of the castle. The outer grounds had several layers of sensors so that when it was turned on, it would signal and display visuals in his office whenever anything crossed on to the property. He had not felt the need to use this security yet, but he wanted to be prepared. When Jennie arrived, he intended to keep her safe.

The hardest thing in the world for him was what he had to do now—wait. He had never been good at waiting. He wanted to go get her; he couldn't stand this waiting. He never worried like this on other jobs; but this one concerned Jennie. Doubts assailed him as he walked down the steep incline. He tried once again to justify uprooting her life and bringing her here. He had never really doubted that Jennie would come once she knew he was alive. The bond they had formed in their youth was too powerful for either of them to deny.

"Can I keep her safe?" he questioned himself for the hundredth time. So far, there had never been a hint that anyone knew where he was, no suspicious happenings. He did have in place a chain of informants all around the country, from Washington, DC to England, and even further. He trusted them implicitly, or at least as much as one human being can trust another.

The president only knew a number to call to reach him. Davenport had never told anyone the location of his safe place. They had talked of the possibility of Jennie joining him when he retired. The president had even offered his aid in getting her there, but Davenport was hesitant about involving him. Besides, the more people who knew his location, the more danger of the Illuminati finding him. He knew without a doubt that Silverman was still watching.

He was grateful that the president understood and agreed it was time for him to step down. That helped to assuage the guilt. He knew he was lucky to be alive and that he was far past continuing with any degree of safety as an outrider. All the years of stress had taken a toll on his health and last year when he'd been shot, well, that was a bad one.

"Its retirement time," he told himself, one more time. The things he had learned through the years could help someone else. Others can be hands-on and he could work behind the scenes. It wasn't like he was quitting and leaving the president without help. He had been grooming Blakely to take over. Davenport wondered again if he was ready. Bad question, is anyone ever ready for this kind of life?

He set a rapid pace hoping to wear himself out so he would be tired enough to sleep. "It's going to be a long, long night," Davenport said to the mountains.

They didn't answer back.

Chapter 39

MASON SILVERMAN STAYED AT his desk all evening waiting for updates from his agents. When he heard they had lost Jennie Davenport, and she had never shown up at the airport, he was livid but not surprised.

"Then cover the bus and train stations and watch for her there. Use what little mind you have," he yelled at his operative. "Where's Blakely?"

"We found him, roughed him up a bit, but he wouldn't, or couldn't, tell us where she is. We're tailing him."

"Don't lose him. Don't let him find her and go to ground. Report back in one hour. Remember, don't stop her—just follow her. I want to know where she's going."

He had an ominous feeling that he was losing control. The men were stupid; they would screw it up some way. It was evident that she was trying to diffuse her trail. Davenport must be alive and she was on her way to join him. He knew it. He'd always known it. What he had to do now was cover his bases and build a safety net. He poured himself a stiff scotch, sat down and tried to contain his thoughts. Control of situations was his forte—he would manage this one as well.

After taking a deep breath, he dialed the president's office and made an appointment for eight o'clock in the morning. By then he would have his plans in place. The president trusted him; no problem there.

The next call was tougher. Silverman's whole body tensed when the guttural voice answered.

"We have a developing situation, sir," Silverman began. "There's been some unexplained traveling by Davenport's wife. My operatives are

188

following her. She's in Chicago right now. I'll keep you updated as to where she goes."

His hand shaking, he tossed back the rest of his drink and yelled for his aide. "Get Nathan Scott in here ASAP."

Chapter 40

Nathan Scott slammed the bedroom door in frustration and stormed down the hall. He had gone through all Jennie's things, her closet, dresser, and desk, but found nothing that would help him know where she was going. He had to find something.

He was dialing Kris when the doorbell started ringing. Someone was punching the button and not letting go. He banged the phone down and yanked open the door to have G-2 ID flashed in his face. The two men told him he was wanted at headquarters and a plane was waiting. Grabbing his jacket, Scott thought maybe they had found out where Jennie was.

The plane took off as soon as they boarded. It would take several hours to get to D.C.

He should have stopped Jennie when he had the chance, the minute she told him about that damned dream. But she had already called that cop friend of hers.

GENERAL THURMAN WAS RED-FACED and pacing when Scott arrived. Scott had met the general only once before, maybe twice. All his contact had been with Reaves. The general signaled impatiently for him to come in his office.

"Reaves, get in here," the general roared. "Scott, tell us all you know about your wife's activities. Start with where you think she's headed?

"I don't know, sir," Scott answered. He handed the general the note Jennie had left behind. "She didn't leave any clues. She didn't even tell her daughters where she was going. We're all in the dark."

"What made her start looking into Davenport's death?"

"A dream, some sort of a stupid dream, sir. That's all. I thought it best to humor her at first, so we drove to New Orleans and looked around. I knew nothing would come of it because he's been dead so many years."

"There had to be something else. What else did she do?"

"She contacted an old high school friend of hers who's an undercover cop with the Dallas Police. He's been nosing around. He did find a few odd circumstances, such as missing documents at the precinct. The paperwork describing Davenport's physical condition was also missing from the funeral home. What capped it off was when we went to the cemetery and the grave was gone. Initially, Jennie went a little crazy then she became really quiet and unresponsive."

"Why? Why did you let her do this? You were supposed to be watching her."

"I was. My instructions were to make sure she was safe and let you know if she was contacted by anyone suspicious or took any trips. No one has contacted her or attempted to that I've been aware of."

"You weren't supposed to let her get away. Davenport's missing and we haven't been able to find him. She's evidently trying to get to him and she's likely to lead the Illuminati straight to him," continued the general in a low, frustrated voice.

Scott's body wrenched like he had been hit. "What do you mean she's trying to get to him? Davenport's dead."

"No. He's not. His cover got blown in '77 and we had to take him out."

"Take him out. What do you mean take him out?" he yelled.

"His death was faked. It was determined that was the only way to keep his wife and family safe from the Illuminati."

Scott staggered and grabbed the edge of the desk. Reaves poured a brandy and took it to him. Scott's pale face was turning red as he gripped the drink.

"You're telling me Davenport's alive, that you put me there without telling me?" Scott exploded and threw the brandy against the wall. "How dare you put me in a situation without all the facts?"

"Watch it, Scott. I'm in charge of this operation. You're just on the team and information for you is on a need-to-know basis. You know that. We told you to keep close watch, to keep her safe, not to marry her."

Scott collapsed in the nearest chair. What had he done? "Who else knows Davenport is alive?" he demanded.

"You're in no position to be demanding anything, Scott, but I'll answer that. Four men know; me, of course, Reaves, and two senior G-2s. They've been his contacts all these years. Why?" asked the general.

"Because ... I, uh ..." Scott almost told him about his connection with Silverman at NSA then stopped. He had been ordered to keep that alliance secret. He tried to remember exactly what Silverman had told him about his reason for keeping tabs on Jennie. Scott had always felt that Silverman just wanted to be kept informed of what G-2 was doing. He had done lots of "behind-the-scenes" surveillance for him through the years. It paid well. They had lived very well, much beyond his G-2 salary.

"Because what?" the general probed.

"Are you telling me that no one outside of G-2 knows Davenport is alive? Not even the NSA?"

"No. No one else knows. Why are you asking about the NSA?"

"What difference would it make if someone knew? Did I hear you say Illuminati?" Scott demanded, ignoring the general's question about the NSA.

"There are lots of innocent people who could be compromised, his daughters included, if the wrong people found out. Yes, you heard right. The Illuminati as well as *The Brotherhood* would be after them in a flash if they ever found out Davenport was alive. Why did you ask about the NSA?"

"You should have told me this a year ago," Scott stammered. Then he continued sarcastically, "There are things you don't know. We'll just say, it's another need-to-know basis, and you are not on that list." Scott bolted out of the room saying he needed fresh air. The general signaled for Reaves to follow him. Scott ignored the elevators and took the stairs. If Reaves was going to follow him, he could damn well work for it. He ran down the stairs and out of the building.

Careening down the street, his mind was in turmoil. Why would NSA have someone watching a woman whose husband died years before? There was no reason. What a fool he had been. He should have wondered why G-2 had him watch Jennie. He had never really thought about it before.

How stupid. He had been a robot, just following orders. In all honesty, he had to admit he knew something was fishy or Silverman wouldn't have kept his NSA connection secret from G-2.

All that money, the cash he was paid, where did that come from? Silverman said it was unnecessary to report it. "I've not only been a fool, but a stupid fool. Well, no more. It ends right now."

And Jennie, how long had she known Davenport was alive and didn't tell him? Had all their time together meant nothing to her? "Well, I'm not going to play the fool any longer, Mrs. Jennie Davenport Scott. I will stop you."

Red-faced and breathing heavily, he turned into a bar on the corner, sat down, and ordered a double scotch. Evidently Davenport reported for years to G-2 after his death, and now they don't know where he is. Why?

Does Silverman know he's alive? Maybe that should be clarified before anything else. He tossed down the scotch, threw some bills on the counter and left. Signaling the first cab he saw, he jumped in and gave the address of NSA headquarters.

REAVES WATCHED SCOTT GET IN a cab. No other cabs were around. No problem, he got the cab number. He would get Scott's destination from the cab company. He shrugged and went back to his office.

FORT MEADE, MARYLAND

WHEN SCOTT ARRIVED AT NSA in Fort Meade, he found Silverman waiting for him. "You took your sweet time about getting here."

"I didn't know you wanted to see me, but I want to see you. We have to talk."

"You bet we do. Why didn't you tell me the Davenport woman left? That's what you're paid to do. Where's she going?" demanded Silverman.

Scott ignored the question countering with his own. "Tell me why you put me in G-2? Why are you so interested in Jennie?

"Information is valuable, Scott. You know that. In order to serve the president I have to know what's going on. He wants all information. The woman was married to Davenport so we naturally keep tabs on her."

"That's a bunch of nonsense. He's been dead for years. So why are you interested in my wife?"

"We have to make sure no one makes contact with her or attempts to do her harm."

"After all this time, that won't wash, Silverman. Why?"

"I've told you. I keep tabs on everybody."

"Does the president know about this? Does he know about the money you paid me? Where do you get that kind of cash? Who else knows about this?"

"The time is long past for questions, Scott. You're in too deep now. You were happy to take the money, no questions asked. Don't push me."

"What if I tell G-2 you've been paying me to inform on them? Tell me why or I may just do that."

"Don't try to play hard-ball with me, Scott. You can't win," Silverman retorted, bending forward over his desk.

"Just watch me," Scott threatened. Enraged, he stormed out of Silverman's office.

Chapter 41

Late Thursday Night
March 31, 1983
WASHINGTON, D.C.

WHEN SCOTT GOT BACK to G-2 headquarters he burst into General Thurman's office with Reaves on his heels. "We've got to talk. I have to find Jennie," Scott shouted.

The general acknowledged his presence then continued signing documents. After several tense minutes, he pushed them aside and looked directly at Scott. "Okay. Talk to me."

"It's a long story and not a pretty one. I've played the fool out of willful ignorance or greed or both. I'm not sure which. So hear me out before you hang me."

"Keep talking."

"I was assigned to NSA under Silverman for a long time. A few years ago he approached me and said he wanted a man who'd be his ears in G-2. He said he needed to know what was going on for the president. He arranged my transfer from NSA to G-2. My connection with Silverman was to be kept secret. I wasn't to tell you or anyone that I was still in contact with him. You know the rest. I'm here and officially classified G-2. However, NSA has paid me for information, mostly about what G-2 is involved with, but also about Jennie. At least I thought NSA paid me, maybe it was just Silverman. The money was always in cash."

"Damn," muttered the general, his face turning red. "I've never trusted Silverman. He's always creeping about. He's a sleazy S.O.B."

"Yeah, he always has been, but I thought I could handle him. I want to know where Silverman got the cash he paid me. I never thought about that before. Greed is a powerful eye-closer. But my eyes are open now and I want to know where the cash came from."

Thurman leaned back in his chair and stared at Scott. "I've questioned his actions many times before and wondered why the president put up with him. Actually, several presidents have. I've even wondered if he had something on them."

"It's possible," Reaves interjected into the conversation. He'd had many unpleasant encounters with the man. "Silverman is power hungry. I've heard it said that you can get anything you want from him, if you cross his palm with enough silver or enough information."

The general exhaled noisily, took a long slow breath, and then said, "You realize, Scott, you're in serious trouble. If you ever want to see daylight again you had better tell us all you know. That means you cooperate with us in every way."

"I know, sir. I knew that when I came back here. I've got to find Jennie. Who's tailing her?"

"Blakely called in a short time ago. He followed her to Chicago. Two men accosted her in the airport. Blakely got her to a safe house, but the men broke in there and assaulted him. When he refused to tell them anything, he was beaten unconscious. When Blakely came to, Jennie was gone. He's searching for her now. Do you have any idea who the two men could be?"

"It wouldn't be a far reach to say Silverman had a tail on her," Scott said.

"The only ones who would be interested in Jennie would be the Illuminati if they thought Davenport was alive. As far as we know they think he's dead. If they even had a suspicion that he was alive, they'd be all over her. Silverman must be reporting to them. We've got to stop him from telling them about Davenport. It may already be too late. Reaves, get me the president."

"It's late, sir,"

"I don't care, get him. Tell him it's an emergency."

Thurman reached for a bottle and glasses while Reaves made the call. "I think we could all use a drink. Don't throw this one at the wall, Scott."

"I'm sorry about that, sir. This has been a shock." Scott ran his hand through his hair as he slumped down on the sofa with his drink.

The phone buzzed and Thurman grabbed it. "Mr. President, I'm sorry to disturb you this late, but we have an emergency that only you can clarify. It's too long a story to tell you everything now. Have I your permission to shortcut it and skip to the heart of the matter?"

"I like shortcuts, General Thurman."

"Thank you, Mr. President. Briefly, many years ago we had an agent in the

Illuminati who managed to infiltrate the elite hierarchy of *The Brotherhood*. When his cover was breached, it was determined that the only way to keep his family safe was for him to appear to die. He's worked undercover for us ever since. He's now missing and his wife came up missing today. We think she's on the way to him. Problem is, we know she's being tailed."

"I know all about Davenport. How do you know she's being tailed?" asked the president.

"Our man is tracking her and had a run in with two men trying to find her."

"Who's the man?"

"Owen Blakely, G-2. He worked with Davenport for years and he's trustworthy."

"So what's the problem?"

"If the Illuminati are tailing her, we're in real trouble. We can't let her lead them to Davenport. Also, Sir, we have just found out that Silverman, NSA, has had her watched for years and has been forking out cash for information. I need to know if you think it's possible he has sold out to those double-dealing traitors. I can think of no other reason he would have her tailed. To complicate matters further, we found out that Silverman's had an informant in G-2."

"It's not only possible, it's absolute, General. I'm aware Silverman sold out to the Illuminati long ago. We've known for several years and have worked it to our advantage, but it sounds like the time has come to terminate the situation. Bring him in. There's more to the story on my end too, but it's another long one. So you take care of Silverman, and I'll take care of Davenport," ordered the president.

General Thurman was staring at the phone in his hand when Reaves rushed back in the room saying, "General, did you get that? Silverman's a traitor. Can I give the orders pick him up now?" Reaves looked like he had just won the lottery—Silverman had been a thorn in his side for years.

"Go for it," Thurman said, as he dropped the phone in the cradle.

"What about Jennie?" Scott asked persistently. "Those men are still after her."

"Reaves, I want that traitor bound and gagged. Don't let Silverman near a phone, he contacts no one. Get someone in his office to field all phone calls. When his men check in, tell them that the surveillance on Jennie Davenport is over and to report back to headquarters. Chances are, they don't know anything about Silverman's connection with the Illuminati, but we'll have to find out."

Scott looked back at the general as he ran to catch up with Reaves, "I'm going after Jennie."

"Let him go, Reaves, maybe he can stop that woman. Someone's got to."

Thurman plopped down in his chair. He understood the pressures of the job; they all did. It wasn't the type that you could leave at the office when you went home at night. That is, if you went home at night. But he could not and would never understand what caused a man to turn traitor. America was his country; he would see Silverman hanged for this, and Scott right along with him. A traitor in his own department—damn, that rankled.

He would like to know how the president knew about Davenport, and more than that, how he was going to take care of him.

Chapter 42

H ERMAN WILKINS PULLED INTO the cemetery well after dark. He felt better about what he was doing after speaking with Kris and Laurie. They told him about meeting Jennie and how strangely she behaved. She told them she was going away for a few days to think. Somehow, he doubted that. He knew she hadn't told him everything. What he didn't know was why she had become so close-mouthed. Something wasn't kosher, and he couldn't figure out what it was.

Another car pulled in behind him when he was parking. It had to be Kris and Laurie. He could see several men over at the grave waiting. He hoped, once more, that the digging wouldn't be too difficult. With three of them, they could spell each other. Walking back to the other car, he motioned for the window to be rolled down.

"You should wait here in the car; this is going to take a while. I'll let you know when we reach the casket." Kris and Laurie's faces were solemn. What a load they'd had to carry all these years. He was thinking of his own children and the burden his death would have created. He wondered, if Josh was really alive, if he had any inkling of what this was doing to his wife and daughters.

"Maybe the alternative was worse," Wilkins reasoned, as he joined the men at the grave.

"Thanks for helping me, guys. Let's get started."

"Sorry, Wilkins, no one's digging up any graves tonight. Just come along quietly and there'll be no trouble," the man said, flashing his ID.

Wilkins saw G-2 and wilted inside. Now he knew how Carl had felt. At least he couldn't be sent to Greenland, but his retirement was probably gone.

The chief was going to have a stroke. He dropped his arms to his sides and said "Okay. No trouble, guys. What now?"

He slid his hand around to his back and motioned for Kris and Laurie to get out of there and hoped they could see his hand in the dim streetlight. He relaxed when he heard the motor start up and walked over to the grave to distract attention away from the car.

"You only moved the headstone, right?" Wilkins asked. "That was a heck of a thing to do to that family."

"Don't know what you're talking about, Wilkins. We'll take my car and Clark will follow in yours."

They arrived at G-2 headquarters about thirty minutes later. He tried to initiate conversation, but it was like talking to a stone wall. They weren't playing. He was getting the silent treatment.

He was taken into an office, offered coffee, and left alone to twiddle his thumbs for an hour or more. He understood the scene; he had orchestrated it many times. The longer he sat, the more nervous and willing to talk he would get, supposedly.

The main thing that was bothering him was Molly. She knew he'd gone to open the grave—she would be waiting up for him and getting nervous.

"Oh, Molly, my love, hang in there."

Chapter 43

DAVENPORT WAS DOZING, SLUMPED down in his chair by the phone. He would wait one more hour. If he didn't get a call saying Jennie had caught the next flight, he'd go find her. His backpack was ready and on the floor beside him. The helicopter was on the pad.

When the phone rang he grabbed it before the first ring was finished. "Talk to me."

"It's me, Josh," the president said. "We have a problem. I just talked with General Thurman. Someone has figured out your wife is on her way to you. There have been some problems and she's being tailed. Blakely's in Chicago now trying to find her. General Thurman also found out about Silverman's connection to the Illuminati. He thinks he may be the one who is having her tailed. Silverman is being picked up as we speak, but we don't know what all he's passed along to *The Brotherhood*. The general also said he'd just found out Silverman has had an informant in G-2 for several years."

"I should have brought Blakely in to help her from the beginning. Do you know who the informer is?"

"No. I assume he's been immobilized. The major concern was getting to Silverman before he could pass along the information about you. What do you want to do about your wife?"

"My guess is that Blakely already has her in sight. He'd be cautious about saying where she was. He knows there are eyes and ears everywhere." Davenport thought for a moment then said, "I'd call General Thurman directly, but he's not likely to take orders from me. He's irate because he doesn't know where I am. Will you help me, Mr. President?"

"What do you need me to do?"

201

"First, find out if anyone has located Jennie. She's resourceful and has plenty of money to make alternate plans, so she could be anywhere. Next, I want to know who the informer is. Find out if it's Nathan Scott. And finally, I need to talk to Blakely on a secure line, if possible."

"You got it. Sit tight. I'll get back to you shortly."

The president severed the connection.

Chapter 44

SCOTT'S LIFE WAS DISINTEGRATING before his eyes. He had to get to a phone before Reaves got a team to Silverman. He ran down the hall searching frantically for an empty office. It was payback time. Jennie wasn't going to get away with this. He slid to a stop before a dark office at the end of the hall. Grabbing the phone he dialed and paced as far as the cord allowed him to.

"Answer, damn it, answer your phone," he raged. The ringing finally stopped. "It's me, Scott. I've got a deal for you. You give me Jennie's location, and I won't give you to G-2."

"No dice, Scott. I told you not to play hardball with me. You'll crucify yourself." Silverman countered.

"Oh, hell—you want information, I'll give you information. But you have to give me something in return. What's this worth to you? Davenport's alive. Tell me where Jennie is, and I'll give you Davenport."

"How do you know he's alive? Do you have any proof?"

"You hired me to spy on G-2. I'm telling you he's alive. Jennie's on her way to him, that's my proof. Do you want him or not?"

Scott held the phone away from his ear as Silverman exploded.

"Do you want Davenport or not?" he pushed.

"You know damn well I want him. What are your terms?"

"I want to know where she is right now. I know you have operatives following her."

"My last update put her on board a train in Chicago heading for Atlanta. That's all I know at this time."

"What time did she board?

"My man called a couple of hours ago. Don't have a clue which train. Now, where's Davenport?"

"I need transport. Get a helicopter fueled up and ready. I'll tell the pilot where we're going when I board. When I get to Jennie, I can make her tell me. She's the only one who knows where Davenport is. Do we have a deal?"

"Deal, I want that bastard. The chopper will be ready within the hour."

"I'll be in touch." Scott hung up the phone laughing. Everyone always underestimated him. He knew Silverman couldn't resist, however, he would be in prison before he could get his hands on Davenport. He laughed out loud, "But I won't be. I'll get Jennie, and then I'll get Davenport."

He made one more call. The train from Chicago to Atlanta that left two hours ago would stop one time in Philadelphia. That was all he needed.

"Thanks buddy, whoever you are." Scott saluted the empty office as he ran out.

The helicopter was waiting when he got to the field. He climbed in quickly and gave directions to the pilot. He arrived in Philly with time to spare, took a cab from the heliport to the train station, checked the schedules, and bought his ticket.

He was waiting at the gate when the train from Chicago pulled in.

Scott watched the crowd. He expected to find Silverman's men somewhere, maybe Blakely. He was first in line to board. It was a relatively short stop, just time enough to get people on and off. He knew Jennie would probably get a compartment out of Chicago. It was a long trip and since she'd already had trouble, she wouldn't want to be visible. His best bet was to find Silverman's men or Blakely. They would be somewhere near her.

As the train pulled out of the station he started his search. He had boarded at the end of the train so that he could enter each car from the rear. The first two cars he checked came up with nothing. There weren't very many passengers in the third car and most were dozing. The one woman awake was preoccupied with her baby.

Then he hit pay dirt, a guy's head slumped against a window near the front. Watching for a few minutes he knew it was Blakely. Asleep on the job, that made his task simpler. He eased up the aisle and slipped in the seat beside Blakely.

Pushing a gun in his side he spoke quietly. "Wake up, Blakely. Don't make a scene. I just want to talk about my wife. Stand up—we'll walk forward to the door. Come on, move it."

Blakely turned heavy eyes toward the voice and stood up slowly. They walked past Jennie's compartment and through the exit door to the landing between the cars.

"Stop here, don't turn around. Which compartment is Jennie in?"

"I don't know who you're talking about."

"Don't give me that, I know you're following her. Where is she?"

"I told you—I don't know."

In a burst of fury Scott shoved Blakely. Falling, Blakely grabbed at the railing and hung on as the train sped through the night.

"What compartment is she in, Blakely?"

" ... told you ... don't know," Blakely gasped, as he frantically struggled to get a foothold on the swaying train.

"Answer me," Scott screamed. He slammed the butt of his gun repeatedly on Blakely's fingers until Blakely lost his hold and went flying off the train.

Scott leaned back against the railing breathing heavily. Peering out into the night he couldn't see Blakely anywhere. Well, he wouldn't be a problem anymore, besides it was Blakely's own fault; he should have told him where Jennie was. He had a right to find his wife. And he would—if he had to go through every compartment on the entire train.

She had lied to him about Davenport. He was irate when he thought about that. Maybe he would wait where Blakely had been sitting. She was somewhere close, he was sure of that. She had to come out of the compartment sooner or later and he would be there. He'd follow her and take Davenport out while she watched.

He was sick and tired of playing second fiddle. She had been warned not to keep secrets from him.

He'd show her who her real husband was, who the better man was.

Chapter 45

EXPECTING A REPORT FROM one of his field agents Silverman grabbed the phone on the first ring. He froze when he heard the guttural voice asking about Davenport's wife.

"She's on board a train heading to Atlanta, sir. My men are following her. I should have another update when they arrive in Atlanta."

"Have you learned where the traitor Davenport is?"

"Not yet. My man should be questioning the woman as we speak."

"Your man Scott has screwed up. He is jeopardizing our finding Davenport. He threw Blakely off the train and probably killed him. I have taken control of the situation. You assured us Davenport was dead. I told you we don't tolerate failure. You have failed us and become a liability. Your services are no longer required, Silverman."

The line went dead. Silverman turned white as he hung on to the phone. Fear began building inside of him.

He gasped when he heard the sound of footsteps running down the hall from the direction of the elevator.

The G-2 team along with the Lt. General of NSA burst into the office. Silverman dropped the phone. "Too late," he cried hysterically. "You're too late."

"What have you done?"

"I've already made my report. I told the Illuminati Davenport is alive and his wife is on her way to him, that she's on the train to Atlanta. All they have to do is follow her and she'll lead them to Davenport," Silverman wailed. "I've always felt he was alive, but couldn't prove it. I knew Davenport would be my undoing. That's why I transferred Scott to G-2. Big mistake, I should have picked a man with more sense, at least one with enough sense not to fall in love. Too late, you're too late ..." his voice faded, as he continued mumbling, "Too late ... too late ..."

Reaves could not hold back a snicker when the general put Silverman under arrest and asked how he could turn traitor.

Silverman laughed wildly, yanked the desk drawer open, and pulled out a gun.

Before anyone could move, he put the gun against his temple. Still laughing, he squeezed the trigger.

Shocked silence filled the room.

The acrid smell of gun powder permeated the air.

Washington, D. C.

"THE ONLY GOOD PART about this whole nasty affair is that we won't have to spend money on a trial for that traitor," grumbled General Thurman when they got back to G-2 headquarters.

The general told Reaves to get the president on the phone and try to locate Blakely. He walked slowly around his desk and stood staring out the window. He'd had bad days, but this was among the worst. What caused Silverman to sell out, he'd like to know. He was still looking out at the dark streets when Reaves told him the president was on the line.

"Mr. President, the news isn't good," Thurman said quietly. "Silverman took the matter out of our hands. He shot himself."

"I'm not surprised. One way or another he knew he was a goner. He just took the easy way out. Now, let's tackle our next problem, Jennie Davenport. I need you to listen carefully to what I'm about to tell you. You've known Davenport was alive, but what you didn't know was that he has been the president's man since the mid '70s. He's served us well through several administrations. Since you're in the loop now, I will also tell you that we've been grooming Owen Blakely to take over. However, Davenport will continue overseeing Blakely's activities from behind the scenes. Davenport's had a long run, and for a number of reasons, he's stepping down. He's decided it's time to retire. He wants his wife with him, and I concur. We owe him that much, and more."

Processing this startling news, Thurman responded to his commander-in-chief, "I always knew he was too independent for some reason and, lately,

Blakely has been picking up lots of the same habits. Now it makes sense. What do you want me to do?"

The president continued, "Davenport has more in his head about the terrorist groups, the left-wing factions, and the entire structure of *The Brotherhood* than anyone else we have. We need him. If anything, he's more valuable to us now than he ever was. However, his field days are over, that will be Blakely's job from here on out. It's the knowledge in Davenport's head that we have to protect. It's invaluable, so we'll do everything in our power to see that he gets what he wants."

"Where is he, sir?"

"That, my good friend, is the question of the day. I don't even know where he is, only how to reach him. And we'll keep it that way. It's safer for us all. The minute any of these groups find out where he is, he's dead and everybody with him. Now, back to the problem, here's what I need. I want to know where Jennie Davenport is, who the informant in G-2 is, and to talk with Blakely."

Thurman told the president that Jennie was on a train somewhere between Chicago and Atlanta. Blakely was following her, but they would hear nothing more until the train arrived in Atlanta. He explained about Nathan Scott's connection with Silverman, that Scott had voluntarily come in and told them about Silverman. "The last I saw of Scott was when he ran out of my office yelling he was going to find Jennie. I let him go because someone has to stop her from leading *The Brotherhood* to Davenport. I have no idea where he is now. However, orders have been issued for his arrest."

"Call me the instant you hear anything. And have Blakely call me on a secure line," ordered the president.

General Thurman collapsed in his chair. His command would be so much easier if he were kept informed of everything that was going on. The unknowns were going to give him a heart attack. He might rant and rave, but he was loyal down to his toes.

He would move the ocean if the president ordered it, at least, he'd give it his best.

Chapter 46

OWEN BLAKELY PLUNGED OVER and over down the hard, rocky embankment before coming to an abrupt stop in a muddy ditch. He lay sprawled in the mire and marveled that he was alive. The train rumbled on, the wheels clanking on the tracks above his head.

His whole body hurt. He wasn't sure if he could move. He wiggled his feet then tested his legs. They worked somewhat, but when he tried to sit up pain shot through his shoulder to his back making it difficult to breathe.

Slower, he had to take it slower. His left arm was okay, but the right one was another story. The shoulder was either broken or dislocated. He reached across his body with his left arm, lifted the right one, and put his hand inside his shirt forming a temporary sling. Gritting his teeth he rolled to his left side and gradually pushed to a sitting position.

Waiting for the pain to subside, he tried to figure out where he was. It was pitch dark after the train disappeared. Only one dim light was visible about a mile away. Hopefully it was a farmhouse with a phone. That was what he needed. Blakely moaned as he crawled over to a big rock, balanced against it, and arduously got on his feet. He stood up unsteadily. Everything in his body hurt. The shooting pains in his shoulder were making him nauseous, but his legs seemed to be working, if he ignored the pain in his ankle.

Blakely stumbled across the ruts in the field toward the beckoning light. "Scott's run amuck," he fumed. "The man's gone crazy. Thurman always said he was a problem waiting to happen."

Blakely grimaced and pushed his shaky legs faster over the uneven fields. There was no predicting what Scott might do to Jennie if he found her. He had to get help.

By the time he reached the farmhouse the light was out and everything was dark. He banged on the door and cried out for help. After a few moments, the door cracked open an inch and old man peered out. "What do you want?"

Blakely pushed his military ID through the opening. He waited while the man turned on the light and looked at it. "G-2, what part of military is that?"

"It's the Army, sir. I've had an accident. I need to make a phone call. I'll pay for it."

"You look like you've been beat up. Is anyone out there coming after you?"

"No, sir, I'm alone. I was pushed off the train."

The door flew open and a grizzly-faced old man squinted at him. "What's wrong with your arm, son?"

"It's my shoulder, probably broken or dislocated."

"You better get in here and close the door. Don't need anyone coming after you to finish the job. Let's take a look at that shoulder."

"I have to make a call first. Where's your phone? And where am I? What's the nearest town?"

"Nearest town is Price."

"What state, sir?"

"You are lost, aren't you, son. It's North Carolina near the Virginia line. Nearest big town is Greensboro, about 30 miles south of here. Phone's straight down that hall," he said pointing.

Blakely called G-2 while the old man made coffee. When he got off the phone the man was waiting for him with bandages and disinfectant. "You look pitiful, son. Somebody sure got the best of you. Now while the coffee perks, let's take a look at that shoulder. Better sit down."

Blakely grimaced when the old man probed his upper arm and pushed at the shoulder joint. "It's not broken, son, just out of joint. We have to put that arm back in place." He handed Blakely a glass filled to the brim with whiskey. "Swallow that. This is going to hurt like hell."

The fiery liquid choked him and before Blakely could quit coughing, the old man with a strength that belied his age put his knee against Blakely's chest, took hold of his arm and pulled till it popped. He wrapped a long rag around Blakely's neck and made a sling.

"That'll help some. Catch your breath, son. The worst is over. You're going to feel a lot better in a little while. By the way, my name's Joe, Joe Taylor. I'll see about that coffee now."

Blakely couldn't have moved if he wanted to. His head was pounding and his heart was trying to get out of his chest. He had never been through anything like that before. "Name's Owen Blakely," he managed to squeak out.

Joe brought coffee and a few sandwiches over to him. Joe was right; the pain had settled down to a dull throb, and when he tentatively moved his arm it worked. "Thanks, Joe. My arm's easier now. I figured I'd have to get to a hospital."

"It was just out of joint, son. Never went to a hospital for things like that. Just fixed them and went on about my business. It's going to be sore, wouldn't do much lifting for a while. When you get that coffee and some of these sandwiches and aspirin down, you can get cleaned up. You're likely to scare any of the ladies you might run into," Joe chuckled, looking at the bruises on Blakely's face.

"My unit's coming to pick me up shortly. Could you turn the front lights on? It's pretty isolated out here."

"Yep, that's why I like it. Don't like people nosing around." Joe said, turning the outside lights on.

"Bathroom's down that hall when you feel up to it. Your face is a real mess, when you get clean we'll work on it."

And maybe we won't, Blakely thought as he went down the hall. That old man was likely to start sewing up the cut on his forehead.

Chapter 47

"I GIVE UP," JENNIE GRUMBLED. She sat up, felt for the light switch and flipped it on. The drone of the train should have lulled her to sleep but it didn't. Too many things kept swirling around in her head. If this keeps up, she might never sleep again.

She was worrying about Owen. He looked terrible the last time she saw him in Chicago. Guilt was nagging at her for running out on him after he had helped her twice. She really should have checked on him. She could have when she saw him outside the Drake Hotel. She wished she knew if he was telling her the truth.

The constant worry about Kris and Laurie and Nathan and Herman, plus the guilt of leaving them, was nagging at her. She was hurting so many people she loved, but every time she thought about Josh the doubts went away. She loved him, always had, and always would.

The train was scheduled to arrive in Atlanta soon. She pushed the shade up and looked out the window, the countryside whirled past. They had to be in Georgia. She wanted coffee. Actually, she needed coffee; however, not bad enough to leave the compartment. She popped open the last coke and tore the wrapper off another sandwich. Warm coke and stale bread would have to do.

She ate then brushed her teeth, washed her face, and repaired her makeup. When she heard the porter announcing they were fifteen minutes from the station, she shoved everything back in the duffel bag, put on her raincoat, and sat down to wait.

The tour she had booked wouldn't leave until late afternoon so she had several hours to kill. Maybe she should get a cab and go to a shopping mall.

It might be safer than waiting at the airport. If those men were looking for her, they probably wouldn't think of a mall.

She closed the window shade when she felt the train slowing. If anyone was looking for her she wasn't going to make it that easy for them. She peeped out the side of the window just as the train was pulling into the station. People were struggling with suitcases all along the platform. The train rolled to a stop. She heard voices and footsteps in the hall, people were hurrying to the exits; others were already getting off as the steps were lowered on either side of the car. She looked up and down the platform. She didn't see the men who had accosted her at the Chicago airport.

Suddenly, Jennie yanked the shade wide open. She saw Nathan. Two men were pulling him away from the train, one on each side. He was yelling and fighting to get loose. She grabbed her duffel bag on the way out of the compartment, jumped down the steps, and tried to catch up with him. She was dodging suitcases and passengers while trying to keep Nathan in sight when she ran full blast into Blakely.

"Hold on," he hollered, as he grabbed her to keep her from falling. "What's the hurry?"

"I just saw Nathan. Two men are forcing him to go with them. We have to help him."

"You can't help him, Jennie. Not now."

"What do you mean, not now? He needs help. Some men have attacked him …"

"Listen to me, Jennie. He's being taken into custody. For starters, he pushed me off the train last night."

"He did what?"

"You heard right, look at me. He pushed me off the train. The Army is detaining him, and I have to get you out of here before someone else spots you. By the way, that dark wig is good. I almost didn't recognize you in Chicago."

She was torn between catching up with Nathan and believing Blakely. Nathan was no longer in sight and Owen looked worse than he did in Chicago. He did look like he had been in some kind of an accident. His clothes were muddy, his face bruised and bandaged, and his arm was in a sling.

He was holding a restricted entry door open and beckoning for her to hurry. He seemed to know what was happening which was a heck of a lot more than she did so she followed him as he limped through the door. They went down a long hall and entered a room at the end.

"I'm glad to see you, Mrs. Davenport. You've given us quite a chase," said a red-faced man in an Army uniform. "You look a lot better than Blakely. Thought he was a goner for a while. Sit down, have some coffee and we'll talk."

Jennie glanced at Blakely who nodded his head and said, "General Thurman is the head of G-2, the division of the Army Josh is attached to. He can clarify some things for you."

"I wish someone would," she said, sitting down heavily and reaching for the coffee. She wasn't about to turn that down. "What did you mean when you said Nathan has been taken into custody?"

The general sat down and with an uncharacteristic patience explained the events of the night; that Nathan Scott had been working for Silverman, the director of NSA. Scott was providing information that the director was selling to *The Brotherhood*. The general laid out a concise version of Josh's activities while working as a double agent in *The Brotherhood*, pointing out this was the organization responsible for Davenport's untimely demise.

"Scott showed up at G-2 headquarters last night and confessed his alliance with Silverman. He said he'd been selling information about G-2, and also you, to Silverman. He wanted to find you, to stop you from going to Davenport. Scott's been a loose cannon for years. The final straw was when he pushed Blakely off the train last night. He couldn't be trusted not to harm you. We had no other option; we had to take him into custody."

Jennie looked at Owen. She knew he had been beat up in Chicago, she heard the commotion. He looked terrible, definitely looked like he could have been thrown off a train. Perhaps he had told her the truth about Josh.

"I'm sorry, my dear," the general continued. "Scott was originally put in place to watch and protect you. He wasn't supposed to sell information about you to Silverman. And he was certainly never supposed to marry you. That complicated matters. When Davenport found out, well, we'll just say he wasn't happy and wasn't about to let you stay with Scott. He's always felt Scott had some connection to *The Brotherhood*, but never had any proof. There's a whole lot more to this saga, but I'm condensing it because we don't have much time. Davenport has been reporting to the president for years." The general paused. "If it is any consolation, my dear, I didn't know about Davenport's connection with the president, or Scott's alliance with Silverman and *The Brotherhood*, until last night."

"You've lost me." Jennie said, rubbing her weary eyes and finishing her coffee. "You're telling me that I married a man that was in some way connected to Josh's so-called death; that Josh has a secret alliance with the president. Are you talking about my Josh? This doesn't sound right. I don't know who to trust, I'm not sure I can trust any of you."

"That's understandable," the general continued. "However, I'm supposed to mention the *ponies* to you, whatever that means, and tell you that Air Force One is waiting to take you and Blakely to London. From there, you'll be on your own. I understand you know what to do when you get to London."

Shock registered on Jennie's face as she looked at the general and then at Blakely.

"What are you supposed to mention, general? I don't know if I heard you right."

"*Ponies*, I'm supposed to say ... uh ... *pretty little ponies* ..." he said, disgruntled and turning red.

A full minute went by. Then the ghost of a smile flickered across Jennie's tired face before she answered the general.

"Where's Nathan? I want to see him."

The general looked at Blakely. "He's across the hall, but I don't think it's a good idea for you to see him now."

Jennie stood up and walked to the door, "It's not your decision, General. It's mine. You ordered him to spy on me and you let me marry him knowing Josh was alive. Now, the least you can do is let me talk to him."

The general's face turned even redder. He and Blakely followed the determined woman out the door and across the hall. General Thurman opened the door and walked in saying, "Scott, you have a visitor."

Scott turned and glared at the general and Blakely. When Jennie walked in he visibly crumpled. She went over to him and stared directly in his eyes. He wouldn't meet her unyielding gaze. And she knew they had told her the truth.

Jennie doubled up her fist and hit him in the stomach. "You bastard, you're a lousy excuse of a man. That was for Josh."

Then she drove her knee up hard into his crotch, saying, "That was for me."

Scott was doubled over and moaning when Jennie turned to Blakely and the general and smiled.

"I'm ready now. Let's get on that plane."

Chapter 48

JENNIE'S MOOD KEPT SWINGING between happy and sad, elation and anger. Nothing was stable. Her world had collapsed and she felt stunned. She had known it would all change when she read Josh's letter, when she realized that he was really alive, but the changes were shocking.

Overwhelming her was the fact that she had no say in any of this. The manipulation gnawed at her. She shook her head in disgust as she stomped up the steps leading to the plane.

Then there was Nathan. Her stomach churned when she thought of him. She knew everything the general told her was true the minute she looked in Nathan's eyes. He couldn't even look at her. And topping it all off was the fact that she had actually married him, the ultimate insult. She had taken him into her bed, and she could never forgive that.

The way she felt right now she might not forgive Josh, either. "Oh, boy, did it feel good when I hit Nathan," she mumbled.

"Sorry, Jennie, I couldn't hear you," Blakely said, leading her up the ramp into Air Force One.

"I guess I was thinking out loud, Owen. Ignore it."

"Anything I can do?"

"No. Everyone's done quite enough," Jennie said defiantly, "More than enough."

"I'm sure it feels that way, Jennie. No one meant to hurt you," he said.

She shook his hand off her arm. "Back off, Owen, I don't need you hovering over me."

Anger carried Jennie into the plane ahead of Owen. A subdued Blakely

216

showed her around and where they were to sit. Then he joined the Secret Service men.

Jennie plopped down in a chair and listened to them quietly talking. Shaking her head and feeling nauseous, she knew she had no reason to take her anger out on Owen. All he had done was try to help her and look at where it got him. He looked terrible, he was limping, his arm was in a sling, and his face was several shades of purple and yellow.

It was entirely too much to take in. General Thurman had told her things about Josh infiltrating *The Brotherhood* that was beyond her imagination. She could not reconcile this with the man she knew. But then, the general knew about the *ponies*. He couldn't have unless Josh told him. Did Josh really do what the general said? Owen said he was Josh's partner so he was involved with that group, too.

It must be true because here she was, sitting in a leather chair aboard Air Force One somewhere over the ocean. This was unlike any plane she had ever flown in. There were actual rooms, not just row after row of seats. She and Owen, the two Secret Service agents, and a steward were the only ones on board, except for the pilots.

Feeling guilty about Owen, she went over to him and started to apologize when the steward interrupted asking if they would like a drink. Owen declined saying he wanted to get out of the muddy clothes first, that this was the first chance he'd had to change. He told Jennie that the Secret Service agents had found some clothes for him. "They probably won't fit, but at least they will be clean," he laughed.

Jennie smiled and watched him go down the short hall, then turned back to the steward and requested white wine. Unlike commercial airlines, he opened a regular bottle instead of giving her a little one. When he handed her the wine glass a faint feeling of recognition crossed over her. She had seen him before, but where?

Blakely looked a lot better when he came back and the clothes fit quite well. He signaled the steward that he was now ready for a glass of wine.

Jennie watched the steward while he served dinner, but nothing more came to her. Leaning over to pick up her tray, he asked if she wanted coffee with her dessert. Jennie caught her breath. She was right, he was familiar. It was the voice, she had heard his voice before and it registered as something unhappy. She picked at the brownie and sipped her coffee.

"Owen, have you been on Air Force One before?"

"Yes, several times. It's quite a ride. Nothing like commercial planes. Lean back and enjoy it, you may never have this opportunity again. It's about six more hours to London."

"Is the same steward on here every time?"

"I don't know, never paid that much attention to him. Why?"

"He seems familiar. I think I've met him before. Could he be one of those men from Chicago?"

"Definitely not, he probably looks like someone you've known in the past. I wouldn't worry about it. Everyone on board Air Force One has been thoroughly checked out and cleared by the Secret Service."

"I guess so." Jennie said dubiously, as she looked back toward the galley. "His voice was familiar; it gave me a funny feeling."

"You've had some difficult days, Jennie, to say the least. Don't let your imagination run away with you. Just concentrate on seeing Josh again. Speaking of him, what are we supposed to do when we get to London?"

"I, uh … we have to go, uh … I don't know. …" Jennie rambled uncomfortably, feeling eyes on her back. She turned and saw the steward standing at the back of the cabin listening. He was staring directly at her, his eyes were hard and cold and she flinched at the impact. Turning around quickly, she gasped and put her hand over her mouth to keep from crying out. There was no doubt about it; she had seen him before, but, when, and where?

"I didn't get that, Jennie. What did you say?" Owen asked.

"I said, I'm very tired, Owen. I'm going to try to sleep." A cold chill shook Jennie and she snatched the blanket from the chair beside her and pulled it to her chin. She turned her back to Owen and looked out the window. It was dark and she couldn't see anything except the reflection of his puzzled face. Tilting her head slightly, she could see the galley where the steward was putting away the dinner trays. She saw him glance her way occasionally. She wiggled down in the chair trying to find a comfortable position where he couldn't see her.

BLAKELY WATCHED JENNIE WONDERING WHAT was going on in her mind. She was acting very strange. She seemed excited about flying on Air Force One. It was odd though, she had not mentioned Josh, but she had asked a few questions about what would happen to Nathan. He could hear the anger and hurt in her voice. She had a right to be, a lot had been thrown at her the past few days.

He was curious how she had found out Josh was alive. But there again, she wouldn't talk about it anymore than she would tell him what they were to do when they got to London. He had questioned her several times, but she either changed the subject or ignored him.

Blakely looked up as the steward approached him and asked if he would like the lights dimmed. "Yes, thank you. Dinner was excellent." The steward was unfamiliar; he had never seen the man. He was definitely not one of the men from Chicago. This man was older than most stewards, polished and sure of himself. He spoke very softly, sort of a drawl. Was that what made Jennie uneasy? Something sure had.

Jennie's nervousness was rubbing off on him. Standing up, he stretched and walked around. His arm was aching and he was really stiff. The Secret Service guys were laughing and playing gin rummy and Blakely was drawn to them. He sat down and watched them play. While they were shuffling he questioned them about the steward. They said he was new to them, but as he had told Jennie, the man had been thoroughly checked or he could not be on this plane. They laughed and told Blakely that this was not a casual place. You didn't merely apply for a job; you had to go through all kinds of background checks and other formalities.

Still, Jennie's instincts were good in Chicago, and his respect for her had grown as he watched the way she handled the news about Nathan. He would have to stay alert.

He had to stifle a laugh when her knee doubled Nathan over. He wanted to yell, *Bravo, Jennie.*

He wandered around, checked out all the rooms, and then went back to the galley and watched the steward making coffee. The man asked if he needed anything.

"I'd take a cup of that coffee, if it's not too much trouble."

"No trouble at all, sir."

JENNIE CLOSED HER EYES PRETENDING she was asleep. She was picturing the steward in her mind. It had to be a long time ago for her to forget. Perhaps someone connected with Nathan. That wouldn't be a far reach since Nathan worked for the government. She tried to visualize all the people he had introduced her to. Not that there were many, he had been such a loner. That should have tipped her off that something was wrong. It was much clearer looking backwards.

Don't go there. You can't change the past. She could even have met him with Josh. Just seeing that man's cold eyes made her feel like something terrible was about to happen. He's connected to something bad, she was certain of that. No matter how hard she tried, she couldn't pull out any details, only how he made her feel. She was an emotional mess, maybe that's the problem. She pulled the blanket over her eyes so it would block the light. Jennie felt herself dozing off and fought to keep thinking, but she gradually fell into a restless sleep.

"Good," Blakely whispered. She was finally sleeping. Her breathing slowed and her head fell to the side. Maybe he could get a nap, too, goodness knows, he needed rest. No telling what was ahead of them in London. He swallowed more aspirin and pushed his chair back. It wasn't long before he was snoring.

Nearing London

"Mrs. Davenport," the steward said, gently shaking Jennie's shoulder. "I'm sorry to disturb you, but we're about an hour from London. Breakfast is available whenever you want it."

Startled, Jennie looked up into his face and was transported instantly into the nightmarish time when Josh had died. Her face paled and she gritted her teeth to keep from screaming. She knew where she had seen him. He was the soft-spoken man at the hospital who helped her find Kris and Laurie. What was he doing here? She watched him wake Owen and then check with the Secret Service men.

The lights in the cabin were dim and the window shades had been pulled down. Afraid he would see the recognition on her face when the lights were turned up, she jumped, ran to the restroom, and locked the door. Her legs were shaky and she felt faint. Bending over the sink, she splashed water on her face. Straightening up, she yanked off the wig and ran her hands through her hair. Who is he and why is he on this plane? She had assumed he was a minister that night in the hospital, but he hadn't acted like one.

Jennie turned away from the sink, dropped down heavily on a small step stool and put her head in her hands. Did he ever tell her he was a minister or had she simply thought he was? He had compassion in his eyes that night, but now, his eyes were cold and terrifying. And, he had just called her Mrs. Davenport, he knew who she was. Did Owen or the Secret Service tell him? No, they had been cautioned not to use her name.

She wished she could remember more about that night, but most of it had faded. Time, maybe. More than likely it was the shot the doctor had given her. Maybe if she could piece together what happened that night it would help.

When the paramedics came, they put Josh on a stretcher and took him away very quickly. Then a young patrolman drove her to the hospital. The emergency room staff never let her go into Josh's room or even look at him from the door. She knew now it was because he was alive. Kris said she heard her daddy's voice. Anger flared, she stood up and paced about the tiny room. How could Josh have done this to her and the girls? It was cruel, really cruel. And now she was in a real mess. Tears threatened and she wiped her eyes impatiently, she was through with crying. She had to find the connection.

She had seen men in dark suits standing in the doorway to Josh's room. They didn't look like doctors. They were probably G-2 since they arranged all this. She had been leaning against the wall outside Josh's hospital room feeling sick at her stomach, just like she did now. She remembered sliding down the wall to the floor because her legs wouldn't hold her up.

That was when the nice man she thought was a minister or chaplain came into the picture. He helped her up and to a chair then suggested she call some of her family. Somewhere in all this, she asked him to find her daughters. That's it. The steward is definitely that soft-spoken man from the hospital. That would account for her feeling he was connected to something terrible. And his voice, she couldn't mistake it.

Then her aunt and uncle got there, and that horrid man with autopsy papers demanding she sign them. It still made her mad thinking about it. Next, the doctor pulled her in his office and gave her an injection, telling her it wasn't a sedative. But he had lied. It must have been a strong one because after that everything got very fuzzy.

She remembered voices, harsh, commanding voices saying that it was all over. She had no memory of a soft voice there at the last. Where was he then? If he had been a minister or hospital chaplain, he should have been there helping her. If he wasn't, then why was he there? More to the point, why is he here now?

"Jennie, are you all right?" called Owen, knocking on the door.

"Yes, I am. Would you please bring my duffel bag to me? It's on the floor by my chair."

She opened the door, took her bag, and assured him she was fine, that she wanted to freshen up before they got to London.

Locking the door again, she sat back down on the little stool. Her mind was in turmoil. Nathan had been giving information to that man in NSA, and he was passing it on to *The Brotherhood*. They were evidently the group that was after Josh. The group that had caused him to have to die, the same group that Josh had stumbled upon when they lived in Kansas City.

Good heavens, this goes back more than twenty years. So Josh had to die to keep these people from killing all of us. G-2 sent Nathan to watch and protect her and the girls; but Nathan was a traitor, he sold information. He was the link. He knew about it all, her weird episode and attempts to find Josh. He knew all that Herman was doing.

That's why Carl was sent to Greenland, and why the police records, Josh's military records, and the grave disappeared. That was why Herman's boss told him to quit helping her. Nathan was feeding everything they were doing to G-2 and probably to the traitor in the NSA. That means *The Brotherhood* has known exactly what we were doing all along. That's why Josh was so upset about Nathan. He knew, he should have told her.

Boiling mad and feeling betrayed, Jennie stood up and tugged at Nathan's ring on her left hand until it came off. It was very satisfying when she dropped it in the toilet and flushed it away.

Her thoughts were leading her to some chilling conclusions. *The Brotherhood*, Josh said, had people in every area of the government so why not on Air Force One. They know he's alive and have sent the steward to watch her, that same man who watched her the night Josh died. He was at the hospital to make sure Josh died. If Josh hadn't, he must have been there to kill him. And now he was watching and listening again. He was here to follow her to Josh. Of course he knew her name.

Jennie shuddered and closed her eyes. What could she do? She wasn't about to lead him to Josh. She couldn't talk with Owen without the steward listening, who knows what he could do. Thankfully, she hadn't told Owen anything. She felt for the key pinned in her bra and sighed, it was her lifeline to Josh.

Biting her lip, Jennie sat quite still for some time. When she lifted her head, she knew what she had to do. She knew the rules now.

One way or another, she would lose that man and get the instructions Josh had left for her. She got up, opened her satchel, stripped off her clothes and washed as best she could. It was better than nothing and actually it felt great. She felt like a soldier getting ready for battle. She redid her makeup to match her blond hair, no need for the wig now. She put on navy slacks, a pale yellow shirt, the new navy blazer, and sprayed on Josh's favorite perfume, *Hope.*

No way was she going down now. She had come this far, and no one was going to stop her from getting to Josh, no one. She had already been through hell, and they couldn't do much more to her.

Adrenaline kicked in giving her a strength she never knew she had and a very different woman left the restroom. She dropped the bag by her chair and went straight to the galley. Locking eyes with the steward, she asked him what his name was.

"Mason, ma'am," he drawled.

"I'd like fresh coffee and some breakfast, Mason. We'll be landing soon so make it fast."

Chapter 49

Saturday
April 2, 1983
LONDON, ENGLAND

AIR FORCE ONE LANDED at the city airport about ten miles from central London. It was a heady experience standing at the top of the stairs looking down at the runway. The two Secret Service agents had gone in front of Jennie. One was at the foot of the steps and the other about halfway down waiting for her to move.

An official-looking car flying the American flag was parked at the foot of the steps, obviously from the US Embassy. Two men in dark suits got out of the car and were staring up at her.

Glancing around her, she saw Owen and directly behind him, Mason was still lurking.

They were all waiting for her; everyone was waiting for her to lead them to Josh. She looked beyond the car to the terminal. Baggage was being unloaded and put on carts to be towed into the building. Planes were taxiing around the airstrip and others were flying in huge circles in the skies waiting for clearance to land. It crossed Jennie's mind that they had landed immediately, no circling at all.

She felt very presidential as she went down those steps to the waiting limo. One of the men extended his hand, welcomed her, and introduced himself as Philip Kennedy and the other man as Donald Carlisle from the US Embassy. They made a point of calling her *ma'am* with no mention of her name. She was curious to learn if they knew who she was. Owen followed her to the car leaving the steward standing at the top of the steps. She was sure this official ride was no surprise to Mason and wondered who would be following her now?

When the limo pulled away, she looked out the back window and saw

Mason running down the steps as another car pulled up. Well at least she'd know who to watch for.

"A room at the Embassy has been put at your disposal, ma'am. We'll be there in about fifteen minutes."

"Thank you, Mr. Kennedy. I appreciate the consideration. However, I have other plans. Please take us to the Dorchester Hotel. Mr. Blakely and I will get out there." Surprised, Blakely stared at her, but did not contradict what she said.

The drive to the Dorchester didn't take very long. The doorman opened the limo door and welcomed them to the hotel. Jennie and Owen got out, retrieved her duffel bag, and she led the way inside without pausing. She went directly to the restaurant on the right of the lobby and asked for a table for two near the windows. When they were seated, Jennie smiled broadly at Owen and ordered tea.

THIS CHANGE OF ATTITUDE IN Jennie was confusing and Blakely wasn't quite sure what to make of it. She'd been relatively okay when they first boarded the plane. She started once to explain what they were to do in London, but stopped mid-sentence and asked him about the steward. He evidently reminded her of someone. After that she closed up like a clam, turned her back to him, and had gone to sleep. Upon awakening she ran immediately to the restroom without saying a word. When he took the duffel bag to her and saw her pale face he knew for sure something was wrong. Apprehension was written all over her and she had shut the door quickly.

However, she had changed when she came out thirty minutes later. Not just the fresh clothes and the absence of the wig, but her stance and her whole demeanor were different. She was like another woman. The way she had demanded breakfast instead of ordering it, the look on the steward's face had been priceless. Blakely caught him staring at Jennie several times.

Looking around the hotel, he asked, "What's with the Dorchester? Are we meeting Josh here?"

"No, we're not. I love having tea here and I'm hungry. I couldn't eat the breakfast on the plane. Josh and I enjoyed this hotel very much back in the '70s. It doesn't look like it's changed."

Blakely was irritated. He was tired, hurting, and didn't like being kept in the dark. "Jennie, don't you think you should tell me what Josh's instructions are?"

"Yes, I should. But not right now, there are eyes and ears everywhere. Haven't you figured that out yet?"

He stared at her bewildered by this new attitude. "Okay. We'll wait on that. Tell me what happened on the plane that made you so jumpy? I need to know."

"Nothing happened. I just remembered some things. I'm really all right. I'll explain later. I promise. Let's just enjoy this long enough for me to eat my breakfast and drink my tea."

There was nothing else he could do, so a frustrated Blakely leaned back and waited. He noticed Jennie had positioned herself so she could see the hotel entrance. She seemed to be watching for someone. He wondered if it was Davenport. He tossed down more aspirins.

"That was wonderful and quite refreshing. Thanks, Owen, for going along with me. I'm ready now."

When they left the old hotel, Jennie looked back at it and smiled. "So many good memories here—I wonder if Josh still remembers?"

She paused and looked up and down the street. "If memory serves me right, that's Hyde Park," Jennie said, pointing across the street. "Look, Owen, I can see the Marble Arch from here."

"What are you doing now, Jennie?" Blakely asked impatiently, he was about to lose it. "This is no time to go sightseeing."

"You're wrong, Owen. It's exactly the right time. If I remember the last few days correctly, the idea is to confuse the issue, muddy the waters, and generally make no sense of anything so that nobody can figure out what you're doing."

"Well, you're doing a fine job of that. I certainly don't know." he snapped. "I'd really appreciate it if you would clue me in."

"In time, Owen, in due time," Jennie laughed.

SHE LOOKED AT HIM AND almost felt sorry for him as they scurried down the pathway. He looked like she had felt in Chicago following him through the Drake Hotel and down the dark alleyway. She just hoped she was confusing the man tailing them. Finally she found an isolated bench, sat down on it, and patted the seat beside her. Jet lag was catching up with her and Owen looked terrible.

"Sit down, Owen. Let's rest." She looked all around the park; she hadn't spotted Mason or anyone else that looked suspicious. "I think this will be a good place to talk. I'm sorry to run you around. I just had to be sure of something. Mason followed us from the airport. He came in the Dorchester shortly after we were seated, and he hung around the lobby while we were in the restaurant. I haven't spotted him out here, but I'm sure he's watching us. I don't think he can get close enough to hear without our seeing him."

"Are you positive?" Blakely asked looking all around the park, he was going to feel pretty stupid if Mason was following them. It was his job to know that, not hers.

She answered with a nod. "Oh, yes, I'm positive. I was afraid to tell you anything on the plane after I saw him. It took me some time to get it all straight in my head. You asked me what happened, well, here goes. When we got on Air Force One, I was okay considering the situation with Nathan. I thought we were safe until I saw the steward. It was just a feeling, nothing definite, nothing I could put my finger on, but I felt I had seen him before and I couldn't figure out where. More than that, my feelings were associating him with something bad. I watched his reflection in the window until I fell asleep. He kept staring at me."

Owen took her hand. "You should have told me, Jennie. After you asked me about him I talked to the Secret Service agents. They said he was new, but nobody, and I emphasize, nobody can be on that plane without radical background checks."

"I know. You told me, but it didn't help the way I felt. Eventually I fell asleep, not a good sleep, I kept dreaming about the night Josh died. Next thing I was aware of, the steward was shaking my shoulder and saying, 'Mrs. Davenport, we're about an hour or so from London.' I almost screamed. He called me by name—and no one was supposed to know who I was, but he did. Suddenly everything began to fall in place. He was at the hospital the night Josh died. There's no way I could mistake his voice. That must have triggered my dream about Josh's death. That's when I ran for the restroom. I didn't want him to see that I recognized him."

Jennie told Owen about seeing Mason in the hospital the night Josh had died. How she'd assumed Mason was a minister and that he had disappeared after the doctor had sedated her.

"You're sure he is the same man, Jennie? Not think, but absolutely sure."

"Yes, without a doubt."

Jennie explained why she had started searching for Josh; and how everything kept disappearing, including her friend Carl, the part Nathan had played, and how it had all come together for her on the plane. "I've just hit the highlights of the last couple of months, Owen. I hope this helps you understand what has been going on."

"It does. Mason pretty much confirmed your suspicion when he showed up at the Dorchester. I know he is not G-2; they're not following us now." Blakely stopped and thought for a minute. "Right before Silverman shot himself he told the general he had already informed the Illuminati that Josh was alive. Mason has to be from them. Josh and I had several brushes with them years ago. This means *The Brotherhood* also knows. They never fully accepted that Josh was dead and issued standing orders to find and terminate him."

"Even so, that doesn't excuse the way I've been treated. G-2, Nathan, Josh, and maybe you have moved me around like a pawn in a chess game. They stuck that thing in me and watched and listened to everything I said and did. General Thurman even let me marry Nathan knowing Josh was alive. The only thing I've had to hang on to the last few days was that Josh tried so hard to tell me something when he died. I think he changed his mind at the last minute and was trying to tell me to remember the *ponies* so that he could get back to me. It was a private signal of ours. What I do know now is that I am through being manipulated, Owen. I will get to Josh and no one is going to follow me, except maybe you." Jennie's voice shook with anger. "Sorry to dump on you, but this has not been a good week."

"You're right, Jennie, you've every right to be angry. I believe we could say this has been one of the worst weeks ever."

"I owe you an apology, Owen. I was starting to tell you how sorry I was when the steward interrupted us. I'm sorry that you got beat up in Chicago and thrown off the train because of me. I had no call to yell at you when we were getting on the plane and tell you to back off. I'm sorry about that, too. You've only tried to help me, I know that now."

"That's okay, Jennie, I'd do that and more for Josh. As I told you, I owe him."

"It all fits, Owen, it's the only thing that makes sense. When we left in the limo, I looked back and saw Mason running down the steps of the plane toward a car. The thing we need to do next is find a way for me to get Josh's instructions."

"You're doing all right, Jennie. I'm amazed you've been able to pull all this together." Owen stood up and stretched. "Let's walk for a while. That will give us time to make plans. Keep your eyes open. You know they could have someone else on this end that we won't recognize. Where do you get Josh's next instructions?"

"I have a key to a locker in Victoria Station. I also have a room reserved at the Victoria Hotel with the tour group that I booked in Chicago. It's under the name of Christy Logan. Do you think we could use that?

Chapter 50

BLAKELY REACHED OVER AND took Jennie's duffel bag from her, she looked worn out. The hotel was a good idea, they could both use some rest. The trick was to get her in without Mason following them. He was familiar with London and was steering them toward the crowds at Buckingham Palace. *If he could locate Mason, detain him—yeah, that might just work,* Blakely considered. *It was worth a try.*

"Jennie, I've an idea. That's Buckingham Palace in front of us. Lots of people are milling about and there will be some cabs over at the far side. When I see Mason, I'm going to talk to him, distract him some way. I want you to keep moving, get in a cab and go to the hotel. Here, take your bag. Let's mingle with the crowd. I'm going over to the fountain, up the steps and try to spot Mason. You angle toward the cabs but keep me in sight. When I get Mason's attention, I'll scratch my head and you run for a cab. I'll call your room in a couple of hours. If for some reason I don't call, you get Josh's instructions and then do what he says."

"You better call me, Owen. Don't forget, the reservation is under Christy Logan." Jennie slung the satchel over her shoulder and walked toward the guards. She stood where she could see the fountain and Owen. She watched him climb to the top and stop by the large statue. He looked around, gave her a thumbs-up then rushed down the steps. Evidently he had spotted Mason. She worked her way through the crowd toward the area where the cabs were parked. When she saw him scratch his head, she ran and jumped in the first cab she came to.

"Where to, ma'am?"

"I'm not exactly sure, just drive right now." The cab pulled away from the curb and was driving down the wide street when Jennie had an idea. "Take me to Harrods, please."

The cab made its way through the traffic and stopped at the front door of the department store. Before Jennie got out she asked the driver how long it would take to get from Harrods to the train station.

"Which station?" the driver asked.

"Victoria Station."

"About twenty minutes."

Jennie thanked him. Lots of cabs were waiting nearby so it would be easy to find one later. She located a directory and map of the store. A quick look showed the women's clothing on the second floor. No one appeared to be following or even interested in her.

Exiting the elevator, she went to the hat section and asked about wigs or hairpieces. The clerk had a few to show her. Jennie found a short auburn one she thought would do. Asking the clerk to suggest a casual hat to wear with navy and camel-colored clothes, Jennie sat down at the vanity and waited. It was good to sit; they had walked a long way across the park. The store behind her was reflected in the mirror and no one was paying any attention to her.

"This would be nice, ma'am," the clerk said, handing Jennie a wide brimmed navy hat. "You could wear it with navy or camel with or without the wig."

Jennie tried on the navy hat and smiled. She might not even have to wear the wig with it. "This will do nicely. I'll take it and the auburn wig." When she was paying, Jennie asked the clerk for a couple of the Harrods shopping bags.

The ladies restroom was on this floor and Jennie went straight to it with her purchases. She guessed Harrods would have a nice one and she wasn't disappointed. There was a small sitting area with a couch and dressing table, plenty of room to change clothes. She laid her purchases down and opened the duffel bag. Pulling the camel jacket and ivory blouse out of it, she realized clothes got a lot more wrinkled in a soft bag than in a suitcase. "

Oh, well, they'll have to do," she complained, shaking out the jacket. The blouse was in bad shape, but it wouldn't show very much. Folding the shirt and jacket she took off, she put them in the bottom of a shopping bag and dressed in the rumpled clothes.

Jennie dug in her purse, found her small manicure scissors, and cut the tags off the hat and wig. She pinned her hair up and put on the auburn wig, reapplied makeup, and finally added the hat. Standing up she looked in the mirror from all angles. The wide brim blocked most of her face and only a little of the auburn wig showed around her face. Sunglasses hid her eyes. She doubted that anyone would recognize her now.

Jennie emptied her few clothes into a shopping bag, rolled the duffel bag up and put it and her makeup bag in the other one. Looking in the mirror again, she paraded about with the bags and smiled. She looked like a British woman on a shopping spree; she had noticed several women with large hats when she came in. She left Harrods with a confident attitude, hailed a cab and went to Victoria Station.

Several banks of lockers were in sight when she entered the station. Owen hadn't said anything about her picking up Josh's instructions right now, but since he was sidetracking Mason, this seemed to be a good time to do it. Pulling the key from her pocket she checked the number. When Jennie found the locker, she looked around. No one appeared to be watching her. It was at eye level and with her back to the main part of the station her hat shielded the locker when she opened it. Jennie grabbed the padded envelope and slipped it down to the bottom of one of the shopping bags. Leaving the key in the locker she walked rapidly toward the arched portal that said Victoria Hotel.

There was no problem checking in at the hotel. The clerk said that she was the first of the tour group to arrive and handed her a key. As soon as she got to her room she put the night lock and chain on the door, tossed her things on the bed, and dug out the envelope. She tore into it and out spilled another packet of money. What in the world did he think she was going to do with all that? She still had money left from the last one. There was a new passport and driver's license under the name of Jennifer Cameron of Inverness, Scotland. She was thrilled to find she was Jennie again. Interesting, the passport looked used—it already had a number of countries stamped in it.

She opened the note. Her heart thumped when she saw the small pony drawn on the paper. No one drew like Josh. It said for her to take the train to High Wycombe. It would take about forty-five minutes. Then take a cab to the Stuart Farm on the northeast side of town. The cab driver would know where it was. A helicopter would pick her up. Code word was *ponies*. Jennie's face softened, she knew in her heart that Josh had been trying to tell her to remember the ponies the night he died. Six long years of wondering what he meant, now it was so clear.

It had been two hours since she left Owen. She was getting worried about him; he really wasn't in very good shape to have to fight anyone else. She wished he would call. She couldn't stand waiting much longer. There was a knock on the door. She almost opened it, then yanked her hand back and looked out the peep hole.

Relieved, she opened the door—she had ordered tea and sandwiches when she checked in. The waiter rolled in a table. It looked so good and her stomach was growling. She tipped the waiter and locked the door again.

"Come on, Owen, call me. It's been too long," she worried. She couldn't desert him again.

She took her jacket and hat off, sat down, poured a cup of tea and started on a roast beef sandwich. "Umm, this is so good." She was exhausted, probably jet lag. She sighed, finished the sandwich, and sipped the hot sweet tea, then leaned her head against the corner of the high back chair. Stretching, she relaxed her tense shoulders and thought she would just close her eyes for a few minutes.

Jennie woke with a start. It was dark and the phone was ringing. For a moment she didn't know where she was then she jumped and grabbed the phone. Relief was monumental when she heard his voice. "Oh, Owen, I'm so glad to hear your voice. I've been worried."

"I'm relieved to find you at the hotel," Owen responded. "We parted so quickly I've worried about you too. I hoped you understood what to do. Sorry, it took longer than I thought to lose Mason. I was able to get behind him and follow him to make sure he didn't find you. How'd it go?"

Jennie laughed. "Just fine, I changed my looks again and picked up our new instructions. Thought it would be a good idea while you were keeping Mason busy. Where are you?"

"At a small hotel a few blocks from yours. I didn't want to chance leading anyone to you. What are you supposed to do now?"

"I'm to go to a village called High Wycombe and then take a cab to the Stuart Farm where I'll be picked up by helicopter. I have a number to call to tell them what time I'll be there. I checked the train schedule and one leaves in that direction every hour on the hour. It only takes forty-five minutes so it's not very far."

"That's good. We'd better wait till morning. You catch the eight o'clock train. I'll get to High Wycombe another way and meet you at the Stuart Farm between nine and nine-fifteen. That will give us a little leeway in the timing. I assume we just look for the helicopter when we get there."

"The note didn't say anything else. It shouldn't be hard to find it." Jennie paused before continuing. "What happens if something goes wrong and we miss it? I don't have any other way to contact Josh."

"Don't worry, Jennie. We won't miss it. Get some sleep. I'll see you there. Your journey's almost over."

Jennie put the phone down slowly, she was still worried. There were so many things that could go wrong. The train might be late. Owen might not find her. The helicopter might not come. Dozens of things could go wrong.

No, no more *what-ifs* or *might-nots*. They won't do any good. She hadn't come this far to get stopped now. "At least, I know Josh is somewhere near Inverness, Scotland. And I have the phone number, I can call that again. If I have to, I'll go there and look up everyone named Cameron. If that's my new name, Josh must be going by Cameron too."

Oh, my, she forgot to tell Owen about the red hair and hat. Well, there probably won't be very many women getting out of cabs at the Stuart Farm.

234

Chapter 51

WHEN THE FIRST RAYS of light streamed through the windows Jennie threw her arm across her face and groaned. It had been another long difficult night and her mind had gone over and over the last few days. From what the general told her, Josh was a spy. That didn't seem like the man she knew, not her laughing, loving husband. If it was her Josh, she wondered how much he had changed and if he'd still love her. She didn't know.

The worst thing, the very worst thought that kept her awake, was a sneaky horrible doubt that wouldn't go away—that G-2 had confused Josh with another man and her Josh was not alive. Sighing, Jennie rolled over and threw the covers off. She might as well get up. Either way, she had to find the truth.

She thought about all their past years together and how much he loved to sing to Kris and Laurie. She would never believe he could forget his daughters. She knew him, her Josh was there somewhere, and she would find him again. She loved him no matter what, but she owed him a punch in the stomach for what she'd been through. He was not ever going to leave her behind again; he'd just have to get used to it. Whatever he was involved in, she would be too.

She was dressed and ready by six-thirty. It would only take a few minutes to get to the station. She had already eaten breakfast so there was nothing to do but wait. Jennie stood at the window and tapped her fingernails on the wall impatiently. The city was waking up and the cabs were already on the move. She wondered how Owen was getting to High Wycombe.

At seven-fifteen Jennie left her room, went downstairs and checked out.

All her things were still in the bags and she hoped she looked like a woman who had been on a shopping trip and was now heading home. She knew from past trips to England that women who lived in the country made overnight trips to the city for the hairdresser and shopping.

She purchased a ticket to High Wycombe and waited where the clerk indicated. She didn't see anyone who looked suspicious. The *all aboard* call finally came. Jennie closed her eyes a minute hoping that her queasy stomach would go away, then picked up her packages and boarded the train.

Almost there, she had to believe nothing would go wrong and she would see Josh today. She wanted so much to call Kris and Laurie. She had to call them soon and tell them about Nathan. They would have to do something about the house and the mail. Then there would be the bills, Jennie sighed, she would deal with that tomorrow. But today, the only important thing was to get to Josh. It still seemed impossible that he was alive. She wanted to cry and laugh all at the same time.

The train left on time and rolled through the city toward the countryside. The fog was lifting and she could see into backyards of homes along the way. The houses were clustered tightly together and the yards were small and compact. There were a few children already playing outside. As they rolled away from the city, the lots grew larger and the homes more inviting. The train lumbered into the countryside. There were more trees, wooded areas, and larger gardens. Even a few flowers were blooming. The countryside was peaceful and pretty. Jennie leaned back against the seat and enjoyed the views.

The forty-five minute ride passed fast and the train was slowing down. It stopped next to a small building with High Wycombe written in large letters above the entrance. Several people got off when she did and they walked rapidly away from the station. It was evidently a familiar stop for them. No cabs were in sight and she had to ask the stationmaster. He pointed and told her that they queued across the street by the park and one should be there soon. It was a pretty little park. There were several empty benches and a children's play area, but it was too early for anyone to be there. Anxiously she paced until the cab arrived. Tossing her bags in, she told the driver to take her to the Stuart Farm.

"Yes, mum. It'll only take a few minutes," he said.

The farm was near the edge of town. A little brook ran along one side of the property and was flanked by trees and bushes. Jennie got out, paid the driver, and looked around. She didn't see Owen. There were fewer trees behind the house so that had to be where the helicopter would land. All she found back there was a dusty field.

She was beginning to wonder if the cab driver had left her at the wrong place when she heard a distant roaring. Shielding her eyes from the sun, she saw a helicopter coming toward the farm. Jennie backed up against the house. She wished Owen would show up.

The chopper settled to the ground covering the area with dust and debris. The wind from the rotors hit her and almost knocked her down. Struggling against the barrage of dirt and leaves, she hooked the shopping bags over her arm, grabbed at her hat, and was fighting to stand up when she saw the door open. Then her heart almost stopped.

It was Josh. He climbed down and walked over to her. Her mind seemed to turn off, she couldn't move. "I decided to come get you myself," he said grinning. "You didn't think red hair and a hat would fool me, did you?"

"You're here, I didn't expect you here," she mouthed breathlessly when Josh put his arms around her and held her tight. It was her Josh. He was really alive.

"I think I like the red hair. You look wonderful."

Jennie let out the breath she'd been holding and reached up and touched his cheek. Tears streamed down her face. "It's really you. I can't believe it. Oh, Josh, I was so mad at you, but I don't care now. You're really here. We have to call the girls; they will be so excited when they hear your voice."

"We'll have to do that later, honey. Right now we need to get going," he said, steering her toward the chopper. "I know Blakely was on Air Force One with you, I thought he would be with you."

"He said he would meet me here, but I haven't seen him."

Davenport looked toward the house and then turned toward the trees. His demeanor changed as he scanned the area.

"Josh, when I was on the plane from America to London, I recognized the steward. He was at the hospital the night you died. I know that sounds crazy, but he was. He said his name was Mason."

Josh twisted instantly back to face Jennie. "Did you say Mason?"

"Yes, and he followed Owen and me around London. That's what the wig and hat were for, not to fool you, just anyone following me. Owen sidetracked

Mason while I grabbed a cab and got away. When I talked to him last night he said it took him a while to lose Mason. He didn't want to lead him to me so he stayed in a different hotel. He told me to take the train and he'd find another way. Josh, I'm worried. He's hurt; he got beat up in Chicago and was pushed off the train on our way to Atlanta."

"If he said he'd meet you here, then something's wrong." He pushed Jennie in the direction of the chopper and walked toward the trees calling out for Blakely.

Suddenly the bushes parted. A shadowy figure came toward them.

"Get in the chopper, Jennie," Davenport ordered.

"That's Mason," she yelled, running toward Josh. Conscious of every sound, she heard the wind stirring the bushes, Josh's heavy breathing, but most of all, the sound of leaves crunching under Mason's feet as emerged from the bushes.

"Very touching scene, Davenport, she led me right to you. You didn't really think you'd get away with this, did you?" the man asked in that slow drawl Jennie had come to dread.

"Get in the chopper, Jennie," Davenport demanded again as he pushed her away. "Where's Blakely, Mason? What have you done with him?"

"He's out of commission; he kept getting in my way. You've led us on a long chase, but it's over now. You had a chance to come clean with me. We were friends, Davenport. I'd have gone to bat for you."

"We can still be friends. You can come over to my side," Davenport said, shoving Jennie behind him.

"It's too late for that—you know better. You were in too deep. When you became part of *The Brotherhood's* elite thirteen and privy to all their long-range plans, you knew you could never get out. Hell, man, you were keeping all the records." Mason paused a moment. "You remember the system. I drew the black ball. Sorry, my friend, this isn't going to give me any pleasure."

Mason pulled his hand out of his pocket and pointed a gun directly at Davenport.

"Say your goodbyes."

Without hesitation, he aimed and fired.

Jennie screamed and wrapped herself around Josh as the gun exploded.

Her head jerked backwards. She shuddered then slid down Josh leaving a trail of blood on his clothes as she crumpled to the ground.

A second shot rang out from the nearby bushes that lifted Mason off his feet and threw him to the ground.

Josh fell to his knees and covered Jennie. The bullet had hit her shoulder. Her jacket was rapidly turning red.

"Josh," she cried clutching him.

"Damn it, Jennie, I told you to get in the chopper."

Davenport looked fiercely around. He couldn't see where the second shot had come from. Or how many were there—or where Blakely was.

All he could do was shield her.

The pilot was scrambling out of the chopper; gun in hand.

Then Davenport saw some dense bushes part—Blakely was laboriously crawling out and pointing a gun at Mason.

"Get Jennie out of here," Blakely shouted, "I've got him covered."

Davenport grabbed her up in his arms and ran toward the waiting chopper. He shoved her in and turned back to help Blakely.

Blood was running down the front of Blakely. He pushed against a tree and got himself up, then limped over to the man on the ground. He kicked him over with his foot, bent down and felt for a pulse. There was none. He looked around, but didn't see anybody else.

He stumbled toward the chopper, blood pumping out at a furious rate.

Davenport jumped in and buckled Jennie in a seat then bent down and pulled Blakely in. Blakely's face contorted and he cried out in pain. Davenport grimaced and yelled at the pilot to take off.

"I hope you're not as bad as you look," Davenport said. "Where are you hit?"

"Bullet—left side. Missed heart, I'm still here, stuffed handkerchief in it … bleeding's slowed. I'm getting pretty groggy … Jennie?"

"She took my bullet. It hit her in the shoulder, it's painful and bleeding, but it's not deadly. It will take about thirty minutes to get us to a safe place. Can you hang on?"

Blakely nodded and inched further into the chopper. He couldn't get off the floor. It took all he had just to get his feet inside. Jennie was buckled in a seat above his head. He looked up at her bloody clothes and mumbled, "I didn't do a very good job of protecting you, did I?"

"You did fine, Owen. We're safe now." Blakely's head fell sideways and his eyes closed.

"Do something, Josh. Help him," Jennie cried.

Davenport felt for the pulse in his partner's neck. "He's passed out, Jennie, but he's still alive. We're going as fast as we can."

She couldn't quit staring at Josh, it was really him. And it wasn't a dream. Her head was swimming. She wanted to keep looking at him, but her eyes wouldn't stay open. She heard a voice telling someone to have medics and stretchers waiting at the pad. He had two down, one chest wound bleeding fast. Then Josh said AB positive blood would be needed. The last thing she heard was that damage control was necessary at the Stuart Farm.

Davenport looked at Jennie, then down at Blakely. He was losing too much blood. The floor around him was turning red. "We don't have thirty minutes," Davenport told the pilot.

The pilot looked over at the bloody passengers and told Davenport to hang on.

Chapter 52

JACK HARRELL PUSHED THE black armored chopper to its limit. He had been Davenport's pilot for the past two years and had never tested the chopper's 309 miles per hour capability, but today was the day.

He landed the chopper in exactly twenty-three minutes at a small private medical facility on the outskirts of Skegness, a seaport town on the North Sea.

Davenport opened the door of the chopper before it was completely on the ground and beckoned to the waiting men. He helped lower the unconscious, but still breathing man onto a stretcher, then picked up Jennie, and started running toward the building.

The man pushing an empty stretcher urged Davenport to put her on it, but he wouldn't let go of her.

Dr. Colin Fitzsimmons met them at the entrance and rushed Blakely to the operating room.

Doc Fitz was already cutting the shirt off Blakely and giving orders to the nurse by the time Davenport got in the room. He motioned for Davenport to put Jennie on a nearby table where another team was prepped and ready. Davenport's hands were shaking when he reluctantly laid her on the table; he didn't want to let go of her. Her eyes were closed and her face was white. He pulled the red wig off Jennie then stepped back as the nurse removed his wife's blouse.

Heart thundering, he gripped his hands tightly. Jennie's wound wasn't a mortal one, but he knew Blakely didn't have much of a chance; he had lost too much blood. He crawled out of the bushes and saved them. With that blood-pumping wound, Blakely got up, made sure Mason was gone, and got himself to the chopper while Davenport was getting Jennie inside. All that time Blakely's blood was draining out at a furious rate.

Scenes from the past bombarded Davenport. He had seen too much of this. His face was a black cloud as he watched the doctors working on them. He was responsible for all this, and he had caused Jennie pain. He would never forgive himself for that.

"What was I thinking?" Davenport paced around the patients beating his fist into his hand. "All these years I've worked to keep everyone safe, and now, I've jeopardized Jennie and my partner."

The bruises on Blakely's face weren't recent. Jennie had indicated they were from the Chicago incident.

If Blakely dies, Davenport's eyes veiled over with anger; cold, hard, and unapproachable. "There's no place on earth where *The Brotherhood* will be safe from me," he raged through clenched teeth.

Davenport twisted violently around when a hand touched his shoulder.

"Whoa, take it easy, man. It's me, Jack." Hands in the air, Harrell backed up saying, "You have to let the doctor work on your wife. Besides it won't help her for you to watch."

Harrell pulled him to the door, but Davenport refused to leave the room. Harrell found a couple of chairs and pushed Davenport into one.

"She'll be all right. It's a shoulder wound," Harrell said. "I heard the doctor say that it was a clean one; it won't take long to get the bullet out. I don't know the doctor working on your wife, but I do know Doc Fitz. He knows what he's doing and he wouldn't have anyone here who doesn't. Remember how he took care of you last year. You were in worse shape than Blakely. Doc's the best in the business."

"I know, I know, but it's my fault they are hurt. Jennie took the bullet meant for me. I can't get that scene out of my head."

Davenport ran his hand through his hair then dropped his head to his hands; it was suddenly too heavy to hold up. *God, if you're really there and care, I need you now. I'm asking for Jennie and Owen, let them live. This isn't their fault. Punish me, not them.*

After all this time, after all his careful planning, they still got to her. They had to pay. He would make those bastards pay for her pain. With a heavy heart he realized there was no way he could get out now—not until *The Brotherhood* was stopped.

Harrell watched him a minute, then left the room and went down the hall to Doc Fitz's office. He knew the way well; he had spent enough time here. Going to the file cabinet in the corner, he opened the bottom drawer and pulled out a bottle of single malt whisky that doc always stashed there. Looking around the room, he grabbed a couple of paper cups. He'd never seen Davenport lose his cool before, and he had been with him in some pretty tough situations.

"Here, drink this," Harrell said, pushing the paper cup in Davenport's hand.

Davenport looked at it, wiped his eyes, and tossed the drink down. "It wasn't supposed to happen this way, Jack," he stammered, coughing.

"I know," Harrell said, pouring more whisky in his cup. "There was nothing wrong with your plans, but fate has a mind of its own at times. I don't know how he found us. It came down so fast I didn't have time to get out of the chopper. I'll check on Blakely. Wait here, my friend."

Davenport nodded and looked toward Jennie, then at the commotion around Blakely. He swallowed the second whisky slower and set the cup on the floor. A little color returned to Davenport's face. He felt like a cornered tiger ready to spring.

Harrell was reassuring when he came back. He listened and watched Doc Fitz working on Blakely. It wasn't a pretty sight, but he had seen worse. The bullet had missed the heart and lungs and was wedged in the rib cage. "Doc says he has a chance if they can get enough blood back in him. It was a good thing that you knew Blakely's blood type. He said that saved some precious minutes. All in all, he has a chance."

Harrell told him Jennie looked better now and was making moaning sounds. "The bullet is out and they are stitching her up. She is going to be fine. The nurse told me she'll be waking up shortly."

"Thanks, Jack. This is different, you know, this is my wife. She's the reason I left years ago. I had to keep her safe. And now, I got her hurt. It's a whole different game when it involves Jennie, I can't remove myself from the situation."

"It's your right, man. I'd feel the same. Look, the nurse just nodded at you. You can go see Jennie now."

Davenport took his first deep breath since the whole thing went down. He could think again. He stood up and saw Jennie's doctor walking toward him. Some of the tension went out of his face when he saw the doctor was smiling.

"The lady's fine. The bullet didn't do any major damage. It was pretty clean, blood loss was minimal. We're giving her antibiotics to be safe. She'll have a small scar and will be sore for a while. If there's no fever tomorrow, she'll be able to leave. You can go see her now—she's been asking for you."

"Thanks," Davenport said, running toward Jennie.

"Jennie, I'm so sorry. I wouldn't have brought you here if I had known you'd be hurt ..."

"You couldn't have stopped me once I found out you were alive." Jennie reached up with her good arm and pulled him down for a kiss. When he lifted his head and looked at her, she was smiling. Her blonde hair was all over the pillow—this was his Jennie.

"What do you mean you wouldn't have brought me here? I just want to know what took you so long to come after me." She paused and looked around the room. "Where are we, Josh? I remember the helicopter and you talking to someone."

"We're in a hospital. You and Owen needed help. You're going to be all right, honey."

"I know, the doctor said I was shot in the shoulder." She opened her hand and showed him the bullet. "He thought I might want this for a souvenir," she laughed weakly before a frown took over. "Josh, how is Owen?"

"The doctors are still working on him. The bullet hit him in the chest and lodged in the rib cage. I think he'll be okay. He's tough."

Jennie turned her head toward the other table where the doctors were working on Blakely. Tears rolled down her cheeks. "Josh, he's been beat up, thrown off a train for me, and now this. He has to be all right. Please, Josh, make him be all right." Jennie's voice faded and her tearing eyes closed.

The doctor tapped Davenport on the arm. "She's okay, it's just the sedation. She'll sleep most of the day. Best thing for her. The nurse will stay with her."

Halfway home, he mused. Davenport turned anxious eyes toward Blakely. Then he looked back at Jennie. She had turned on her side and was sleeping soundly.

"Thank you, Lord," he whispered.

By twilight, Doc Fitz said the young man would make it. Being young and strong was in his favor. "I don't want himself moved for at least a week, can't chance that wound bleeding again. He told me his shoulder had been dislocated and some old man popped it back in place. It looks okay in the X-rays, but he can't use that arm for some time. The other side of his body took the bullet and shattered a rib. I got the bullet out and stitched himself up. And somewhere along the way, he must have twisted his ankle. It's swollen and multi-colored. He has several bruises on his face and also a cut that I stitched up. All in all, he's a banged-up mess."

Relief flooded over Davenport when Blakely opened his eyes and mumbled something about where he was.

"You're in the hospital, partner. You're going to have to be here for a while. It's safe here. Doc Fitz took care of me last year when I was shot. He bloody well saved my life, and it looks like he has saved yours, too. We're going to owe him."

"So, where are we, still in England?"

"Yes, for a few days."

"How's Jennie?"

"She's okay. Bullet's out and she's sleeping. Baring infection, she'll be able to leave tomorrow."

Davenport paused, swallowing with difficulty. "Owen, I don't know how to thank you for taking care of Jennie." His voice broke and he angrily swiped at his eyes. "I owe you. There's no way I can ever repay you."

"Well, I wouldn't say no to a shot of whisky. You smell like a distillery so I know there's some around," Blakely mumbled.

The tension broke and Davenport's laugh echoed in the high-ceilinged room. "You got it, buddy. Just as soon as the doctor lets you, in fact, you can have the whole damn bottle."

Chapter 53

"IN ME OFFICE, NOW," Dr. Colin Fitzsimmons commanded, glaring first at Davenport and then at Harrell. Rudy-faced with a shock of bushy white hair, the Irishman opened the operating room door and motioned impatiently for them to follow him. He marched down the hall and turned on them when he entered his office.

"What in the name of the blessed virgin do you mean getting that woman injured? And that young man was half dead. It's only by the grace of God he's still alive. What have you been up to this time?" he fumed, as he yanked open the bottom drawer of his file cabinet.

"All right, who's got it?"

Harrell sheepishly handed over the whisky. "Sorry, Doc, it was medicinal."

"Medicinal, bah humbug. I should have known you took it, you young scallywag. You drank enough of it last year. Well, don't just stand there, get the cups. So, who's the woman?"

"She's my wife, Jennie" Davenport answered with a faint smile.

"Who shot her? You know I'm supposed to report all gun shot wounds to the authorities."

"But you didn't report mine last year, Doc," Davenport grinned at him. "The bullet was meant for me, but she threw herself around me."

"Brave woman, and the man?"

"Owen Blakely, he's my partner. The one I told you about last year, who was doing my job while I was here in the hospital. Is he really out of danger?"

"For now, depends on infection and your interference." Doc Fitz poured

246

a round of drinks and told them to sit down. "There are some things I need to get clear and some things you have to understand. When Jack brought you here last year he asked me not to notify the authorities. I did it as a personal favor for Jack and me old friends, his grandparents. Jack's a good lad. I've known himself since he was a wee lad running up and down the beach acting like he was an airplane. Me wife and I never had laddies. Jack sort of filled that spot in our lives, at least during the summers. So I have a right to be concerned about what he's got himself into. You're going to have to explain what's going on, and you better convince me that what you're doing is not illegal."

Davenport wrenched around to look at Harrell. "You never told me you had grandparents around here."

"Not anymore, they died a few years ago. They lived next door to Doc and I used to spend every summer with them. My dad's from here. He and my mom moved to the States before I was born. I had to do what I thought best last year when you got shot, you were unconscious. Doc patched me up on a regular basis when I was a kid. He was the only one I could think of that I trusted, so I brought you here. He's always run a private surgery. He's never been part of the National Health Service."

"Too many restrictions, a bunch of bureaucrats telling me how to doctor me patients," Dr. Fitz said disgustedly.

"Anyway, I knew doc would take care of you, and I knew he'd make his own mind up about telling the authorities." Harrell faced the red-faced Irishman saying, "Doc, we're not doing anything illegal. You have my word on that."

Doc Fitz nodded and looked at Davenport.

Davenport thought for a minute and then made his decision. "Doc, you've been more than fair to me. I owe you the truth. I work for the United States Army and have been involved in undercover activities. Officially, I am listed as dead; very few people know I am alive. I do special assignments for the president."

Harrell interrupted him. "I need to tell doc what you did for me." He stood up and stared out the window for a minute, then turned to Doc Fitz.

"In 1979, the Navy began an operation in the Barents Sea to tap into a communications line that went to and from the headquarters of the Soviet Union's biggest fleet. I was making reconnaissance flights in my chopper. In 1980, a former National Security Agency employee alerted the Soviets to the operation and compromised the entire Pacific cable tap operation. The result was that I got shot down. I wasn't injured, but the Soviets had put my chopper out of commission and I went down."

Harrell paused, clearing his throat. "Davenport's job was to get me out of the Soviet Union prison where they were holding me. He came in, got me out, and over the Wall. I'm still amazed when I think about it. That's what he does, Doc, he does impossible jobs that no one ever hears about. We got to know each other pretty well. After I left the Navy, he asked me to be his private pilot, and I jumped at the chance. We've done some incredible things these last couple of years."

"You might have told me about this, Jack. You're too damned close-mouthed for your own good. You should have told me last year."

Doc turned from Harrell and fastened on Davenport, "Now you, Davenport. You told me last year, if you survived, you were gonna retire from all these nefarious activities."

"That was my plan," answered Davenport. "I have a home in a secure location under another name, and I am trying to get my wife there. However, there's always things you can't anticipate. This time it was a mole in one of the major government offices. He passed classified information to a group that has dedicated itself to killing me. Through him they found out Jennie was joining me and followed her. They shot my wife and my partner. He's the man who is supposed to take over my job."

"Well, that isn't gonna happen for donkey's years. That young lad's got a lengthy, murderous recovery ahead of himself," doc snapped.

Doc Fitz stood up and got a glass of water. "I believe Jack, and I'm grateful to you he's here now. The authorities can go to hell for all I care. If I tell them, there would be such a bureaucratic snafu we'd never get it straightened out."

"Thanks, Doc."

"Don't interrupt me. Here's what we're gonna do. I'll have me staff move your wife and partner to their rooms. Then I'll send them on their way, except for Scully. She stays. They don't need to know anything about what's going on. Your wife, if there's no infection, can probably leave on the-morra. But Blakely can't be moved, he'll have to stay. I only have a couple of patient rooms so if anyone else comes, Scully can send them to another surgery. She can tell them I'm on vacation and we're closed. I close periodically because I don't trust anyone to run me surgery. All me patients know this. They may get mad, but they won't think it's unusual. They are used to me ways. Josh, you can bed down on the cot in Jennie's room. I'll stand watch over Blakely the-nite. Jack, there's an extra cot in the operating room. You'll have to make do there. Scully can arrange some grub for us. Now, I suggest we all get some rest while we can."

"Thanks, Doc," Davenport said with relief. "I need to report in. I better do that from the chopper. It's got a secure phone line." He motioned for Harrell to join him when he left the office.

"Yes, Mr. President, both Jennie and Blakely will be all right. Blakely's going to be out of action for quite some time. His injuries are serious. I'll keep you updated. I'm grateful for all your help and concern," Davenport said.

Pausing for a moment, Davenport slowly continued. "We have several major problems—the man, name's Mason, the one who shot Jennie and Blakely, was a member of *The Brotherhood*. I knew him when I was working undercover with them. They have long memories and evidently never believed that I was dead. They must have shadowed Jennie all these years, but I never had a glimpse of them or heard a rumor that they were still looking for me."

"It had to be Silverman," the President said. "The general told me the last thing Silverman said before he shot himself was that he never believed you were dead. Then he mumbled they were too late, he'd already reported to *The Brotherhood*. He's evidently the one who sent Scott to watch Jennie. You had no way to know that."

"Yeah, I guess, but I should have. Silverman and *The Brotherhood* were naturals. Neither of them got where they are by trusting anybody or any circumstance. My fault, I should have anticipated Silverman would question my death."

"You can't cover everything, Davenport. We both know that."

"I know, but this was bad. We don't know what all, if anything, Mason passed on to the group. It's unlikely they know where I am exactly, however they're sure to know I'm in the British Isles. I have some history with the doctor who is taking care of Jennie and Blakely, and I'm confident he won't give us away, but here's the main problem. Jennie told me Mason was the steward on Air Force One. Your plane has been compromised. We don't know whether he's the only one or if there are others. That means the Secret Service falls under suspicion."

"Not a surprise, Davenport. *The Brotherhood* appears to have penetrated everywhere. Since we're both sure of the general, I'll get him started on this. We'll keep you informed of what we find."

"Mr. President, you do understand that it may not be safe for you to fly until everybody is checked out again."

"I know. I won't be planning any trips until this is worked out."

"Until Blakely's up and functioning, I'm still on board. They have to be stopped. They shouldn't have shot my wife," Davenport said angrily. "Secret Service is the first priority. That has to be sorted out before anything else. You have my number and you can call me as usual." With a worried look on his face, Davenport hung up the phone.

Harrell secured the chopper, and they went back into the building locking the door behind them.

"Do you want first or last watch?" asked Davenport, "Your choice."

Chapter 54

HARRELL QUIETLY SLIPPED OUT of the building and stood in the shadows. He looked past his helicopter at the night sky. The new moon didn't give much light, but he could make out the waves as they broke across the shoreline. He remembered how he used to look forward to coming here every summer. He wished he could walk along the beach. It was a magical place in his mind.

He had already made rounds inside the facility and all was secure. He would check the exterior of the building in a little while. It would be an hour before Davenport relieved him. He reached in his pocket to pull out his lighter when a movement near the chopper caught his eye. Dropping the lighter back in his pocket, he stepped behind a post where he wouldn't be seen. Someone was out there.

Hoping it was just some kids checking out the chopper, he stood still and watched. No, they were too big, it wasn't kids. Two men dressed in dark clothes were testing the doors. One man stooped down and crawled under the body of the chopper. "What the hell," Jack whispered, and started out there, then stopped. The man slid out and motioned the other one to follow him.

All Harrell's instincts wanted to confront them, but Davenport's words roared through his mind, *Watch and wait. Don't confront until you know what you're up against.* A couple of minutes later the man came back, crawled under the chopper again, then he scooted out and ran through the hedges to the road. A couple of minutes later the sound of a motor starting up broke the silence of the night.

Harrell stayed in the shadows and waited for fifteen minutes. No one came back so he ran out to the chopper. A quick inspection didn't show any

251

obvious problems. He circled the building and tested all the windows. They were secure.

He went back to the helicopter and checked it thoroughly. Then he crawled underneath it. There was some reason the man went under it. He wanted to know why. He didn't like anyone messing around his chopper. Harrell turned on a tiny penlight and ran the light around the underbody. Then he saw it, they had attached a tracking device. "Damn, they've found us."

He looked around cautiously before leaving the cover of the chopper. No one was in sight. He ran back inside the building, locked the door, and hurried down the hall.

"We've got trouble," he whispered, touching Davenport's shoulder. Davenport woke instantly and looked over at Jennie. Then he followed Harrell out of the room.

"What's up?"

"Two men were messing around the chopper when I went out for a smoke. They've attached a tracking device to it. Someone knows we're here."

"I was afraid of this. We'll have to get out of here. Can you remove the device?"

"Yeah, no problem—how about I attach it to one of the fishing boats anchored out there. They'll be leaving before daybreak."

"Good idea. I'll wake Jennie and get her ready. Then we'll check on Blakely. It will be a little harder to get him out of here. If Doc's asleep maybe we can roll the bed out into the hall. We don't want to move the tracker until the last minute. Be sure you attach it to a boat that's moving so whoever put it there will be drawn away from the chopper."

Jennie woke easily and Josh told her that they had to leave. She sat up on the side of the bed while he slipped the IV out of her arm and stuck a piece of cotton and tape over the spot. "What's wrong, Josh?"

"Someone has found us. I'm not sure who, but we have to get out of here. Can you walk?"

Jennie stood up slowly. "Yes, I'm fine, Josh. I'm just a little dizzy. What do you want me to do?"

"Find something warm to wrap around you, a blanket will do. You'll freeze in that hospital gown. I'm going to get Blakely."

Harrell was pushing Blakely's bed slowly, but the rollers kept squeaking. Frowning at the noise, Davenport took hold of the foot of the bed and lifted it slightly to see if he could stop the squeaks. Doc Fitz stirred in his sleep. Suddenly, he bolted up asking what the hell they thought they were doing.

"Sorry, Doc, we have to get out of here. They found us."

"Not with me patient, you don't." Doc went over to the bed and checked Blakely's pulse. He's in no shape to be moved."

"We have to chance it. I can't let what happened yesterday happen again. If we stay here, we'll be sitting ducks."

Doc Fitz looked at Blakely. "Then I'm going along. I'll not be letting you two kill this young lad." He turned to Harrell and asked, "How steady can you fly that thing?"

"I'm the best, Doc. If you say steady, then steady it is."

"I'll need me bag and some medicines. Will we be going to a hospital?"

"No, sir, can't chance that. We have to get to a secure place. It'll be about an hour and a half flying time," Davenport replied.

"No hospital, no doctors, is that what you're saying?" Doc looked at Davenport's nodding head. "In that case, we'll take Scully with us. I'll need her help. Will that thing out there carry all six of us and me supplies?"

"Yes, it will. Are you sure you want to do this, Doc? What about any other patients?"

"Don't have any critical people right now. Scully can put the usual note on the door and tell everyone to go over to Dr. Bodwin. I've done it before."

"You'll have to hurry, Doc." Davenport ordered. "I want us out of here in fifteen minutes at the longest. Stack whatever you need in the hall and we'll load it up. I've already taken the IV out of Jennie. She's ready to go."

Doc gave Davenport an angry look and went off down the hall yelling for Scully. She came out of the end room buttoning her blouse and looking very sleepy. He turned back to Davenport. "You better not touch Blakely 'til I tell you to."

Doc boxed his supplies up, checked his bag, and was helping roll the sedated Blakely to the chopper within ten minutes. Scully followed holding Jennie by the arm. Harrell loaded the boxes and a couple of suitcases into the rear of the chopper then belted Blakely into the makeshift bed they had rigged. Doc crawled in and sat on the floor beside him.

Scully climbed in and buckled herself in beside Jennie. Then she looked down at Doc Fitz sitting beside his patient and warned him, "If you're planning to stay on the floor, you better find something to hang on to." She checked Jennie's bandages muttering under her breath that the good doctor was going to be the death of her yet.

Harrell scooted under the chopper, removed the tracker, and ran down the beach to the docks where a couple of fishermen were getting their boats ready for the day. Harrell slowed down and walked over to the first one, asking what time he would be going out.

"Inna couple of minutes, young feller, ay likes to be out at the banks before daybreak. What's got you out so early?"

"Couldn't sleep," Harrell said, as he leaned across the edge of the boat. "You've got a nice set up here."

"Thanks. Make yourself useful and untie that rope in front o' you."

Harrell untied the rope and tossed it to the fisherman. When the motor turned over, he gave the fishing boat a hard shove away from the dock and wished him a good catch. The boat pulled sharply away leaving a small wake behind. Harrell grinned and ran back to the chopper.

He nodded at Davenport when he got in. "All's well. The tracker's on its way out to sea," he said, as he revved the engine up for take off.

Chapter 55

AFTER TWO LONG HOURS with Doc yelling every couple of minutes *to quit rocking the damned machine*, Harrell set the chopper down as easy as he could, then breathed a sigh of relief. The temperature was in the thirties, but he was sweating. He pulled a handkerchief out of his pocket and wiped his face. This had been one of the hardest trips he'd ever flown, almost on the same scale as combat, almost. He had forgotten what a pain Doc could be.

Davenport had alerted Duncan they were on their way and would need a conveyance on which to carry the injured Blakely. He opened the chopper door and saw an old iron cot sitting there. "Oh, no, that damn thing is going to weigh a ton," he said frowning. He made a mental note to get a stretcher.

Doc Fitz took over, got Blakely out and settled on the cot. It took all four of them, Doc, Harrell, Davenport, and Duncan, to carry the sedated Blakely to the castle. Scully was in charge of Jennie. She and Darcy walked her in.

"Is all the security turned on, Duncan?" Davenport asked. "Even the perimeter sensors?"

"Aye, sir, everything is on. Angus is monitoring the cameras. I told him to warn ye or me immediately if there's a breach of any kind, nae matter how insignificant, just like ye said, sir."

"Thank you, Duncan. We've had lots of problems." He looked at the men standing around Blakely and nodded toward the curving staircase. "We have to get him up that."

Scully and Darcy followed with Jennie and settled her in a huge bedroom that was warmed by a roaring fire while the men took Blakely to his room.

Jennie looked around the incredible room. The bed was massive and she gratefully crawled into it. "Thank you for helping me, Scully. I'm not sure I could have made it without you. I am a little shaky."

"Of course you are, my dear," said Scully, tucking the down comforter tightly around Jennie. "You've been used for target practice and you've had surgery. You'll be weak for several days." Scully glared at Davenport when he walked into the room. "She needs rest now."

"I'm not going to bother her," he laughed. "I just want to make sure she's comfortable."

He kissed Jennie and sat down beside her. "Welcome home, honey. Not exactly the homecoming I wanted it to be, but the important thing is—you are here." He waved his arm about the room saying, "This is the castle we always dreamed about." Davenport motioned to Darcy. "I want you to meet someone. Jennie, this is Darcy, she takes care of all of us. If you need anything, she's the one to ask. She's been anxious to meet you."

"Welcome, mum. I'm glad yoo're finally here. Mr. Alex has been so lonely. It's nae right for a man to be separated from his guidwife."

"Darcy has told me that on a daily basis ever since I moved in, Jennie." Davenport laughed.

"You're right, Darcy. Thanks for reminding him. I'm happy to meet you and be assured I am here to stay," Jennie said, looking into the kindest face she had seen in a long time.

"No more talking, you need to let this poor woman rest. She's had enough for one day." Scully tolerated no argument as she ushered Davenport and Darcy out of the room. "You can see her after she's had some sleep. I'll be on that lounge chair in the corner so don't you come sneaking back in here."

When Davenport came out of the room, he found Harrell and Duncan talking in the hall. Duncan turned and said, "Mr. Jack told me that your guidwife threw herself atween ye and the gunman and took the bullet meant for ye. She's quite a lady. We knew she would be."

Darcy's eyes widened and she said, "We'll be honored to care for her, sir."

"Scully, get in here," Doc's voice bellowed. "We've got problems." Davenport ran to Blakely's room with Scully close on his heels. "He's bleeding again. Where's me bag and supplies?" Doc was holding a towel against Blakely's chest and looking anxiously at Scully.

"Downstairs," yelled Davenport, as he tore down the stairs. Scully grabbed Doc's bag the instant he got back with it.

"Stand back, don't crowd us. Give Doc room to work," she ordered.

Doc and Scully worked on Blakely for the next fifteen minutes. They were quite a team, neither said a word as Scully handed Doc everything he needed. Harrell had never seen his old friend look so tired and worried. He wondered for the first time how old the man was. He had to be in his late sixties, maybe even seventies, or older. Doc looked like an old man when he was a kid. He'd taken care of Blakely the day before, had very little sleep, then that horrendous ride here.

"You must be worn out, Doc. What can I do to help?" Harrell asked.

"You can clean up the mess on the floor, Jack. We've got himself stabilized for the moment," Doc said, as he continued to stare at Blakely. "If that wound opens up again, we could lose the lad. The body won't tolerate much more." He turned and glared at the group standing in the doorway. "The sedation I gave himself for the trip hasn't worn off. He'll sleep for several more hours. The lad absolutely cannot be moved again. He has to stay still and that's all there is to it."

"No more moves, Doc, you have my word. It's safe here. We're not going anywhere for a long time." Davenport went over, took him by the arm, and led him to the big leather chair by the fireplace. "Sit down. You look like you're about ready to drop."

"Darcy, bring a tray up here with something hot to drink and a few sandwiches for Doc and Scully. They're exhausted; it's been a hard twenty-four hours. Better add a bottle of whisky to that tray. I'll go with you and get a tray for Jennie. Jack and I will come down later and eat in the kitchen."

Harrell cleaned up the room while Scully checked Blakely's bandages, straightened the bed, and tucked the covers around him. She shoved a table near the bed and arranged the medical supplies on it.

Doc's eyes had closed as soon as he leaned back in the chair. Scully picked up a blanket from the foot of the bed and gently covered him before she tiptoed out of the room.

"Well, I'll be," said Harrell, as he sat down in the chair on the other side of the fireplace. "She's got a heart after all."

Chapter 56

THE MINUTE DAVENPORT LEFT Blakely's room he went to the control center and checked the monitors. He had to see for himself that all the areas were armed and functioning properly. He activated the overhead sensors then studied the perimeters carefully. Everything was quiet.

He set the system to sound the alarm throughout the castle if there was a breach. All was secure and he told Angus to go get some rest.

Looking out the window, he watched dark clouds forming on the horizon. It would be raining before long. He was so glad they had made it back before it started. Doc Fitz would have really been issuing orders. *We're all here at last. We survived, one more time,* he thought gratefully.

Now he had to see about his daughters. He sat down at his desk and made several phone calls.

IT WAS LATE IN THE day when Jennie awoke. Scully helped her to the bathroom and she soaked in a hot bath. It was heavenly and she felt like a new person. Darcy brought her a gown and a big terrycloth robe and she put them on. When Josh came in she was sitting in an armchair by the window with a tray of food in front of her.

"This soup and bread is wonderful, Josh. I didn't know I was hungry until Darcy brought it in."

"She's always feeding me, too. It's a dream come true to see you sitting there. I wasn't sure it would really happen." He pulled a chair beside her and sat down. "You're beautiful, Jennie."

She laughed. "Wait till you see me stand up. This robe would cover two of me, but no complaints. It's warm and clean and not bloody. I guess my bags are still at the Stuart Farm. I must have dropped them when I saw you. I didn't even think about them until I bathed earlier."

"I didn't have time to get them when we were leaving. If you remember, my darling wife, we were a little busy—guns were going off," he laughed. "I talked with the men who cleaned up the Farm and they have your things. Harrell can pick them up later when he goes for supplies. Doc's already made a list of things he needs. So just make a list of whatever you need. The important question is, how are you feeling?"

"I'm a little shaky and sore, but I'm not hurting anymore," she said, standing up and holding on to Josh's arm. Doc changed the bandages and said *I'd do*. When I asked about Owen, Doc said he was holding his own and that he'd sleep most of the day."

"He was awake a little while ago and making a few wise cracks. He's still got his sense of humor."

"That sounds good, makes me feel better," Jennie answered.

Anxious to look around, Jennie left the bedroom and went over to the staircase. When she looked down into the entrance hall of the castle she was overwhelmed. "Josh, is this castle yours? I mean, do you own it?"

"Ours, Jennie, we own it. Your name is on the deed with mine. Plus all the land you can see, more than a thousand acres. It's the castle we dreamed about."

"A thousand acres—what on earth will we do with all that land? While I'm asking questions, Darcy called you Mr. Alex. I assume that's your name here? I've had so many names the last few days I scarcely know who I am anymore. I don't even know where I am—so where are we? England?"

"Scotland, honey, we're in the Highlands not far from Inverness. Alex is my name here. I'm known as Alexander Cameron. There's a lot I need to tell you about."

Davenport pointed over the railing to the large hall below them. "That is the oldest part of the castle. The medieval carvings on the staircase and the stained glass on the first floor date back to the time of the Crusades. You'll have fun exploring when you feel better."

They continued down the hall and into the library. "I've wanted you to see this room ever since the first day I came here. Look out that window, Jennie." When she looked out, Josh started humming and then softly sang the old lullaby ...

> *Go to sleepy, little baby,*
> *Go to sleepy, little baby,*
> *When you wake, we'll play patty, patty cake*
> *with all the pretty little ponies.*

Her heart pounded. "The ponies, there are little ponies out there. I see a couple of them, no, there are five ponies. Oh, Josh, there's even a maze," she said excitedly. Jennie turned and looked around the huge room at the leather couches and chairs and more books than she had ever seen outside of a public library.

She looked up at Josh. "It's unbelievable, this castle, the ponies, this room, and you. I look at you, and it's hard to believe you're alive." She reached out and pulled him to her. His arms went around her and he held her tight.

"I have to touch you to know you're real," Jennie whispered. "Every time you leave the room, I wonder if you were a dream. If I am dreaming, Josh, I don't ever want to wake up."

She leaned back and looked directly in his eyes and said, "You do know that you have a whole lot of explaining to do, not only to me but to your daughters."

"I know, honey," he said smiling. "But let's just take this a little at a time."

"What about Kris and Laurie, Josh? I'm worried. I had nightmares about them all day; that Mason and Nathan were chasing them. I have to talk to them and tell them about Nathan. I have to tell Herman too. Herman Wilkins, you remember. He's probably digging up your grave by now. I promised to tell them where I am." Jennie paused. "Do you think *The Brotherhood* will go after our daughters?"

Josh put his fingers over Jennie's lips to shush her.

Then his face changed to someone she didn't know; the man the general told her about.

"I've taken care of that. Guards are already watching Kris and Laurie. They are safe for the moment, but we may have to bring them here. I need you to tell me everything that's happened since you left Dallas, everyone you talked with, how you recognized Mason, how you and Blakely got together. And I want every little detail."

Jennie nodded and started to answer, but Josh shushed her again.

"I want to know about Kris and Laurie and all the years I missed. I want to know everything you've done these past years. I want to know all about our family. We have so much to talk about. I promise you we will talk about all of it."

His face turned back into the man she knew, he grinned at Jennie and his eyes softened.

"But right now, honey, the next few hours belong to just you and me."

Epilogue

THE GOLD GAVEL SLAMMED against the marble table, and *The Brotherhood* was called to order. The huge man in the wheelchair thundered at the eleven other men gathered around the table.

"Gentlemen, we have two critical situations. First, one of our own has been assassinated. Mason, our comrade from Texas who drew the black ball six years ago, is dead. I only have limited information about how that happened. Second, I have absolute confirmation that Josh Davenport is still alive and responsible for the assassination. The latest report puts him in the British Isles. He left the scene in an armored helicopter. My watchdog managed to get a tracker on it. He followed the chopper to a medical clinic in Skegness, England. He switched the tracker for a more powerful one at the clinic, but it was discovered. It was removed and attached to a fishing boat and my man followed it out to sea. Bottom line, Davenport, along with the chopper, has vanished again."

He paused, his eyes piercing each man sitting at the table. Each of these men had proven themselves trustworthy, time and time again. Only one breach had ever occurred and that was the traitor Davenport. His face turned redder at the thought. He had trusted Davenport—he had trusted him with all the plans. He would never forget or forgive the bastard's treachery. He had fooled them all.

"Davenport has to be stopped." His hands gripped the marble table and it vibrated with the force of his anger. "As long as he lives, he compromises our plans for a unified world under our control."

"The contract to exterminate Davenport has escalated to a new level of urgency. We voted on this situation six years ago, another vote is unnecessary.

Here are the new facts. His wife is now with him. The daughters are grown, married, and each has a child. The value of the daughters' husbands is unknown at this point. My informant tells me that the daughters are worried about their mother and don't know where she is, which also means they don't know where Davenport is."

He spun his chair around to the console, picked up the dark red drawstring bag, dropped two black balls in it and drew it closed.

"The procedure is the same, gentlemen, with one exception. There are two black balls in the bag. This is unprecedented, but the situation is unprecedented."

He handed the bag to the man on his right. Each man reached in and drew out one ball in his closed fist and immediately placed it in his pocket.

"As usual, you will examine your selection privately. We'll convene here one month from today at 1800 hours. The two who drew the black balls will work together. You will meet at 1100 hours tomorrow in the lobby of the Hotel Waldstatterhof in Lucerne and formulate your plans. If you need additional manpower, call the hotline. Whatever you need will be made available to you."

The chairman laboriously pulled himself out of his chair and stood up. He looked intently in the eyes of each man. "Gentlemen, it is critical you fully understand our situation. The future of *The Brotherhood* is in dire jeopardy. No matter what it takes, Davenport must be eliminated."

He fell back into the wheelchair gasping for air.

Then the chairman issued a chilling new command.

"The daughters and the two grandchildren are now your leverage. Davenport will come out of hiding if he thinks his family is in danger."

The gavel crashed against the marble table and the chairman bellowed, "Failure will not be tolerated."

Author's Note

This is a story of fiction, most of it anyway ...

To the best of my knowledge, *The Brotherhood* including the Illuminati, the Inner Circle, and the European Alliance do not exist as represented in this story. The events and people, including the president, military personnel, and the tales of NSA and G-2, are merely figments of my wild imagination.

For the part that is real ...

In 1995, I had a *dream* about my husband who died in 1977. It was so real that when I woke up I was actually disoriented for a time. I searched the house and ran down to the dock trying to find him. The *dream* was unlike any I have ever had, before or since. The strangeness of it continued to worry me.

In my desire to put the *dream* to rest, I went to New Orleans and visited Tulane University; looked through several of the buildings culminating with a thorough search of the yearbooks in the library. As you might suspect, I found no trace of my deceased husband. What I did find was the place in my dream where I got out of the car and ran across the field. I also found the *For Sale* sign on the Jung Hotel just as I dreamed about it. I have pictures of both these places.

My husband was a G-2 in the Army in the 1950s, and his records are unavailable to this day. Many of the events in Kansas City are true including the News Center, Fort Leavenworth, and the early discharge.

It took years for me to come to some sort of peace about that dream. What I knew for sure was I had the bones of a story, one I wanted to write, but was too emotionally involved to do so immediately. I shelved it for a long time ...

Was the dream real …? Was it precognition …? Or was it something else entirely …?

I really don't know. The answer still eludes me.

There's an old saying that reiterates over and over in my mind …
There are more things in heaven and earth, Horatio,
than are dreamt of in your philosophy.
William Shakespeare

Does the dream still plague me?

You bet it does.

If it had happened to you, how would you feel?

CPSIA information can be obtained at www.ICGtesting.com
Printed in the USA
LVOW081435160213

320105LV00004B/10/P